C000157040

Sons

of the

Wolf

Book One
by
Paula Lofting

LONGSHIP
Publishing

Copyright © Paula Lofting 2012
This edition published by © Longship Books, 2016
Longship Books is an imprint of © Longship Publishing

All rights reserved.
Except for brief quotes in critical articles or reviews,
no part of this book may be reproduced in any form
without prior written permission from the author.
Cover design © Dave Slaney
Artwork by Charlie Kirkpatrick
And Gayle Copper

About the Author

Paula Lofting was born in Middlesex and grew up in South Australia where she nurtured a love of history as a youngster. She returned to England in the late 70's and now lives in West Sussex with her family. A psychiatric nurse by day, she spends as much of her spare time writing when she can.

The sequel to *Sons of the Wolf*, *The Wolf Banner*, is also currently available and she is now working on the third in the series, *Wolf's Bane*.

Paula is also a reenactor with Regia Anglorum, well known re-enactment society of the early medieval period.

You can catch up with what Paula is up to and writing about on her blog, *1066: The Road to Hastings and Other Stories*, a home for all her research and other interesting things.

ACKNOWLEDGEMENTS

This edition is the second in Sons of the Wolf: book one. The original was written in 2012 and is largely still the same with the exception that editing errors in the first have been rectified. Though some of the prose has been re-written, this edition still retains the essence of the story, which leads me first to thank my dear friend and proof-editor, Louise E Rule, who spent hours with me getting this edition right. A big thank you to cover designer, Dave Slaney, and Charlie Kirkpatrick, who produced some fine artwork for the book in creating my fighting horseman; plus, Gayle Copper for Wulfhere's sword and the images that head each Part.

I would like to remember all those who helped me when crafting the first edition, Rob Bayliss for his assistance in helping me wax lyrical for Skalpi's song and Ian Weston and Stephen Pollington for their valuable help in understanding the Anglo-Saxon language. Thanks also to Paul Waddington for his advice on Wulfhere's war gear and re-enactment Society Regia Anglorum, www.regia.org, which has been a huge help in sourcing evidence for everyday life in Anglo Saxon England.

Lastly thanks to all my family and friends who have also helped me, encouraged me, and saw me on my journey to becoming an author.

PRONUNCIATION OF NAMES

Old English is a complex language. There are many spellings of the same names and many different ways of pronouncing them. I hope I have made it a little easier by providing this list for some of the more difficult Anglo-Saxon names. Please email me at sonsofthewolf1066@googlemail.com if you wish to know more.

Alfgyva – *Alf-giv-a*
Eadgyth – *Eead-gith also pronounced Eea-dith*
Ealdgytha – *Eeald-githa (or Alditha)*
Godgyva/Godgifu – *God-giver (Godiva)*
Leofric – *Leyo-fric or Leyo-frich*

PLACE NAMES

Pronunciation where given in brackets

Cantwarabyrig – Canterbury
Dyfflin – Dublin
Englalond – England
Gleawecestre – Gloucester
Iralond – Ireland
Jorvik – York
Lundenburgh – London
Northymbralond – Northumbria/Northumberland
Norweg – Norway
Súþrigaweorc – Southwark
Súþ Seax /Súþseaxa – (sooth-say-ax/a) South Saxons, Sussex
River Waeg – River Way
Westmynstre – Westminster
Winceaster – Winchester

LANGUAGE OF SONS OF THE WOLF

ANDREDESWALD: refers to the forested area that covered the South and North Downs of Sussex and Surrey.

ANGLO-SAXON: refers generally to the peoples of who made up the population of England. The Angles were said to have come across the North Sea to Britain from the area that is now southern Denmark and the Saxons are thought to have migrated from northern Germany. There were other tribes who also migrated, such as the Jutes and Frisians, but the nomenclature that developed seemed to have favoured the Angles and Saxons to form the term 'Anglo-Saxon'. The 7/8th century historian Bede referred to these peoples generically as the Englisc (English).

ATHELING: Title bestowed upon an Anglo-Saxon prince or nobleman of royal blood, who was deemed to be throneworthy.

BEOWULF: Old English Epic Poem found in a manuscript dated somewhere between the 8th and 11th centuries. It was said to have been a favourite of King Edward.

CEORL: A free man, lower than that of a thegn, but his status was the peasant aristocracy. His free status was marked by his right to bear arms and his attendance at local courts. He would have been a tenant with land or own land granted to him from a lord.

COTTAR: A term for the lowest rank of the peasantry classes. Often these were semi-skilled craftsmen such as tinkers, foresters, sawyers or hurdlemakers or the villager miller. Their houses, five acres of land and tools were provided by their thegn and, in return, they paid no rent but worked for him ploughing his land as well as their own.

EARL: Derived from the previous English Ealdorman and Danish Jarl, vernacular equivalent of a range of Latin titles such as dux, praefectus, comes. It came to describe a leader of noble or royal status who had jurisdiction for the king over several individual shires.

FYRD: Refers to the king's national or local army. The populace of each five hides was obliged to provide and equip one man from the area (although this varied in some parts of England). Sometimes this could be the landholding thegn or a man he appointed. During a national crisis, such as when the Normans invaded, every man who could fight was expected to turn out when summoned. The select fyrd, the professional warriors, the huscarles, would have been better equipped than the general fyrd.

GEBUR/VILLEIN: A villain or gebur were the more substantial peasants who owned about twenty or thirty acres. Their property was gifted to them by the thegn, reclaimed upon their death and gifted back to the heir to renew their bargain. In return for their property, equipment, land and oxen, they owed a formidable list of duties for which he would need strong sons and daughters to help him, thus making his landholding a family business.

HIDE: A hide was a measurement of land, enough to support one family. In Sussex, a hide could be roughly 40 acres; however, in East Anglia, it was 120 acres. A thegn's landholding was usually not less than five hides.

HUNDRED: England was divided into earldoms, earldoms into shires and shires into hundreds. In ancient times, Hundreds were so called because they contained a hundred hides but, as more land came into cultivation, some hundreds contained more hides.

HUSCARLE: Meaning house-man, and introduced into England by the Danish, King Cnut, as one of an elite band of warriors who made up a lord's personal body guard. Many would have acted as shire officials too, such as reeves etc.

LAMMAS: In some English-speaking countries, August 1st is Lammas day (loaf-mass day), the festival of the first wheat harvest of the year. In the Anglo-Saxon Chronicle, where it is referred to regularly, it is called 'the feast of first fruits'.

NITHING – (Níðing): A term referring to someone who was 'without honour' and therefore an outlaw. Probably the worst punishment a lord could pass on one of his retainers.

NORMANS: Ethnic name for those whose origins lay in Normandy. King Edward's (known as the Confessor) mother was the sister of the Duke of Normandy and therefore William's great aunt, linking him to Edward as his second cousin. Edward brought many Normans over to England with him when he was invited to be king.

NORMANDY: Normandy is a principality of northern France founded in the early 10th century. King Charles the Simple of France granted Rouen and its surroundings to the Norse settlers of the Seine, Rollo and his companions, to help defend it from other Vikings.

SCOP/SKALD: Old English/Norse for poet. Entertainers in great halls.

SHIRE – scīr: A division of land. England was divided into earldoms, then shires within the earldoms and then hundreds. The shire court was where legal proceedings took place.

SHIRE-REEVE – scīr-reefa: The king's personal representative in the shire. Tax- collecting and policing, were most likely some of his duties, along with administering justice.

THEGN: literally means 'one who serves'. Considered to be a member of the nobility or landed aristocracy. He would own at least five hides of land and possibly owned other property (perhaps in a town) other than on the estate where he lived. Some thegns were substantial landowners with properties spanning several counties. All thegns owed both military and administrative services, a number of them (for example, those who were king's thegns) held special office in the king's household. Some were shire-reeves. They owed allegiance to their king but might be inclined to offer it to an earl or another party if predisposed to protect their own interests. Earls and bishops could have their own thegns who held their land directly from them as opposed to owning it directly from the king.

WERGILD: Blood price of a person, a legal value set on a person's life, and could be demanded from the victim's family of the murderer. All classes were protected by the Wergild except slaves. For example, a thegn's wergild, 1,200 shillings, ceorl 200 shillings, with an intermediate payment for varying statuses.

WITAN: The king's council which literally means 'wise men'.

WITANAGEMOT: meeting of the Witan. Those who could be included in the Witan were members of the royal house, the two archbishops, bishops, prominent abbots, earls and leading thegns. This could also include women such as the queen, queen mother and sometimes leading abbesses.

Dedicated to Mum and Dad

Tony and Maria

Forever in my heart

Prologue

In the autumn of 1052, two young boys were set on a journey to a place where they would remain hostage for many years. Wulfnoth and his nephew Hakon were the sons of earls Godwin and Swegn, and they were not to see a familiar comforting face for many years. They were whisked away across the sea to the court of Normandy by Robert Champart, former Archbishop of Cantwarabyrig. Champart was fleeing the return of his nemesis, Godwin, the powerful Earl of Wessex, as he came storming back from exile. His part in Godwin's downfall, meant that Champart's life was now in danger. If he stayed in Englalond, it would be at his peril, for Godwin's revenge would be devastating.

Some said that the boys had been meant as hostages sent with King Edward's consent as surety that he would name the bastard born William, Duke of Normandy, as his heir. Others say the archbishop took the boys out of hatred for Godwin. Whatever the motive this ill-fated abduction was to be the start of a thread that would eventually spin the downfall of the once mighty House of Godwin.

Onginnen þa spinnestran…

(Let the spinners begin...)

Part One

Horstede

Chapter One

The Homecoming

Late Summer 1054

Wulfhere rode wearily through the great lush woodland once known to the ancient Britons and their Roman conquerors as the forest of Anderida. It was now called Andredeswald by the people who knew themselves as the descendants of the Súþseaxan, who, in the dark days that followed the death of Rome, settled in the lands south of the great river Temes.

Wulfhere's companion, Esegar, his servant and righthand man, rode beside him. Half asleep in the saddle, eyes all but closed, Esegar nodded as he fought to stay awake. The horses, too, were tired, heads low, pace no more than a lumbering amble. Their destination was home, Horstede, in the heart of Andredeswald, on the marshy slopes of a shallow valley. They had been travelling many days along the ancient trackways, which for centuries had witnessed the various comings and goings of the many different peoples of this ancient land. They were wearing their armour so as not to over-burden the packhorses. The feel of it against Wulfhere's skin was chafing but familiar. It was a sensation both he and Esegar had got used to over the last few months, campaigning hard in the north.

Wulfhere wore the formidable trappings of his warrior status as he journeyed home. Beneath his gleaming helm, strands of his long, sun-bleached hair blew in the cool breeze. The mail shirt hugging his torso emphasised strong broad shoulders across which was strapped his battle-scarred shield. The chips, dents and holes in its facing had been made by Scottish spear tips, a testimony to the recent bloody encounter with Macbeth's army. Even the shield's deadly metal boss had not escaped damage and was now crushed beyond repair. His sword, the most precious weapon he possessed, hung in a decorative scabbard secured to a leather belt worn around his waist. The pommel, inlaid with gold banding, rested against his upper thigh; the silver lobe at the end of the grip, was decorated with the figure of two intertwined wolves. The sword had been in his family for many years, handed down to sons through the march of generations. Its name, Hildbana, meaning 'battle slayer' was inlaid along the flat surface of the blade. Warriors were inclined to give their weapons fierce names to enhance the reputations of their owners. For a fighting man, his sword was more than a battlefield tool; his sword was a companion, a lover, a life-giver, and a death-bringer. For Wulfhere, Hildbana was like an extension of himself, another limb into which his heart pumped his life's blood. As he and Esegar rode over hills, marshes, and along ridged valleys, people eyed him with the respect a man of his status could expect, deferring to him as he met them on the trackway, or standing still in salute as they passed them by.

Despite his magnificent weapons and polished war gear, Wulfhere was more a man of reasonable means than a man of great wealth and land holdings. He held roughly five hides of village and pastoral lands direct from King Edward, the minimum amount a thegn might possess. It had been endowed to his ancestors by subsequent royal lines in return for both official and military services and he was now returning home after more than two months of brutal campaigning with the Earl of Northymbralond against the Scottish king, Macbeth. Although he had not been eager to travel so far from his family, Wulfhere accepted his duty with the unquestioning loyalty of a king's faithful servant. The battle had been hard-won, with many lives lost on both sides.

It was natural for a man like Wulfhere to take up the mantle of warrior, for he came from a long line of such men. However, nothing had prepared him for the carnage he had witnessed that day on Dunsinane Hill. Death in battle was no stranger to him, but never had he seen it on such a scale as this.

Riding deeper into the forest's heartland, Wulfhere observed that the track was becoming more like the path home. As the day drew toward evening, the August heat began to cool through the forest. Thoughts of being home were becoming a reality.

"Not long now, lord," Esegar said sleepily, as they ambled along.

Wulfhere nodded in agreement, "It will be a good homecoming, I think, lad." He always called Esegar 'lad' although at twenty-seven he was only Wulfhere's junior by seven years.

"Aye, lord, it will be good to see my wife and the little ones again," Esegar replied with a smile. "And you, my lord? You must be looking forward to seeing Lady Ealdgytha after all this time."

Wulfhere laughed good-naturedly as he thought of the differences between Godgyva and Ealdgytha and said, "Of course! What man would not miss the warm comforts of his wife?"

Wulfhere envied the younger man, for Esegar's homecoming would be geared to meet his every comfort. Enviously, he pictured Esegar being pampered by the willingly attentive Godgyva who, he had been assured by Esegar, might be a gentle soul, but was a wildcat in bed. Where Esegar's wife was easy-going and obliging, Ealdgytha was fussy and difficult to please. Wulfhere visualised his wife now, knowing that he would be arriving any day, buzzing around the household purposefully and driving the maids to distraction with her painstaking demands. They would be scrubbing, cleaning, cooking, and sweeping like souls possessed to keep her happy. Amongst all the mayhem it was *haerfest monath* and there would be crops to bring in, adding more work to the already busy hive of activity.

In the earlier days of their marriage Wulfhere had been in awe of Ealdgytha; dazzled by her beauty and believing himself to be the luckiest man on earth. He was the eldest son of a middle-ranking thegn. His father had secured him a far greater match in Ealdgytha, than he may have hoped for. Ealdgytha was a granddaughter of Tovi the Proud, the closest of King Cnut's counsellors. Not only did she have noble blood, she also possessed great beauty, an enchanting wit, and a vivacious spirit, appealing to any man.

Young and naïve, Wulfhere was soon to find out just how adept Ealdgytha was at using her womanly guile to her advantage. With the gullibility of a lovelorn youth, Wulfhere conceded to her womanly charm. However, time and maturity would see him shed his youthful innocence, and as he did so, Ealdgytha's ability to control him eventually began to diminish. Nowadays she was still apt to remind him of her noble lineage whenever they had a disagreement, but Wulfhere was no longer easy prey to her attempts to belittle or dominate him.

Now they came upon the place where a low-lying bridge forded the river. Interrupting Wulfhere's thoughts, Esegar called out, eagerly, "Look, this is our crossing!"

Wulfhere's earlier lassitude transformed into wakeful excitement at the prospect of nearing home. He nodded and urged his mount Hwitegast, so called for his ghostlike hue, to move faster. He was looking forward to finally feel his feet on the ground again.

They left the track to join the path on the other side of the river, the last leg of their journey home. The evening was drawing in now and the dying embers of the sun spread their flames over the leafy branches of the trees, bathing the whole forest in a vibrant glow of pink and gold. As they passed the homes of the forest-dwellers, the men were greeted with horns of ale and barley bread spread with honey.

"My lord! *God æfen*! Glad tidings to see you home and hale!" Inewulf, the charcoal worker called out to Wulfhere.

Inewulf's wife, Eanflaed, handed him a most welcome horn full of refreshing ale which he shared with Esegar.

"The ale is welcome, Eanflaed."

"*Aye, þu airt welcumen*, lords. We heard news that the battle was hard and that many men were perished." Eanflaed replied, endowing Wulfhere with a concerned expression on her rugged features. "We prayed that you were not amongst them, and that you would be returning home whole and hearty."

"Aye, we are happy to be returned safe and well, indeed," Wulfhere replied, handing back the horn to Eanflaed who took it with a grubby charcoal-blackened hand and a toothless grin. "I see your little Ymma and your lads are working diligently as usual!" He nodded to a small girl and two older boys who were tending to the burning charcoal mound some yards away from their house.

"Aye lord, they are hardworking children," nodded Eanflaed proudly, her bleary eyes beaming.

Wulfhere handed her a couple of coins. "Here, take this for them. They deserve it."

Eanflaed looked at the silver coins with amazement. "My lord, you are so gracious!" she cried, as she humbly bowed her head.

"Hemming! Eadric! Fetch water for our thegn's horses," called Inewulf to the two boys. "And you can assist lord Wulfhere in his journey back home!"

The boys left their work and hurried toward the adults, hoping for a bigger slice of their lord's hoard for their efforts. They took the reins of the pack horses and followed Wulfhere and Esegar as they continued their journey.

As they approached the forest clearing, Wulfhere recognised the familiar aroma of hearth smoke from the village and felt safe in the knowledge that their journey was all but over. There would be many things for him to do around the homestead and village over the next coming weeks. For now, however, Wulfhere anticipated sharing some time with his family and relaxing without the uncertainties that being on campaign brings.

It was twilight when Wulfhere discharged Esegar into the arms of his relieved family, expressing genuine gratitude for his fyrdsman's loyalty and fortitude.

"Thank you, Lord Wulfhere, for bringing him back safely." Godgyva said after she had hugged Esegar warmly. Her young eyes brimmed with tears of joy. "The whole village was filled with fear that you would not be coming home to us."

"Your husband did his duty with great courage, Godgyva. He served me admirably, and I have rewarded him well. If it was not for his bravery, I would not be here."

"My lord, stay awhile and refresh yourself for some moments," Godgyva invited him, smiling with unrestrained delight as she clung to her husband.

Wulfhere could not help but notice the look of longing in their eyes and politely declined. "Nay lady, I will be on my way. I have a desire to be home before the light fades even further into night."

He left them to greet each other happily with their two small children skipping around them, squealing with glee to have their papa home. He carried on up the slope through the settlement of little cottages, the forest youths still trailing behind with the pack horses. As he passed through the village of smoking chimneys, his people came out to acknowledge him with warm greetings. He observed with envy that there was the usual intoxication and merry making. *Haerfest monath* was a time for the reaping of a long year's hard work. He returned their welcome, smiling and waving, but as he approached his steading, a hint of anxiety fluttered in his stomach. He wondered what kind of welcome he was about to receive at home. When Wulfhere had last left Horstede, he and Ealdgytha had not been speaking. *Will she greet me coldly? Will she even greet me at all? Would she embrace me as Godgyva had done Esegar?* He knew the likelihood of that was small.

Wulfhere approached the strong wooden palisade that surrounded his longhall. He reached for the blowing horn that hung on a leather thong around his neck. Putting it to his lips he blew a couple of short notes, then a long shrill high one to sound his approach. Wulfhere was answered by the appearance of his blacksmith's nephew, Yrmenlaf. The sandy-haired lad shouted a hearty greeting as his red-cheeked face peered above the rampart before swiftly disappearing to run down the steps to open the gates.

The horse's weary hooves trudged across the wooden planks of the ford, clattering as they crossed the defensive ditch. Wulfhere looked up proudly at the familiar sight of his formidable twin towers, made by his own hands from the strongest timber. He passed through the gate, opened eagerly by Yrmenlaf, and gave a contented whisper of thanks to the Lord for his safe arrival. The sight of his longhall was welcoming, standing as a symbol of safety from the outside world. It was surrounded by smaller out buildings that served as sleeping bowers, work sheds, animal byres and storage huts.

The little wooden chapel comforted Wulfhere as he passed it. He crossed himself piously, grateful to be home and safe at last. The stallion's ears pricked at the clanking of Aelfstan's smithy hammer as they passed the forge and Wulfhere breathed in the familiar aroma of horse dung that wafted from the stables nearby. As he approached the house, he imagined that Ealdgytha might be tending her garden to the rear where she grew herbs and vegetables; or perhaps she was in the orchard where the sweet succulent apples grew abundantly. He heard the recognisable laughter of children at play and knew he was finally home in the place he thought he would never see again.

Two boys tumbled from the stables, fighting to be first to greet their father. Wulfhere barely had time to ease his aching body from the saddle before they threw themselves at him in a whirlwind of excitement. Laughing, Wulfhere grabbed a twin in each arm and embraced them warmly against his mail shir. "Father! Father is here!" they both shouted, leaping about with unbridled enthusiasm. "Everyone, Father is home!"

Wulfhere ruffled their auburn hair and stood back to study them. In the two months he had been away, the twins, approaching their twelfth birthdays, had grown at least two inches, and their once round, child-like features were sharper and more becoming of their approaching adolescence.

As Wulfhere embraced his sons, other members of the household gathered in the courtyard. He looked up toward the porch and saw Ealdgytha, carrying their baby, Drusilda. The second youngest of their brood, Gerda, clung shyly to her mother's skirts. Wulfhere felt his heart pound as his eyes met those of his wife. Ealdgytha, the Lady of Horstede, was a diminutive woman, with delicate elfin features. Her temperament, however, did not always as reflect the delicacy of her appearance.

As he held his wife's gaze, a feeling of nervous apprehension threatened to overcome him, but Ealdgytha gave a hesitant smile. Wulfhere felt a rush of relief to see her usual austerity was absent. He watched as she handed the baby to Sigfrith, her servant girl, and descended the steps to meet him. He removed his helmet and gave it to one of the twins. Wulfric immediately set it on his head as his brother, Wulfwin, tried his best to snatch it from him in an amusing display of mock sibling rivalry. The thegn stood before his wife with the reticence of a child and waited for her to speak.

"Welcome home, husband!" Ealdgytha smiled with genuine warmth, her arms open. She pushed herself in to him and he enclosed her in an embrace, her face against his cheek as she softly breathed the words again into his ear.

Anxious that his armour should not chafe her, Wulfhere pulled away but she resisted and held onto him, kissing his cheek with soft lips. This surprised him, for it was a far cry from Ealdgytha's usual reserve. The warmth of her against him reminded him of happier times. He allowed her to hold on to him until she turned her head and looked up at him, her comely face marked by the rings of his hauberk. He smiled and tried to rub the marks off with his thumb. Wulfhere marvelled at the affection he saw in her eyes. It seemed a lifetime ago that he last saw that look.

For a moment, they held each other's gaze as though frozen in time. At thirty-one, Ealdgytha was maturing, though many other women her age would not have done so quite as well. There were few lines on her face; her heart-shaped lips still held their colour and her up-turned nose remained small and delicate. Her blue-grey eyes were almond-shaped and still unlined, like the eyes of a young girl, creasing only when she smiled.

For that moment, Wulfhere wanted nothing more than to sweep up his wife and carry her to their bed and shut out the world whilst they made up for lost time.

"I've missed you, Ealdgytha," he murmured gently.

Her long eyelashes swept downwards, reminding him of the young demure bride she had been when he had first brought her to Horstede as his wife. "It gladdens me to have you home," she replied quietly. "And the children, too, are happy to see you."

She took Drusilda from Sigfrith and held the baby out to her father.

"Even this one?" Wulfhere laughed and planted a kiss on the baby's face. "Is she walking yet?"

"Almost."

Ealdgytha laughed as the baby, having no idea who her father was, screwed her face up to cry before being keenly whisked away by Sigfrith. Wulfhere bent down to Gerda, still clinging to her mother's skirt, and lifted her up into his arms. The usually bashful little girl squealed with delight at the attention she received.

"We heard that the battle was hard and that many men had died," Ealdgytha said, as Wulfhere threw Gerda in the air playfully.

"Aye," Wulfhere solemnly confirmed, settling the little girl down. Ealdgytha looked at him sadly, touching his cheek. She had not shown him such tenderness for so long now that he felt awkward. He quickly lightened his mood. "And what of my other children?" he asked, forcing the joviality back into his voice. "I count only four! I could have sworn that I had three more somewhere! Ah, Tovi – Winflaed! Come greet your father!" His son, a boy aged about ten and his daughter, somewhat younger, came forward form the porch and allowed themselves to be hugged. "And where is my eldest, Freyda?"

"I'm here, Father," called a girl, joining the welcoming party.

At fourteen summers, Freyda was the eldest of Wulfhere's brood and secretly his favourite child. Wulfhere endeavoured to treat his children with equal amounts of love and affection, but for some reason he loved Freyda the most. Perhaps it was nothing more than a father's love for his firstborn. Nonetheless, she was dearest to him. He gave his daughter a warm embrace.

"Have you brought anything for me father?" she asked, delivering him a coquettish smile.

Wulfhere laughed indulgently "Of course!" he replied. "And not just for you, my dear daughter, but for all my children!" He turned to where his baggage had been unloaded to see the twins rummaging inside the sacks like two ferrets in a squirrel's nest.

"Wulfric! Wulfwin! Stop looting the loot. Hell's teeth! Have you no patience, you *Sons of Loki*?"

Ealdgytha took his arm in hers. "Come inside now Wulfhere, you must be exhausted… and hungry!" she said as she ushered everybody to the longhall. "Boys, leave your father's things alone and help him remove his armour. Wulfric, hang up his shield and sword. Wulfwin, you and Sigfrith fetch the mead from the cellar."

Ealdgytha gave the lads from the forest a couple of coins and sent them out to spread word that a great feast was to be had on the morrow to celebrate the return of their lord. She called to Aelfstan, the blacksmith, and his nephew, Yrmenlaf, to unsaddle the horses and see that they were fed and watered in the stables. Then she joined the rest of her household in the hall, thankful that her husband was home at last and able to share some of the burden of running a farm and bringing up a family. Although Wulfhere often went away on the king's business, this had been the longest absence for some time. They had one of their many fights before he left, and she had been sorely angry with him. The thought that he might never return however, made her realise what his loss would mean to her and how much she valued him. As she walked inside the building a smile of pleasure formed on her lips. Her husband was home at last and, for the first time in a long while, she was content with that.

After supper, Wulfhere dished out the gifts, booty from the war in Scotland. He sat with his family around the hearth in the longhall, listening as Ealdgytha relayed to him everything that had happened in Horstede while he had been away. His late brother's wife, Gunnhild and her teenage son, Leofric, joined them for supper. They had their own small plot of land a little way south of the village, but Gunnhild, a large opinionated woman, spent more time at Horstede than both Wulfhere and Ealdgytha liked. Wulfhere knew Ealdgytha only tolerated her out of his concern for her welfare. The two women did not see eye to eye on good days, and Leofric, named after his father, was bad-tempered and mostly sullen. Nonetheless, Wulfhere was duty bound to see to their welfare, especially because of the guilt Wulfhere felt around the death of his brother, who had been Gunnhild's husband and Leofric's father.

The hall glowed with the light from the hearth and the smell of the newly laid rush-mats mingled pleasantly with the aroma of smoking wood. Wulfhere listened with interest as Ealdgytha told him that the carpenter's son had requested a marriage with the miller's daughter, but the miller and the carpenter's wives had fallen out over an unpaid for bag of corn and now the wedding was off. He grinned when Freyda regaled him with the story about how their milk cow, Buttercup, took exception to Sigfrith's milking technique and chased her out of the byre. He almost cried with laughter when the twins eagerly spoke of Sigfrith's father's attempt to catch a pig for their supper, ending up with him jumping out of a hay loft and nearly breaking his back. Joy turned to sadness when he discovered the reason his dear mother could not join them for supper. She was very ill and confined to her bed. The illness was thought to be a stomach ailment, but she had been ill before, and survived. Lady Gerda was a strong old lady. He was hopeful that she would pull through.

The children were longing to hear tales of their father's exploits in the north, but Wulfhere shook his head and declared that it would have to wait until tomorrow for he was bone weary and needed his bed.

"Oh no, please tell us!" pleaded the twins.

"Yes, father, tell us!" added Winflaed, settling herself on his lap. "Tell us how you killed the Scottish warriors with your spear!"

Ealdgytha hushed them and ordered them to bid their father goodnight and go to their own beds. Then Ealdgytha and Wulfhere took themselves up to their bed chamber above the hall.

Wulfhere allowed his wife to remove his grimy tunic, conscious of his body odour. Ealdgytha was usually so fastidious about such matters and yet there was no sign that she minded, then, that his scent was less than sweet. He saw the wash basin by the bed but gave her no time to set about his body with a sponge. Wulfhere was filled with an urgency that was difficult to contain. He pulled at her clothes until he could feel her lithe nakedness against him. Ealdgytha tried to stop him. He knew that she wanted to talk, but he did not want to. When she tried to speak, he sealed her mouth with a kiss. As he stroked her tenderly, he felt her arousal build. She tilted her head back and her eyes closed. He sensed that she had missed the sensation of him against her and the way he made her feel when he touched her. Her resistance crumbled, and she gave in as they fell onto the bed together. The lovemaking that followed revealed a passion neither of them had shown each other for some years.

Afterward, they lay in a haze of sweat and astonishment as they took a few moments to gain back their breath.

"My God, woman! What's come over you?" Wulfhere laughed as he kissed her temple. His breaths were short and came quickly.

"I could ask you the same question," she replied, quietly.

"You've changed, my love," he said softly, barely able to find the words as he still fought to catch his breath.

"What makes you say that?"

"It's a long time since you've been so attentive and loving," he replied carefully. He knew how changeable she could be at times and did not wish to spoil what had just passed between them. "The last time I was home, you were barely speaking to me."

"I am sorry for that," she replied. There was a long moment of silence before she continued. "I was worried that you would be killed," she said at last. "I did not want to lose you to a Scottish sword."

Wulfhere was stunned by her words. He cupped her face between his hands and saw that she was crying. The glow from the candles were burning low and could not show him what he wanted to see; her inner most thoughts. She continued as he held her face. "You have been away for long times before, Wulfhere, but when word came of the ferocity of the battle and that so many men had died, I feared for you. It made me realise just how much you mean to me and that my life would be empty without you. When we received the news that you were coming home, I vowed that I would never argue with you again."

"Then I must vow never again to give you cause for displeasure." He gave a tired laugh and rolled onto her and kissed her.

Too tired to do anything else, they fell asleep in each other's embrace, more content than they had been for a long time.

Chapter Two

Children of the Forest

Ealdgytha gave an exasperated click of her tongue as she fixed her eyes on the unacceptable state of her longhall. Hands braced on her slim hips, she surveyed the empty clay lime washed walls with a pained expression. Except for the weft of cobwebs that draped from beam to beam like decorative wall hangings, they were indecently bare. Exasperation turned to disappointment as she continued to gaze around her. Her favourite curtains were missing from their wall hooks and the rushes had not been swept or laid anew with fresh herbs and meadowsweet. She had been planning Wulfhere's homecoming feast for days. With his sick mother to look after and her other duties to attend to, she thought she might have relied on her daughters to carry out the few tasks she required of them. What was the point of having daughters if they could not be of any use, or follow simple instructions? She might as well do everything herself.

"Sigfrith!" she shouted irritably.

"Yes, mistress?" The young servant woman hurried out from behind the partition that separated the hall from the food preparation area. She was closely followed by her charges, baby Drusilda and three-year-old Gerda.

"Are Freyda and Winflaed in there with you?" Ealdgytha asked, knowing that the inevitable answer would be no.

The two young children crawled and toddled to their mother, smiling as they reached out to her to be picked up. Ealdgytha absently bent down and lifted the baby, swinging her onto her hip. Although she ignored Gerda, the little toddler was satisfied to tug on the skirts of her mother who was tapping her foot impatiently for a reply to her question.

Sigfrith wiped the vegetable debris from her hands onto her apron, and tried to tuck in some strands of hair that had escaped from under her linen cap. "No, mistress," she replied cautiously. "I have not seen them for a good while. I have been hard at work in the kitchen."

"Just look at the state of my longhall!" Ealdgytha swept her arm wide to emphasise her disgust. "The whole village will be attending tonight and nothing has been done as I ordered!"

"I saw Lady Freyda and Lady Winflaed tending to it this morning," Sigfrith replied. She followed Ealdgytha's gaze. "Oh, I see there is still much to do, Mistress."

"This is not good enough, Sigfrith!" Ealdgytha cried. "I cannot do everything myself! The floor will have to be swept and the rush-lights made; and then there is the table linen and the cooking, and I have my husband's sick mother to care for. Where is Freyda now?" Ealdgytha held her hand up to her forehead in a dramatic gesture to show how exasperated she was.

"I cannot say, Mistress," Sigfrith replied. "I have not seen her since I saw her last working in here."

"And Winflaed?"

"You sent her into the forest, Mistress, to pick herbs and cures for poor sick Lady Gerda," Sigfrith murmured. "Do you not remember, my lady?"

"Of course I do!" Ealdgytha snapped indignantly, even though, truth be told, she had forgotten in the rush to prepare everything. She was not going to admit that, however, especially not to a mere servant girl.

"Do you wish me to help you in here, my lady?" Sigfrith asked.

"It seems that you may have to! Fetch some others. Bring your mother and that aunt of yours and her daughters… and any others who are willing to give a hand."

The women came quickly, dipping quick curtsies to Ealdgytha, and in a short while all was as it should be. Her precious wall hangings were hung, the floor was swept, and fresh rushes dipped in candlewax. The tableware was laid out and water was collected from the well and set to boiling in the pot above the stone hearth.

As she stood back to survey all her efforts, there was a sudden clamour as Wulfwin and Wulfric tumbled through the doors of the hall, a ball of entwined arms and legs, locked in a vigorous play-fight. The hollow sounds of their wooden practice weapons could be heard as they crashed to the floor, still clutching them in their hands. Amongst the mayhem of flying furniture and utensils, two lively hounds bounded in after them, barking and leaping about on slender hind legs with wagging tails and flapping tongues.

"By all the saints! What on earth…? Look what you have done to my hall! Stop it at once!" cried Ealdgytha in frustration, hardly believing that in a few moments all her hard work had been mercilessly destroyed.

She wielded her broom at the boys but they were oblivious to their mother's protestations as they focused on their game. They untangled themselves, leapt apart and stood facing each other. They were panting and snarling, rocking on their heels and brandishing their wooden practice swords and shields threateningly.

"Wulfwin! Wulfric!" Ealdgytha raised her voice to catch their attention. "Get outside if you are going to fight! And take those hell hounds out with you!"

Wulfwin turned to look at her. "Sorry, Mother!" he cried just as his brother Wulfric took the opportunity to land an unsuspecting blow on his brother's shoulder.

Wulfwin let out a painful yelp but recovered quickly to retaliate. The two of them clashed their swords and shields together, growling, and grimacing like wolves fighting for supremacy. The door of the hall opened and their younger brother Tovi, a heavy golden fringe sweeping across his piercing blue eyes, stood smiling in the doorway. He laughed with amusement as he watched his brothers' battle.

"Hey, Wulfric!" shouted Wulfwin, cocking his head toward the boy at the door, distracted by Tovi's sudden presence.

Wulfric, believing it to be a trick, refused to look.

"Over by the door!" Wulfwin said, gesticulating at their younger brother standing obliviously in the doorway.

Wulfwin's eyes flashed as a devilish grin shaped his brother's lips. Wulfric nodded approvingly at his twin and they leapt toward the doorway as Tovi, whirled out of the hall.

"Get him!" shouted Wulfwin as they ran after him, hotly pursued by the hounds, leaving their infuriated mother to clear up the mess they had left in their wake.

*

Winflaed knelt beside her basket in the grass. It was mid-morning; the late summer heat, cooled by the dense branches of the majestic yew trees. Nearby, the stream trickled its way deftly over rocks and sediment, onwards to the millpond. This was a good place to find the medicinal plants her mother required for her sick grandmother, and it would afford her some peace from the relentless teasing of her older brothers. She often came here to escape the chaos of her household, finding solitude in the natural beauty that surrounded her home.

This was her special place. On the grassy bank by the stream, she would daydream of the stories told in her father's hall: tales of handsome warriors that slew fearsome giants in the forgotten lands of *Middeleorðe*. Legends of lovelorn heroes, fallen under the spells of warlocks and sorceresses. Myths of the beautiful nymph-like creatures who dwelt within the ancient lakes and caverns of forest-laden hills. All the sagas that she loved. Winflaed found her own company pleasing, feeling at one with the woodland and privy to its hidden secrets. Here she felt a sense of belonging, like a true child of the forest.

As she unfolded her strips of linen and laid them out on the grass to encase the roots and herbs she'd picked that morning, she thought about the sick grandmother for whom the herbs had been sought. For some days now, Grandmother had been bedridden with a fever that had been preceded by excruciating stomach cramps. It vexed Winflaed to see the old lady frail and prostrate, looking all of her fifty-three years and more. She had always been so full of life. Now, laid up in her sickbed, it was as if some dark magic had sucked the energy out of her.

Winflaed sorted through the herbs and laid them out one by one. Coltsfoot for the fever, fennel, and chervil to mix with buckthorn, to ease stomach cramping; chervil and comfrey mixed with wild cherries to help calm the pain. She wrapped them carefully into their linen strips, hoping that her mother would be pleased with her morning's work. As a reward, she might allow Winflaed to assist her in making them into effective remedies for her grandmother's ailments, a thing that Winflaed enjoyed very much.

The heat began to increase as the day shifted towards midday. Winflaed picked up her basket and was now collecting berries and nuts to add to her collection. A sense of lightness entered her as she skipped further along the bank of the millstream, eyes seeking anything else that she could bring back with her as she enjoyed her surroundings. The sounds of the forest lightly reverberated, encapsulating everything around her, whilst the sweet-smelling aroma of the honeysuckle plant gently caressed her senses. Birds fluttered between the trees as little woodland creatures scurried into their hiding places. The soft drone of insects tickled her ears as sun-dried twigs crunched beneath her shoes. She loved the woodland and the wonders that its nature revealed. Here she could escape the trials of being a tormented younger sibling. If she was not carrying out chores for her mother, she would be running the gauntlet of Wulfric and Wulfwin as they bestowed their abuse and insults upon her with arrogant impunity.

Winflaed approached her favourite spot, where the stream became deep and wide and had been dammed with rocks to make a pond. Here she knew she would find the water plants for which her mother had various uses. The bank was low and access to the water was easier here than at other parts of the stream. She placed her basket down away from the pond's edge and lay flat on her stomach, rolling up her sleeves so that she could plunge her arms deep into the water. She waved her fingers through the pockets of green sludge to search for any useful plants, smiling to herself as the little fish slipped in and out of her fingers.

Without warning, something thudded on the ground next to her. She leapt up in fright, heart pounding, but it was only Tovi, the youngest of her three brothers. He gave her a devilish grin as he sat beside her on the damp grass.

"Tovi!" she said crossly. "What are you doing here?" She felt a wave of irritation that her peace had been spoiled.

"Mother's looking for you, Frog Spawn."

"She knows where I am. She sent me here." Winflaed frowned at her brother. "Have you been following me?"

"Mother sent me to find you," he said with a shrug. "She said you have been gone such an age."

"The gathering of herbs and special roots takes time and care. It cannot be done just like that!" Winflaed snapped her fingers with an air of importance. "You have to know what you are looking for."

"You've been out here all morning, so you can't be very good at it." Tovi leaned forward over the water. "What were you doing with your arms in the water anyway, Frog Spawn? What are you supposed to be looking for in there?"

"You can find plenty of useful plants in there!"

"Show me."

"You have to lie down like this." Winflaed pushed her long fair braids back over her shoulders. She lay forward onto her stomach. "Come on, clever braies, lie as I am."

Tovi laughed. "All right, if you say so, but I can't see what you're going to find in there, apart from frogs and tadpoles." Tovi rolled up his sleeves, lay on his stomach and dipped his arms into the water as his sister had instructed.

"You have to put your head under to find them of course," Winflaed said.

"What? Under the water?"

"Yes, under. Like this." Winflaed leaned forward over the pond's edge and submerged her face into the water. When she emerged, Tovi was looking at her astounded. "You have to," she told him. "It's the only way to see what you're trying to get. You can open your eyes under water, can't you?"

"What am I looking for? All I can see is green slime and maybe a few tadpoles." He stared into the murky green water.

"The plants I need are like big white flowers. You can't mistake them. Look…" Winflaed put her face close to the water again. "There's one!" she cried.

As Tovi copied her, Winflaed seized the moment and pushed her brother's head hard into the water so that his shoulders and chest were submerged. Having succeeded in getting the top half of his body into the water, she proceeded to push until the rest of him slid in. All Tovi could do was thrash about desperately in a futile attempt to escape the inevitable.

He eventually made an undignified appearance from beneath the water, a mass of green slime hanging off his fair hair. Winflaed let out a hearty chuckle at the sight of her brother resembling a sun-bleached frog. She beamed triumphantly as she watched him make several unsuccessful attempts to clamber out of the water.

"Who's the frog spawn now?" she teased.

Tovi's good-natured smile turned to loud laughter as he finally managed to leap toward the bank and get himself onto dry land.

Winflaed turned to run but her foot caught on the root of an oak and she tripped. "No!" she squealed, as Tovi swung her into the pond with a mighty splash. "My basket!" she cried, but it was too late. The basket and all its contents tipped into the water and began to sink.

Tovi leapt in after it, but, when he hauled it back up onto the bank, Winflaed could see that it was filled with nothing more than wet slime and pond life.

"Mother will be furious if I go back with nothing." She was close to tears as she sat down on the grass, wishing that she hadn't been so foolish.

"We can find some more. I'll help you," offered Tovi.

"It'll take forever to find everything again. Mother will certainly punish me now. And the herbs for Grandmother... they were not easy to find."

"At least we will dry out as we hunt for them!" Tovi jumped to his feet and held out his hand to help her. Suddenly he began to laugh.

"What are you laughing at?" Winflaed demanded as she scrambled to her feet.

"You look like a drowned hare!" he declared, pulling at her waterlogged braids.

She was glaring at him irritably. "So do you," she replied, trying to squeeze out the water from her tunic. "We're definitely going to be in trouble now. Not only have we lost the plants, we are wet through!"

"Not if we take our time and dry out." Her brother picked up the basket to begin their hunt. "The sun really is warm today. Exactly what we need."

Winflaed had one last try at wringing out her clothes but, as she squeezed a handful of her skirts, she became aware that Tovi was listening intently to something. "What is it?"

He brought a finger to his lips. "Ssh," he whispered. "Listen!"

"What?" Winflaed lowered her voice.

"Someone's coming."

Then Winflaed heard it too – a young man speaking and the familiar laughter of a girl. She caught sight of two figures walking arm in arm through the trees, making their way towards the pond.

"It's, Freyda, and who is that?" Winflaed whispered.

Tovi caught her arm, and jerked her into the prickly undergrowth so that they were out of sight of the approaching pair. "That's Edgar Helghison," he hissed. "Father will have our dear sister's hide bloodied if he finds out."

Winflaed shivered. There had been a feud between the two families for years. The reasons for it were never really clear, but she knew that her sister's friendship with Edgar Helghison would spell disaster if their elders should gain knowledge of it. "Mother will kill her," she whispered. The next moment she wondered whether Freyda's misdemeanour would deflect from her own.

"Ssh," Tovi said. "We don't want them to catch us."

"Why not?"

"Frog Spawn! You don't know anything, do you? When we tell our sister that we have seen her trysting with a son of Helghi she will be at our mercy!"

"What is trysting?"

"Meeting in secret," Tovi explained.

"Like secret lovers?" Winflaed asked in awe and Tovi nodded. Truthfully, she was quite impressed at her sister's daring.

The two of them fell silent. Winflaed processed the idea in her mind, slowly registering the implications of Freyda's actions. She pictured her sister parting with the gold-plated hand mirror and jewelled brooch her father brought back for her from the wars. With glee, she imagined the infuriated look on Freyda's face as she handed over the coveted items. She would be helpless in their hands. From their hiding place, Winflaed and Tovi watched their sister and Edgar sit down, closely together, at the water's edge.

Winflaed drew in her breath. "He's kissing her!"

"Excellent. This will be one secret she will have to pay dearly for!" Tovi sniggered.

"She's half naked!" Winflaed exclaimed.

"And more excellent!" Tovi laughed. Winflaed noted that he looked thoughtful and was most likely still considering the advantages that their newfound knowledge might bring them. There was no way that his sister would have gained permission for such a meeting. She noted that her brother had an evil grin on his face.

Freyda felt a shiver of excitement as she responded to Edgar's kiss. She had been attracted to his tall physique and dark handsome looks for some time. At eighteen, he was four years older than she was. Whilst he was undoubtedly handsome with a lean, well-developed body, there was one flaw that marred his charm: his left leg was crippled, causing him to limp quite noticeably. The cause of Edgar's damaged leg was the source of the current bad blood between their two families, but Freyda suspected that the origin of the feud went back further than their generation.

Eleven years ago, the young man's father, Helghi, had insisted on buying an unruly pony from Wulfhere for his son, before he had been properly broken in and trained. A horse like that was not suitable for anyone let alone a boy of seven and Freyda's father had tried to deter his neighbour from purchasing the stallion. Unfortunately, Helghi was a determined, proud man, and would not listen. When the boy was thrown from the horse and his leg badly broken, Helghi accused Wulfhere's blacksmith of not having shod him properly. Freyda had heard that her father had denied this, arguing that he had tried to dissuade Helghi from buying the horse, and had advised him to purchase another. Wulfhere won the suit by swearing on oath with twelve men vouching for him. Though the case was settled, a feud had been born between the two thegns that would affect the lives of their people for years to come. However, Freyda was not going to let the bad feeling ruin her new friendship with the handsome, virile young Edgar.

She removed her homespun tunic and climbed into the water wearing nothing but her shift, a light linen undergarment that barely covered her knees. She smiled at Edgar as he watched from the bank unaware of the peeping eyes currently fixed on them.

"Freyda!"

She swam further toward the middle of the pond, treading water with ease as she teasingly cajoled him into joining her. Freyda enjoyed the way he was watching her, transfixed as the water rippled around her milk-white skin. He gasped as she removed her cap and unknotted her hair at the nape of her neck so it flowed unbound in long golden sunrays that seeped around her into the water.

"Come in, if you dare!" she called.

He stood up and began to undress. "As you wish, m'Lady!" He beamed as he stripped down to his white linen braies. He left his tunic, hose and *winingas*, the bindings that covered his calves, with Freyda's clothes in a pile by the water's edge before taking a dive into the pool. He swam to her and she twisted teasingly away from his grasp and swam away. She was not quick enough and Edgar lunged, locking her in a watery embrace as she squealed with delight.

Locked in their lovers' clinch, the young couple were obviously unaware of what was happening only feet away. Winflaed and Tovi crept from the bushes to the pile of clothing, quickly grabbing them and running away. Edgar and Freyda were fully occupied with each other, eyes closed and blissfully unaware of the thieves until it was too late.

Slightly disturbed by rustling, Freyda opened one eye and saw them. "The little snakes!" she cried, opening her other eye. She dragged herself to the bank. "They've taken our clothing!" Angrily she climbed out of the water with Edgar moving swiftly behind her. "What are we going to do?"

"I don't know, but there will be hell to pay if we don't get it all back." Edgar was half smiling. He was amused at the children's fearlessness and gave a sudden laugh.

"I don't know why you're laughing!" Freyda exclaimed. "You won't be if my father hears about us!"

Wasting no time, she took off after them. The ground underneath her bare feet was rough and dry, obstructed by twigs and thorns. Edgar followed her as best he could, but the lameness of his leg was not advantageous to speed. Freyda ran as fast as she could, threatening her younger siblings with a multitude of calamities.

"You'll both pay for this!" she bellowed, waving her fist furiously at them. "Just see if you don't!"

"Run!" Tovi shouted just as Freyda was within a few yards of them. As they ran, they dropped an item of clothing every few feet until they had relinquished all of the garments. All Freyda and Edgar could do was collect each piece until they had found them all, allowing Winflaed and Tovi to escape further into the woods; their laughter fading into the distance.

"The little pig droppings!" Freyda fumed as she rescued a shoe from the branch of a tree. "I am going to make them suffer! How dare they?"

"I think we might actually be the ones who will have to suffer, my love," Edgar said pragmatically, pulling her to him as she struggled to get her tunic back on over her wet, muddy shift. It seemed that Edgar was less concerned with what the children might divulge, and more concerned with continuing what had started earlier in the pond.

Freyda broke away from his attempts to kiss her, protesting that she would have to catch up with them and somehow ensure their silence. "I must go, Edgar. There could be a lot of trouble for us if I don't persuade them to keep their mischievous mouths shut."

"How are you going to do that?"

"I don't know, but I will think of something."

"When will I see you again?"

"If all is well, I will meet you here again tomorrow after the morning work is done." She pulled away from him, her fingers slipping reluctantly through his grasp.

"Tonight, meet me tonight?" he begged.

After a thoughtful moment, she nodded and broke away with a brief kiss.

Edgar watched his sweetheart disappear further up the woodland path until he could just see her golden hair glistening through the patches of forest sunlight in the distance. After he had put on his clothes, he turned and began to make his way down the track that led to his village of Gorde. He wondered wistfully whether Freyda would be able to keep their tryst that coming evening. Would she be able to persuade her brother and sister to keep their secret? He knew that her father had returned from the campaign in the land of the Scots. If their secret was exposed, there would be trouble between the families. His heart ached with a yearning for the girl and the loss of what should have been that day.

Chapter Three

The Dream

Horstede's longhall was a rectangular building large enough to hold at least two hundred people. It was not the grandest of buildings, but Ealdgytha had transformed it with her fine embroidered wall hangings, depicting a mixture of tales from the scriptures and ancient sagas. An elaborate display of old shields and weapons covered the spaces on the walls between the hangings. In Pagan times, weapons would have gone with their owners into their grave, but these were Christian days, and such practices were forbidden by the Church. Nowadays they were used to decorate the halls of their masters as a reminder of the bravery of the forefathers that used them. At one end of the hall was an ante-chamber separated by a wicker-woven partition where guests would enter and leave their weapons, cloaks and other personal items not needed. The wooden rungs that accessed the bed chamber above the hall were made private from the view of the guests by a wide curtain which ran across it.

"Is the food to your liking, husband?" Ealdgytha asked Wulfhere, observing him as he dipped a chunk of white bread into his stewed pork.

"Mmm! Of course, 'tis delicious, made more so by the fact that Herewulf nearly broke his back killing it for me!" Wulfhere answered, still amused by the story from the previous night.

He and Ealdgytha were sitting on colourfully painted high-backed wooden chairs in the centre of their raised table at one end of the hall. Esegar and his wife sat next to Wulfhere in a place of honour. To the right of Ealdgytha were her sister-in-law, the odious Gunnhild and her equally offensive son Leofric, who still remained as their guests despite Ealdgytha's efforts to get rid of them.

There were rows of trestle tables set up for Wulfhere and Ealdgytha's guests from the village. Everyone had come, even the children, to celebrate their thegn's homecoming. It had been a good harvest so the food was plentiful. There were honeyed griddlecakes, followed by the main course of pork, stewed with leeks, onions, and carrots, accompanied by newly baked bread; and for dessert they were served a compote of mixed berries and cream.

Everyone took full advantage of the generosity of their lord and lady, drinking their fill of strong beverages and eating till their belts needed loosening. Once Wulfhere was finished satisfying his hunger, it was time for him to address his guests. He praised Esegar, his brave shieldbearer, who had accompanied him on his first campaign and had protected his lord in the shieldwall with much courage and fortitude.

Esegar grinned with embarrassment as his wife, Godgyva, proudly kissed him and leant against his shoulder lovingly. The village guests wanted to hear stories of the battle for they were isolated most of the time, and loved to hear of life beyond their community.

After a while, Wulfhere handed over the evening's entertainment to Esegar who, despite his reticence, soon began to enjoy having a captive audience. He returned his lord's appreciation, describing Wulfhere's skill and heroism in battle, and speaking of the bravery of the wild Scotsmen, to enhance the valour of his lord. As he spoke, Freyda played a piece of music on a harp that her father had brought back amongst his booty. The hall was dark, lit only by the candles in their sconces and the fire that crackled in the hearth. All were silent as they listened intently to Esegar speak of the Battle of Dunsinane. Even the hounds made no sound as they lay sleepily under the tables, amongst the debris of scraps dropped for them.

Wulfhere sat in his chair, leaning comfortably to one side as Ealdgytha refilled his drinking horn. He smiled at her and drank deeply from it. Then he offered it to her. She put her hand on his and for a moment their eyes locked and everything else seemed to fade into the distance. Her almond-shaped eyes glistened with the glow of the hearth and they both smiled.

"It seems you killed a thousand Scotsmen," she whispered to him.

"Nine hundred and ninety-nine to be exact," Wulfhere replied with a sigh.

"You are tired, Wulfhere. I should like for us to go to our bed now. You are in need of rest. I should like to make you more comfortable than you are here."

"You, too, are in need of rest." Wulfhere smiled again. "After all, you have been busy these past few months with the harvest, the children, and all the work."

"Let me just check on your mother and send the children to bed. Then we can retire ourselves."

"That does sound good to me, but what about our guests?"

"I don't think we can accommodate everyone in our bedchamber, do you?"

"You jest very badly, my love," he chuckled and pinched her thigh playfully.

"Not as badly as you, dear husband!" Ealdgytha replied with a mischievous smile and a kiss for his forehead as she stood to her feet.

He grabbed her wrist and held it. "What happened to the miserable woman I left behind?"

Playfully, she thwacked his head and trod carefully through the mead benches to leave the hall.

That night Wulfhere and Ealdgytha made much gentler love than the previous. When they were both satisfied, they lay basking in their passion. The noise from the hall was beginning to subside and they were drifting into sleep when someone let out a great guffaw. This jolted them awake and they both broke into peals of their own laughter.

"Must be Herewulf, the old fool!" Wulfhere chuckled. "Only he has a laugh like the braying of a mule!"

"Don't let Sigfrith hear you say that about her father!"

"Not bloody likely. One look from that she-devil and she'd turn a man to stone!"

Ealdgytha clicked her tongue in mock disgust. "Heavens, I have such a thirst. Drink?" she asked, rising from the bed to fetch a pitcher of light ale. They both drank from it. "Now, let me bathe you."

"I have a better idea... why don't you let me sleep?"

"No, husband. You have not been anywhere near a basin of water since you got home! It's time you did." She dipped the sponge into the water before he could object further and began to wash his face first and then his chest.

"It's cold." He shivered.

"It will cool you down."

He yielded to her, knowing he would lose anyway, content to let the water wash over him gently. He felt relaxed and at ease, his senses still reeling from the unexpectedness of it all. This was not how he had envisaged his homecoming. He had expected nothing more than a grudging acknowledgement of his presence. Certainly not lovemaking, nor affection.

"Now let me do your back," she cajoled, easing him into a sitting position. She climbed across and knelt behind him. He could feel the softness of her skin against his back as she sponged the perfumed water soothingly down his aching torso. "At least you are all in one piece," she remarked as she studied him intently in the fading light. She noted some old scarring, but was glad to observe that there was nothing new to worry about.

"I still have all my fingers and toes," he commented.

They were quiet together for a few moments. The noise from the hall had begun to abate, signifying that the celebrating was coming to an end. The villagers had either gone home or were now asleep where they had passed out. Ealdgytha began to dry his back with strips of linen. Wulfhere sat silently whilst she wiped the dampness off his skin.

"Ealdgytha?" he whispered, breaking the silence.

"Mmm?" She began to massage his shoulders with agile fingers, probing every muscle.

"Ealdgytha, you do forgive me... don't you?" Wulfhere asked suddenly, as if he was disturbed by some thought or other on which he had been quietly pondering.

Ealdgytha's hands stopped working. "Forgive you? Forgive what?"

He bent his right arm across his chest to grab the hand that was massaging his shoulder. He held it gently, but firmly. "You know what for," he said earnestly.

Ealdgytha pulled her hand from his grasp and swung round beside him on the edge of the bed. She held her braid in her hands and twiddled it anxiously. "I don't want to talk about that woman, Wulfhere. Not tonight of all nights."

He saw that she was looking down at her hands, playing with the end of her hair. It was something she had always done when she was nervous or unhappy. His face reddened in the darkness. "I need to know that you have, Ealdgytha."

"Wulfhere, please don't... it was five years ago. You have never asked forgiveness. Why ask for it now?"

"Last night you told me that you wanted our marriage to be content and peaceful. It can only be so if we put the past behind us and talk about that which has been a thorn in our side all these years."

"It happened, Wulfhere, what more can be said? Why must we talk about it now?" A lone tear trickled down her cheek.

"I am sorry, *luflic*," he told her, a lump forming in his throat. "I should not have opened the wound. But I often wonder if it has ever truly healed."

"If it is forgiveness you want then I forgive you," she said tersely and gave a barely audible sob.

Wulfhere pulled her round and they lay down on the bed. He gently pressed her head to his shoulder and put his arm about her comfortingly. "No, not like this," he whispered. "I cannot ask for it until you are ready to give it, and now does not seem the right time."

Neither said any more. They pulled the woollen coverlet over them and lay in each other's arms until deep exhaustion drew them into sleep.

He stands on the crest of a hill, and stares through blurred vision at the terrible carnage surrounding him. Gazing upwards, he sees the black carrion eaters circling the sky, their mournful cries piercing the air as they wait to feed. His sight becomes clearer and congealed masses of human entrails, and bloodied tissue, scatter the hill slope. His mail feels unbearably heavy. Sweat pours, tickling his skin in rivulets. Instinctively, he clasps his sword. But as perspiration runs from his sleeve into his palm, he finds he cannot hold her. She slips from his grasp and the blade glints in the sunlight as it tumbles down the slope.

The sky is suddenly dense with dark clouds. The mist grows around him, dank with the stench of death and blood. He feels dizzy and wants to gag. Instead he forces himself to breathe hard to avoid expelling the bile that is rising in his throat.

"Pick up your sword, Lord Wulfhere!" urges a familiar voice.

A terrible throbbing pounds at his temples and he fights the need to lose consciousness. "It is lost!" he cries. "I cannot find her."

"You must!" the voice shouts in earnest.

Wulfhere staggers down the hill, recognising the faces of the fallen among the human carnage. They speak through lips that do not move; words he cannot discern. His feet slip in the ooze and he feels his heart racing. The voice continues to implore him to find his sword. Below him, at the foot of the hill, he sees a morass of jumbled men and spears. His head throbs as he moves toward them, fearing that *Hildbana* is lost somewhere amongst the chaos.

Suddenly, he is in the midst of the growling shieldwall. The sound of battle deafens him as he is heaved, pushed, and stabbed at with spears, axes, and swords. The enemy are in front; snarling, wolf-like faces. Wooden shields slam into the phalanx, trying to break their way in. Wulfhere is jostled this way and that, as if he is a coracle tossed in a stormy sea. He wants his sword. How can he fight without her?

"Where is my sword? Where is *Hildbana*?" he hears himself shout. And, though he knows it is his voice, it feels as if it belongs to another.

His head spins.

He stares down in an attempt to avoid unconsciousness and sees that his feet are bare... and the air is freezing against his naked body. *Where is my armour? I am naked!*

Terror grasps at his insides and fear tears through his veins. No spear, no sword, no armour to protect him...

"My lord, your sword!" He hears the voice calling out to him as though it is caught in a strong squalling wind. "Where is your sword?"

He looks up from the ground and stares into faces that are no longer fleshy. Faces of bone; skeletons, wearing dark hoods. He screams – a long, agonising cry that is eventually broken by the familiar voice calling him again.

"My lord! Open your eyes! Can you hear me?"

I know that voice. Esegar!

He is pulled by his ankles out of the scrum of heaving shields and thrusting spears.

"My lord! 'Tis I.... Esegar! Can you hear me?"

Wulfhere lies on the grass, dazed; tries to sit up. His head pounds. Around him he hears the roars and cries of the men in the shieldwall; the agonising sound of men dying.

"Here, take your sword!"

"You have it?" Wulfhere asks. Relief overwhelms him. He is alive and Esegar has found his sword.

Esegar's face flashes above him, and then he is no longer lying, but stands, face to face, with his shield-bearer. Wulfhere feels reassured. Then, almost instantly, the flesh begins to deteriorate, leaving a mass of hideously rotting skin, until it is no longer Esegar, but the hooded figure of *Déapscufa*, the Shadow of Death, surrounded by darkness.

Déapscufa smiles; a repugnant grim contortion, as the jawbone drops open to spill forth evil laughter, and with it, disgusting creatures, bugs, worms, and all kinds of ghastly things from hell.

"Your sword is broken, my lord," the jaw of Death says, rasping, and mocking like the voice of an old hag. A pair of bony hands hold forth his beloved *Hildbana*, she is broken in two.

The darkness disappears and Wulfhere feels himself rising into the greyness of the clouds. The world is drifting away from him and a scream is rising within him as the sky spins. It pierces through him and he is sure his head will break open and scatter its contents. Unable to breathe or move, his whole body is paralysed. The scream reaches a crescendo, and suddenly, he forces his eyes open, and he hears someone gasping for breath; not knowing that it is he.

"Wulfhere!" It was Ealdgytha's face now before him. "Dear God, what is it? A nightmare?"

He sat up in the darkness of the chamber and saw his wife at the end of the bed, holding up a lighted candle, the flickering flame reflecting the horror in her terrified face. He was soaked in sweat and shaking uncontrollably. He realised that it was he who had been gasping.

He struggled to speak. His eyes were moist with tears. She went to him, no longer afraid. As she put her arms around him she whispered, "You saw terrible things, my love, didn't you – in that battle?"

He breathed in deeply and gulped before pulling away, replying softly, "Many of my friends were killed... and I too... would have been, if it were not for Esegar... He fought over me as I lay amongst the fighting. He saved me."

"Oh, my sweet Jesus!" Ealdgytha whispered, horrified, covering her mouth with her hand.

"I took a blow to my head when my helmet was lost and I was knocked out, but Esegar got me out of there. He saved my sword and my life!"

"But neither of you said when you both told your tales of the battle! All you said was that Esegar fought bravely!"

Wulfhere shook his head. "It is hard for me to remember, or even speak of it. Esegar is a modest man. His humility prevents him from bragging. And, besides, he would not wish to shame or embarrass me."

"There cannot be any shame in taking a blow in battle, surely. Nor can it be shameful to be saved by one's loyal hearth-man."

"I am a warrior, Ealdgytha. The son and grandson of warriors. Esegar is not. I am supposed to be the stronger."

Wulfhere was no longer shaking now, knowing he was safe and that it was just a vivid nightmare. Up until then, the horrors of Dunsinane Hill had stayed only in his mind during the day when he could distract himself from the memories. This was the first time that they had manifested themselves in his sleep. He was accustomed to seeing men die, but not like this. The war with the men of Scotland had been bloody, brutal, and terrible. He had hoped that he would not experience anything like it again. The worst was what they had done to the civilians – women and children burned out of their homes and forced to flee in terror.

He had told himself that such things were inevitable in war, just as he always did. Nonetheless the guilt was still entrenched in his mind and heart. Guilt for the terrible atrocities committed by the men he fought with and guilt that it had not been him who had died instead of his friends. Surely it was a cruel God who allowed such wickedness to happen.

Ealdgytha pushed him gently back down on the bed. "Come, I will comfort you, husband," she told him soothingly. She began to stroke his hair. "You are home now and safe, with those who love you. Sleep, my love... all is well now."

Wulfhere closed his eyes, exhausted. He wanted to tell her what he had seen, the guilt which he felt and the fear which drove him to insanity, but he could not. He wanted to hear her tell him that he was safe and that there was no shame in being afraid. But he could not. To the world, he was a warrior and protector; he should not flinch from blood nor should he fear death. So, he was quiet. He would keep his demons within; his own beasts, locked away in the far corners of his soul.

Chapter Four

The Flames of Love Burn Brightly

Freyda stepped furtively from the hall out into the chill of the night air. She shivered with expectancy, knowing that she ran the risk of being caught. But she had promised Edgar that she would meet him that night and did not want to let him down. She had chosen her moment cárefully – her parents had retired for the night and Sigfrith was occupied looking after Grandmother in her sick bed. Thankfully, the watchful eyes of her younger brother and sister were no longer upon her as they, too, were also abed. A few of the village diehards were still carousing in the hall, but most had returned home to sleep off the effects of ale and strong mead.

Earlier, Freyda had sneaked out to the stables to saddle her horse, Aelfwyn, and tether her round the back of the building so that she was hidden out of sight. That way, her compliant mare would be ready and waiting for her when she could make good her escape. Seeing that the way was clear, she hurried across the courtyard in the dark, hoping that she was not too late and that Edgar would still be waiting for her at the usual place. After she had opened the gates just enough to allow space for her and Aelfwyn to exit them, she galloped out into the forest, hopeful that she would find Edgar

Her heart sank when she reached the pond and he was nowhere to be seen, but she had gone to a lot of effort to make the meeting and was not going to give up that easily. If she set out now, with the light of the full moon, she might encounter him returning home and the night would not be lost after all. She crossed her fingers, clipped her heels into Aelfwyn's flanks and cantered off along the track that led to Gorde, where Edgar dwelt with his family.

A sheath of grey cloud began to encase the moon, deepening the shadowy gloom of the outstretched branches. Despite the eerie darkness, she was not deterred in her mission, nor was she discouraged by the sounds of the rustling bulrushes or the night owl overhead. The forest had always been a welcoming place by day when the woodland spirits either slept, or watched quietly as humans invaded their domain. Night-time in the forest was quite the opposite. Stories about unfortunates who had met their doom in the forest at night, were plentiful, so that only the very brave ventured there after the sun had gone down. Freyda was definitely not in the habit of wandering through dark woodlands at midnight, but the anticipation of meeting Edgar thrilled her, tapering any fear she might have about a calamity befalling her.

Edgar was trudging, along the path back to his homestead. He had given up hope of seeing Freyda that night. When he heard a horse cantering in the distance behind him, he turned his head cautiously, expecting it to be the *nihtgenga*, a deadly dark rider who terrorised the forest at night. Waiting alone in the shadows had played fanciful tricks on his mind, and in the murky distance, a ghostly figure, red cloak billowing out behind it, was thundering fiercely toward him. He was about to turn and run when he heard his name, and to his relief, realised it was Freyda. She leapt from the horse and threw her arms around him in delight.

"Freyda! You came after all! I thought…"

"Did I scare you, *min lufestre*?" she laughed. "You look like you've seen a ghost! But I am so pleased that I have caught you. I thought I'd not see you tonight!" Her breath was heavy on his face as she kissed him.

"And I thought the little rascals had given the game away and your mother had packed you off to a nunnery. I thought I would never see you again!" he beamed, lifting her off the ground as they embraced. "Did the brats do their worst?"

She shook her head. "Would I be here if they had? I made sure they kept their damned mouths shut! It cost me dear, but I let them win, and only for now. No, I am late because of my father's homecoming feast. There was such a fuss! The whole village came to the hall and I just couldn't get away!"

"Is this one of your father's?" Edgar asked, stroking Aelfwyn's nose.

"No, Aelfwyn is mine," she said proudly, patting her horse's neck. "My father gave her to me on my last birthday. She matches my spirit, he said: fast–like the wind!" She tossed her head as she spoke. "Anyway, let us go to your place. We need somewhere warm and sheltered. 'Tis perishing cold out here tonight in the forest!"

He thought for a moment, wondering if it was such a good idea. How would his kin react should they catch him with the thegn of Horstede's daughter – in their domain?

"As you wish, then," he finally agreed, his reluctance overcome by the twinkle in her eye and her pouting lips. "But it must be the cattle byre for us, I am afraid."

"Really, so I am to be treated like a fat-arsed cow, am I?" Freyda broke into laughter and pushed him towards the stirrups, urging him to mount.

"If you are a cow, then I must be a bull! And I'm a very rampant bull tonight!" he chuckled, and did a very bad impression of a horned animal on heat.

She giggled as he swung his leg astride the animal before leaning down to pull her up onto the saddle before him, and away they went.

As they rode, they whispered endearments to each other and a sense of excitement began to seep through them. They took a path through the meadow that ran alongside the village so that they would not be seen or heard by any of the inhabitants. Gorde was a less imposing landholding than Horstede, with a smaller perimeter. Unlike Wulfhere's larger and more formidable longhall, Helghi's homestead had no boundary fence which separated it from the homes of his tenants. Nor were the defences properly maintained. There was no strong, high palisade, or ditch, nor earthen rampart, to surround the village, like at Horstede. Although Helghi was a landholder, he did not receive the same rights or title of thegn, for he did not hold the five hides of land that a thegn was expected to hold. He was still a free man nonetheless, and like Wulfhere, he owed service to the king for his land.

Edgar and Freyda left Ælfwyn tethered outside the village fence, just in case her hoof falls alerted the household. Hand in hand, they ran across the ground to the cattle byre, giggling, as they closed the wooden door. From a drawstring bag, Freyda produced tallow candles and a blanket that she laid out on a pile of hay, serving them sufficient comfort on which to lie.

"You've thought of everything!" Edgar marvelled.

He was totally in awe of her. She was beautiful, charming, and, amazingly, she seemed to be as enamoured of him as he was of her. Recently, he'd been pinching himself just to see if he was dreaming. His father called him *áwerde*, a useless cripple. He had grown used to the insults, believing that he was worthless, but Freyda seemed to look beyond his affliction.

They both knew something of the story as to why there was contention between their fathers, though both suspected there was more to it than that which had happened to Edgar's leg. That their love was forbidden made their tryst even more exciting.

"Do you have a flint?" Freyda asked as she lined the candles on the earthen floor, pushing them hard into the ground. She had brought the stone but had lost the flint.

Edgar reached for a lantern that had been left burning low and used the wick to kindle the end of one of the candles. Freyda took it from him and set all the candles alight. The glow was sufficient for them to see and they made themselves comfortable. The place was quiet apart from the odd movement or sound coming from the animals and they felt a chill of excitement that at last they could be alone together.

"Wake up, Freyda!" Edgar was shaking her anxiously. She sat up rubbing her eyes and gazed at him, disorientated.

"I smell smoke!" she cried, as the acrid smell of fire infused the air around her.

"Quick! We must get out of here!" Edgar cried, grabbing her wrist.

He dragged her to her feet and pushed her toward the door as she hastened to set her cap and clothes straight. They had both been so tired that they had barely shared a kiss before they fell prey to slumber. When Edgar woke, he was shocked to see flames spreading fast across the stacks of hay. The overturned lantern and a candle lying on its side, gave him a clue to what had happened. He knew there was no time to waste and his mind raced with thoughts of what to do next. He wanted to get Freyda out of there and away from Gorde, safely, before anyone noticed her – for if they were discovered, there would be all kinds of seven hells to pay.

Once outside, he knew that they would have to move quickly. "You must go, Freyda!" he ordered, pushing her toward the gate. He could hear the distressed noises that the animals were making and turned his stricken face toward the cattle byre.

"What are you going to do?" Freyda cried.

"I have to try and get the animals out."

"But you can't! It's too dangerous!"

"Go, Freyda!"

"Let me help you!"

"You cannot! If they see us, we are done for!"

"Edgar, I'm afraid for you! Please -"

"Go Freyda, you cannot be seen here!" Again he pushed her, more forcefully this time.

"I will get help!" she told him determinedly, and before he could protest, she gathered her skirts and ran. He watched her, with dread-filled horror, at what was about to happen.

Freyda felt a strong wind slapping the side of her face as she ran swiftly to the gate. She stopped briefly, her hand on the latch, and turned to look back at the byre. She saw to her horror, columns of flame, raging up the wooden sides of the building. The thatched roof had caught light and was collapsing onto a large building next to it. Such a construction must be Helghi's hall, she thought, the living quarters.

Villagers were waking up, and coming out of their dwellings; she could hear them shouting for water. She checked the desire to run back to make sure that Edgar was safe. Instead, she thought better of it and leapt onto Aelfwyn's back and galloped off into the forest. These people were going to need help if they were going to save their homes, their harvest and their livelihoods, although what she was going to say to her father when she got there, she had no idea.

She and Aelfwyn flew like the wind back through the woods. Branches caught at her cloak and hair, scratching her face until she bled. Luckily her father had taught her to ride well and she arrived, quickly, back through the gates of Horstede. She left Aelfwyn in the yard as she hurried up the rungs to her parents' chamber and burst through the curtains. Ealdgytha sat up in astonishment as she was confronted with her daughter, eyes wide with terror, hair full of twigs, cloak torn, and her arms flailing like a wild banshee. She was trying to waken Wulfhere, shouting, "Father, come quickly! There is fire at the Helghisons'!"

"Freyda! What is the meaning of this?" her mother cried, reaching for her shift. "Look at the state of you! Where have you been at this hour? How dare you come crashing into our bedchamber without permission?"

Freyda ignored her. She knew that this would spell disaster for her and Edgar, but she was beyond caring. Right now, help was what was needed and there was no time to concern herself with the consequences that would follow.

"Father, wake up! I need your help!" She was shaking him vigorously, enough to wake up a dead person.

Wulfhere opened his eyes and sprang up to a sitting position. He stared at her uncomprehendingly, rubbing his eyes and gasping at her appearance. "Freyda? What is it? You're making enough noise to wake a thousand armies!" he demanded, grabbing her by her shoulders. "Has someone attacked you? Who has attacked you?" He moved to sit on the edge of the bed and fumbled for his braies, visibly shaking as he struggled to secure them.

Ealdgytha grabbed her daughter, muttering angry words of chastisement. Freyda shook her off. "No, Father, I have not been attacked but there is a fire at Helghi's and they are in need of help!"

"What? A fire? At Helghi's?" Wulfhere asked, his voice full of disbelief.

"Yes, Father," she replied. "Do not look so confused, it is true. Their homestead is burning. Just as we speak, people could be dying! We need to hurry, we may be of use if you come now!"

"Freyda, what is this madness?" Wulfhere's voice was incredulous.

"Father, I cannot explain that now. We must hurry to their aid before it is too late! Get dressed and I will rouse the others!"

He tossed his head sternly, securing the last thong to the belt of his braies. "How do you know this, Freyda?"

"Please, there is no time for me to tell the tale, just come!"

"There is truly a fire? 'Tis not one of your pranks?"

"A prank? At this hour? No, Father, 'tis no prank. Please, we must make haste!"

"Let me at least put on my shoes, daughter! By the Holy Rood, girl, you have got some explaining to do. Even the Scots had to wait for a man to get dressed before we met them in battle. Fetch my boots, wife!" he commanded.

Ealdgytha began to protest. "Wulfhere, don't go. It is not our problem."

"If what our daughter says is true, I should go. I cannot leave them to burn. Where are my boots?" Reluctantly, Ealdgytha found them for him and he put them on. Freyda bent down to secure them, wishing anxiously he would hurry.

"Can you forget so easily how they left us to burn?" Ealdgytha said, her voice bitter.

"I have seen enough burning this year, I would not stand by and see another in my own neighbourhood," Wulfhere muttered.

When he was done, Freyda followed her father as they clambered down the steps, Ealdgytha hurrying behind them to the ante-chamber.

Wulfhere peered through the curtain into the hall and surveyed the scene. "Ealdgytha, you and Freyda wake up the men and tell them each to take a horse and follow me down to Gorde. Tell them to bring buckets and rope if they can find it. They might as well help with this fire if indeed there is still time."

"We must hurry!" Freyda urged.

"And I would like to know what it has to do with you, daughter?" Ealdgytha asked tersely, then added, "Wulfhere, you cannot go! Remember the last time..."

"Ealdgytha, if there is a fire, my conscience would not let me rest if I did not try to help."

Freyda sighed with relief as her mother gave her blessing. "Then, if you must go, I pray that God goes with you."

Freyda watched Wulfhere push open the door and followed him outside where they could smell the faint aroma of burning. He turned to her and she shrank from his infuriated glare. "Freyda, where do you think you are going?"

"I must come with you."

"No, you will stay here," he ordered and pushed her gently back into the hall. "And later you will explain to me how you came to know of this." Reluctantly, she obeyed and went to rouse the other men with her mother, scheming a way to get back to Gorde.

When the men from Horstede arrived, Wulfhere ordered them to join the line the villagers had already started. They were passing wooden buckets with water taken from the stream to the burning buildings. He had already ascertained that their efforts had little effect on the fire for it was burning well now, fanned by an easterly wind in the cool dawn hours, and threatening to spread to the homes of the villagers as the wind propelled burning embers towards the nearby houses.

Wulfhere hoped that their presence would give heart to the already beleaguered people of Gorde if nothing else. Seeing that his men were deployed usefully, he then went to find his neighbour to let him know that they were there to help and see what he could do for him. He did not relish the prospect of confronting his old adversary; there was much enmity between them. Nevertheless, Wulfhere knew it was the Christian thing to do, and hard as it was given their troubled history, he faced the challenge boldly.

Helghi's hall was almost devoured by the flames. He was brought to mind of the time when his own stables had caught fire and he had lost five of his best horses. The blame had rested squarely on Helghi's shoulders and also those of his evil kinsmen, whom Helghi had called upon to help him. There had been a fight and Wulfhere's brother, Leofric, had been killed. That had been six years ago, and Earl Godwin had ordered the two men to stop their feuding or face heavy fines. An uneasy truce followed, each man keeping their distance and only willingly crossing paths when the king, or the earl's business required it of them.

Wulfhere spotted his neighbour at the head of the queue, passing buckets back and forth. Helghi was a big man, large and stocky. In his more youthful days he had been well-groomed, with muscles honed by regular fyrd duty and a strength that matched a powerful frame. Nowadays he neglected himself, was more rotund in shape and paunched in the midriff. His once handsome features were now tarnished by broken veins and an almost purple complexion from an over-indulgence of strong mead and rich food. Despite his loss of vigour, Wulfhere saw that Helghi fought like a mad boar for his home that night. Everyone in the village capable of hauling a bucket full of water was there, both young and old. Wulfhere suspected, with humour, that the prospect of having their lord as a house guest was enough to inspire the villagers to do their best to save the hall. Helghi was a surly man at the best of times. At his best, even, he was a cruel drunk with a head full of resentment for anyone and anything. He would not make a pleasant guest.

Wulfhere move towards him nervously. In front of him, flames lit up the early morning sky. He paused with some distance between them. He was unsure about the response his presence would provoke, or from any of the others for that matter. So far, there had been a lot of mixed reactions. Some were stunned to see the men of Horstede there; some silently accepted their presence unquestioningly; a few others asked what had alerted them, but none had made any objections. Most likely all were relieved and too busy with the task in hand to concern themselves with their mysterious arrival.

For a moment he stood almost enthralled, as Helghi fought like a mad bull to save his hall from the fire. He summoned up the nerve to approach. Around him was chaos. Men were yelling as they ran from burning houses, salvaging what they could whilst their women chased the livestock here and there to safety. As Wulfhere edged tentatively closer to his neighbour, he was suddenly aware of a woman screaming, somewhere near to the far end of the hall. It was bloodcurdling; he had heard the like before in Dunsinane.

A dishevelled middle-aged woman, her hair uncovered, ran toward him. She grabbed him desperately. "Come help us, good sir," she cried and then exclaimed, "Oh Lord, save us! What are you doing here, Lord Wulfhere?"

"I and my men have come to aid you," he reassured her gently.

"Then help my lady save her child!" the woman gasped.

He followed her as she ran around the side of the hall to where a group of women were restraining a younger woman he knew to be Mildrith, wife of Helghi. She was on her knees in the grass, screaming as her women prevented her from running into the burning hut.

"My baby!" she screeched, her hands clawing her face and hair. Every time she made to break free, they held on to her fast, sobbing and begging her to cease struggling. Looking at the hut, Wulfhere assumed that some embers from the byre, fuelled by the wind, had fallen onto the roof of the building and set it aflame.

"Why did I think it would be safe to leave her in there?" Mildrith was crying. Her shoulder-length hair was matted, her face tear-streaked and dusty. "I should have known that the hut was too close to the hall."

Wulfhere shook his head and looked at the distraught women. He knew instantly that he had to do something. If he walked away and did nothing, he would never forgive himself for leaving a child to burn. "Get me a blanket or something doused in water," he shouted at the woman who had brought him there. "Your cloak will do!"

The woman nodded and dashed off to do his bidding. The other women looked at him, their mouths dropped open in surprise as they recognised him. Wulfhere reassured Helghi's hysterical wife that he would get her baby for her. He grabbed her shoulders, put his face close to hers and spoke earnestly to her. She seemed to look right through him and Wulfhere realised there was great fear for her child. He glanced round at the hut and saw why. The fire had taken hold with a firm grip, and the chances of the building collapsing in on him were ominously high. Just then, the woman returned with the cloak doused in water, and he threw it over his head ready to enter the burning hut. For a moment, he marvelled that only two nights ago, he'd returned home after surviving a bloody battle with the Scots; now, here he was, risking his life to save the child of a man whose hatred for him rivalled any enemy he had ever met on the battlefield.

He said a quick *Paternoster*, and gazing upwards, added, "I hope you reserve a nice comfortable seat for me up there, oh Lord!" Then he kicked the door of the hut, which came away easily, and entered, gingerly.

The intensity of the heat was overpowering. His eyes streamed and stung with the smoke. He was coughing and spluttering and smoke-blind, fearing he could not go in but when he heard a baby's whimpering, he knew he could not give up.

Flames burned on the front right side of the hut. This was the area of the little building that was nearest the hall. As he tried his best to focus, he heard the child choking from a corner of the hut somewhere behind the flames. He had to get there quickly, for the flames were growing and if she wasn't burned to death, the smoke would fill her lungs and kill her. As he peered tentatively from underneath the protection of the cloak, he could just about see her outline; the baby was bouncing in fear, and his heart lurched. She was a little thing of no more than a year or so, same age as his Drusilda. She was pressing herself against the wall. Her piercing wails broke his heart as she cried out frantically in her cot. Within seconds, the flames had moved closer to her. Through the smoke, he tried to see another way round. Above was a loft, the floor of which had just started to burn. He hoped that the timbered base would hold out until he could get to her, for he knew they would be done for if it came down. He thought about running back out for water, but the thatch on the roof in the middle was beginning to burn and he knew there was no time.

"Stay with me, God. Help me," he prayed. "And Lord, if you let me live today, I promise to do more good deeds." He crossed himself, kissed the little iron crucifix that hung about his neck, and lunged forward.

His outstretched hands felt for her, but he could barely see because of the flames and the smoke. Behind him, he heard something crackle and collapse, and he tried not to think of it. What mattered most at that moment was what was before him. He managed to grab the screaming infant and tucked her under his right arm. With his free hand, he drew the cloak closely over them both. When he turned to get out, he saw that the way was now blocked by the blazing thatched roof which had collapsed into the interior. He felt the heat searing toward them and the smell of burning oak was almost suffocating. The little girl clung to him, smothered against his heart, whimpering with terror. He had to find a way to get her out.

Looking along the back wall, he could see that it was scorched but not yet burning. The shuttered window was also still intact. A strange mixture of fear and calm possessed him, and he began to slide along the wall until he reached the window frame. He pushed out the shutters and exited the baby as carefully as he could out onto the grass; then he squeezed himself through the aperture to land beside her. The little girl was sobbing and vomiting, and he felt weak as he took a moment to recover from the burning, painful coughing. His heart was beating fast, but he knew he couldn't stay so close to the building, for burning thatch was falling about them; he had to get them both away. He could hear women screaming as the building continued to burn and collapse in flame. He imagined that they must have thought the worst, believing that he and the infant had both perished. It was not hard to see why as he gazed momentarily at the hell from which he had just escaped.

His eyes roasting, he gathered up the babe and staggered through the billowing smoke. He saw the women huddled together, hysterical with grief and eyes wide with terror. They were staring at the blazing hut but one of them caught sight of him.

"Lord save us!" the woman cried, and clutched Mildrith's shoulders, "Look!" Turning Mildrith to face him, the woman thrust her forward to take her child. "He has her! He has your little Ealswith"

Wulfhere held the baby to her relieved mother who grabbed her from him and smothered her with kisses and words of endearment. As he lay on the grass, he felt himself heave and could not stop himself from vomiting. As the women were fussing around the child, one of them withdrew to kneel beside him and ask how he fared. He was coughing savagely but managed to respond with a nod that he was all right. Someone fetched him some ale and he drank gratefully.

Watching the group of women weeping and laughing together, Wulfhere felt their emotion permeate through to him. He was glad that he had been able to save the child, even though it was spawned of

Helghi. This moment would touch him forever, like at Dunsinane, when he had looked around at the carnage in the aftermath of battle, and heard the screams of women and children as the soldiers brutalized them. And the burning fires… He would never forget. Perhaps he had been driven to risk his life for the child to make amends for what happened in Dunsinane. Whatever the reason, maybe now, he had absolved himself by this selfless act, risking his life to save that of another, not in battle for his lord or fellow warriors; just a simple act of goodness, to save a life other than his own.

For a moment he felt at peace. A sensation of calm, like a warm breeze blowing through his body, washed over him. Looking at the hut, savagely consumed by the raging flames, he realised they should not have gotten out alive. God had answered his prayer. He watched the group of women for a minute as they embraced. The older woman who had brought him her dampened cloak, realised the danger of remaining so close to the fire, and ushered them to a safer distance.

As Mildrith walked away with her child hugged closely to her, she turned and mouthed "Thank you", an expression of immense gratitude in her wide, fawn-coloured eyes. He acknowledged her with a nod, and as her image disappeared into the smoke, raw pain throbbed in his scorched hands. His feet were also smarted, where blazing embers had dropped onto his boots, leaving them his footwear beyond repair. He removed them and flung them away; they were useless, now. He had been oblivious of the pain whilst the need to get himself and the child to safety had been paramount but now that the crisis was over, the awful burning he felt in his extremities created a new need, to bathe his injuries in the cold water of the stream.

He hurried there and dipped his hands and feet in the cold water. Looking around, he observed the disorder. Some of the men were only half-heartedly fighting the flames now. Others had given up and were lying about on the ground in exhaustion and despair. Helghi was trying to rouse them, but it looked as if even he was beginning to realise that he could do nothing now other than wait until the fire had run its course. To try and fight it was futile, and he slumped on the grass, his pretty wife comforting him, babe in her arms, watching as his home was destroyed.

Wulfhere felt Esegar's presence beside him. He was still coughing as his friend crouched down beside him. Like Wulfhere's, Esegar's face was red from the heat and dark smudges mingled with the sweat that layered his cheeks and forehead.

"My lord, you have swallowed the smoke into your lungs," Esegar said, looking down at his lord's injured hands and feet. "And I see that you have been busy."

"Just a little," replied Wulfhere, with a cynical grin.

"Your daughter is here," Esegar told him nodding towards a group of women who were soaking strips of their tunics as cold compresses for those who had suffered burns.

Wulfhere felt a surge of anger. Why can't the damn girl do as she is told for once? In his anger, he ignored his pain and rose to his feet. He stormed across the village green to where Freyda was helping the women tend to a group of injured men.

As he got closer, he saw that she was engaged in a heated discussion with a lad; a younger version of Helghi. A crowd had begun to gather round them. Worried, Esegar hurried beside him. Wulfhere felt him touch his arm but he ignored his friend's efforts to calm him.

"I had nothing to do with this!" Freyda was shouting at the boy as Wulfhere pushed past the curious villagers, grabbed his daughter by the arm and pulled her away.

"I saw her," the boy was telling the crowd in an angry voice. "I saw her, riding out of here, just before the fire started."

The boy was Helghi's younger son Eadnoth, a stocky youth about two years Edgar's junior. Wulfhere pushed his daughter behind him, just as Helghi appeared, weaving his way through the growing crowd. Helghi came to stand by his son. The two men faced one another, the atmosphere threatening. Helghi was Wulfhere's elder, by only three years, though his weight and complexion, and the effect that the night's devastation had wrought on him, made the difference seem more like twenty.

His neighbour, clothing scorched. face darkened by smoke, looked curiously at him. "So, I am homeless now," Helghi grunted. "How happy must that make you, to see me ruined." A wealth of bitterness simmered in his eyes. "Have you come to gloat at my misfortune?" Helghi's dark hair, peppered with white strands, was matted with sweat and bits of thatch. His beard was singed, and he looked a pathetic sight.

Helghi's words were not quite what Wulfhere expected. He found it amusing. He looked down at his bare feet, beginning to blister. "I too, have lost something – my boots." He smiled wryly, gesturing downwards with his hands. "Not quite equivalent to your loss… but nonetheless a nuisance. Alas, they were a good pair of boots."

"It gladdens you to see me so humiliated, does it not? What are you doing here, anyway?" There was no mistaking the suspicion in Helghi's voice.

"I came to help you, Helghi -" Wulfhere began to explain.

"Father, this man's daughter started the fire!" interjected Eadnoth, animatedly pointing at Freyda.

"It was not me!" protested Freyda. Her attempts to step forward were obstructed by Wulfhere.

"I saw her," Eadnoth insisted.

"If my boy says he saw her, then it must be true," Helghi said. "What kind of a man would send his little daughter to do his dirty work?" His villagers chorused their support.

"If I wanted to set fire to your hall, Helghi, I would do it myself. I would not send my daughter to do the deed. But I didn't, nor did my daughter." He gave Freyda a look of disapproval, as if he were daring her to deny it.

"Then who did?" Helghi bellowed. "Who else could it be but you?" He pushed his face close to Wulfhere and spat the words into his face. "You've been waiting for this moment, haven't you?" He swept the scene with his arm, "Are you happy now?"

Wulfhere faced him, with his hands on his hips and legs apart, staring back at him grimly.

"Yes, that's the truth of it," Helghi continued menacingly. "You have always blamed me for what happened to your stables, and this is your revenge." He looked round at his people gathered behind him, just as Wulfhere's men were assembled behind him; two villages at war with each other.

Wulfhere folded his arms. "If I had wanted to get my revenge for that night, the thing would have been done before now, and you would not be standing there with your foul breath and ugly face staring into mine." He supressed the thought to cut the man's throat with his seax, letting the anger that had risen within him out with a long, deep breath.

Mildrith pushed her way through to the centre of the crowd. The little girl whose life Wulfhere had saved was clinging to her mother's neck with silent bemusement.

"Husband stop this at once!" Mildrith implored. "It is thanks you should be giving Lord Wulfhere, not accusations. He came here to help to us."

Suddenly Wulfhere was reminded of his promise to God only a short while ago. How was it possible to save a life one minute and then want to destroy one a moment later?

"How did he know there was a fire? Tell me that." Helghi gesticulated at his wife then turned back to face Wulfhere, eyes wide and watery.

Wulfhere fought the urge to break into laughter at the irony of the situation. He failed. His laughter rang out, unrestrained. *So Helghi thinks I set the fire then came down here to put it out?* Such an elaborate scheme not even he would have thought of.

"You think this is funny?" Helghi stormed. "You see?" He turned to his people. "What more proof could we have than the guilt he cannot hide in his mirth."

"No, Helghi, I do not think it a matter for mirth that I would go to all the trouble of sending my daughter here to set fire to your homestead – and then come down here in the middle of the night to help you put it out, especially when all I wanted to do was spend my first night home from warring in the north in my own bed with my wife!" His voice rose in a crescendo of ire.

Wulfhere was not the only one to find this a humorous prospect. His men, gathered around him, began to laugh as well. Much to Helghi's annoyance, it was contagious, and before long, his own people began to join them. Helghi, his face already flushed with vitriol, looked as if he was about to explode in rage.

"Stop this amusement now!" he roared. His fury had an immediate effect on everyone, compelling them to quieten instantly.

Thinking it was a good time to leave, Wulfhere placed his hands on Freyda and Esegar's shoulders, moving them towards the gate and encouraging his men to do likewise.

"Don't you walk away from here, Wulfhere, *horningsunu!*" Helghi called after them, his voice getting louder the further away they got. "You won't get away with this. You think because you are a thegn you can do as you like? Burn a man's house to the ground, and just walk away?" he continued, shaking his fist. "You and that daughter of yours are as guilty as hell. You are not above the law. I will see to it that you are outlawed for this. You will be *Níðing!*"

Freyda broke away from her father's grip and turned to face her accuser as the morning sun began to brighten the dancing shadows, cast by the fire. "For the last time, I did not start the fire... Edgar! Tell them, tell them the truth!"

Helghi turned and looked at his son. Edgar's guilt-ridden face was as red as the dye from a madder root. Shaking with fear, he took a few tentative steps forward toward his father. He hesitated, licking lips that were dry and blistered.

"Edgar..." The desperation in his Freyda's voice made Wulfhere's heart beat faster as he suddenly comprehended what was happening. Something was going on between Edgar and his daughter. What a fool he had been not to have realised it.

Edgar was gazing at Freyda, looking to her for courage. "The fire was not her fault. It was mine, I..." His voice broke off, nervously.

Helghi went to speak and then hesitated, as if he was checking what he had heard. Then, as he opened his mouth to speak again, Edgar reaffirmed, "It was m-me – Father." He stared at Helghi, apprehensively.

Helghi's mouth remained open but the words did not come. He suddenly laughed; an insane cackle of disbelief. When he finally spoke, it was with disbelief. "Come on, lad, are you out of your wits? What is this nonsense? Has something crushed your head?"

"Yes, Father. No doubt I am out of my wits, and I will as like suffer for it, but it was not Freyda's fault."

"We are both to blame," Freyda cut in. "Yes, I too... I am to blame – with Edgar – but it was an accident, you see. An accident..."

Wulfhere gave an inaudible moan. The truth was suddenly dawning on him – "the familiar way they looked at each other, the way he said her name, her urging him to speak, and the fact she had known there was a fire; it was all adding up. She had been there with him when it started. *But why?* And then realisation came to him, the scene unfolding piecemeal in his confused consciousness. *Helghi's idiot son must have lured her there for his own foul purpose.*

"Tell him everything, Edgar," Freyda urged. "Tell him all of it. It will be all right, I promise... it will be all right."

Edgar shook his head at her. "I cannot, Freyda..." His voice was no more than a whisper.

There was a curious murmuring amongst the crowd as Freyda lunged toward Edgar. Wulfhere attempted to restrain her, but he was stunned, weakened by the shock, and let her go as if she was a puppy, escaping from her master. He watched as she scampered past an open-mouthed Helghi, and stood by Edgar, taking the lad's hand firmly in hers. In the crowd, gasps and whistles of amazement could be heard.

Taking heart from her show of courage, Edgar lifted his downward gaze to meet everyone's disbelieving eyes.

"Freyda and I were together last night. We were in the cattle-byre together and fell asleep. The fire was an accident. We had some candles for light and accidentally kicked them over and the hay caught fire."

"We love each other, and want to be together," Freyda asserted. "But we knew that if we openly displayed our friendship then we would be prevented from being together. We did nothing sinful, just slept... until the barn caught alight." She paused, and the silence hung in the air until she said, "It is our wish that we be betrothed."

Helghi stared at the pair open-mouthed. A few others sniggered in the crowd, but most dared not show any reaction for the atmosphere was tense and a feeling of unease saturated the smoke-filled air.

Wulfhere swallowed, sensing trouble, his heart palpitating as the battle fever flowed through his veins. Here, on Gorde's territory, the men from Horstede were doubly outnumbered. If there was to be a clash like the last time, they would come off worse.

"Lord, we have to get out of here. If there is trouble, we are likely to lose," Esegar whispered, with urgency.

Remembering the death of his brother Leofric, Wulfhere nodded. He knew it would give Helghi great satisfaction to fight him here on his home ground and win, but he was not going to give him that. He eased Esegar's fears by nodding with ice-cold control, replied quietly to himself, under his breath, "Another time maybe."

The air was silent for some moments until he gestured to his daughter. "Freyda! Here, now!"

"Father, I -"

"Don't even dare to speak to me, girl. We will go home now!" he roared at her, startling her.

"But, Father -"

"You will come now! Our work here is done." He shot Edgar a venomous look and added, "…it would seem."

Freyda did not move. It was Mildrith who stepped forward and touched her shoulder gently, suggesting it would be best for all concerned if she went. Edgar, too, encouraged her to go. Daring to move toward her, he spoke softly, barely louder than a whisper, reassuring her that, *nothing on this earth will keep us apart.*

Suddenly, it seemed that time was standing still, but after a moment, she stepped forward, and kissed Edgar gently on the cheek. He clasped her hands, and as she moved away, their fingers remained locked until she was out of reach and could no longer hold on. Reluctantly, she let her arms fall. Freyda seemed to float away, still looking back at Edgar, until she reached her father, waiting sternly, his arms folded in disgust. He turned his back on her and began to walk with the rest of his men to their horses. In the distance, Helghi continued his stream of invective, but it was ignored.

Wulfhere found his mount. He turned in his saddle for a last look at the wreckage of Gorde. He was some yards away but could see the fire was still burning, though subsiding somewhat now that the wind had dropped. The people looked stunned, but at least the flames had not spread from Helghi's buildings to their own homes, and thankfully they had managed to save most of the grain they had harvested.

Then he flinched as Helghi gave his son an almighty blow to the side of his head with the back of his hand. The blow felled him, and he lay sprawled in the dust as Helghi rained down blow after blow upon him. Wulfhere turned as Helghi, tired of using his fists, began to kick Edgar, mercilessly. He could watch no more and gently clipped his horse's flanks and rode after the others.

Chapter Five

A Dutiful Daughter

Freyda stood before her parents, waiting in silence for the inevitable chastisement she knew was about to begin. The longhall was grim, her parents' anger permeating the atmosphere like breath from a dragon. She had been summoned to give an account of herself. As her eyes, bloodshot from endless crying, took in the harsh expressions of her parents, she lost any hope that they might be prepared to consider her marrying Edgar. She tried hard not to blink or yawn, but stared at them, defiantly. The events of the previous night meant that it was well into morning by the time the weary band had returned home from the fire.

Eventually the dreaded silence was broken by her mother, eyeing her reproachfully as she spoke. "So, what do you have to say for yourself, daughter?" Ealdgytha demanded.

Freyda felt herself shrink under her mother's disdainful gaze. She turned away from her, looking to her father for support. He returned her glare steadily, but there was no flicker of emotion in them, just an unfamiliar coldness. He was unrecognisable to her. Gone were the laughter lines and the smile that she thought was only for her. She studied him keenly, as if the real Wulfhere would somehow reappear if she searched long enough. It had always been her custom to tease and cajole him, ensuring that he gave her his full attention. She had ensnared him long ago, when she was just knee-high to him; like a treasure that must be hidden away, she had locked him into her heart. But now, it seemed, he had broken free of her spell, hardening himself against her.

"Well?" demanded her mother after a moment. Her voice was chilled. "Have you nothing to say?"

Freyda continued to ignore her, remaining focussed on her father. Once upon a time, Ealdgytha had been a kind and loving mother, but not anymore. Something had changed within her mother over the years, and lately Freyda's own rebellious nature had resulted in her being in constant conflict with her.

"Wulfhere, make her answer!" Ealdgytha turned to him for assistance.

Father shifted uncomfortably in his seat and gave her mother an angry glare. Then he looked back at Freyda. She knew by the burning in his blue eyes that he was seething. Growing up witnessing many of her parents' arguments had given Freyda enough insight into their relationship to know that Mother had quite a gift for making Father feel inadequate.

"What were you thinking, Freyda, running off to tryst with this fellow in the woods without your mother's knowledge?" Wulfhere demanded.

Freyda could tell he was forcing himself to look at her and steeled herself for the coming onslaught that would follow her next words. "We could not help ourselves. We are in love."

"Love?" Wulfhere retorted. "Don't be foolish, girl. What could you know of such things? You have been listening to the songs of too many *scops*."

Freyda looked down. She knew it would be imprudent to argue. "I am sorry, Father, if I have disappointed you in any way." She attempted to sound meek.

"She should have a good whipping!" Mother broke in angrily. "My father would have skinned me alive had I dared to behave so disobediently!"

"I have always been a dutiful daughter," Freyda objected. "Surely that has to count for something."

"You know who this youth is?" Wulfhere asked.

"Of course she knows who he is," Ealdgytha interjected impatiently.

Speaking with confidence, Freyda said, "I know he is the son of Helghi and that there is disagreement between you and his father, but it has nothing to do with Edgar, nor me, for that matter."

"It has everything to do with you, and since you have described yourself as a 'dutiful daughter', I would not have expected you to go running into the woods with a lad whom you know to be the son of your father's sworn enemy, a man who caused the death of your beloved uncle!"

The harshness in Wulfhere's voice sent a shiver down Freyda's spine. She could see him clutching the scrolled arms of his chair with such force that his knuckles blanched. "'Tis true, daughter. My brother Leofric's life was lost because of Helghi, the night my stables were burned to the ground, some of my best horses killed."

Freyda felt the tears gather in her eyes but she refused to let them fall. She lowered her gaze and said in a quiet voice, "T'was not Edgar's doing, Father, and it was never proved that it was Helghi that caused your stables to burn. Please, Father, I want you to end the feud and allow me to marry him."

Wulfhere ignored her request, taking a different approach now. "Does this man have carnal knowledge of you?"

Freyda shivered as her boldness gradually diminished. She was losing the battle, and for the first time in her life, was afraid of her father.

Wulfhere lunged forward in his chair causing a startled gasp from her mother. "Answer the question! Or so help me, God, I will skin and gut him and stick you in a nunnery quicker than you can spin thread!"

Father's eyes were ablaze with anger and his handsome features contorted with rage. Though Freyda shook with fear, she did not flinch, and she remained steadfast in her resolve, determined to stand strong against them. The desire to hurt him as he was hurting her, burned within her. She was a cornered animal whose only recourse was to fight back. She knew that he would be deeply wounded to know that she had lain with the son of his greatest enemy. And, so what? Was that not justifiable retribution for the pain she was feeling now? She loved Edgar, and wanted to be with him.

"Answer the question!" Wulfhere demanded again. "Am I to take from your silence that you are guilty of having given yourself to this man?"

When no answer came, Wulfhere suddenly stood to his feet. Enraged, he took hold of the heavy oak table, and lifting it, flung it forward, causing it to crash off the dais onto the floor in front of Freyda.

She sprang out of the way as the remains of her parents' lunchtime meal flew in all directions; wooden bowls and clay cups crashed to the floor. She let out a wail as one of the cups smashed by her foot and a shard cut her ankle. Sigfrith had been watching from the other side of the hall and instinctively ran to her.

"Answer your father, Freyda!" Ealdgytha ordered, trying to seem composed. But she looked as shaken as Freyda had been, at the ferocity of Wulfhere's rage.

"No, he does not have carnal knowledge of me!" Freyda declared, and pursed her lips defiantly.

She looked up at her father as he stood on the dais. His anger had reached boiling point. She had seen him display such rage before but never thought she would be the cause of it. Her resolve was beginning to crumble, her mouth and chin, quivering. Sigfrith threw her arms protectively around her. Freyda was grateful for Sigfrith, the maid's presence lent courage to her. She continued to glare at her father. His brow furrowed, his chin, like hers, also quivered. His hands clenched into fists, as he towered over her. Every part of him was shaking with rage. Her heart beat anxiously. *Is he going to hit me*? she wondered.

"You will never see Edgar Helghison again. Do you understand?" Wulfhere glowered.

Freyda gave no reply. She kept her head high, refusing to hang it in shame. She wanted to scream that she *would* see him, that it would be futile for them to order her not to; but after observing the explosive nature of her father's anger, she was terrified to see the whiteness of his fury again so soon.

"Do you understand?" he repeated forcefully. "I have never beaten you before, daughter, but I can assure you that I will not baulk at giving you the whipping you deserve if you ever defy me again!" Freyda looked toward her mother whose smug expression galled her. *She is enjoying every minute of it*, thought Freyda. She narrowed her eyes wickedly at her mother.

"Your father has spoken, Freyda," Ealdgytha said disdainfully. "There are to be no more secret meetings with this boy."

Freyda nodded passively and made an obeisance. She left the hall, her face burning with rage; like players in a board game, her parents had won the first round and her mind was already scheming her next move.

She was waiting for him in the courtyard, astride a small grey horse, accompanied by a handful of men from Gorde. The men were carrying the buckets that Wulfhere had left behind in the hurry to depart. Wulfhere studied them, their faces, and clothes, still blackened by the smoke, their expressions dominated by weariness. Mildrith wore no pretty wimple for going abroad. Instead, she wore a plain linen scarf that she had tied at the nape of her neck to cover her hair. Her garments were tattered and smudged with the residue of fire smoke.

"My Lord Wulfhere, I come to return your buckets and bear you a message from my husband. He expresses his regret that he laid the blame for the fire at your feet. He was most shamed when I told him what you had done for our child." She lowered her eyes.

Wulfhere nodded curtly as Aelfstan, Yrmenlaf and the twins retrieved the buckets. He did not believe for one minute that Helghi had expressed any sort of regret, but he felt a tinge of sympathy for this pretty young woman and her humbled, wretched men.

"Lady Mildrith," Ealdgytha said as she emerged into the courtyard from the hall. "I am sorry for your unfortunate circumstances. Have you lost everything?"

Mildrith, poised in her saddle, turned her head to look at Ealdgytha; proud eyes in a face filled with humility. "The hall and its surrounding buildings have all gone, but the villagers still have their homes, thanks be to God. We managed to save some of the harvest grain but lost some livestock, I'm afraid. Some of our people have been sorely hurt but at least no one was killed, or badly maimed."

"That's very fortunate," Wulfhere said soberly.

"Thank you for your assistance last night, my lord. We are truly grateful." Mildrith pulled on her horse's reins and turned to leave.

"Wait there, Mildrith, until I have put together a basket for you. It is the least we can do," Ealdgytha said, and she hurried toward the hall.

"And what does your husband really say of the matter?" Wulfhere asked.

Mildrith's pained expression suggested that Helghi had offered no such apology and that she had taken it upon herself to extend those words of regret.

"He thought you had come to gloat, not to help. But he *is* repentant, my lord – angry at Edgar and your daughter, but repentant that he blamed you."

"He feels stupid is the truth, is it not?" Wulfhere said, unable to disguise a smirk.

For a moment, they looked at each other. Her face exuded such sadness that he felt ashamed of his harshness. She was, after all, doing her best to make amends.

"My lord, I admit that it is I alone who extends the apologies, but it is not for Helghi's sake that I do. 'Tis for my people's sake. This situation between our villages might escalate, and we desire only peace." She looked back at the men standing miserably behind her. "This feud between you and my husband should stop before someone gets killed."

"Like my brother, you mean?" Wulfhere said reproachfully.

Mildrith recoiled a little. "I was too young to remember that, sir. I'm sorry."

"'Tis no fault of yours. Pay no mind to my bitterness." Wulfhere smiled briefly and shrugged his shoulders.

Ealdgytha returned with a basket filled with goose and duck eggs, a loaf of bread and honey cakes. Mildrith took it gratefully.

"You should come for more if you have need," Ealdgytha said gently.

"I am thankful for your kindness, madam." With that Mildrith turned to leave again.

"Lady?" Wulfhere called to her.

"My lord?" her voice cracked and Wulfhere realised that she was holding back a sob.

"The child, your daughter? She thrives still?"

"Lord, she does. Only by the will of God who sent you to save her life. I'm sorry, I should have thanked you properly. I am…we are forever in your debt, Lord Wulfhere."

Ealdgytha and Wulfhere stood hand in hand as they watched Mildrith leave. "It must be difficult for the girl, being married to a man like Helghi," Wulfhere said. "I wager he beats her for the littlest thing. There is much sadness in her eyes. If I were her father –"

"Wulfhere, I feel sorry for her too, but our own daughter is our concern now. What are we to do about her?"

"We need to find her a husband – soon!"

"But first, you had better fix my best oaken dining table," his wife said with a sprinkling of humour.

Grandmother's bower was pungent with the smell of sickness. Freyda pulled aside the leather curtain that covered the doorway, letting in the grey sunlight. There were no window openings in Lady Gerda's hut, making it difficult for fresh air to circulate inside the room. This compounded the acrid stench that filled the room. Freyda felt a pang of guilt as she eyed her grandmother's face, pale and sunken against the bolster. She had been so concerned with her own needs that she had neglected to remember that her grandmother was sick and in need of great care.

"Ealdgytha? Is that you?" The old woman spoke in a whisper, the effort of speaking being too much for her.

"No, Grandmother, 'tis Freyda. I have brought you some thin broth."

"You have let the air in. I can feel the freshness on my face." She began to cough, a harsh guttural sound.

Freyda rushed to her bedside and bent down to help her sit up. She was afraid that her grandmother would choke on her vomit as she had almost done before. She held her grandmother as she coughed into a wooden bowl and brought up granules of dark-coloured globules. When Lady Gerda was finished, Freyda wiped Grandmother's mouth and laid her back upon her pillows.

Exhausted, Gerda let her head fall back. The whites of her eyes were rheumy and yellow. Freyda turned away with the bowl to dispose of its sickly contents.

"You are filled with anger, child," she heard Grandmother say, as she washed out the bowl with water from a bucket.

Freyda, surprised at the sudden clarity in the sick woman's voice, turned to see her looking at her with clear eyes.

"Yes, child, you are… and there is much defiance within you." Gerda gave her a wan smile. Her once vibrant skin stretched painfully across features that were now hollow. "I feel it."

Freyda felt her face flush hotly but said nothing. Her grandmother was as perceptive as ever, with an infuriatingly intuitive mind. It surprised her though that the old lady should be able to assess her current emotional state, given her illness.

"Tell me, child, are you in trouble with your parents? Everyone thinks that because I am halfway to my maker, I cannot hear what goes on in this place. But I still have all my senses. My wits have not left me yet, nor have my ears."

Freyda smiled briefly. She sat down on a stool by her bed and held a spoonful of broth to her grandmother's bloodless lips. Gerda pushed away the spoon. "Besides, Sigfrith tells me everything that goes on."

"Please, Grandmother, take some. It will help you to feel better," Freyda gently urged.

Gerda shook her head with a pained expression. "There is no time for me to get better now, child. My time is over. I've had a good many years and I am grateful to God for them all. But you, dear child, have many years yet."

Freyda pulled the stool closer. Gerda reached out and touched her face with a cold, bony hand. She kept it there for a minute before letting it fall. Freyda caught it again clasping it in both her hands.

"Such a pretty girl, just like your mother. I remember the day your father brought her to Horstede." She smiled wanly. "Just a girl of sixteen summers... no, seventeen, I think."

"Did my mother love my father, back then?" Freyda asked, intrigued.

"Well, I don't know if Ealdgytha did, but your father was enamoured by her."

Freyda watched the life come back into Grandmother's eyes as she reminisced. Touched by the old lady's memories, she smiled at her.

"But I think she came to love him as much as he loved her, if not more," Gerda continued. "But she was a feisty girl. I liked her for that. She could charm him with a twinkle in her eye; just like you charm your father, little lovely. He was always a weakling where pretty girls were concerned."

"He was?"

"Aye. And probably still is. That is why you and your sisters always get your own way." They laughed together, spurring another coughing fit. When Gerda had recovered, they resumed their conversation.

"Grandmother, did you love your husband?"

"No, never. But I came to respect him and we had an understanding of sorts. But I did love another –"

"Grandmother! Should you say such things?"

"What does it matter now? Both the old goats are dead."

"Did Grandfather ever know?"

"Perhaps. Perhaps not. I never spoke of it with him."

"And the other man?"

"He didn't know either!" Gerda smiled.

"Oh, Grandmother!"

"Your mother is lucky to have your father. It is not often that a girl is wed to a man not much older than herself. My man was much older than my fourteen years. Almost double my age."

"That is my age," whispered Freyda. She could barely imagine being wed to a man she did not like or one so much older than herself. "Why did you marry him if you didn't love him?"

"The law says that a woman has the right to say 'no' if a man is not pleasing to her. But I didn't know that then. How could I know?

Nobody told me and my father said I must marry him. And I always wanted to be with someone else. But I dared not say; otherwise I would have been beaten black and blue. So, I stayed silent."

Freyda felt a tear run down her cheek. Her grandmother's message could not have come at a more pertinent moment.

"Follow your heart, Freyda. Remember, you have the right. The law of the land says it is so." Her words were no more than a whisper, but Freyda heard them well.

Chapter Six

The Earl

Early Autumn

With summer lingering a little longer than usual, the autumn winds waited patiently before scattering dying leaves over the succulent forest bed. There, in Horstede, with the days growing shorter as the evening cast its shadows over the village, life carried on much as usual despite the excitement of recent events. It was threshing time for those who worked the land; the time when the grains were separated from the ears of the newly harvested sheaths and stored in the barns. For Sigfrith, the domestic chores in her mistress's household spared her from having to pick up a grain flail. However, this might have been a preferable option given the current mood of the household: Ealdgytha was more demanding and Freyda, frustrated at not being able to see Edgar, was taking it out on her younger siblings. Wulfhere was surly and unusually offhand, and everyone was walking around him tentatively so as not to provoke another angry outburst. It seemed that the much-welcomed peace that had newly settled over the lord and lady's hall, had been shattered in just one night, by the wanton transgression of a wayward daughter.

It was early morning and the sun had just begun to dry the dew on the ground. Carrying two pails of Buttercup's newly extracted milk into the dairy, Sigfrith sighed at the sound of raised voices. Only moments ago, she had been enjoying the tranquillity of the cow-shed with a placid Buttercup. Now her quietude had been disturbed and she put down the buckets and faced the subjects of her irritation.

"There is no need for you to have them now. Not now that the whole village knows!" Freyda was shouting. The paddle of the milk churn was raised threateningly toward her younger sister.

"It was not me who told them," Winflaed retorted. "So, I should keep them!"

"I told them, little sister, and now that everybody knows my secret, the necessity to pay for your silence is no longer needed. Therefore, I have removed those items of my property you extracted from me in bad faith!" Freyda scowled.

"Freyda, put that down before you hurt someone!" Sigfrith ordered. "Is it not enough that the whole household is on tenterhooks because of your behaviour, and now you have to argue and fight with your little sister?"

Freyda stuck her tongue out at Winflaed, but lowered the paddle as Sigfrith stepped toward her. "I was not going to hit her with it. She was going to hit me, so I was just defending myself."

Sigfrith huffed loudly and shook her head. "If I get wind of you two fighting again, I will feed you both to the pigs!"

"Oh, please don't feed them all to the pigs. Save some for me," a male voice chuckled from the doorway. "And make sure they're roasted first, right through. I like my meat well done."

All three girls, startled by the intrusion, spun round to face him.

"Lord Tigfi!" exclaimed Sigfrith.

The young man gave a curt bow and a wide grin. He was one of the Earl of Wessex's huscarles, and also the reeve of Framling, the hundred in which Horstede lay. He was dressed in a finely embroidered tunic of green linen, with brown hose covering his legs, overwrapped with sturdy tablet-woven *winingas*, wrapped around each calf. A richly decorated scabbard hung from his belt as he stood, arms folded and face beaming like the morning sunlight as it poured in through the doorway. He was known as Tigfi the Yellow-haired, for the long, well-groomed golden locks that fell about his handsome face.

"So, Sigfrith, do we skin and gut them now?" the young huscarle asked. "Or shall we wait until they are a little plumper?" He was rubbing his hands. "This one's a little too skinny for my liking. Let me have a closer inspection!"

Winflaed gave a squeal as he darted toward her, but she managed to escape by diving through his legs and exiting the building in a flurry of screams and yelps.

"See how she squeals as if she is stuck already! Goodbye, little piggy!" Tigfi laughed. "So now we are left with only this little piggy."

"I dare you to come near me!" Freyda shrieked, waving the paddle at him.

"On second thoughts, perhaps I had better settle for a piece of cheese," Tigfi said with mock solemnity. He reached for one of the cheeses on the work trestle, sliced off a piece with his seax, and munched on it appreciatively. "Mmm, it's good!"

Sigfrith was laughing; Freyda was trying her best not to.

"So, what brings you here, Lord Tigfi?" asked Sigfrith. She was eyeing him up and down with interest.

Tigfi returned her look. Sigfrith felt her knees shake and her heart fluttered as his eyes met hers. "I have a message for Lord Wulfhere from Earl Harold: he and his family will be calling on him in a few days, so the necessary preparations must be made."

"Earl Harold is coming here?" squawked Sigfrith with obvious delight. If the earl was coming, that meant more handsome young men like Tigfi would be at her disposal.

"Well then, now that I have delivered my news, I should be on my way. Would one of you young ladies kindly see me to the gate?" Tigfi said, adding a wink to his request.

"I will, lord," Sigfrith replied eagerly.

Freyda shook her head, admiring Sigfrith's boldness as she headed off with him. She returned to her cheese-making, laughing to herself as she imagined the turmoil her mother would be in after hearing news of the earl's visit. Then a little glint came to her eye as she realised that, with her mother's attention focused on their visitors, she might well be able to steal away to meet Edgar.

Tovi and Winflaed watched in awe from the porch, as the Earl of Wessex's fearsome warriors, the famed huscarles, filed in through the open gates of the compound. All were mounted on impressive steeds, resplendent in their finery. Tovi had counted fourteen of them, not including the earl himself. Each man wore a magnificent scabbard hung from a strong leather belt, gold buckled with fine inlaid decorations on them. Their cloaks were dyed in bright shades of madder and their tunics were garnished with ornate tablet-weave. The earl numbered about three hundred huscarles in his service, but these few were from his own personal bodyguard, the most favoured and elite fighters amongst his men.

"The earl has brought his whole army," whispered Winflaed in Tovi's ear.

Tovi gave her a look of derision. "Silly Frog Spawn. Do you think he would bring his whole army to our hall? Don't you know that he has more men than the king himself? Thousands! There would be no room for them all!"

Somewhere in the middle of the line-up, Tovi spotted a horse-drawn litter. A small, wide-eyed child peered curiously through a colourful curtain. She appeared to be about six years of age, and her eyes widened excitedly, when she spotted Tovi and Winflaed standing on the porch. Every now and then she would turn her head back behind the curtain, as if she were describing them to others inside the litter.

"Who is that?" Winflaed asked curiously.

"Obviously, the Earl's children," Tovi replied in an impatient tone. He was more interested in the warriors. His gaze switched and rested on the earl as he dismounted from his horse. The boy examined the man who was far more magnificently attired than any of the huscarles, if that could be so. Tovi needed no introduction, for Harold Godwinson possessed a commanding presence, which made him prominent amongst all men. There was something noble about him, regal and imposing; a leader of men.

In wonder, Tovi watched his mother offer the earl some ale from a horn. His eyes widened when the earl greeted his father with warm familiarity, and Tovi felt a sense of pride that his father was so favoured. Harold was not unlike his father, being of similar age. They had the same fair, collar-length hair, the typical fashion of the Englisc nobles, the same strong angular features, clean-shaven except for the heavy moustache that draped each side of their mouths; and the same blueness in their eyes. It was a blue that sparkled brightly when they smiled.

Harold's rich attire reflected his nobility. His tunic was of the finest woven linen, dyed a rare shade of the deepest blue, hemmed at the edges with skilfully embroidered braid of gold and silver threads. He wore a dark green summer cloak, also decorated in braid, and made from a cloth of lightly woven wool. The elaborately wound *winingas*, covering his brown hose, were tucked into boots of the highest quality. Harold exuded authority by his very demeanour; a power which was pertinent to a man in his high position. Yet, despite his commanding appearance, his smile showed the warmth of a charming, affable fellow. Even Tovi could sense the agreeable wit and charm.

Next to Harold, mounted elegantly in side-saddle fashion, was the Lady Eadgyth, the woman, who for many years had been his loyal handfasted wife. She was dressed as a lady of high-status would be; strands of her hair could be glimpsed from beneath her comely silk wimple, showing it to be a shade of the fairest blonde. She radiated gentle beauty; with bright eyes that illuminated a flawless pearl complexion, giving truth to her name *Swannehaels*, 'Lady of the swan neck.' Tovi thought her as magnificent as her lord.

Tovi nudged his sister to attract her attention to the earl and his lady, and saw that Winflaed seemed to be drawn to the boy assisting Lady Eadgyth to alight from her horse. He was tall with long limbs and a head of thick chestnut hair. He was handsome and taller than average, but his features still retained a youthful appearance indicating that his height most likely belied his true age. The boy caught her staring and he smiled and winked at her, causing Tovi to smile to himself. His sister blushed and averted her gaze, looking embarrassed that he had caught her.

"So, this is the Earl's fine Lady Swannehaels," Freyda whispered to Sigfrith as they stood watching the arrival of their guests. "It is true what they say... she has a most beautiful complexion."

"Aye," nodded Sigfrith, enviously. "Are they not the most beautiful couple? It is hard to understand why the earl has never married her."

"You mean she is his mistress?" Freyda asked.

"No, she is not his mistress, though some would see it that way. Evidently, they were handfasted, which is lawful, but the marriage has not been blessed, before God, on the church steps, nor witnessed by a king's official."

"Why?" Freyda asked, thinking about her own situation.

"Because his father forbade it. He was the son of an earl, and as the king has no sons of his own, Lord Harold might have to make a far greater alliance one day."

"Then… he could cast her aside?"

Sigfrith nodded.

"I would never allow myself to be treated like cast-off shoes!" Freyda said, shaking her head. "The shame of it!"

"Kings and nobles have always done such things. It is not unusual. And after all, the woman and her children always have the same rights as a woman whose marriage is witnessed by the court and the church. I find the idea quite agreeable."

"Well you would. You are a low-born maid. I, for one would not bear it with comfort." Freyda glanced haughtily at Sigfrith. "How is it you know such things, Sigfrith, being the simple maid that you are?"

Freyda tutted as Sigfrith paid her no heed. The older girl was deeply engrossed in amorously eyeing one of the young huscarles.

"*Waes hael* Wulfhere, *Ic grete þe*! Good tidings to thee and yours! 'Tis good to see you are returned safe and well from the northern lands. I heard there was much loss and suffering on both sides." Clasping Wulfhere's hand, Harold drew him into a hearty embrace. "And greetings to your lovely wife also." He acknowledged Ealdgytha with a smile and she genuflected lightly.

Harold turned back to Wulfhere and nodded over to where his men were having their weapons inspected with great interest. "Your boys, they have grown heads taller since I last saw them!" He threw a concerned look at them as the twins launched themselves upon the huscarles. "Watch that axe, boy; it will take your fingers off if you touch the edge!"

"Wulfric!" called Wulfhere as his son ran an inquisitive hand along the flat of the fearsome blade. "Do you hear the Earl? Stop it at once! I am sorry, my lord." He gave an embarrassed shrug. "They are a little exuberant, but they mean no harm."

"Do not apologise. My own sons annoy my men constantly. They're used to it. 'Tis good to see young lads showing such enthusiasm. I trust they are learning their fighting skills well?"

Wulfhere nodded. "Indeed, my lord."

"Wulfhere, I can see all seems undisturbed here. However, I do not think your neighbour fares as well as you do. We just passed by Helghi's place and it would seem that he has had some great misfortune. Nothing to do with you, I hope, Lord Wulfhere?" Harold asked, a hint of sarcasm in his voice.

Wulfhere averted his gaze and stared down at his shoes.

Harold leaned towards him. "You know it is my business to know what goes on in my earldom? I know that my father once had cause to intervene in your feud with Helghi. You both swore an oath to him to keep the peace or face a heavy fine."

Wulfhere continued to stare at his shoes, feeling uncomfortable, and searching for an explanation.

"Tell me about it later," Harold suggested, noting his discomfort. He placed a genial arm about his host's shoulder. "Now, introduce me to the rest of your household and lead us to where the refreshments are. By Christ on the Cross, I have worked up a thirst on this journey. Do you know that we have been travelling since daybreak? And I am not without a ravenous hunger too, come to that. God's bones, how my belly is rumbling! I fear I could eat one of your fine horses, never mind ride one!"

"Ranulf's mother was a cousin of mine," Harold explained, as later that day, at the earl's request, Wulfhere proudly showed him and the boy around his stables. He leaned closer to Wulfhere so that Ranulf could not hear. "His father is Guy de Rouen, a Norman, but I don't hold that against him!" He laughed and Wulfhere reciprocated in kind. "My father," continued Harold, "had arranged Guy's marriage to our cousin, and had always been on good terms with him. However, Guy needed to return to his ancestral lands in Normandy, and left Ranulf here in my care. I have wardship over his mother's lands until he comes of age. In the meantime, he has been schooled at my collegiate in Waltham. But now, unfortunately, Guy's eldest son was killed in a tragic riding accident and that has left him with just one other, apparently not in the best of health. Now he requires that Ranulf return to him, and I would like to send him home with a fine steed. I hear you have a good strong mare breeding excellent young stallions, the type that our Norman friends are breeding to use in warfare."

"Aye," nodded Wulfhere as they stood in the stable-yard. "The king's nephew, Lord Ralph, is intent on bringing cavalry to police his Wéalas borderlands. These stallions are indeed better at this. But what of your own fine stables, my lord? Is there none such a beast of your own stud that would serve the purpose?"

Harold waved a hand dismissively. "I have nothing such as that which would satisfy a great Norman baron at the moment. The Normans apparently like their horses to be swift and lithe, and strong. My stables do not seem to be capable of breeding such a horse as yet, alas. Do you have such a creature, Lord Wulfhere?"

Wulfhere looked over to the stall that belonged to a young stallion of three years. Ranulf spotted him first and made for his stall, stroking the horse's nose as it poked its head out of the stable door. "That one there has just been broken. He's a little frisky, somewhat spirited, but has the promise of a fine steed. I was saving him for Lord Ralph, but..."

"Lord Ralph will understand my need," Harold said and Wulfhere wondered why it was so important.

Harold and Wulfhere watched from the fence as the boy put the spirited young stallion through his paces.

"He is a good rider. He has been well instructed at Waltham," Harold remarked proudly.

It was clear that Ranulf had been taught to handle energetic and lively horses by the way he demonstrated that he could bring the horse under control with ease. As they watched, Harold was telling Wulfhere about the current circumstances at court and elsewhere. Ealdred, Bishop of Worcester, Harold informed him, had been sent on a mission by the king to seek out his nephew, another Edward. This other, was the son of Edmund, King Edward's elder half-brother. When Edmund died after fighting Cnut's forces, his wife and infant son had been forced to flee abroad in fear of their lives. No one had known exactly where on the Continent the son of Ironside had been secreted away, so Bishop Ealdred and his delegation had gone to appeal to the Holy Roman Emperor for his assistance in seeking them out.

"So, if the king is thinking of bringing this Edward to Englalond," Wulfhere said, "what of his 'so-called' promise to William of Normandy?"

"I am not such a fool to think that, whilst my family were in exile, William had not taken the opportunity to come across the sea to seek an agreement of some sort. I am sure that Edward dangled the crown in front of his nose as if he were dangling a carrot in front of a donkey. I am also certain that William must have brayed like one too, for I know that Normandy has long looked at our shores with envious eyes. Even our illustrious Queen Emma, a Norman herself, was so determined to retain her Englisc crown that she married Cnut after Aethelred. But with her son, Harthacnut, in the grave with no issue of his own, and her first born, Edward, also without an heir, the Norman connection will end with Edward; which means that William is now their great hope. And I am not holding my breath for my sister to get herself with child. Edward has shown little interest in her in that department, and it looks unlikely they will sire a son between them in this lifetime."

Harold smiled at the look of concern on Wulfhere's face and continued, "Do not fear, my friend. Edward knows that no Englisc man would be happy to put a Norman on the throne. The presence of Edward's Norman friends is tolerated, but to have one on the throne would be incontrovertibly unacceptable. If Edward has offered the crown to William, it has most likely conveniently slipped his mind by now," Harold winked and smiled, "for he is determined that, Edward the Exile, should be found, and brought home. Plus, there is another contender for the throne: Ralph of Mantes. The king's nephew may be half Norman, but he also has the blood of the kings of Wessex, unlike Duke William. Furthermore, I happen to know that Edward harbours great resentment against the duke. Apparently, when he was a lad, he was none too kind to our Edward. According to my sources, William saw him as a weakling, and would often deride him for his pious nature and lack of fighting skills."

"Then how did the duke get the king to allow him an audience when he came?" Wulfhere asked.

"The duke may be an uneducated man, but he is not an idiot. He would have had something to offer Edward in return, such as: refusing to allow the Norse pirates to continue using his ports to launch their raids on our coast; perhaps a new wife for him, seeing that, at that time, he had cast off my sister; some good Frencisc wine, perhaps, a favourite of Edward's. Who knows?" Harold looked amused for a moment. "God knows; it was Frencisc wine that secured his marriage to my sister!"

It was Harold's nature to remain resilient in such matters, and since the Godwins' return to power after a spell in exile, relations with Edward were much improved, especially after the sad demise of Godwin himself. It was well known that there had been no love lost between Godwin and the king, but Edward seemed to hold no ill-feeling towards Harold or his brothers.

"If he had indeed offered the crown to William, why would he go to all the trouble of finding Ironside's sons?" Wulfhere pointed out, matter-of-factly.

"Knowing Edward, toying with William as heir was probably a good idea at the time, just as it was when he agreed to marry my sister!" Harold gave a hearty laugh and then just as quickly became serious again. He looked at Wulfhere darkly. "Wulfhere, the real problem for us now, is the plight of my nephew and brother, stolen away by that cowardly piece of humanity, Robert Champart, the former Archbishop of Cantwarabyrig. I am hoping to secure their return. The horse is a gift for the lad. If I can ingratiate myself with Ranulf's father, I am hoping he will use his influence at the duke's court to help secure their release. Know you, that my father was forced to hand over two of our boys as hostages before we were so impolitely banished?"

"Of course." Wulfhere nodded.

"Know you also, that Robert Champart, my father's mortal enemy, and craven leech of Edward's, had fled into exile upon our return? And well for him that he did. But not well for our boys, Hakon and Wulfnoth, for he fled with them, to Normandy."

"Aye, I know the story," Wulfhere replied. "Some say that the Archbishop influenced the king to allow him to take them with him to Normandy, so that William would know that he still wished to honour his pledge to him, despite your family's return."

"Most likely there was a plot of sorts, but we cannot be certain that Edward agreed to their kidnap. I believe that when Champart knew his time was up, he seized the opportunity to take the boys with him, using them as shields with which to protect himself should anyone try to stop him from leaving." There was a twist of disdain in Harold's reply. "After all, they were in his care; it would have been easy. If he took them with him, he could kill several birds with one stone. Firstly, Robert Champart supported William's claim to Edward's throne, and so could use the boys as surety, just as you said, to prove that he would honour his promise. Secondly, the boys' presence would ensure that he came to no harm as he tried to leave. Thirdly, they were a bargaining tool for him to worm his way back into Englalond, should he wish someday to do so, and finally, he took them to spite my father; his greatest enemy."

"My lord, this must be an insufferable thing to have to bear," Wulfhere replied, shaking his head in disbelief. "I know it is customary to insist on hostages to ensure the good behaviour of someone, but they are usually treated well, especially if they were children of noble birth. But to have sent them so far from their homeland and family seems such an unnecessarily cruel act."

Harold nodded. "Edward knew this would have twisted the knife further into Father's guts; helpless in exile, his boys used as pawns, and forced to sit idly by as the kingdom fell into the hands of his enemies."

"So, my lord, with the boys held abroad as hostages, Edward was able to ensure the good conduct of your father."

"Aye, it was the last bit of control that Edward had over my father and he was going to hold on to it, so that even in death, Godwin was not safe from Edward's revenge."

They were quiet again for a moment, watching the boy enjoy the feel of the horse.

Then Harold added grimly, "Champart took them, Wulfhere, and he needn't have done that. He could have left them at Ness where he boarded the ship, but the spiteful bastard took them across the sea, and now God knows how they fare. And the thing that angers me most is that they must think we have abandoned them. They are young and my mother yearns to have them back. Wulfnoth was scarce a man, and Hakon, just an infant."

"I cannot imagine what it must feel like to have your sons ripped from you like that," Wulfhere sympathised. "So, you hope that Ranulf's father might be of assistance in securing their release? That he may hold some sway with the duke?"

"That is what I am hoping, if indeed they truly are with the duke. It would seem that no one is willing to divulge their whereabouts at this moment." Frustration furrowed the earl's brow. "Ranulf's father has influence at William's court, so I am hopeful that he can use it to help us get the boys back. After all, his wife, God rest her soul, was my kinswoman and his son my ward."

"Has no one thought to plead with Champart himself about the matter?" Wulfhere enquired.

"Let us just say, my friend, that our former Archbishop has no love for our family and has been less than forthcoming in answering any of my mother's letters; nor has the Duke of Normandy for that matter." Harold looked thoughtfully out across the exercise yard at the young boy. "But then I hear that the duke has problems of his own at the moment, and may not have a mind to consider the plight of two young Englisc boys, far from home."

"What of the king? Can he do nothing to help with the matter?"

"Edward avoids the subject every time it is brought up. My sister tells me she has requested him to write to Duke William, and he apparently says that he will, but so far there has been no indication that he has done so. My feeling is that, in time, he will send for Champart. Perhaps he will use the boys to bargain with us, though I cannot be sure I would be able to stomach such a thing. Nonetheless, if I have to, I shall accept it if it means the return of Wulfnoth and Hakon. But the king remains very mysterious about the issue. It is as if he is playing a game; he has placed his counters around the board but only he knows when he will use them."

"You think that the king would allow Champart to return, knowing the strength of feeling against the man in this country."

"I cannot rule it out. Now that my father is gone, he may think he can restore Robert as archbishop again. I hear he has papal support on that matter. Edward still smoulders at losing his little lickspittle, Champart. He was completely devoted to the wretch. More's the pity that such a love for someone should cause such catastrophe. He only let him go because he was backed into a corner. The relationship between the king and myself is, shall we say, polite and workable, but not necessarily relaxed. However, he does seem to have found a replacement for Champart: my brother Tostig. He is often in his company these days."

"And what of the boy, has he been long with you?"

"He has been at Waltham since he was a small boy. I think he was enjoying his education with the canons there. I detected a look of sullenness when I informed him of his father's request that he re-join him in Normandy!" Here, Harold laughed a little, allowing some of his old humour return. "After all, you could hardly blame him for not wanting to swap our merry Englalond for the austerity of Normandy. I hear you need permission to smile at William's court these days... Actually, I think Eadgyth will miss him most. She seems to have become quite fond of the boy. He is a good lad really, despite his Norman blood."

"Then it must be his Englisc blood that makes him so." Wulfhere smiled and Harold nodded in agreement.

"Let us hope that it will stand him in good stead. He will probably need it where he is going," mused Harold as the boy approached them and dismounted. "Wulfhere, I have something else to ask of you."

"My lord?"

"I need to leave the boy in your care until his father's men in Normandy, come to collect him. If you could escort him to Pevensey, at the end of October; word should reach you before then of their expected arrival."

"I would be happy to assist in any way, my lord."

"Well, Master Ranulf? Think you that this is the horse for you?"

"Yes, sir. Thank you, sir!" Ranulf enthused.

Harold looked down at him, and felt genuine pleasure at the innocent delight in his dark eyes. He was breathing heavily and there were beads of sweat on his forehead and his top lip from the ride.

Harold ruffled his thick, glossy chestnut locks. *They'll soon have those curls lopped off in Normandy,* he thought to himself in silent amusement, visualising the closely shaven heads of the Normans. He wondered about his brother Wulfnoth and little Hakon. Would they, too, have had their heads shaven in the Norman style?

"Then the horse is yours, Master Ranulf," Harold said, with a flourish of his hand. The boy's expression was filled with obvious pleasure. "What are you going to name him?"

Ranulf looked thoughtful. "He anticipates commands and possesses a great spirit, perhaps lacks patience, but I think I can tame that. I think I should call him, Woden, after the old God."

"Good choice of name, but don't let Father Leofgar hear you utter it," Harold joked. "Now go and untack him and give him water and fodder. You have worked him well."

Harold turned to Wulfhere as the boy, face beaming with delight, led the horse back to the stables. "It is a fine creature, Wulfhere. Now we must find mounts suitable for my son and daughter. After that you can tell me what you know about poor Helghi's plight. After all, 'tis my business to know what is going on in my earldom. And I fear you know more about it than you are content to let on."

After two of the smaller horses had been selected for the children, Wulfhere and Harold found themselves a quiet corner in the stable yard, with a pitcher of mead and block of cheese to share, Wulfhere began to relate the story of Freyda and Edgar, and the fire at Gorde. Harold listened intently to his recounting of the night Helghi's homestead caught fire, shaking his head, but with a smile. No matter how sombre the tale, Harold almost always saw the humorous side of any situation. He was a man often given to laughter and had no great liking for the gravity of pompous ceremonial occasions. But, for all his dislike of formality, he was well-educated and had a rare intellect, able to speak and read in at least four languages, fluently. He enjoyed intelligent conversation, often sitting into the small hours with the most learned men, discussing anything and everything from hawking to literary subjects, such as the translations of King Alfred and the works of the great scholar, Aelfric of Evesham. Yet he was as equally at home enjoying the ribald humour of his favourite huscarles as they sat round the fire at hearth time in their great hall.

Listening to Wulfhere, he understood his concern for his daughter. He had a daughter of his own, but secretly empathised with Edgar's attempts at seduction being thwarted at every turn, reminding him of his own misspent youth. And what a price to pay for their forbidden love: the loss of his father's longhouse was a very dear one indeed.

Harold sat quietly with that pleasant smile of his never leaving his lips as Wulfhere expressed his uncertainty as to what to do about the situation. But he had an idea that he knew Wulfhere was not going to find very pleasing.

"Don't you think it is about time you ended this damned feud of yours with Helghi?" he asked. "What good has it done the pair of you? Here you are with a daughter who has dishonoured you, and there he is with his homestead destroyed and his life in ruins."

"My lord, are you saying that this misfortune is because of the feud between us and that I am to blame?" Wulfhere asked defensively.

"No, I am saying that it is because the boy and girl had to keep their love for each other a secret. If they had not had to hide their love, then perhaps they would not have caused the fire. Wulfhere, it would be funny if it were not so lamentable!"

Wulfhere looked at Harold open-mouthed. "Are you saying, my lord, that they should be allowed to marry?"

"Would it be such a bad thing?" Harold sighed as Wulfhere gave him a perplexed look.

"But he is a cripple... and the son of a *ceorl*," Wulfhere protested.

"He has a crooked leg, so what? He can walk and hold a shield and spear. He may not be a thegn, but Helghi is not poor and there is still land for him to inherit, is there not?"

"Such land that there is. I was hoping for a better match for Freyda..." and, muttering under his breath, he added, "...a much better match."

"Wulfhere, you have another three daughters to find husbands for. You think you can find four wealthy thegns for them all?"

"With respect, my lord, I had hoped for the son of a wealthy thegn for Freyda," Wulfhere replied petulantly. "Lord, I have great regard for you, but it really is too much to expect me to allow my daughter to make a match with Helghi's son. Where would they live for a start? And how can I tolerate the accusations Helghi threw at me about setting fire to his homestead? How would a union between our families be of any benefit to either of us?"

"It would put an end to this ridiculous enmity between you. Then perhaps you can all live in peace, instead of pieces. And they love each other, Wulfhere. 'Tis a good basis for a marriage. I chose Eadgyth because I loved her and she still tends my hearth for me and bears my children after all these years."

"I cannot have my daughter live in a corn shed, my lord."

"Then let them live here with you."

Wulfhere shook his head. "I cannot even contemplate it. My wife would certainly not allow it."

"You are a stubborn man, Wulfhere, and proud too," Harold said but he was not to be deterred. "Some years ago, you and Helghi agreed on oath before my father to stop this quarrel, and it seems you have both broken your oaths. My father may now be gone, but the oath still stands, and I have inherited that pledge. I could take further action against you both and impose some heavy penalties for not keeping the peace, but I would rather we resolve this amicably. Have you not forgotten that this ill-fated quarrel between you cost you your brother?"

Wulfhere hung his head shamefully. "Upon reflection, I know you speak the truth. I have been neglectful in extending the hand of peace to Helghi. But the rivers of hatred run deep between us. The divide is too wide to cross, and I am unable to abnegate the feelings of anger I feel toward him, and I am certain that Helghi would feel the same. There must be some other way to make restitution? Do I have to sacrifice my daughter and my dignity?"

"I do understand your concern about the lad's lack of prospects, Wulfhere. If it were my daughter, it would concern me too. But let them be betrothed, and if things do not work out between you and Helghi, then it can be withdrawn. If they wed in, say, two years' time, I will throw in thirty acres of land for your daughter to do with as she likes. A wedding gift for her."

Harold waited patiently for an answer as Wulfhere studied his shoes and kicked the dirt.

"What do you say? Do we have a bargain or not?" Harold asked after a few moments. "You know I have the power to force this upon you, Wulfhere, but I do not wish to. It would be better if you came to it of your own volition."

"It is a generous offer, my lord, and I expect that there would be some benefits… though I cannot for the life of me see what they can be."

"Then you agree?"

"Perhaps a betrothal would be acceptable at this stage – if Helghi will agree to it, of course. What if he doesn't?"

"Oh, he will. Don't worry about that," replied Harold meaningfully. "So, you agree to a betrothal?"

"Aye... in principle," Wulfhere muttered reluctantly. He sighed and crossed his arms tetchily.

"And you will agree to assist Helghi with the rebuilding of his house?"

"What? Lord, this really is too much!" Wulfhere nearly jumped up off his seat.

"Well, you wouldn't want your son-in-law's inheritance to be a wasteland, would you?"

Wulfhere shook his head and laughed cynically. "What am I going to tell Ealdgytha? She will have my balls for this!"

"Then I'll lend you one of mine, Wulfhere. Or perhaps you'll grow another set with any luck! Come, let's tell your wife the good news. Perhaps my presence will save you from a gelding. On second thoughts, perhaps I'd better guard mine too, knowing how temperamental women can be."

"Especially my woman," agreed Wulfhere, drily.

To say that Ealdgytha was furious at the strange turn of events was an understatement, but thank heavens the earl had been there to curb Ealdgytha's livid tongue. Ealdgytha knew her place and wouldn't have dared to express her anger openly in front of Harold and Eadgyth. Instead, when she could catch his eye, she glared impotently at Wulfhere, and all he could do was shrug and give her an apologetic look in return. When Harold suggested that he send Tigfi for Helghi and his son so they could discuss the plan, Wulfhere thought that Ealdgytha was going to have a fit of pique, but somehow, she managed to keep her thoughts to herself.

Helghi and Edgar skulked in through Wulfhere's longhall behind Tigfi. Helghi's face was morose; Edgar's eyes were wide and fearful. Wulfhere suspected that they had not been told why they were summoned. The earl requested that they sat at the bargaining table opposite him and Wulfhere. Ealdgytha moodily presented them with a jug of mead and it was poured into a horn which was then passed between them. Wulfhere watched his adversary with interest. Helghi's expression was belligerent. Edgar, looked down cast and ashamed.

Wulfhere felt some pity for the lad when he noted the faded bruising around his cheek bones.

"Well it seems that we have a problem here gentlemen," Harold said in his usual genial manner.

Helghi grunted and fingered his beard. "Do we, lord?" he replied with hostility. "I thought it was I who had the problem, since that brat of his and my brainless son burned down my longhall!" Helghi glared at Wulfhere resentfully. Wulfhere couldn't help his lips curling into an unwanted smile. "I see you still find my situation amusing, Wulfhere! I want compensation!" Helghi thumped his fist down on the table and Harold put his hand over his to contain him.

"Lord Helghi, there is something I want to discuss, now if you will bear with me, I will explain what I propose to do with you two," Harold said, firmly. "I want an end to this hate between you, and there is only one certain way to do it."

Helghi looked at both men opposite him with grave expectation, as Harold released his hand from his. Wulfhere watched Helghi taking in the scene, his eyes sweeping the hall suspiciously. The earl's huscarles stood in the background, as witnesses. Wulfhere wondered if Helghi felt threatened at that moment. He looked like a cornered animal and Wulfhere enjoyed his neighbour's discomfort.

Harold continued, ignoring the suspicion in Helghi's eyes. "This enmity and ill-blood between you, grows like a wild beast and will cause disharmony throughout these parts, especially when men start taking sides. I need an end to this and since young Freyda and Edgar are somewhat love-struck, I would see them betrothed. A joining of their hands in wedlock should end the feud between your families and expel the curse that has haunted you both in all these years."

Helghi was open mouthed. "Never! Never in a thousand years!" he exclaimed. He thumped the table again, causing the horn of mead to spill some of its contents as it sat in its iron stand. "I will *not* permit it!"

Wulfhere was smiling secretly, but when Helghi caught his gaze, he removed the smile from his lips. "I agree with Lord Helghi. It is wholly unsatisfactory," Wulfhere said. He stared briefly at Helghi and then saw that Edgar was looking hopeful. "I would rather die than see my daughter married to this scum," he said pointedly, his gaze settling on Edgar. He wanted to see the lad's misery as his hopes were dashed.

Helghi rose to his feet, enraged. "And what makes you think I would have your little bitch in my home?" Helghi ranted.

Wulfhere also leapt to his feet, clutching his fists at his sides.

"Lords!" Harold called in his commanding voice. Two of his huscarles had closed in on them protectively, hovering just in case the highly-charged meeting turned volatile. "Sit! I shall not tolerate this! I mean to settle this feud, here, and now, and I will not have you both gainsay me!" Harold was fuming. Wulfhere sat down, sheepishly, and Helghi followed suit, pouting obstinately.

"I cannot agree to this, lord," Wulfhere said, shaking his head.

Helghi smiled. "Well, perhaps I *could* be persuaded..." Helghi sneered, "...with some more mead…"

Wulfhere suddenly went cold, wondering if his protesting had encouraged Helghi to change his mind. Helghi's eyes said it all. He was relishing the fact that Wulfhere was the one who was squirming now.

"Good, because now I want you two to give each other the kiss of peace," Harold ordered.

Wulfhere knew he had no choice but to comply. Helghi had given in and there was no way out. He felt like a fool as he reluctantly sealed the peace agreement by planting his lips as lightly as he could against Helghi's cheek. He felt sick and somewhere in the hall he could feel his wife's eyes boring into him.

Then, Freyda was brought to them, and she and Edgar did their best to contain their glee. The agreement was finally made and cast down in writing by Father Paul.

"Good!" Harold exclaimed, his humour returning. His impatience had receded, now that the deal was cast. "Tomorrow," he announced, "we shall have a feast in honour of the bride and groom, and the new peace between you all! "Drink! *Waes hael*!" he cried and he replenished the horn for all parties to drink from.

As he stared mutely at Helghi gulping down his share, Wulfhere realised that he had lost the first battle already.

That evening, when Ealdgytha and Wulfhere were getting ready for bed, Ealdgytha was in a mood for grumbling.

"What on earth in God's name, compelled you to agree to this alliance, Wulfhere?" she complained as she ran a comb through the long, golden waves of her hair. "Our daughter deserves better than Helghi's son."

"I had no choice, my love." Wulfhere sighed and climbed naked under the bedcovers. "The earl was determined that the betrothal go ahead."

She began to pace from one side of the chamber to the other, the comb still in her hand. "You could have refused. You *are* a king's thegn remember, not an earl's."

"How could I refuse? Harold wanted to fine us for feuding again. He does not tolerate bloodfeuds in his earldom. He sees marriage as a peaceful means to end it."

"But there has been no feuding – not for many years, at least. The problem lies with Helghi, not us," she snapped. "If only Freyda had not embroiled us in this mess by meddling in the fire... You should never have listened to her, Wulfhere."

"Maybe so, Wife; but there is nothing much I can do about it now. Harold will have his way."

"Well then, your wonderful revered, Lord Harold, is as wily as a wolf. He uses cunning to control people and get what he wants," Ealdgytha said irritably. "He stole Waltham from my Uncle Athelstan, you know. He is just like his father, a conniver, and a schemer. It is well known that the Godwins have risen in status through the underhandedness of their father; gaining their lands by misappropriation. Harold has obviously inherited his father's shrewdness."

"Harold did not steal Waltham. It was awarded to him by the king after your uncle neglected his duties. I would remind you not to be so disrespectful, Ealdgytha. I may hold my land from King Edward, but Harold is our lord and protector, and our guest. Besides, he has promised to give our daughter land as a wedding gift, and for that we should be grateful at least."

She gave him a sarcastic look. "Thirty acres, as much as a *ceorl's* holding. How generous of him!" She scowled. "I feel as if we have been very well manipulated."

"Stop that wretched whinging and come to bed, woman. There will be much to do tomorrow."

"How will I sleep with this hanging over us? I cannot help but think of my poor Freyda married to a cripple for a husband!"

"Poor Freyda? Yesterday she was the worst daughter in the whole of Súþ Seaxa," Wulfhere sighed. "Stop worrying about your daughter for a minute and come here and worry about your husband." He patted the empty space in the bed beside him as Ealdgytha climbed in next to him with an air of indignation. He drew her close to him and pulled up her shift. She murmured contentedly as his hands caressed her body.

"I suppose the worrying can continue on the morrow," she said softly as he kissed her neck.

"Mmm, tomorrow. Worry about it tomorrow..."

Chapter Seven

The Reluctant Hero

"Out of the way, *Cicen Sceancan*! What do you think you're doing?" Wulfric shouted and barged his way past Tovi into the stable yard. Tovi grimaced. He hated it when Wulfric called him 'Chicken Legs'. Somehow, he could never think of anything witty enough to match him. The twins were getting the horses ready for the day's hunting and it was Tovi's plan to join them. Unfortunately for Tovi, it was not his brothers'.

It was early morning and the sun had not yet raised its glorious globe high enough to send rays of warmth over the stables. There was a light frost in the air as Wulfric spoke and Tovi imagined his brother as a fire-breathing dragon, scorching all in his path. In his mind, Tovi unsheathed his battle sword, drew his shield in front of him and steeled himself for a fight unto death.

"I want to hunt too," Tovi replied, insistently.

Wulfwin, who had been attending to chestnut mare, Flame, looked over and scowled. "Do as he says and go away, *earsling*. This is to be *our* first blooding. We don't want it spoilt by you, so go and play with the little ones, for that is where boys like you belong!"

"I can hunt just as well as you! Father said I could ride the black short-nose." Tovi squared his stance, crossing his arms. The twins were a head taller than he, a fact that would normally have induced submission, however that morning, he was determined not to miss the excitement of hunting. He wanted to be there amidst the magic and the mayhem; the noise of hunting horns, the squawking of hawks, the barking of dogs, and the earl and his huscarles riding out in all their finery. Since Lord Harold and his men had arrived he had been drawn to them. In his wild imaginings, he was among them, fighting side by side in their shieldwall, sharing their laughter in their lord's meadhall and riding out to fight the beast Grendl. If he was left behind today, it would feel like the end of the world.

Wulfric smirked, mirroring Tovi's crossed arms. "*You, hunt?*" he spat on the ground. "*We* are the men here, not you," he said, indicating himself and his twin brother. "*You're* still a boy and *you're* not coming!"

Tovi retreated into the fierce warrior within his mind, seven foot tall and just as broad. He chopped at Wulfric with his Dane axe and his brother fell to the floor, head cloven in two, his brains spilling out like a slaughtered pig's. Tovi pulled out the axe from the pulp of his brother's head and stepped over him as he lay in a mass of blood and gore.

"Where are you going?" Wulfric demanded, stretching out an arm to bar him.

"I am going to get my horse," Tovi replied.

"*You're* not going anywhere, so get back to your play, baby."

Tovi tried to push past his brother but Wulfric caught at his tunic and held him back.

"Oh, just break his face, Wulfric. That's the only thing he understands," Wulfwin called, storming across the yard toward them. Tovi reminded himself that he had just killed Wulfric, so he could do him no harm, and went to move past him, but Wulfric was doing very well for someone whose head had been cloven in two. Tovi suddenly felt his arms locked behind his back and Wulfwin thrust his face at him as Wulfric held him, fast.

"Hearken to me, you little piece of *scite*! This is *our* hunt. This is mine and Wulfric's day to hunt with the earl. We don't want you getting in the way and trying to make us look bad."

"Because you know I am better with a bow than either of you? And I wouldn't have to try hard to make you look bad, you can do that for yourselves," Tovi argued, squirming like a little insect caught by two hungry spiders. "That's why Father said that I could go, because he knows that you two couldn't hit a tree even if it was right in front of you."

"He is rather good with a bow, Wulfric," Wulfwin acknowledged.

"Yes, he is," Wulfric agreed.

"All the more reason for him not to go then, is it not?" Wulfwin added.

"Aye," agreed Wulfric. "If he goes, he might make us look bad, Wulfwin."

"You're going to tell Father that you've got a stomach-ache, and you can't go to the hunt after all, aren't you, little brother?" Wulfwin said, turning his attention back to Tovi and giving him a menacing grin that made him look like a demon.

"But I don't have a stomach-ache," Tovi protested.

Wulfwin glanced at Wulfric and his brother nodded, reading his thoughts. Wulfwin grinned and slammed a forceful fist into Tovi's midriff. "You have now, runt!"

Tovi doubled up, clutching his winded guts, and tried steadying himself. He made a determined attempt to skirt round them but it was futile. He could not get past them. They started taking turns to punch him. As was usual practice for them, they targeted the parts of him where the bruises would be hidden, knowing that a black eye or bloodied nose would be noticed by inquiring adults.

"He's not going to give up, Wulfwin. He's a stubborn little *bæcþearm*, I'll give him that," said the other twin.

"Aye, but an arsehole is useful, Wulfric. He isn't!" Wulfwin laughed loudly.

"Think of something!" Wulfric shouted, frustrated, and growing tired of holding Tovi.

"I am thinking," Wulfwin replied, a finger poised on his nose pensively.

"Better hurry, they will be waiting for us."

"You won't stop me. I'll tell Father!" Tovi cried, his anger bursting from him in a stream of tears.

"Right, Wulfric, get some rope," Wulfwin ordered, suddenly catching an idea. He took charge of Tovi from his brother whilst Wulfric looked blindly around.

Wulfwin pointed and shouted impatiently, "Over there, by that water trough." Then, as Wulfric handed him the rope, he threaded it through his brother's belt. "Now, go get your horse saddled, brother, before we are too late."

They were both laughing as Wulfwin threw the rope over a high branch of a tree and began to hoist a struggling Tovi off the ground. He then secured the rope to a lower branch so that Tovi's legs dangled.

"Let me down!" Tovi cried, kicking out his legs. He struggled uselessly, shouting all manner of obscenities at them.

"Look at him dance in the air! Dance, Tovi, dance! Do the hanging dance!" Wulfric sang as he and Wulfwin led their horses out of the yard.

"Good day to you, little brother, enjoy your jig," Wulfwin added. "Next time you cross us, it will be the water well for you!" They slapped their hands together in a congratulatory gesture for a job well done.

Tovi tried to swing himself at them and missed miserably.

"Hoy, Tovi, don't wear yourself out!" laughed Wulfric.

"At least he won't be able to follow us now," Wulfwin commented to his brother.

"Aye, but we might just be in trouble for this," Wulfric replied a little more seriously. "Should we let him down?"

Wulfwin looked momentarily thoughtful, and then shook his head. With a malicious grin, he glanced up at Tovi and declared, "No, leave him, it will be worth whatever trouble it brings."

The horn was blowing in the distance, and the boys hurried to join the hunt. No one even knew that Tovi was missing... except for his tormentors.

It was at least half an hour before Tovi was back on solid ground again. Luckily for him, Yrmenlaf had heard his cries for help and cut him down. He had fallen to the ground and the impact caused him to graze both his knees, tearing his hose. Mother was not going to be pleased about that, but experience told him that if he went running to her to complain about his brothers, she would not listen anyway. Most likely he'd get a good ear boxing for his trouble instead. After all, Wulfric and Wulfwin were such 'good boys' and would 'never do such a terrible thing'. If they did, it would be because he deserved it for something *he* had most likely done to *them*. And it was no use relying on Yrmenlaf. He would not support his story for fear that he would fall victim to the same treatment. So, there was no point. Even if his mother did believe what had happened to him, his brothers would somehow manage to talk their way out of it. They always did.

Nor was there any point in trying to join the hunt now for it would be well underway, and things would probably get even worse for him if he did. Feeling dejected and thwarted, he limped away to find consolation in the company of Winflaed, vowing future vengeance against his brothers. One day his time would come, he promised himself.

Like Ealdgytha, the Lady Eadgyth was the daughter of a well-to-do thegn, and despite being an earl's lady, she was not above helping with the household chores. She had insisted on assisting Ealdgytha in the dairy, had swept the hall and had even assisted in nursing Lady Gerda. It was no trouble; she had told a grateful Ealdgytha. It made a change from sitting down and embroidering all day. Eadgyth had even offered some of her own remedies that Ealdgytha had not yet tried, but Gerda was deteriorating daily, and although everything had been done to improve her health, there appeared to be little that anyone could do except make her as comfortable as possible, until the end inevitably came. It appeared that it was just a matter of waiting for her demise, and whilst there was a betrothal to celebrate, there would most likely also be a time of mourning, very soon.

Ealdgytha was enjoying the Lady Eadgyth's company. She found her innocent simplicity refreshing. Eadgyth, being in her mid-twenties, was some years younger than Ealdgytha and it pleased Ealdgytha that the younger woman consulted her for advice on childrearing and other wifely matters. It gave her a sense of importance that the earl's lady should seek her counsel. It was also a chance for Ealdgytha to learn a little of the world outside Horstede, for she seldom had the opportunity to leave the homestead, except for the occasional visit to the burgh of Lewes at market time.

"You have such beautiful children," remarked Eadgyth as she and her hostess were laying out the table linen. Drusilda sat on a rush mat surrounded by her plaything, toying with her mother's keys, given to her to keep her amused. She was gurgling contentedly, enjoying the sound of the keys as they jingled in her hand. Ealdgytha looked over at her proudly and said, "Thank you, my Lady, I am truly blessed. All my children are strong and healthy, as are yours." She followed her companion's gaze and saw that she had fixed her eyes on the child. There was a wistful expression on Lady Eadgyth's face.

"Yes, they are... but there was one... one that we lost." Eadgyth looked saddened momentarily.

"Oh, I did not know, my Lady. I am sorry."

"Aye, the babe was born dead. She would have been three years this autumn."

Ealdgytha contemplated for a moment, calculating the years. It must have happened in the months when Harold had been exiled. Perhaps the shock of losing him indefinitely had been too much for Eadgyth, and had caused her baby to die within her womb. Such things were known to happen. It was often advised that women who were with child should avoid stressful situations. However, there were some things that could not always be avoided in uncertain times.

"Aye, it happened when Harold was sent into exile," Eadgyth said anticipating Ealdgytha's thoughts.

"Then that was a terrible thing to happen, my Lady," empathized Ealdgytha.

"It was God's will," Eadgyth replied resignedly. "I would have liked another daughter though. Boys are wonderful, but girls are such a help to a mother, don't you think? I was an only child and my mother, God rest her soul, always said how blessed she was, that I was a girl. Boys can be such a handful most of the time."

"Sometimes, my Lady, raising a daughter can also prove to be just as difficult." Ealdgytha sighed. "Still, Lord Harold's good lady mother has five sons and they are all a credit to her."

They had finished laying out the tables and were now placing the wooden bowls and drinking vessels on them.

"Well, she did have *six* sons. We all know what befell the eldest, Swegn." Eadgyth glanced at her hostess sheepishly, as if the mention of Harold's now deceased elder brother would elicit disapproval from the other woman.

"I understand he was a rogue." Ealdgytha smiled.

"Oh, he was, truly; a handsome one at that!" Eadgyth confirmed with a mischievous smile. "But his roguish quality was to be his ultimate downfall."

"And is it really true that he seduced the Abbess of Leominster?" enquired Ealdgytha curiously.

"Indeed... *and* he abducted her!" Eadgyth replied enthusiastically.

"And they had a child?" probed Ealdgytha further. *So, the tales were true about Harold's infamous brother*, she thought. She was interested to know more.

"Yes, they did. Swegn even desired to wed her but was not permitted to marry her as she could not forsake her vows. He was ordered to return her to her abbey."

"What happened to the child?"

"Hakon would be seven now. He was given up as a hostage with my lord Harold's youngest brother, Wulfnoth, and taken to Normandy. We believe them to be residing at the court of Duke William. As for Swegn, Lord Godwin ordered him to embark on a pilgrimage and perform penance. Sadly, he died returning home from the Holy Land before he could fully repent of his crimes. He was a great trouble to his father and mother. Do you know he even tried to claim that his real father was King Cnut?"

"Really? How absurd."

"Harold's mother never forgave him that last insult. As for his father, he was always trying to see the good in him. Even when he murdered his cousin, Beorn, in cold blood, he convinced Lord Godwin that he'd been defending himself against Beorn, Godwin forgave him, God rest his soul."

"Poor Lord Godwin. How sad to have a son that breaks your heart so," murmured Ealdgytha.

"Aye, Godwin was beside himself when the news of his death arrived, but I'm not sure I can say the same for Lady Gytha. As for Harold, well, he had always fought with Swegn, but I think he, too, was saddened by his brother's loss. Harold had been very close to Swegn as boys growing up, but he had come to dislike the man he became. He saw the hurt that his bad behaviour caused his parents. But now he has Tostig to fight with!" She finished her sentence with a little laugh.

"Oh?" Ealdgytha said curiously, hoping that Eadgyth would indulge her further. "I thought as brothers they would love one another as brothers should."

Eadgyth looked guilty, as though she was about to disclose some great secret that she knew she shouldn't. "No need to worry, my Lady," Ealdgytha said, trying to put her at ease. "You may trust that I will keep your confidence."

Eadgyth smiled and took a deep breath before saying, "I am afraid that Tostig finds it difficult to accept Harold's increasing importance since he inherited his father's Earldom of Wessex. They are frequently at odds with each other."

"It is true that brothers can often be rivals. Wulfhere's own brother and he were forever vying with one another for their father's approval. Wulfhere's brother, Leofric, has been dead these past six years, but there are times when I still see the sadness in his eyes whenever he remembers him. Having three sons myself, I know how spirited and competitive they can be."

"Aye," nodded Eadgyth knowingly. "They can indeed. I look at my own boys and I wonder how well they might grow up. I hope that none of them inherit any of their Uncle Swegn's traits, but Gytha seems to keep them in line, the little madam. Harold dotes on her, more than the others, I do think."

Ealdgytha smiled cynically. "He should have a care then, not to spoil her. I fear Wulfhere's indulgence of Freyda has resulted in her headstrong ways. If he had been more inclined to discipline her instead of indulging her every whim, we may not be in this situation."

"Then we must conclude that all children can be troublesome whatever their sex!" Eadgyth laughed. "There is no hope for any of them!"

"None, at all," agreed Ealdgytha. The Lady Eadgyth may have been jesting, but she was deadly serious. She had an ominous feeling the problem with Freyda was going to prove more troublesome than ever, now that they were being forced to betroth her to Edgar. Still, at least there would be time for she and Wulfhere to devise a plan that would see them out of this damned agreement – if only they could find a way.

Winflaed watched with envy as the hunt went off in a flurry of horses, hounds, hawks, and hunting horns. She enjoyed hunting, and sometimes Father would take her out with her brothers, but today was men's work and she had been given the responsibility of looking after the earl's children. Tovi found her entertaining them, playing with a ball made from a pig's bladder, whilst their mothers busied themselves, organising Freyda's betrothal. Godwin, brown-haired and thickset, just like his grandsire and namesake had been, was the eldest at eight; and six-year-old Gytha, like her brother, was also named for her grandmother. Five-year-old Edmund came next, followed by Magnus, who had just reached his fourth birthday. The two younger children were boisterous, noisy little creatures, with the swan-white fairness of their mother.

"I thought you were going on the hunt, too?" Winflaed queried as Tovi limped toward the group of laughing children. She looked down at his ruined hose. "Oh my, what happened?"

"You cannot guess?" he asked, sarcastically.

"The beasts! What did they do this time?"

"Never mind, little sister. What are we doing here?"

The Godwinson boys gathered around him shouting, "Play with us!"

"Yes, come play with us, Tovi!" demanded Gytha, grabbing his hand.

"Come, Tovi, you can help me look after this lot. Let us go into the forest and play on the rope swing. I'm bored here."

Tovi sighed. It was not how he had planned his day, playing with little children, but it was better than moping around the homestead, or being given work by his mother.

It was nearly midday and the autumn sun was still warm enough, that time of year, to warm the forest. An old oak tree stood on ground where the embankment along the stream was higher. On an outstretched branch, hung a swing made of rope, projecting over the pool. Using the ground to propel oneself, it could be leapt onto and swung out over the water. If nimble enough, an intrepid person could land on the other side without too much trouble. Tovi demonstrated first, swinging with the ease of a seasoned acrobat. Then, when Winflaed dared her brother to drop from the rope into the pool, he did not disappoint her, crashing into the water as the younger children laughed and clapped appreciatively. Not to be outdone, Winflaed swung herself higher than her brother, dropping down into the water not far behind him. Then, in a closely run contest, they raced back to the bank with Tovi the winner, but only by a hair's breadth.

"I want to do it now," Godwin shouted determinedly. Tovi leapt up the steep bank, shoes squelching, to where the younger boy was struggling to grab the rope, as it swung tantalisingly out of his reach.

"Careful, don't lean out too far. You might fall," Tovi warned, snatching the rope when it came close by. He handed it to Godwin who took it eagerly.

"It's all right, I *can* swim," Godwin informed him. "My father taught me."

Tovi helped Godwin to jump onto it. When he could not quite make it, Tovi demonstrated, showing him how to push from the verge and use his thigh muscles to clasp the rope between them just above the knot. Then Tovi handed Godwin the rope again, and after a couple more attempts and a push from Tovi, he managed to swing out over the pond and back again with a gleeful shout. But he was not brave enough to let go and jump into the water as the two elder children had done. Tovi caught him safely, and made sure his feet were firmly back on the ground before he released him.

"My turn! My turn!" shouted Edmund and Magnus together as they fought to be next in line.

"Not before me," insisted their sister, Gytha, brushing past them roughly. "I am next."

Before Tovi could stop her, she grabbed the rope with all the confidence of one who had done this a thousand times before, leaving her brother to watch indignantly as she swung happily out over the pond. Tovi chuckled to himself as Godwin watched her sourly. He had seen that same look on Winflaed's face a thousand times before.

Winflaed clapped approvingly and Tovi shouted, "Well done, Gytha!" much to Godwin's chagrin. Even the younger children shouted out encouragement to their sister as she swung to and fro, squealing with delight at her own cleverness.

"I think you had better stop now," Tovi called to her, as there was no sign of Gytha returning. She ignored his pleas, and carried on swinging.

"Gytha, stop now!" Winflaed pleaded. She and Tovi tried to grab Gytha when she swung close.

Gytha continued to make no effort to return it to the bank, and swung out into the middle of the pond again as the others watched and moaned in annoyance. Then their moans turned to gasps of horror as, without warning, the little girl let go of the rope and fell straight down into the water with a great splash. Tovi and the others watched her, powerless on their high perch, to do anything to help. They looked down, waiting anxiously for her to resurface but there was no sign of her; just the water rippling after the impact.

"Gytha!" shouted Godwin. He turned his face to look at Tovi, his eyes full of dread. "Help her, please; she can't swim!" He began to struggle down the precarious mudslide to the water's edge.

Leaving Winflaed to deal with Godwin, Tovi leapt into the water, using the rope to position himself over the spot where he thought Gytha had fallen. He submerged himself again and again in the pond, desperately searching for her. The water was about a foot deeper than Tovi was tall, but he was a competent swimmer and the depth was not a problem to him. The problem was the disturbance of mud and slime, creating a murk that hindered his vision.

Winflaed and the children watched anxiously from the bank as Tovi frantically searched for the little girl. Then Winflaed heard in the distance, horns blowing, and an idea came to her.

"Godwin, stay here and don't let your brothers into the water. I am going to get help," she cried and scrambled up the grass verge, struggling as her wet shoes sank into the mud. She kicked them off and ran as fast as she could into the woods.

Following the doleful sound of the horns, she ran through the trees and undergrowth to where she met the woodland track. Her senses had been right and she met the hunting party just as they were coming up the track toward her. Her father and the earl were leading the group as they meandered home at a relaxed pace after the morning's hard exercise. The men behind them carried their quarry proudly. The hart was a limp, lifeless mass of reddish-brown fur, carried upside down along a spear shaft, tied by its hooves.

"Winflaed!" Wulfhere called in surprise as she ran out of the trees in front of them. "What the devil are you doing out here?"

Diving deeply into the murk, Tovi found her and was using all his strength to pull her to the surface. He struggled to hold her head above the water, keeping her nose and mouth clear so she could breathe. It seemed an impossible task lay ahead of him. How was he going to get her back to the bank? His arms and legs were tiring, his lungs felt as if they would burst and he was unable to avoid swallowing water. He was frantic, concerned that he would lose his grip on her and she would drown. All he could think of was that everyone would blame him, should he not be able to save her. He tried to swim with her, his arm secured around her neck; but his efforts were thwarted as he found it impossible to hold onto her and they both went under.

Suddenly, the last of his strength almost sapped, he felt Gytha's unconscious body swept from him; and then, he was pulled to shore by a sturdy pair of hands he knew to belong to his father. As Wulfhere dragged him onto the grass, he could vaguely make out what was going on around him. His father's cloak was draped about his shoulders to keep him warm, he sat up and watched, as Harold lay his daughter down on her side, gently, to expel the water from her nose and mouth. He heard Godwin, tearfully asking if she was alive. His heart sank, believing that Gytha was either dead, or almost dead; and it would be his fault. Surely they would hang him. Closing his eyes, he held his head in his hands. Then he heard a small child coughing and spluttering, and a faint little voice saying, "I couldn't get off the swing, Father, so I let go, and the water swallowed me. I'm sorry, Father."

"You are safe now, *deorling*, thanks to this young lad," he heard the earl say in a mellow, comforting voice. "How is the boy, Wulfhere?"

"Alive and breathing, my lord, thank God," his father replied, as he rubbed him down with his cloak. "And your daughter?"

"She will recover. She could not have been under for too long. I am sure she will be fine, thanks to your son."

Tovi heard squelching footsteps across the grass and a voice asked, "What are you called, boy?"

He opened his eyes warily, and stared at the pair of wet boots standing before him. Tovi was cold, soaked through to the skin, and shivering. The earl's shadow towered over him, and he dared not look up. His chattering teeth meant that he could not speak. Instead of answering, he waited expectantly for the earl to admonish him.

Wulfhere nudged him. "Look at the earl, Tovi, and answer him," he urged, whispering in his ear.

Reluctantly, Tovi lifted his gaze. He was relieved to see that Harold's face held a kindly expression, not the angry scowl he had imagined.

"Don't be shy, boy. Surely you have a name?" Harold asked laughingly.

Tovi was encouraged by Harold's bright smile. Rays of light were shining through the trees and the earl, whose tallness seemed to go on and on, appeared to be illuminated by the glow of the sun. Spellbound by the magic of this golden warrior before him, Tovi stared wordlessly until, eventually, he found his tongue.

"Tovi, sir. M-m-my name is Tovi, sir."

Harold hunkered down and put a hand on Tovi's quaking shoulder. His smile was still radiating his face and the boy felt at ease in his presence.

"Well, Tovi, 'sir', I give you my heartfelt thanks for saving my daughter. Consider yourself a hero, lad. I could have lost her, today; I shall never forget what you have done. And Gytha, I am sure, will be forever grateful to you, for her life."

"But I almost let her go, sir. If you had not come when you did..." Tovi protested, believing that the earl, with all his heavenly golden light, could see right through him.

"And if you had not held her until I came, then we would not have pulled her out alive. You could have been drowned yourself, lad, yet you chose to hang on to her, and for that I will be eternally indebted to you." Then Lord Harold looked straight at Wulfhere. "You have a courageous boy, Wulfhere, but he is far too modest."

Wulfhere beamed, and nodded. "I fear he has an overly humble nature, lord."

"He shall be rewarded for this good deed," Harold said, rising and holding out his hand to Tovi to pull him to his feet.

"Thank you, but there is no need. She was in my care and I feel it was my fault," Tovi said, imagining himself a warrior who had just defeated an army of ogres, single-handedly rescuing a beautiful princess, and, having returned her to her father, the king, was kneeling before him to receive honours and praise. Then reality brought him back and he knew he was just a boy again.

The earl laughed, good-naturedly. "Wulfhere, you're right, your son is overly humble. I like humility, but not too much. You must remedy this."

"I will, my lord." Wulfhere smiled.

"What's this then? Lord above what has happened to all of you?" demanded Ealdgytha as the hunting party and children returned home. "Heavens! This boy of mine looks half-drowned!" she cried, glaring at her son and husband with displeasure.

Wulfhere dismounted and then assisted his son from the saddle.

"You could say that, could she not Tovi?" Wulfhere replied. "Our son saved the earl's daughter from a drowning."

Tovi was wearing his father's cloak and was still shivering. He felt damp and uncomfortable and desperate to get out of his wet clothes.

Inside the hall Tovi found himself smothered by his mother, fussing over him with melodramatic concern. "Goodness me!" she exclaimed as she rubbed him with fresh linen towels. "Always up to mischief, you and that sister of yours!"

Lady Eadgyth left Gytha in the care of her nurse for a moment to swamp Tovi with grateful kisses. "Thank you Master Tovi, for saving my little girl's life! May God reward you with good fortune for such an act of bravery!" she said graciously.

Tovi was thoroughly mortified by all the commotion. He was glad when they left him by the hearth to dry out and change into the clean clothing his mother had left for him. As he was not suffering the effects of anything too dramatic, Ealdgytha turned her concerns to helping Lady Eadgyth attend to her daughter.

Tovi thought he had managed to escape any taunting from his brothers, knowing how angry they would be at him for having stolen their limelight, even after all the trouble they went to keep him away from the hunt – but no chance of that. Just as he was trying to put on his trousers, Wulfwin picked up a fire poker and started prodding his buttocks with it, laughing menacingly at the same time. Trying anxiously to avoid the poker and desperate to rid himself of his vulnerable nakedness, Tovi stumbled and tripped as he hopped about with one leg in and one leg out of his trousers.

"See, Wulfric? See how his legs are so skinny! He thinks he is Beowulf, but he's more like Sparrowulf! It was only an ugly, rat-faced girl anyway! Why go to all that bother for a girl?"

"Hey, Wulfwin, he probably pushed her in the pond on purpose, so he could save her and win favour with the earl!"

"Aye, he wants to be one of the earl's huscarles – but not with a skinny arse like that!" The twins fell about laughing and Wulfwin swapped the poker for his seax. He started prodding the tip of the blade against Tovi's shivering buttocks, much to his brother's delight. "My, Tovi, your arse is so hairy! Let me shave it for you!"

"Leave me be!" Tovi pleaded, trying to get the other leg in his trousers whilst dodging the point of Wulfwin's seax. "Ouch! Get off, Wulfwin! It hurts!"

"Aye, leave him be, you two *Sons of Loki!*" The sound of their father's voice startled the twins. "Go and help the men prepare the dinner, you two. Make yourselves useful and let your brother alone. He has been through enough for one day."

The twins uttered a terse, "Yes, Father," but threw a threatening look back at Tovi when they thought Wulfhere could not see them. Wulfhere ignored them and helped Tovi with his trousers.

"Pay no mind to those two. It was their first hunt and they thought they should have had all the glory."

Tovi did not reply but just stared despondently down at his feet. Wulfhere lifted the boy's chin and studied him. "Why do you let them bother you?"

Tovi shook his head. "They don't," he replied. But it was a lie; now that he had become an object of envy in his brothers' eyes, they would dislike him even more. He had always longed to be accepted by them, but had been subjected to their tormenting as long as he could remember. Despite the strength of his animosity toward his brothers, he would rather eat horse dung than admit how he felt to his father.

"So why the long face?" Wulfhere persisted, helping Tovi into a clean tunic. "Is your newfound status as a hero not to your liking?"

"I don't know…" murmured Tovi quietly. He did not want to look his father in the eye for he knew that, if he did, Wulfhere would know that he was lying.

"There may be a reward for you."

Tovi's expression remained bland. A reward would just make matters worse, most likely, he thought, and his eyes fluttered before looking down at the ground again.

"She's not just *any* little girl, you know. She is the daughter of an earl. Who knows, one day she may marry a king! Then you can say, 'I am Tovi, son of Wulfhere, the fellow that saved the queen from drowning!'"

Tovi bit his lip and shrugged his shoulders as Wulfhere put both their shoes on the stones of the hearth to dry out.

"They said I pushed her in the water on purpose," Tovi said. "They said I did it to gain favour with the earl. But I didn't, Father. She fell. She fell off the swing."

"I know that, son. And so does the earl. I swear – out of all my sons, you are the one I least understand!" Wulfhere shook his head. "You put your own life in danger to save the girl, and all you can think about are your brothers!"

Tovi looked up at his father through the thickness of his fringe; a shield to hide behind.

Wulfhere pulled a bench close to the hearth so they could both get warm. "How unlike you are to the other two. If it had been one of them who had saved the girl, they would have sung their own praises from the highest mountain. In fact, I would wager my life on it that *they* would have pushed her on purpose to win favour."

Tovi shrugged and stared again at the floor, feeling his face blush. His father continued. "You don't think that they will accept you unless you stand in their shadows and not their sunlight?"

Tovi nodded reluctantly and tilted his head to one side. "I do not want them to think that I wish to be better than they." Then he added dejectedly, "Their hatred is already enough for me."

"'Tis not hatred they feel, Tovi – it's just rivalry amongst brothers. You will all grow out of it." Wulfhere smiled as he put an affectionate arm about Tovi's shoulders. "You cannot change the way they are right now. Not even I can do that. They will be put out for a while, but they will get over it!"

Tovi looked down at his hands folded in his lap and half smiled. "Perhaps," he murmured. "But one day, I should like to kill them. They tied me up, Father, so I couldn't join the hunt."

Wulfhere shook his head in disgust at Tovi's disclosure. "Hearken to me, boy, there will be plenty of times in this life when you will need to kill to stay alive. Remember that when the world is full of madness, it is not always the taking of lives that makes us strong; but not to kill – that takes more strength and courage than you'll ever know."

Someday, Tovi thought, *I may need to remember that, when I want to kill my brothers.*

Chapter Eight

The Betrothal

Freyda seated herself next to her mother at one end of the long table. She glanced down at Edgar who was taking his seat with his father and young stepmother at the further end of the table. She caught his eye, and he winked at her, making her tingle with excitement. She sighed contentedly. *I am going to enjoy this evening*, she thought to herself, knowing that she would take great pleasure in seeing her mother squirm uncomfortably as she danced with her beloved. It was her betrothal feast, and she beamed with the radiance of a new bride to be. Glancing down at her gown, she fingered it lovingly. Her mother had given her one of her own best linen gowns, a garment that had been dyed using the root from the madder plant to create a rich dark shade of red. Her under-tunic was of bleached linen with embroidered, close-fitting sleeves, longer than the sleeves of her over-dress. She wore her golden hair in two long braids that reached to her thighs, covered by a white linen cap and wimple, held in place by silver pins. To complete her dress, around her neck she wore a little silver cross on a leather thong with a couple of coloured glass beads on either side. She was pleased with her attire and hoped that she looked as resplendent as she felt. The idea that she would be the focus of attention this evening filled her with great anticipation.

She tried to remember the advice her mother had given her on how to conduct herself in the presence of the earl. Her head spun with such excitement that she could barely remember what was permissible and what was not. Her mother had imparted her knowledge, stony faced and empty of the loving words she had hoped for. In truth, she had not expected anything other than disapproval; nonetheless it still caused her great hurt. But she would not let it affect her that night. It was her night and she was going to enjoy it.

The table, she observed gratefully, was magnificently decorated. Her mother, she knew, would have seen to it that it was dressed with her best table linen and utensils. Despite her displeasure at the betrothal, Mother wanted to impress the earl and his lady. Father had broken their best oaken table and they had had to use an old trestle, which, once it had been laid with the best tableware, sufficed well enough. Soft seat coverings and furnishings had been brought out of storage to add comfort for those fortunate enough to sit at the high table. Freyda felt a sensation of satisfaction that all this fuss was for her.

At the other end of the table, Edgar's cheeks glowed brightly. Freyda leaned forward and flashed her large green eyes, flirtatiously. As he replied with a smile, she retreated, teasingly, behind her mother's shoulder. She was pleased that he had made an effort with his appearance: neatly combed hair, trimmed moustache and shaved chin.

When all the guests had arrived and were seated, the festivities could begin. Freyda looked around her, feeling a pang of sympathy for her little sister, who was helping Sigfrith and some of the other village daughters to serve the food that had been prepared by Herewulf. It was Winflaed's first time serving at a big feast like this and Freyda was aware that her younger sister looked anxious, just as she had done when it had been her first time. The choicer cuts of venison would of course go to the top table, served with a rich sauce, dressed salads and vegetables. Then the dishes would be served to the other guests in order of status. Winflaed would have to know who was to receive what. The huscarles were to be served first, followed by the more substantial *ceorls*, such as Esegar. Next, those of lesser standing within the hierarchy of village life, the cottars, who would mostly be consigned to sit on the floor should there be no room at the tables. There would be boiled pig stew for them. Venison was a commodity that only the wealthy were entitled. Amongst the guests were Helghi's kin. They had paid with honey for the privilege of attending. Village children sat on their mother's laps or at their feet under the table. Freyda's younger sisters would be on a table of their own with the earl's children, supervised by Lady Eadgyth's nursemaid and Sigfrith. Her brothers, the twins and Tovi, sat amongst the huscarles and were expected to ensure that the men's drinking vessels were kept full throughout the night.

Then came the time for speeches. Harold started with a dialogue about women being *friðuwebban*, peacemakers between families, in an obvious but polite reference to the hostility that had hung over the two families for so long. He spoke of the age-old custom of how a woman was not only a weaver of clothes, but a weaver of peace, reconciliation, and compromise. He praised Helghi and Wulfhere's decision to opt for a peaceful solution to their problems by the binding of their families together in matrimony, thus abandoning enmity and embracing friendship and kinship. He also formalised the gift of land that he had offered to Freyda on receipt of their marriage, announcing it publicly and having Father Paul write out a charter.

Helghi managed to be congenial, in his own gruff manner; when it was his turn to make a speech, he offered his prospective daughter-in-law a terse welcome into his family, announcing that her bride gift should be a cow, six goats, a gold brooch and some other trinkets that had belonged to Edgar's deceased mother.

Freyda watched her father with interest as he gave his speech. She could tell he was doing his best to be polite and courteous which was more than could be said for her mother, judging by the look of obvious hostility that darkened Ealdgytha's face.

When all the speeches were over, Earl Harold stood again and called everyone to listen. "I have one more speech to make this eve." The sound of the earl's commanding voice quietened the hall. Everyone turned their eyes toward him in anticipation. "Today my beloved little daughter decided it was a good day to try and drown herself. She would have succeeded if not for our host's son, young Master Tovi." He gestured toward her brother. Freyda could see from where she sat that he was cringing with embarrassment. She knew he hated being singled out, whether it was for negative or positive reasons.

Harold continued. "Gytha has a gift for him in gratitude for saving her life today. Gytha…" He beckoned his daughter to him and placed in her hands a tanned leather scabbard, and nodded to where Tovi was sitting. As Gytha walked over to him carrying the scabbard in both her hands, 'oohs' and 'aahs' echoed around the hall. Freyda was almost embarrassed for her brother, knowing that he would be mortified. Tigfi stood up, dragged him out of his seat, and pushed him into the centre of the hall where Gytha stood waiting for him.

"Thank you for saving me," Gytha said, just as her father had instructed her. She was smiling confidently, and there were plenty more 'oohs' and 'aahs' as her saviour stood in awkwardly silence, staring at the thing in her hands with confused, wide eyes.

"Go on, lad, don't be shy. Take it!" someone shouted and the boy grabbed the gift and hurried back to his seat to cries of such like, "Well done, lad!" and "*Waes hael*, Tovi!"

It was then that Wulfhere signalled to the musicians to play and Freyda felt a sense of relief for her brother's sake. It was time for the real merrymaking, the dancing. She looked to Edgar, he nodded, and the crowd clapped and cheered as they took the floor to dance together.

Tovi leapt from his seat and escaped the hall, weaving through the dancers until he found the door to outside. He wanted to have a better look at his gift, away from the covetous eyes of his brothers, whose malevolent looks had intensified after the gift was given.

Outside, the sun was slowly setting, providing the homestead with a beautiful golden halo. Tovi sat down on the steps of the porch and examined the weapon's scabbard whilst music from inside the hall drifted painfully out through the open doors. Out here, the noise was not quite so loud and he could concentrate on studying the leather casing on the scabbard, decorated with entwined serpents. He gazed in awe and amazement at the craftsmanship. He carefully caressed the decorated heads of the copper rivets that secured the scabbard, noting there were leather loops on copper rings, to hang it from a belt. His heart glowed. He had never imagined possessing such a thing of beauty.

Suddenly, he felt a presence next to him. "Let me see what the earl has given you." Winflaed's voice was cheery and pleasant. She sat down beside him on the step.

Tovi drew the seax from its scabbard and held it carefully between his hands. It was a little longer than the knives they used for everyday use, about eleven inches from the handle, inlaid in silver and copper along the fuller. They both gasped, studying the horn and silver mounted hand grip. Looking closely, they saw that there was some text etched in the fuller. Tovi held it closer to see.

"It's beautiful. What does it say?" Winflaed asked, leaning against his shoulder. Neither she nor her brother had paid much heed to Father Paul's attempts to teach them to read.

"I don't know," Tovi replied.

"It says *Eorl Harold is min hlaford*, Earl Harold is my lord," Wulfhere said joining them. Squeezing in between them, Father sat down on the step and stretched his long legs out onto the bottom treads. Tovi looked at his father incredulously as Wulfhere continued, "It once belonged to Lord Harold himself, but now he has gifted it to you. 'Tis a measure of how high in his esteem he holds his daughter, and how grateful he is that you saved her precious life."

Tovi studied the weapon with even greater amazement as Wulfhere gazed on. "My first seax," the boy whispered. "My very own." *Given to me by the most renowned warrior in the kingdom*! He smiled proudly at his father, his earlier embarrassment lost in the glory that the gift endowed him.

"Well it saves me from the expense. Think yourself fortunate, son. Your brothers will be green with envy, for I doubt I shall be able to supply each of them with such a piece," Wulfhere said, and laughed. "Here, let me put it away for safekeeping. You will have no need of it yet, and we do not want those two *Sons of Loki* getting their hands on it."

Tovi allowed his father to take the weapon from him, though he did so somewhat reluctantly.

"What are the lessons to be learned here, son?" Wulfhere asked, eyeing Tovi intently.

Tovi shook his head. "I am not sure, Father."

"Then I shall tell you. Our fate is already determined by God, but the manner of how we choose to live our lives is determined by ourselves, and so our worth is counted. We prosper through our own deeds, be they good or bad. Good deeds are always rewarded in the end, but bad deeds will inevitably be our downfall when we are called before God to account for ourselves." Wulfhere ruffled his son's golden head and Tovi thought him the wisest man he ever heard speak. Much to his annoyance, Winflaed jumped into Wulfhere's lap. It had been his moment and she had to spoil it.

"What do daughters get if they are good?" Winflaed demanded to know, hanging onto her father's neck.

"If they are good, they grow up and get good husbands." He laughed and kissed her cheek. "Fine men like their fathers!"

"I don't want a husband. I want a sword, bigger than that one!"

"It isn't a sword, *dwæslican mægþ*. Stupid little girl! Besides, girls do not have swords, Frog Spawn," Tovi said.

"Why not?" his sister retorted, pursing her lips.

"Because your purpose in life is to weave and spin, and bear your husband children – not to fight," Tovi replied with an air of superiority. "Don't you know anything?"

"And if girls were given swords, they would kill their brothers and their fathers!" Wulfhere laughed again, as his daughter attempted to wrestle him to the ground, pounding him playfully with her small fists when she couldn't. "Come now, let us go back inside. We are missing the entertainment!" He cocked a cynical expression as he listened to the noise from the hall. "Such as it is," he added, laughingly. Catching Winflaed in his arms, he swung her behind his back, she wrapped her limbs about his torso, and they went inside to re-join the festivities.

Ealdgytha sat rigidly in her seat and watched, disapprovingly, as her daughter danced with her future son-in-law. *He is so clumsy*, she thought to herself. *My daughter... betrothed to a cripple...* And she is so besotted by him. The fact that Freyda appeared oblivious to what she perceived as a great disability, irritated Ealdgytha greatly.

"He is so unsuitable for our Freyda," she whispered to Wulfhere as he sat down beside her. "And she seems not to care a jot."

"Well, there is nothing we can do about it now." Wulfhere's tone was one of impatience. He leaned toward her. "And I would ask you to keep your voice down, wife. I would not have the earl hear your disparaging remarks."

Harold was locked in a conversation with Helghi. Ealdgytha could hear him giving Helghi permission to cut down the trees he would need to rebuild his home.

"And of course, Wulfhere, I am certain, will assist you in any way that he can," Harold was saying to Helghi.

"Thank you, my lord," Helghi replied.

Ealdgytha dug her elbow into Wulfhere's ribs as Helghi gave them a smug smile. "Did you hear that?" she whispered hoarsely. "I cannot bear it."

"Nor can I, Ealdgytha, but you are not making me feel any better about things."

"Just look at him, Wulfhere, he has already had more than his fair share of my best mead. Even his wife has been giving him looks of disgust. I wonder how the earl manages not to flinch at the man's vile breath."

But Harold was not flinching. "And I hope that you and Wulfhere will put your differences aside now and live peaceably with one another," he continued, emphasising the word 'peaceably'. Helghi, it seemed, was the earl's new comrade.

"Of course, my lord, you have my word," Helghi's speech was slurred. "May I ask how long this betrothal is meant to last?"

"No longer than tonight, I hope," Ealdgytha whispered to Wulfhere again. He glared at her.

"I mean, my lord, when should our lovebirds formalise the union?" Helghi smiled, sickeningly, as Ealdgytha looked on in horror.

"I would suggest that a year or two of peace between you two should seal the deal. That is, if you can both manage such a task. If one of you breaks the peace then there may be serious consequences," Harold replied, as if he were laying down the law to two wayward sons.

"I am sure a year should be enough; perhaps sooner," Helghi said, shrugging his shoulders, and gesturing with open palms.

"My lord, two years is what we agreed," Wulfhere said hurriedly.

"Two years, Helghi," agreed Harold.

"But what if Wulfhere recants his promise?" Helghi queried suspiciously.

"He won't, will you, Wulfhere?"

Ealdgytha's heart sank as Wulfhere was forced to agree. Still, in two years anything could happen.

Helghi took another gulp of mead as he gazed over at the young couple dancing together and gave a satisfied smirk. *Such a shame she is not the sole heir to his land*, he thought, pensively fingering his beard. *If she was, his land would fall to Edgar if she was to see her demise before him. But she would have to outlive those damned brothers of hers. Still, such things were known to happen. Yes, it was not impossible. In two years, anything could happen...*

"This music is terrible!" laughed Freyda as she caught up with Edgar in the circle dance. He whirled her into his arms. Her eyes were shining with excitement and her face flushed with a concoction of happiness, mead, and fire-glow.

"I know," an amused Edgar said in response to her complaint as the musicians' attempts to play in tune were fumbled. "Can you believe what has happened to us?"

"Pinch me, I must be dreaming!" Freyda said with a husky laugh.

"I want to do more than just pinch you," replied Edgar, winking.

"Edgar!" She laughed again as he drew her far closer to him than was respectable.

As she went to pull away, he said, "I love to hear you say my name. Say it, say it again."

"Edgar," she whispered as she twirled on to the next partner, looking back at him with a flutter of her lashes. She could hardly wait for the round to be completed so that she could dance with him again. When she came back to him, she pulled him out of the circle and dragged him into the food preparation area, separated from the hall by a partition and curtain. The hall was crowded and she was sure that no one would notice their exit. Happily, there was no one in the kitchen where it was darker so they could be alone. She hung her arms around his neck and kissed his lips passionately.

"We will not be seen?" Edgar asked, pulling away. He sounded concerned.

"I just wanted a moment with you, but we should be careful."

They kissed once more and then Edgar said, "I cannot believe our good fortune. Why, just a few days ago, we were walking in the forest, your hair loose and feet bare, dressed plainly like a forest waif." He smiled, stroking her face. "Now, look at you. You are the most beautiful – loveliest – creature…" They both laughed and embraced. "You are a thegn's daughter and I could never have hoped or dreamed of a wife like you."

"Would that my parents were as happy about our betrothal as we are," she said dolefully. "My mother was positively scathing toward me all day."

"There were no words of encouragement for me either, not from my father anyway. He has constantly berated me for my treachery; oh, and for starting the fire, but I do believe he is secretly revelling in your father's discomfort."

"At least we have that in common... and each other," she said softly.

"Wulfhere, do you think you could have employed a better band of musicians? This lot are bloody awful!" Harold exclaimed, nudging Wulfhere's elbow with his own.

"They were the best I could do given the time in which I had to organise it. Good musicians are hard to come by in these parts – and at such short notice. Perhaps someone else could take over the entertainment? Skalpi, I hear, is an excellent *scop*."

Harold shook his head and said, "Not Skalpi! He will frighten the children with a face like his."

Hearing his name mentioned, Skalpi turned and gave his master a rude gesture which Harold returned with infectious laughter.

Wulfhere knew Skalpi of old. He was one of Harold's chief huscarles and an old war veteran. He was powerfully built, stocky and shorter than most of his fellow Danes. A leather patch covered his left eye and his deeply scarred face bore the evidence of many a past battle. He had acquired the scars as a young warrior serving with Harthacnut in his troublesome Scandinavian kingdoms.

"On second thoughts," reflected Harold, "I do believe that he scares me just as much as he does the children. I'd better be careful. Skalpi does not like his feelings hurt." He laughed heartily as the old Dane swore and scowled at him. Wulfhere chuckled, knowing that Harold's easy-going nature meant that he could trade insults with his men and not be offended. This was a side of Harold that he loved.

"Hoy, Skalpi!" Harold called loudly.

The Dane looked round with mocking eyes. "Ah, Lord Harold, at your service."

"Lord Wulfhere has heard that you have a fine singing voice. He wishes you to perform," Harold called from the dais, cupping a hand to his mouth to project his voice above the din the tuneless musicians were making.

"My lord knows full well that my employment with him is that of personal bodyguard. If it is a *skald* that he desires, he needs to seek one," replied the huscarle. Wulfhere noticed he used the Danish term *skald* instead of the Englisc *scop*.

Skalpi turned his back and Harold threw a silver coin that bounced off his shoulder.

"As you know, Skalpi, I pay well." Harold laughed as Skalpi retrieved the coin from where it had fallen.

"One silver coin, my lord, does not make a generous and benevolent patron. Skills a good *skald* might possess cannot be bought for a mere silver coin." he remarked, mockingly.

Harold sighed and brought out a small purse. "You want to ruin me," he complained good-humouredly. "Is this your fee?"

Harold threw the purse and Skalpi deftly caught it. He felt the weight and appeared to be satisfied with the payment. Then he stood and said with a flourish, "It will do, so fetch me a harp. For tonight I am Skalpi, Lord of *Skaldr*."

Wulfhere sent someone to fetch a harp and signalled to the musicians to stop. The Dane took the instrument and checked its tuning. Then the hall fell silent as he began his recital. He introduced the piece he was about to perform as a saga of his ancestors: one of men spending the last night before battle in their lord's meadhall, feasting, drinking, and making merry with their women.

> *"Death stalls not, its bloody hand*
> *From steel sundered vein they spill*
> *Their heart's blood*
> *And their soul's release*
> *Upon the scarlet field of slaughter*
>
> *"The span of lives lay hidden*
> *The destinies of all good men*
> *Fates woven from birth to death*
> *When with sword in hand*
> *Draw their last earthly breath*
> *"I see my lord, I see my father*
> *They call me unto them*
> *We fight and drink freely*
> *In the Lord's golden halls, forever*
> *Spared of the pains of mortal men*
>
> *"Once again mail-clad and weapon fierce*
> *When Armageddon calls to us*
> *We mere black raven's carrion*
> *The Almighty's angelic horde*
> *Loyal shield companions of Christ our Lord."*

There was a roar of approval as Skalpi ended his performance. Wulfhere joined in the appreciative applause as Skalpi was urged to play more, though not until Harold had thrown him another silver coin. Later, a few of the guests took turns to play the instrument until Wulfhere, keen to show off his daughter's talent, suggested that Freyda play.

Luckily for them, Freyda and Edgar had managed to sneak back into the hall without being seen. She took up her harp, and entranced them all with both her beauty and her voice. Greatly impressed by her performance of the Wife's Lament, Lord Harold congratulated his host for fathering such a talented beauty.

"I can see why the lad was so smitten with her," Harold whispered to him. "She is indeed a beauty and has the voice of Christ's angels. You, Wulfhere, are a man of hidden talents. Not only are you a fine breeder of horses but of women too."

Wulfhere smiled at the earl's flattery, but the situation marred any pleasure he may have felt, for he was still reluctant to accept it. He looked down the table at Helghi's family and tried hard to find fault with Edgar. *The lad does not possess his father's unpleasant nature,* he thought silently but, after visualising his daughter living at Gorde, he felt a jolt of disgust burst through him. *Ach, I cannot accept this. My daughter dwelling in that hell's spawn's den. I cannot bear the thought. There must be a way of extricating myself out of this damned contract.*

Watching Helghi's drunken pawing at his wretched little wife, Wulfhere felt nothing but repugnance at the thought that Freyda was to be married into his family. He wondered how this alliance was ever going to work when his own loathing for them was so intense. *I must have been out of my wits to agree to this. Well, on the other hand, it was only a betrothal... and could be rescinded if there were good reason. Anything could happen in two years. But Freyda looks so happy, damn her. And look at that pig, Helghi!* He wanted to wipe the obtuse smugness off his ugly face. *Damn the impudent worm-eating vermin. He has always coveted that which I have worked hard to maintain: a substantial landholding that gives me reasonable affluence, thegnly status and a place at the royal court, a beautiful wife and healthy offspring, fine horses and... Alfgyva, Lady of Waldron.* He thought of her, the woman, who, for a while, he had loved and had fathered a child with. When Helghi had wanted her, and had tried to force her into marriage with him, she had turned to him as her friend and neighbour for protection. Wulfhere had not meant to fall in love with her, but had been captured by her mysterious, dark beauty. After the child was born, he had vowed to Ealdgytha not to see her again and, although so far, he had stuck to the bargain, the affair had been a bone of contention between them for a long time afterward. As for his enemy, Helghi, it was just another log on the fire of his burning jealousy and hatred for his neighbour.

Ealdgytha interrupted his thoughts, nudging him to suggest that, as it was getting late, maybe now was the time to slow down the entertainment. As was the custom, the men gathered around the hearth to tell riddles and swap amusing anecdotes whilst the womenfolk set about clearing the tables and trestles to make room for the bedding. Even Father Paul eagerly took his place by the fire. Although he was a man of God, he was not averse to a bawdy riddle or poem.

"Edgar, as we have not heard much from you this evening, perhaps you would grace us with a riddle?" Harold said placing a persuasive arm about the lad's shoulders, once they were seated around the fire. Edgar's face glowed with embarrassment as some of the men echoed the earl's encouragement.

"Come on, lad, this is your night," Skalpi called out. "I'm sure you know a riddle or two."

Wulfhere noticed with disdain how Edgar constantly looked to his father for approval. He wondered if it was usual for him to seek his father's consent for everything. Had Helghi known about his son's relationship with his daughter all along? The thought sickened him.

"Aye, my son is not without a riddle or two, or three… are you, son?" Helghi slurred and drained his drinking horn of its contents. "Tell them the one about the…" and Helghi got up, leaned across to Edgar and whispered in his ear. When Edgar hesitated, his father slapped his shoulder in support. "Go on, lad!"

Edgar began the riddle falteringly at first then more confidently as he picked up the rhythm.

"A man came walking where he knew
And came upon a maiden
Reached beneath his skirt and drew
Something stiff and brazen

"Beneath her belt he worked his will
They both began to wiggle
Weary of the work and tired
His handy helper bidden

"Less strong now than she at last

127

There swells inside her belly
The thing that men praise with their hearts
And pay for with their pennies."

"I know what the answer is," yelled one of Harold's younger huscarles. "An army camp whore!"

"That's too obvious," said someone else.

"I know, it's an alewife!" came another suggestion, as laughter sounded around the hall.

"Peeling an onion!" shouted Herewulf in his raucous voice.

Edgar shook his head at each wrong answer, which became more ridiculous with each attempt.

"It's milking a cow," shouted one of the women from the other end of the hall.

"No, it's my wife's mother – mistaken for a cow," the woman's husband joked and was consequently beaten about the ears by his wife.

"I think we should allow Edgar to tell us the answer," Harold said after some more attempts. "Go on, Edgar, what is it then?"

Edgar's face grew red once more as he looked for Freyda and caught her mother's glare instead. "A-a-a milk churn," he replied, blushing.

Wulfhere saw his daughter smiling dreamily at Edgar and felt irritated by their obvious affection for one another. Then he caught Edgar's eye and gave him an evil glare. The lad looked away, red-faced, and Wulfhere angrily willed him to meet his gaze. He wanted him to know that he did not have his approval.

"A milk churn. Of course, very good," Harold said, amused, as the hall thundered with applause. "I would never have guessed it was a milk churn. Now, who's next?"

"I have one I would like to tell," Father Paul spoke up with unpriestly enthusiasm. His chubby chin wobbled with excitement and his rosy cheeks had been made rosier by the evening's immoderation.

"Then tell away, Father," Harold said indulgently.

"Thank you, lord, I do love a good riddle." Father Paul cleared his throat and began somewhat animatedly amidst the howls of laughter that boomed around the hall.

"I am round and hairy underneath
I grow tall and erect in a bed

A satisfier of women
And they rob me of my head

"A beautiful girl with plaited hair
Grabs my reddish skin
Dares to take me in her hand
And grips me there within

"That maiden with the plaited hair
Takes me to the pantry
Wipes her moistened eye
And remembers our meeting sadly."

"That's an onion!" Herewulf shouted. "He's told it countless times before."

"Well guessed, Master Baker," Father Paul agreed, laughing uproariously.

Inside the hall, the riddles continued as Helghi staggered out from the doorway and lurched down the steps of the porch, belching and breaking wind loudly as he did so. He had no wish to leave the comfort of the hall, but was unable to contain his need to relieve himself any longer. He had made sure that he'd more food and mead than was considered gracious of a guest. After all, was it not small compensation for the troubles that Wulfhere had caused him over the years? He made a mental note of them in his head: a crippled son for one; that was definitely Wulfhere's fault. Then there was the loss of his crops over the years; he was convinced this was the doing of Wulfhere's wife, Ealdgytha. *She had evil eyes, that woman.* Hadn't the witch also poisoned Helghi's wife and caused her to die? Then there was Alfgyva... ah yes, beautiful, dark, bewitching Alfgyva. *The woman should have been mine, dammit! And she would have been had it not been for Wulfhere's interference.* There were countless more reasons for him to hate Wulfhere. Helghi was convinced that previous Horstede clans had, for generations, been responsible for obstructing his family's advancement.

He made his way along the side of the longhall, hands groping like a blind man's, flinching as a splinter from one of the timber posts caught his finger. It was useless for a man to try and find the midden pit in this state, he thought, and then a smile came over his face as he pulled up his tunic. Squatting unceremoniously on the grass, exposing his bare buttocks to the chill of the night air, he defecated, effortlessly, on the ground, right beside his host's hall. He smiled at the thought of Wulfhere or one of his grubby, barefoot children stepping in it. His hands found the ground in front of him, and he levered himself to his feet, adjusted his clothing and turned to go back inside, stumbling drunkenly. Rounding the corner, he paused. Swaying unsteadily, he stood aside to allow a girl to hurry down the steps into the yard.

Sigfrith was making her way out into the dim moonlit darkness to Lady Gerda's bower to check on her. Intent on her purpose and used to drunken men's stares, she paid no heed to Helghi's lewd observance of her. She made her way along the coarse pathway and paused for a moment to observe two figures stealthily dart across the yard, and disappear amongst the darkened shadows of the outbuildings. They appeared to be a male and female, one being tall and slim of build and the other much smaller and slighter. In the darkness, she could not have been sure, but was almost certain that it was Edgar and Freyda. Her tongue clicked the roof of her mouth, scornful of their disregard. *If they are caught*, she thought to herself, *they will be whipped*.

For a moment, she stood in the chill of the night air, holding her lantern aloft in an effort to see better, where they had gone. She saw that they had vanished and, deciding not to warn them after all, made to move on when suddenly she felt an unexpected hand on her shoulder. She turned in surprise only to have a large, hairy face with foul stinking breath, shoved into hers. Slobbering thick wet lips sucked at her own as she was pushed roughly up against the wall of the hall. Sigfrith tried to fight but, despite his inebriated state, Helghi was strong and she felt her skirts whipped up and his hands groping at her groin.

"Son of a… Look at that fool," exclaimed Tigfi, who had just been sharing a joke with Esegar on their way back from the urinal pit. "Not the best place to seduce a wench, in full view of anybody on their way for a piss. The man must be as full as a cow's udder on a winter's morn."

They both laughed but stopped when they heard the girl's muffled cries.

It was dark, and light was sparse, but it dawned on them that the girl's cries were not moans of pleasure after all, and that she was struggling with the man who had her pinned against the wall of the longhall.

"'Tis no seduction, my friend. That girl is the Lady Ealdgytha's servant girl, the baker's daughter. Looks like that filthy scum, Helghi, is attempting to be free with her, and she is not liking it very much."

"Nor would I, for that matter," Tigfi replied in disgust. "Best we put a stop to it, my friend."

"Aye, but we must not make a fuss. Wulfhere cannot know of this or he will fly into a rage, end the betrothal or, worse still, kill Helghi and thus incur the earl's greater displeasure!"

Tigfi nodded. "There is nothing like a good bloodfeud to alienate Lord Harold. He hates bad blood amongst his people. He says there are better enemies to fight than ourselves."

"Then it is up to you, and I, Tigfi, to keep the peace," Esegar said and the two men hurried to the girl's aid.

Sigfrith was fighting hard against Helghi's groping hands, and Tigfi thought that she looked to be losing the battle when they approached. He and Esegar pulled Helghi forcibly away from her, and watched as the girl stared with pure hatred at her assailant. They held him back, spitting and snarling like an angry bull.

"Are you all right, lass?" Tigfi checked, as Helghi struggled to break free.

Sigfrith took a deep breath and nodded. Then, to both men's amazement, she lifted her skirts, swung back her leg and kicked her attacker full between the legs. The blow took them all by surprise, and as they staggered back, Sigfrith took the opportunity to hurry away.

Tigfi and Esegar chuckled as Helghi bent double. "The bitch. Fucking wild cat!" he spat as he rubbed his private parts in agony. The blow had left him breathless. "She was asking for it all night," he spluttered, a poor attempt to excuse his behaviour.

Enraged, Tigfi swung Helghi round and slammed him up against the wall of the hall, eyes blazing in anger. Harold's reeve was a lad of no more than twenty, but powerfully built from the rigorous training that huscarles were expected to take part in. Helghi, even when clear-headed, would have found himself no match for the younger man.

"You dare to dishonour the earl and Lord Wulfhere, by forcing yourself on his servant girl in his own home?" bellowed Tigfi angrily. "At your own son's betrothal feast?"

He held Helghi by his neck, feeling the older man's flesh between his fingernails.

In the background, could be heard the laughter from the hall.

"What are you going to do about it?" Helghi snarled defiantly; his hands covering Tigfi's to draw off his hold.

"Nothing, Helghi. It's what *you* are going to do that is important."

Helghi stared at Tigfi uncomprehendingly.

"You are going to get your fat arse back inside, and behave with the propriety of a good guest," Tigfi continued, "with grace and decency toward his host and lord."

"What if I said I didn't want to?" Helghi said through clenched teeth.

"Now, now, Master Helghi. Let's not be childish about this." Tigfi tightened his grip on the older man. "I don't want to have to explain to the earl why your bollocks are impaled on my fingernails. If you follow my advice then we won't tell, and the earl won't have to punish you for raping a servant girl. What's the punishment for rape these days, Esegar? Is it still castration?"

"I didn't rape her," protested Helghi, looking frustrated. "Didn't get the chance."

Tigfi grasped Helghi's balls and squeezed them painfully as if to emphasise what he was threatening.

"Ooow! All right!" Helghi gasped as excruciating pain struck him in the crotch. "Don't you think they've had enough for one night?"

"Good man. Good man. Then we won't have to tell the earl that you raped a servant girl?" Tigfi made sure that Helghi shook his head before continuing. "Good. We won't tell him as long as you conduct yourself in the manner of a courteous guest from now on. Now, run along, like a good little peasant!"

Tigfi wheeled Helghi around in the direction of the hall and watched him stagger back up the porch steps. Just as he entered through the doorway, a group of young men came out on their way to relieve themselves. They smiled suspiciously at Esegar and Tigfi as they passed, for the two of them were loitering, as if they had just been up to some mischief.

"What of the girl? Do you think she will tell?" Tigfi asked, when the others had passed out of earshot.

"I will speak with her."

Tigfi looked thoughtfully at a coin he had pulled from his pouch. "Maybe this will ensure that she keeps her silence."

"That, and your charm," Esegar smiled.

Tigfi grinned broadly. "They have been known to work for me before."

"She won't mind, but she's evidently choosey, that one."

"Apparently so, judging by her treatment of Helghi. Where do you think she was going?"

"Probably to check on the old lady in one of the bower huts over there," Esegar replied and pointed into the darkness.

"Wish me luck, my friend. Let's hope my bollocks get better treatment." Tigfi disappeared across the yard to a cluster of buildings.

"Rather you than me," Esegar called after him.

"Come, let us leave here," Freyda suggested, whispering in Edgar's ear as they sat together in the hall. The riddles had continued into the night long after most of the women and children had withdrawn and gone home to their beds. Only the younger unmarried females were still awake, some hoping to share their charms with Harold's huscarles for the night. It was quieter now, and more subdued with the drowsiness that a good supply of mead and ale brings. They were listening to Aelfstan recite the classic poem *Beowulf*, an ancient tale that had been handed down through generations, telling the story of a brave warrior who was sent to kill a beast that was plaguing a tribe in the old lands, over the seas. It took great skill to recite such an epic with eloquence and perfection, and although the storyteller's memory occasionally had cause for prompting, he was doing an acceptable rendition.

Few had seen Edgar leave the hall with Freyda, and those who did would most likely be too drunk to remember on the morrow. Of course, there were those who would not have approved. After all, a betrothal was not the same as a wedding. Still, they could leave unchallenged, and without any fuss. Once outside, they headed for the weaving shed. It was the safest place, Freyda suggested. The stables were out of the question, for there was a good chance that some others would bed down there for the night. Freyda unlocked the door of the shed, and lifted the latch. They slipped inside, and drew each other into an embrace.

"Now we can be alone," Freyda whispered. "No one should discover us in here."

"How can you be sure that we cannot be caught?" Edgar asked cautiously.

"Because I am in charge of the key, and Mother says that this room is always to be kept locked," she replied confidently.

"As usual, you have thought of everything," Edgar whispered as he nuzzled his nose up against hers.

"No candles," she giggled, remembering the last time he had said that to her. "Nothing can possibly go wrong this time."

"Except for a hailstorm and flood... or maybe lightning will strike us," replied Edgar drawing her close to him again. Just as he did so, there was a clap of thunder that made them jump.

"Shush, don't wish for misfortune. Be still," Freyda whispered. Her lips sought out his and they kissed.

She felt awkward, as if it were the first time their lips had ever met. The thrill of being alone together at last, permeated through them as they clung to each other.

"You are shaking," Freyda said, feeling him shuddering against her.

"'Tis what you do to me," he replied in between their kisses. "I can hardly believe that this is happening. Only two days ago, we had not a hope in heaven of being together." He pulled his head back then leaned his forehead against hers. "Now here we stand and you are promised to me."

"And we have the Earl's endorsement, so nothing can stand in our way. If anyone tries to stop us now, they will have to answer to him."

"Then I am always to be beholden to the Earl," Edgar said as he lowered his head to kiss her once again.

She moved her head aside. "Tell me that riddle again?" she teased.

"No," he whispered, and she felt him shake his head. In the inky darkness, she could just about see the outline of his face. He leaned forward to kiss her but she withdrew and groped for an oil lamp and flint. Then she lit it, leaving it on the safety of a shelf.

She turned back to him. "Please?" she entreated.

"Come here!" He fumbled for her and she avoided him playfully.

"Not until you promise to tell me the riddle again."

He sighed and gave in. "All right then. But you must come here."

She moved closer to him. Light shone dimly from the lamp, creating an intriguing shadow across his face. She shivered with excitement, and willingly allowed him to pull her toward him.

"A man came walking where he knew..." he began, and drew her closely. She felt his breath close to her ear as he continued, *"And came upon a maiden, reached beneath his skirt and drew, something stiff..."*

She gave a little gasp as one of his hands grasped her buttocks and pulled her lower half close to him so that their groins locked together. He kissed her passionately, his tongue searching eagerly for hers. With his other hand, she felt him gathering her skirts, and she breathed more heavily as he felt under her clothing and between her legs.

"Continue," she demanded. "Beneath her belt..." she urged.

She permitted him to pull her to her knees, and shaking, lay back compliantly on the floor. He lifted her skirts, and when she was ready, entered her gently.

"He worked his will, they both began to wiggle," he whispered and moved within her.

She bit her lip to stop herself from crying out, not knowing if it was pain or pleasure that she felt. He moved her with him, and she wondered what she should do, but after a while, she began to relax, and felt herself enjoying this new sensation. He worked faster and seemed to be reaching a crescendo, when he pulled himself out of her and started to finish himself with his hand.

She sat up and grabbed it from him and took over. *"...weary of the work and tired, his handy helper bidden..."*

Suddenly he gave an unintelligible shout, falling forward against her, and she felt him spill his seed over her. She laughed, and he rested on top of her saying breathlessly, *"Less strong now than she at last, there swelled inside her belly, the thing that men praise with their hearts..."*

"And pay for with their pennies." She joined him in the last verse and they collapsed laughing together.

She lay blissfully in his arms, wondering at the strange but pleasing turn of events. For Freyda, the initial virginal pain of their lovemaking had eventually turned to something akin to pleasure, but it was more the act itself that was so agreeable to her.

"I hope I did not hurt you, *lufestre?"* Edgar asked her when he had gotten his breath back.

She shook her head. "I liked it, though I hope your seed did not reach mine. If it should cause me to get with child..."

"No, I made sure that did not happen," he whispered, kissing her head reassuringly.

And so, the young lovers fell asleep, exhausted but content as they lay amongst the wool, looms, and other trappings of the weaver's shed, with hardly any thought to the consequences that might follow should they be caught. Their only concern was the strange but happy fortune that had brought them together.

Chapter Nine

Friends

Winflaed struggled as Wulfric wrapped one of her long braids around the fence post whilst Wulfwin was doing the same to her other. Her hands were tied tightly with rope, and the more she tried to move, the more it pulled on her hair, causing her to flinch with pain.

"Winflaed, daughter of Thegn Wulfhere, of Horstede, you have been found guilty of the casting of evil spells, to affect a boil to burst upon your brother's arse and causing him to experience great pain!"

Horrified, Winflaed looked on as Wulfwin displayed the afflicted area that had been the apparent cause of agony, whilst her other brother leapt about with great peals of laughter.

"I didn't do such a thing. I don't know any spells like that!" she protested.

"Are you denying that this boil on my arse has burst?" Wulfwin demanded, exposing his backside once more.

Winflaed cringed at the sight of her brother's spotty bottom cheeks. "It *is* a terrible sight, but —"

"Then you are guilty and will therefore suffer the penalty of death by hanging!"

"No, I didn't do it. I am not an evil spell-doer!" she cried defiantly. "Father, Father!"

Wulfwin put his knife against her throat. "Quiet! You dare to speak, witch? If you alert your demons to rescue you, it will only be worse for you. Wulfric, prepare some rope for a noose," he commanded as Winflaed whimpered.

Winflaed could hear her hound, Elf, as he barked in response to her distress. She knew the faithful beast would have come to her rescue, but the twins had thoughtfully tied him to a tree. The dog strained against the lead, whimpering and barking.

"Hmm, brother, the hound may have a point; hanging might be a bit excessive. What about that pile of rotting vegetables over there," Wulfric said, pointing over to a midden heap by one of the storage huts. "We can improve our throwing aim whilst covering her in decomposing vegetation at the same time."

"Good thinking, Wulfric. Stay here and guard her, I will fetch the stuff," Wulfwin said, thrusting his seax into his brother's hand, and picking up an empty bucket as he went.

"No!" protested Winflaed. "Let me go, I have done nothing wrong."

"Silence, witch! You must endure your punishment like the fiend you are," Wulfric yelled. She felt him put Wulfwin's knife to her throat. "Utter another word, and I will cut out your witchy voice."

They were in the middle of administering her punishment when Tovi, hearing her screams, rushed at them, roaring, with all the fury of an enraged bear. He hurled himself at them, and for a few moments, lay sprawled across their prone bodies. Before he could gather his wits, Wulfwin, uttering profanities, pushed him off and leapt upon him, pinning Tovi to the ground, forcing his face into the dirt.

Tovi, his nose and mouth filled with mud, was powerless to move or breathe. Certain that he was going to faint as his brother pushed him deeper into the dirt, he began to give up all hope of surviving when, a few moments later, he felt himself freed.

It was Ranulf who had come to his rescue. Taller and stronger than any of them, Ranulf grabbed Wulfwin by his scruff, and rescued his suffocating victim. Whilst Ranulf saw to Wulfwin, Tovi leapt at Wulfric who had been about to throw another handful of compost at Winflaed. But Wulfric quickly steadied himself, and Tovi felt his brother's fist smash into his face. Then Wulfric turned to charge at Ranulf who, thinking quickly, threw Wulfwin straight into his twin brother's path, headfirst, so that their skulls cracked together with a satisfying thud.

"Get your sister," Ranulf shouted, and holding a hand over his bloodied nose, Tovi leapt to his feet.

"Get me out of here," Winflaed, covered in muck, screamed as Tovi rushed to her aid. Once he had cut her free, they observed the scene with satisfaction as the twins lay in a heap on the ground, rubbing their bruised heads.

"Why, you dirty Norman scum!" Wulfwin yelled when some sense had returned. He leapt to his feet, a bulbous contusion sprouting viciously on his forehead.

Wulfwin rounded on Ranulf. On the ground, Wulfric was reaching out to grab one of his assailant's legs.

"Look out, Ranulf!" Tovi cried.

Ranulf switched his gaze to the ground and swiftly pulled his right leg out of Wulfric's reach. At the same time, his left arm slammed into Wulfwin's gut, severely winding him. Then he kicked a kneeling Wulfric in the side of his head, felling him with the blow. Both twins crumpled into balls, tears of anger smarting their eyes as they fought to get their breath back. Tovi and Winflaed clapped with delight.

"Help me," Ranulf called to them, and they rushed over to assist him to drag the twins by their legs, dazed and injured, to the fence. Using the rope that had tied Winflaed, they secured them by their arms to the posts.

Now it was time for *their* punishment. Revenge was sweet as Tovi and Winflaed took turns to pelt them. When their lust for retribution was sated, Ranulf went to release them.

"Now, you hell hounds. How do *you* like it?" Ranulf yelled at them in an intimidating manner.

Tovi laughed to see them covered in compost and pigs' dung.

"Unbind me, you Norman *swinescite*!" spat Wulfwin furiously.

"Aye, get us out of here!" Wulfric joined in.

As rage twisted his brothers' faces, Tovi imagined he was staring at two monsters, their tails thrashing angrily – slime dribbling from their gaping mouths as they squirmed in their captive bonds.

"Ha, your brothers stink like pigs, and yet they call me pig *scite*." Ranulf smiled.

Brother and sister laughed heartily. Tovi thought that Ranulf was a hero.

Then one of the trolls screamed, "Wait until my father hears of this!"

Ranulf's hand went over Wulfric's mouth to silence him, and Tovi saw him thrust a warning look at Wulfwin. "So, tell your father. I am sure he'd be interested in hearing our side of the story, too."

"Why should he believe you?" Wulfwin asked, narrowing his eyes.

"Because the Earl of Wessex is my kinsman. I think that leaves me on higher ground, don't you?" Ranulf replied. "I tell you what, if you don't say anything to anyone about this little... ehem, "misadventure, we won't either. Is that a deal?"

He took his hand from Wulfric's mouth and cocked his head questioningly. Wulfric nodded but Wulfwin scowled. "And what if I don't do deals?"

"It's entirely up to you, my friend, but I will tell you this; if you mistreat your brother and sister again, I will tell your father exactly what you do to them. Is that clear?"

Wulfwin nodded. His lip curled as a look of contempt swept across his filth-caked face. Ranulf cut them free with his knife and the victorious trio walked away, congratulating themselves on their success.

Tovi smiled eagerly. "Follow us," he cried, his heart filled with excitement. He was going to show Ranulf their special place in the forest and somehow it felt like a great honour.

"This is our special place," Tovi said as he, Ranulf and Winflaed sat on the cool greenery of the grassy bank. Hazy autumn sunshine visited the afternoon, replacing the cool morning air with a warmer ambience.

"It is truly enchanting," Ranulf murmured looking around him. "I can see why you come here."

Tovi felt a calm wind whisper past him and ripple the water. Across the other side of the pond, a heron gave an indignant squawk at their intrusion into its habitat as it waded in the shallow water's edge, looking for its supper. Winflaed went down to the water's edge and washed the dirt from her face.

"Do they always treat your sister like that?" Ranulf asked, as they watched her splashing her face generously. "Such a skinny little mite too... Someone should teach them a lesson."

"I think you have already." Tovi smiled. "But I get it worse than she," he added somewhat jealously.

"Then I shall see to it that, while I am here, they will not touch a hair on either of your heads," Ranulf said, boldly.

Tovi glanced at him enviously. If only he could be as tall and strong as Ranulf. Today, Ranulf had managed to achieve in minutes what he had been trying to achieve all his life: to defeat the dreaded *Sons of Loki.*

"Is that the swing that the Earl's daughter fell from?" Ranulf asked curiously.

"Aye, it is."

"He will always be grateful for what you did." Ranulf spoke sincerely. Tovi shrugged, unconvinced. "I speak the truth, Tovi my friend. The earl never forgets a kindness done to him or those he loves."

"Do you want to try it?" Tovi asked, looking up and inclining his head toward the swing.

Ranulf nodded. "Show me what you can do, my friend," he replied and Tovi grinned. Suddenly, his world seemed a much better place with Ranulf in it.

Tovi stood on the wharf and waved at the boy who stood abaft the vessel as it set sail for Normandy. He felt the comforting lightness of his father's hand on his shoulder, as they looked out across the grey murkiness of the estuary at the ship that was taking his friend off into the distance. He could see the vigorous waving of Ranulf's hand, but he was getting smaller and smaller as the repetitive movement of the oarsmen glided the vessel further out to sea. Tovi was determined to continue his farewell until all he could see of the ship was a tiny speck disappearing beyond the horizon. He was sad to see his friend leave, knowing that their paths were not likely to cross again. The few weeks that Ranulf had spent with them had been the happiest of his life. Now they were over, and the light of his world was dimming like the darker days of winter that were soon upon them.

As Tovi looked at the shrinking figure, one hand shielding his eyes from the dimming sun, he fondly, but sadly, recalled their time together. He would miss Ranulf's protection and his company and all the things he had done with them. He had taught Tovi and Winflaed to better their hunting skills, showing them the finer points of archery; engaged them in mock battles with their practice weapons, teaching them the techniques he had learned himself. Sometimes they would challenge the twins to a fight, and utilising Ranulf's strategies, the three of them would triumph, leaving Wulfric and Wulfwin to scamper off like beaten cats with their tails between their legs. Like Tovi, Winflaed had welcomed Ranulf's intercessions, and Tovi had felt sorry that she had not been allowed to be part of the party that had escorted him to Pevensey. Sullenly, his sister had bidden farewell at the homestead gates, presenting Ranulf with a coarse woollen drawstring pouch, and a pair of socks that she had sat up late into the evening to bind for him.

With Ranulf had gone the new horse that Harold had purchased for him and various gifts for his father. Tovi, having heard the story of the hostages in Normandy from Wulfhere, made a joke about swapping Harold's kinsmen for his twin brothers. This earned him a dark look from his father and a roar of laughter from Ranulf, which Tovi appreciated much more.

"Come then, son, we must get back home. I still have much to do before I need to go to court again," Wulfhere said, gently steering him in the direction of their tethered mount further up the shore.

"Will Ranulf ever come to Englalond again?" Tovi asked as they walked along the shingles.

"Who knows? If God wills it, then perhaps."

Wulfhere swung his leg over the saddle and pulled Tovi up with him. He took the reins in his hands, clipped his heels, and they cantered off. It was at least a day's ride back to Horstede, and he was anxious to return home. It had been more than four weeks since the betrothal, and that had been followed by the sad demise of the Lady Gerda. Barely had he the time to grieve when he was expected to organise and assist with the reconstruction of Helghi's hall. This he had done grudgingly, but once things were under way in Gorde, Wulfhere was content to leave Esegar in charge of the few men he had been able to spare for the task. There was still much to be done in the fields yet; the earth needed to be made ready for the sewing of next year's crops. Having to send some of his labourers to help Helghi meant double work for those left behind. Then there was the usual work of patching broken fencing and maintaining the bridges that forded the river; all was king's work that he must perform, not to mention that two of his colts would soon need to be saddle broken.

But it was not all work to look forward to, for soon it would be time for the twins to pledge their *áþswaru*, an oath-giving ceremony, an event that took place in the moot hall at Fletching, where all the boys of the hundred who had reached their twelfth summer, were to pledge their loyalty to their king and lord. He would stand amongst the other fathers as they looked upon their sons with pride as they received their first seax, the weapon that had once been eponymous for their ancestors of the Súþ Seaxa. Finally, when that was over, it would be *BlódMonath*, time for the fatted animals to be killed and hung in the rafters for their winter supplies.

Although he was a man of some nobility, there was still much to occupy a thegn during the coming winter days… And soon it would be time for him to attend court again in his capacity as a royal staller. If he was lucky, he might be home for the Yuletide celebrations that followed Christ's birthing day.

PartTwo

Harvest of Sorrow

Chapter Ten

Outlaw

March 1055

Edward's magnificent new palace at Westmynstre was a hive of industry as the royal household prepared for the twice-yearly meeting of the *Witanagemot*. The little Isle of Thornes was dominated by this huge palatial building situated only two miles downriver, away from the unpleasant, often malodorous stench of Lundenburh. Wulfhere was on duty, assisting with the smooth running of the king's household. As he hurried through the narrow walkways that linked the buildings, servants scuttled in and out of chambers, nearly colliding with him in their haste to carry out their tasks. One such was his old friend, Leofnoth, of Stochingham, a grizzled, toothless, tough old veteran who had first befriended Wulfhere's father, and had known Wulfhere since he was a boy.

"So, the palace is finally finished here," Leofnoth remarked after he and Wulfhere had made their greetings. "What do you think? Personally, I'm not too sure about all this cold and unwelcoming stone."

Wulfhere thought the new building quite superb with its white plastered walls, high beamed ceilings, fine furnishings, and Spanish carpets; but he was inclined to agree with Leofnoth. He, like his friend, was much more at home in his timber-framed longhall. Here a man felt swamped rather than cocooned.

"It seems Edward loathes our wood-framed halls in Englalond, ever since his return from Normandy. He constantly complains about our smoky, 'primitive' draughty homes, and his yearning for the comforts of Normandy has prompted these new developments," Wulfhere advised as they dodged through the stream of dashing servants, their arms full of fresh linen, and other preparatory materials for the important members of the *Witan*.

Leofnoth shrugged lightly. "My heart bleeds for our gracious lord," he mocked. "Where are you going now? I shall be on duty down at the wharf shortly, toadying to all the loathsome, sycophantic bastards as they arrive."

"Myself too, but first I am to check the work down at the building site. Accompany me?"

Leofnoth nodded, and they passed from the palace to where work was progressing on the new church. The king was there, escorting some of his newly arrived guests around the embryonic church as workmen toiled around them. Wulfhere drew his cloak around him as a cold wind bit. He gazed across the newly dug foundations and wondered at the immensity of the project, dedicated to St Peter. He watched as an animated Edward and his party walked around the building site. The king was pointing, showing his companions what was going to go where, his excitement plain for all to see.

"This church is going to be far grander than its predecessor," Wulfhere remarked.

"What was wrong with the last one?" Leofnoth said gruffly, plainly not amused at the expense of the undertaking.

"It is going to be his lordship's most ambitious project yet, I am informed," Wulfhere said. "One that will make this a vision of breathtaking magnificence, the like of which Christendom has yet to see. Not only will it guarantee Edward instant entry into the Kingdom of Heaven, but it will also be an impressive attraction for visiting papal envoys."

"Aye," Leofnoth nodded. "Edward's steadfast belief in his own saintliness will enhance his piety before all men. Our devout king, my dear friend, is more interested in ensuring himself a place in heaven than carrying out his kingly duties, those for which he was anointed." His tone was edged with disgruntlement.

"And hunting, Leofnoth, don't forget the hunting," Wulfhere said with a smirk.

Both men clammed up when a well-dressed thegn, Asketil, and his young son, walked by. At court, there were many who would report such criticism to the king. There were few men that Wulfhere trusted. Even Asketil, though he be a distant kinsman of Ealdgytha's, he could not be sure. The man recognised him and nodded a greeting.

"*Waes hael*, Wulfhere," Asketil said with the accent of those northerners whose ancestors had settled in the Danelaw around two centuries ago. He was aging, though still very hardy and sprightly. Wulfhere reckoned he must be approaching sixty. He had long white hair and a ruddy, weathered complexion. His son, Hereward, the boy who bounced playfully at his side, was his youngest by a second wife.

Wulfhere watched the boy swinging a stick around as if he were a warrior in action. Once upon a time, though, young Hereward had not been as full of life as he was now.

"*Waes thu hael*, Lord Asketil," replied Wulfhere. "The boy grows well."

The men watched as Hereward ran along the edge of the ditch, turned a cartwheel, and promptly fell into the foundations on top of the builders. There was a cry of annoyance from the workers and Asketil pretended not to notice. "He thrives. We thank God every day that he survived the sicknesses of his infancy."

"And your other son?" Wulfhere asked, resisting the desire to laugh as the boy was tossed out of the ditch by angry workmen.

"Thorbrand is well. He was eager to join the other youths in the hall."

"Aye, the youngsters enjoy the company of their own." Wulfhere smiled.

They looked across the foundations as a sudden burst of exuberant laughter and voices came from the royal party. Wulfhere saw that they were throwing back their heads with amusement, probably at one of King Edward's inane jests.

"For Edward, the joy of kingship does not come with battles or warfare, but the Church and all things holy," Asketil said, and smiled cynically. "Good day to you, Wulfhere, Leofnoth. I'd better rescue my son before he makes a nuisance of himself with the king. He can be a handful at times, but I would rather have him so than dead."

Wulfhere nodded and chuckled as Asketil moved on. "That boy has already made a nuisance of himself by the look of it."

"Asketil is right," said a man who had just joined them.

"Greetings, Cana," Wulfhere said, and he and Leofnoth clasped hands with their new companion. He was an older thegn like Leofnoth, perhaps a few years his junior.

"Edward sees himself as a divine ruler rather than a warrior king," continued their friend. "The kingship is something he endures for the sake of God and His holy approval… or, more sinisterly, his revenge against those who tried to deny him his inheritance. Even his own mother did not evade his retribution, despite her attempts to be conciliatory. With Edward's hostile attitude towards her, Emma had no choice but to give up and die. There was nothing else in this world for the old lady anymore."

"Such a shame that a noble queen, such as she, should come to such an ignominious end." Wulfhere sighed. "All her ambitions went with the death of her youngest and most precious son, Harthacnut."

"'Tis sad to say, but perhaps she should have afforded her first born with a little more respect and a little less neglect, and then perhaps Edward would have not mistreated her so," said Cana.

"Pah, she was an arrogant old crone anyway," replied Leofnoth. "She deserved what she got. You cannot blame Edward for removing her wealth and lands. Besides, she did all right in the end. It was not as if she lived in squalor."

"But think about it, Leofnoth. The poor woman lives through two royal marriages, gives birth to three sons and the two only sons worth their salt, die, leaving her with the one son she despised the most," Cana said. "What bad luck, eh?"

"Poor woman, indeed." Leofnoth was scornful. "Mind you, Harthacnut was not the king his father was. Edward could not have wished for better luck when his little brother came to an untimely...strange end. How fortuitous could that have been?"

"Aye, Edward should be grateful," Wulfhere added. "Not only did he gain a crown that looked as if it would never be his, but his mother was finally at his mercy, to do with as he wished. He never forgave her for all the years of abandonment. I am sure it pleased him well enough to make the last years of her life a misery."

"Strange? You said Harthacnut's manner of death was strange," Cana remarked curiously to Leofnoth.

Leofnoth grinned and looked about him furtively. "I often wonder how it came that one so young keeled over and died, just like that. Some say he was sickly, but I had never seen so much as a glimmer of illness."

"You mean he was poisoned?" Wulfhere whispered hoarsely.

"Preposterous!" Cana snapped. "He was always a drunken sot!"

Leofnoth grinned and shrugged his shoulders. "Maybe it was just a rumour after all. But, if you ask me, you cannot rule out the possibility."

Wulfhere looked thoughtful. "With Harthacnut out of the way, Emma would be powerless." He knew exactly what Edward had thought of his mother which was why he did not believe the pious, virtuous charade that Edward often played. In Wulfhere's view, Emma had been a remarkable woman. Her ingenuity in forging an alliance with Cnut had brought stability to the kingdom at a time when it was anything but secure. Of course, this was not exactly an act of selfless sacrifice; after all, by agreeing to marry the Danish conqueror, she was assured of all her wealth. Nonetheless, she was a politically astute woman, even in Aethelred's time. You either loved or hated her, and it was true that while there were plenty who despised her, there were also many who loved and admired her.

"The list of suspects could be endless," Leofnoth said, still grinning like a fool.

Wulfhere drove a friendly fist into his friend's shoulder. "You jest too much, friend!" he laughed. "But we must be quiet; this is a place of intrigue. There is always someone ready to pounce and shout treason if they thought it would curry favour with the king."

None would argue with *that* statement.

Wulfhere stood with Leofnoth at the water's edge, their faces turned outwards across the river as the waves gently splashed against the shingle, before the tide drew it out again. Behind them loomed the palace, splendid in the light morning mist that enshrouded the bramble-covered islet. Arriving in their droves, brought there by boat or ferry, or on horse across the ford, were men and women of the highest rank, come from all over the realm to discuss nominations for the new earl of Northymbralond.

The death of Siward the Strong had left a vacancy in the North. The old Dane had been a follower of King Cnut, and had held the earldom since Cnut had succeeded to the throne. Although Siward had not always been popular with the wild men of Northymbralond, he had gained their respect throughout his reign and the hard, but fair, line he took with them. Siward had never recovered from the loss of his eldest son, Osbeorn, who had perished at the terrible battle of Dunsinane. Some said that grief had spurred the aging warrior to his grave.

By his second wife he'd left a young son, Waltheof, but the boy was a mere child of six and could not be considered for an earldom. In the North, with the constant bloodfeuds that existed between the various clans, Siward had wielded a mighty sword. He had managed his people in his own style, curbing their murderous habits and violent ways with strong justice. It would be hard to follow such a man, and whoever the king appointed as Siward's successor would need to possess many essential qualities: he would have to be a warrior and diplomat, a fair administrator of justice, and above all, he would have to be fearless in the face of wild, brutal men. Only a leader who possessed these attributes would command their fealty and respect.

Wulfhere and his companions watched expectantly as the Godwinsons rode across the ford from the marshes of Lambeth, via the road that led from the earl's manor of Suthrigaweorc. This was an estate on the south bank of the Thames that had passed to Harold when his father died. Now, with his father and older brother in their graves, Harold was head of the family, and rode with his three brothers and mother in the fore of his retinue. Together, they presented an impressive image of a noble family. Wulfhere headed the welcoming party, and saluted Harold and his brothers as they reined in before him.

"Wulfhere, we meet again. I trust you have recovered from your daughter's betrothal party," Harold mused. An infuriating grin spread across the earl's face. "You look tired, man. Is it safe to assume that my brother-in-law, the king, has you running about for him like hounds after stoats?"

Wulfhere smiled broadly. Harold's humour could be exasperating at times but also charming. "Aye, lord, as usual," he replied, though the response was not entirely truthful. If he had been of a mind to answer the earl candidly, he would have replied that it was not the king, but the queen who was the cause of their weariness. But since the queen was the earl's sister, he thought it wiser not to. She had been fussing about everything from the décor of the palace to the evening menu. She was constantly changing and unchanging her mind, driving all in her vicinity to despair. When she was in full flow, she reminded Wulfhere much of Ealdgytha, and he found himself smiling inwardly, thinking that his wife would have revelled in the comparison.

"Wulfhere, you know my brothers Tostig, Gyrth and Leofwin?"

Harold's younger brothers nodded to him. He had seen them often in their youth, but now they were full grown, well into manhood. Wulfhere noted that they, like Harold, possessed the same ultra-good looks of the Godwin clan. Harold, in his thirty-third year, was some three years senior to Tostig and the pair were the most alike of the brothers. They were often compared to famous Greek heroes. Their tall, sinewy, muscular frames, displayed their strength and energy, cutting fine figures in their expensive attire. Gyrth, twenty-seven, was darker than the rest, but his blue eyes still twinkled with the same Godwin humour that he and Harold had inherited from their father.

Leofwin, at twenty-three, was the younger of the brothers; blonde and with boyish good looks. He was still trying to stamp his mark in the world, and was sometimes overshadowed by his more formidable brothers. All the siblings were pleasant-natured and good-humoured, except for Tostig. He was not so quick to smile or laugh as his brothers did, and was severe in his nature. Although he acknowledged Wulfhere politely, there was an unmistakeable hollowness to Tostig's greeting, as if he were only paying lip service to common decency. Beneath his mask of magnanimity was a layer of contempt, easily seen if one chose to look closely enough.

"And of course, you know my good lady mother," Harold said, presenting the Lady Gytha of Wessex. She came, mounted on an ambling grey palfrey, aging, but still alert; clad protectively against the chill of the spring air in a thick woollen cloak, hood, and mantle. Wulfhere bowed and kissed the thin scrawny hand she offered him.

"Of course. Wulfhere knows me very well, is that not so, my lord Wulfhere? I have known him from a young boy, and his father before him. Though it has been many years since we last met, I remember you well, sir," the Lady Gytha replied. Her graciousness greatly impressed Wulfhere. A woman such as the old Earl of Wessex' wife would come across many a thegn's sons in her lifetime. He was pleased that she had remembered him.

Wulfhere replied with a courteous nod and recalled that the last time he had seen her was when her husband died two years before. She seemed to have aged much since that unhappy time. The stress of exile and her husband's untimely death had taken its toll on her, and the strain was showing in her wizening features. She was approaching her fifty-third year, and her once handsome looks had begun to diminish. She was too thin for comfort and some of her front teeth had gone, but she still held herself upright, and with dignity. She was, after all, of royal Scandinavian blood, a granddaughter of Harold Bluetooth, the former King of Norweg.

"Reckon the Godwinsons have surly brother Tostig in mind for Northymbralond," Leofnoth remarked, joining Wulfhere after helping another family of nobles to alight from a boat nearby.

"What makes you say that?" Wulfhere asked carefully. Leofnoth of Stochingham was one of the few men he associated with at court that he could trust, but it was too easy for a remark made innocently to be misconstrued if overheard. He knew that the Godwinsons were an ambitious family, and this often made them unpopular. At the moment, Harold was the only brother with any real power, but with three other determined brothers waiting in the wings, the other great ruling families were bound to be a little jittery.

Leofnoth made his thinking face: a frown and then a lift of his eyebrow, followed by a stroking of his greying beard. "How often does the old Countess come to court these days?" he asked gruffly. "She wouldn't come unless the journey was worth her while."

"I have heard that Alfgar of East Anglia is the *Witan's* favourite for the appointment," Wulfhere stated. "The King will have the ultimate word on the matter, no doubt."

"Aye, but 'tis common knowledge that Edward has no liking for Alfgar," Leofnoth said knowingly. "But he does have for Tostig."

"No one has a liking for Alfgar, except maybe his wife, but then she is dead," joked Wulfhere.

Alfgar was the son of the sagacious old Earl of Mercia, Leofric. Like Siward, Leofric was greatly respected; a noble ealdorman of old Mercian blood, who, at the time of Cnut, had managed to win favour, and keep his place in the new administration; much like Harold's father, Godwin had. Leofric's son, Alfgar, on the other hand, was not so popular. A hot-headed, tyrannical personality made him an unpleasant choice of lord, but he was an experienced man, and had been posted to Harold's earldom of East Anglia during Harold's exile. When Harold had been reinstated, Alfgar had been compelled to relinquish the earldom back to him. This he had done through gritted teeth, but his father had managed to assert some influence over him, and that kept his infamous temper at bay. Eventually he got East Anglia back, when Harold was given Wessex upon Godwin's death. Ungraciously and without humility, Alfgar received the earldom like a spoilt child, who'd finally had his toy returned.

Leofnoth grinned as the next party of men came closer, for it happened to be Lords Leofric and Alfgar themselves, and Alfgar's son, Burghred. Accompanying them was a large retinue of Mercians.

"Speak of the devil," Leofnoth said through the false smile he used for those guests he did not like. "Looks like we are in for an interesting *Witanagemot*," he whispered, his smile still fixed. "I feel there may be a little contention in the air. I'll leave the lords of Mercia to you, Wulfhere. Your patience is better than mine." He winked and sauntered off to find something else to do.

Wulfhere remained more ambivalent than his companion, but had to admit that Leofnoth was most likely right, when Alfgar presented himself as cocksure and full of arrogance, greeting him with deriding sarcasm as he looked down at him from his mount. For a moment, he wondered which candidate was preferable: Tostig Godwinson with his cold, superior glare, or Alfgar, full of pride and baleful mockery.

"You men," the wild, bearded earl of East Anglia demanded, "guide us to our quarters and provide us with refreshments immediately. I want our horses stabled and tended to now, and don't waste time; we have come a long way." All the men had dressed practically for journeying in wet weather; however, the quality of their attire was what you would expect from men of high status. Despite his fine clothing, Alfgar had the look of a barbarian about him; dark, unruly hair framing a rugged face stained red by the East Anglian wind, and marred by a prominent scar, running diagonally across his right cheek to the bridge of his nose.

"Of course, my lords, it shall be done," Wulfhere replied, swallowing his annoyance.

He looked around for a couple of *ceorls,* but it appeared that they were already busy with other guests, and so he signalled to a couple of younger thegns, deep in conversation with one another, leaning nonchalantly against a fence, and watching the guests arrive. He recognised one of them as Leofnoth's son, Aemund.

"What are you waiting for? Move yourselves! You dare to be idle when you are in the presence of great earls! Know you who I am?" Alfgar drew his horse nearer to the two youngsters, his father, Leofric, looking on sternly.

One of the lads drew himself to attention, but the other, Aemund, carried on slouching without a care. They were youths in the full flush of adolescence, brought to court for the first time by their fathers.

"Y-yes, s-sir, Lord Alfgar," stuttered the taller lad of the two. Clearly, he knew who this intimidating man was scowling down at him.

"And you, boy?" Alfgar grunted at the other.

"Alfgar," sighed the old Earl Leofric. "Leave the boys alone." He looked tired and sat heavily in his saddle.

Alfgar ignored his father. "Well?" he demanded, shifting his horse round to the other lad. Aemund, however, remained unabashed by the earl's attempt to intimidate him. "You know who I am?" Alfgar leaned forward in his saddle at the lad, a look of indignation upon his face.

"No, my lord, I would be grateful if you could enlighten me," replied Aemund. He had folded his arms defensively and was chewing a piece of bark. His face wore an expression of insolence, and a hint of sarcasm was curling his lips.

Wulfhere cringed at the boy's temerity, and looked around for Leofnoth to come and rescue his son, but he was not anywhere to be seen. Instead, he made an attempt to catch the boy's attention so he could warn him. Alfgar was not a man to rile. *Aemund, you fool,* he thought to himself, and wondered if he should intervene.

"Such impudence will earn you a tanning, lad. Stand straight when you're addressing the new Earl of Northymbralond!"

"Alfgar!" Earl Leofric rode in closer. "Leave it. They are but lads with a lot to learn. We have better things to do right now than tarry here."

"My lords, let me come to your assistance. Excuse the lad; he is new to court and has not yet learned how to conduct himself properly. I will see to it that he does better in future." To Wulfhere's relief, Leofnoth put in a timely appearance.

Lord Leofric thanked him. Alfgar grunted, "See that you do, fellow, otherwise it will fall to me to teach him some manners."

Wulfhere watched them go with Leofnoth leading them, knowing that, underneath the polite, friendly facade, Leofnoth was most likely seething, not just with Alfgar, but with Aemund too.

"You'd better mind your tongue, lad, if you want to survive at court. You are not at home amongst country *ceorls* and cottars here. These men are your betters, and some here would as soon cut out your eyes as look at you. Your father will not always be around to save your hide."

Aemund's face was flushed and he appeared a little discomfited. "The man was insufferable. How was I to know who he was?" he replied. He was looking defiantly at Wulfhere.

Wulfhere shook his head again. "Get out of my sight and go and find something to do. Make yourselves useful, and stay out of trouble."

As he watched them hurry away Wulfhere felt a rush of excited anticipation. There was a storm of trouble brewing, and it was already rumbling.

Refreshments were being served in the main hall, whilst minstrels played, and jugglers and acrobats amused the crowd. Wulfhere and his fellow officials, mostly men of the Súþ Seaxa, sat along the mead benches in the great hall enjoying the food and entertainment their king provided them with. Wulfhere was relaying to his companions the tale of Freyda's enforced betrothal, as they helped themselves to a luncheon of bread, cheese, eggs, cold meats, and smoked eels, washed down by ale.

"What a shame to waste such a beauty on a cripple!" Osward, the young thegn of Ratton declared. The beauty of Wulfhere's eldest daughter was well known throughout Súþ Seaxa.

"Aye," nodded Leofnoth. "A great shame. My boy, Aemund here, has had his eye on her for some time. We were going to make a proposal."

Seated beside his father, young Aemund's face reddened.

"Why the hell didn't you ask?" Wulfhere exclaimed. "You have known me for years, Leofnoth. He would have made an excellent match," he grumbled, gesticulating with his open palm at the boy. "Now it is too late and I am honour bound."

"I was going to say something," Leofnoth said regretfully. "Why the hell didn't you say anything?"

"Wulfhere, you should have kept her better controlled. That is what you should have done," Asgar told him critically. Asgar was another of his wife's relatives; the son of her Uncle Athelstan and, like Ealdgytha, a grandchild of Tovi the Proud.

Wulfhere felt irritated at Asgar's disparaging remark about his parenting, but ignored the urge to bestow him with an angry glare, mainly because he knew deep down that perhaps Asgar was right. He *had* been too indulgent of his eldest daughter, and allowed her too much freedom. But he was often away from home, so it was really the fault of Ealdgytha for not overseeing her more closely. Why should he take all the blame when her mother was in a better position to control her behaviour?

"Well, *I* married for love and that suits me," stated Wulfward, one of the other younger thegns. "Nothing wrong with that."

"Who marries for love?" put in Aelmer, an older thegn. "Love doesn't buy land or gold."

"Nor prestige or honours," added Cana.

"I'd rather have a pretty girl and no dowry than a rich dowry and an ugly wart-ridden wench for a wife," replied Wulfward, "even though I got both the pretty wife and rich dowry."

"My wife had plenty of money but, God's bones, was she ugly!" Leofnoth guffawed loudly and infectiously. Soon the air was filled with their laughter.

Slightly irritated that they were laughing at his expense, Wulfhere looked about for the Earl of Wessex and his brothers amongst the men that crowded the trestles, but they were nowhere to be seen. Most likely, they were having their midday meal in their private apartments, or with their sister the queen and her royal husband. His gaze caught the king's nephew, the Norman born Ralph de Mantes, Earl of Hereford. He and his men were filtering into the hall and finding places amongst the already crowded trestles. De Mantes wore his black hair closely cropped like his Norman companions, its dark strands already beginning to pepper with white, despite only being in his twenty-sixth year. A finely trimmed moustache lined his top lip on his narrow, pointed face. As he observed him, Wulfhere was struck by how much he was beginning to resemble his uncle, the king. He was slender and slight, as was the king, and not at all like his Englisc counterparts who tended to be tall and brawny. Beside him was his good friend, William Malet. Like Ralph, he too, shared both Norman and Englisc blood. His mother was Lord Alfgar's sister, and his father a Norman baron. The two men had come to join Edward in his early days as king, and had remained in his service since. The king was very fond of them, especially his nephew Ralph.

Just then there was the sound of a hostile voice, shouting above the mirth. "Move aside, you men. You've had your fill so now you can go about your business and let us have your places. I am sure you have plenty to do other than to sit around, babbling about nothing and wasting the king's valuable time."

Wulfhere and his companions turned and saw that the offensive interruption had come from one of Lord Alfgar's thegns. Alfgar himself was standing by their table with his arms folded, with a look of menace in his glowering eyes. Beside him was his twenty-year-old son, Burghred, darkly handsome as Alfgar perhaps once was. With them were the intimidating men of his household retinue. Alfgar seemed to attract these types of men into his service; men who possessed hearts of stone and took pleasure in causing fear in others.

Wulfhere and the others began to shift, for they had no desire to get into a brawl with the earl and his men – except for Leofnoth. Wulfhere was aghast, for Leofnoth remained in his seat, eating, and drinking as if nothing had been said.

"Move, you ignorant dogs! My lord needs your place!" The man speaking had pushed his way forward. He was Ragnald, captain of Alfgar's bodyguard. He was a tough looking man, his face scarred with pock marks, which lent more to his thuggish appearance.

Leofnoth did not even flinch. Ignoring Ragnald's orders, he casually helped himself to more bread.

Wulfhere and the others moved quickly away from the table and held their breath as Leofnoth, still chewing, released a noisy fart, and took another swig from his ale horn.

Suddenly Alfgar intervened. "Do you not understand the command, simpleton?" the earl bellowed at Leofnoth, clearly frustrated. "My man told you to move. This table is ours now."

The younger thegns, scuttled away. Alfgar's temper was well known as was his reputation as a fearsome fighter. Osward and Wulfward obviously had no wish to stay in close proximity when Alfgar was in a rage. The elders of the group remained nearby, collectively worried about their friend.

Still Leofnoth did not move, nor did he so much as glance at Alfgar. He continued to sit and asked his friends, "Are you going? Wulfhere, Aelmer, you haven't finished your ale. Cana, sit down and finish your cheese. Aemund, you look as if you've shit yourself, get to the latrine, at once!"

"You son of a bitch, are you deaf? You have been ordered to move!" Alfgar shouted so loudly that the entire hall descended into silence. Heads began turning in their direction.

"He *is* deaf, my lord," Aelmer advised, a conciliatory tone to his voice. "Took a bash in the ear fighting the Scots and hasn't been the same since."

"Then I shall shout louder," Alfgar growled. "Move!"

Wulfhere's heart began to beat fast. Here was the storm that he'd felt brewing earlier. Leofnoth was not going to move, and the old thegn's obstinate grin was the spark that ignited Alfgar's smouldering temper. The earl leaned across the table and attempted to pull the old thegn out of his seat, but Leofnoth took him by surprise, nimbly leapt to his feet, tipped the table up off its trestle, and smiled devilishly, watching as it smashed into Alfgar and his men with a resounding crash. The contents of the table scattered across the floor as Leofnoth squared himself balefully.

"The table is yours now, my lord," he said, grinning.

Alfgar's face was contorted in rage. He threw a punch at Leofnoth, but the upturned table and trestle hindered his reach. There was a scuffle as Wulfhere and his friends pulled Leofnoth away. Alfgar threw aside the table, but as he lurched forward aiming for Leofnoth, he tripped over the trestle that had supported the table.

Suddenly a voice called from the other side of the hall. Heads turned to look at the king's nephew, who, like many others had risen from his bench for a better view. "Lord Alfgar, how dare you behave in such a deplorable manner in the king's peace? Those men are the king's thegns and by dishonouring them, you dishonour him."

Alfgar extricated his tangled feet from the trestle and flung it away from him as he regained his balance. He was sweating and puffing like a charging bull that had run into a fence.

"Tis not *I* whose manners are deplorable; it is this ill-bred cur that is at fault!" Alfgar cried, pointing at Leofnoth.

"I do not take orders from an offensive braggart, earl or no! Besides, you might have asked with some respect," Leofnoth retorted loudly. "We are, as Lord Ralph courteously stated, the king's thegns!"

"So, you are not so deaf now, sir? Do you know who I am?" Alfgar demanded. "I am Lord Alfgar, Earl of East Anglia, soon to be Earl of Northymbralond. You should defer to men of much higher status."

"We all know who you are, Lord Alfgar, and what you are," Ralph interjected. His well-clipped French-accented Englisc was animated, like that of a *scop*. "A fatuous braggart, as disgusting as a pig's entrails, and you bring shame on the title of earl."

There was a vast difference in the two men's character. Ralph was, like his uncle the king, a refined, educated man, with impeccable speech. No doubt Ralph found Alfgar and his men uncouth.

"You dare to speak to me thus? You bloody Norman weasel! How dare you question my status? I have the blood of true Englisc men flowing through my veins; the blood of warriors and kings." Alfgar was crimson with fury. His nostrils dilated and his temples bulged in the red background of his face. He turned to William Malet, "And what of you, my dear Norman nephew?" he demanded, sarcasm oozing from his lips. "Are you of the same opinion as this lickspittle? Do you also think I am unworthy of my earldom?"

William frowned in disapproval. "I am sorry, Uncle, but I am of the same opinion as Lord Ralph. Your behaviour is disgraceful. Those men were doing no harm and just wanted to finish their food in peace. They did not deserve to be mistreated."

"Ah, of course you would say that. Not only do you two share your opinions but most likely you share each other's arses! Which one of you wears the wimple then?" He looked about him for approval, but only his men laughed with him.

Moments later, Alfgar was still laughing, even though the room had hushed as Alfgar's father, the Earl of Mercia, stood in the doorway flanked by his guards. Wulfhere held his breath as he waited for Alfgar to notice.

"Alfgar, cease this diabolical rant instantly!" Leofric bellowed.

Unlike Alfgar, Wulfhere knew that the old earl knew how to behave at court. The shame of Leofric had been witnessed by all at some point, as time after time he was forced to reprimand his son for his rude and unruly behaviour. It was not an unusual occurrence for men to want to fight at court, but to do so was frowned upon, and could be deemed as treasonable. Edward had no liking for troublemakers, especially those who mistreated the men in his service. He would not be impressed to learn of Alfgar's performance today, Wulfhere thought to himself.

Seeing Alfgar now, Wulfhere was brought to mind of a wayward child who, having been found committing some act of disobedience, was suddenly filled with dread. He suspected that the bad-tempered earl was now mentally re-evaluating his chances of getting his prize, Northymbralond, and they were about as likely as the king fathering a child on the queen within the next year. It seemed that Alfgar had just supplied the arrows with which Ralph was able to shoot him, and his aim was perfect.

"Father, I can explain," Alfgar said. "These men were being disrespectful, Father."

"I understand all right, Alfgar. You were gravely insulting the king's nephew, your own sister's son," Leofric replied, dismissing Alfgar's excuses.

Alfgar rounded on Leofric and kicked a discarded drinking cup so it shot across the floor and it came to rest at the feet of his father.

"Will you always go against me, Father?" Alfgar demanded, blazing with anger.

Leofric looked down at the cup with disgust. "Enough is enough, Alfgar!" He turned his back on his son and headed for the doors.

"That's right, mighty Earl Leofric of Mercia, turn your back on your son as you always do. I was never good enough for you, was I?" Alfgar yelled after him.

Leofric reached the doorway and turned to look back at Alfgar in response to his invective. He glared at his son; a look that was a cross between repugnance and sadness.

"I would fight for you, Alfgar, but you do not make it easy for me. I have tried to do my duty by you a thousand times over, but you… Christ's Wounds, you are forever shaming me!" Leofric replied. His voice trembled with emotion as the rest of the hall kept silent.

"Just as you fought for me to keep East Anglia when those damned-in-hell Godwinsons returned?" Alfgar retorted. "Just hand the earldom back like a good boy, you said. We will find you something else to play with. Just keep the peace, you said. Is that what you call fighting my corner?"

Leofric looked to be dumbstruck; beaten. "East Anglia is yours now, is it not?" he said, frustration pouring from him like sweat.

It must have broken the old Earl's heart to have his dirty linen so publicly displayed, Wulfhere thought.

"And the earldom? Will you help me get Northymbralond?" Alfgar demanded.

"God help Northymbralond if I do," replied Leofric in exasperation, and with that, he turned and strode off with as much dignity as he could muster.

The heavy wooden doors of the hall banged loudly behind the earl as he and his retainers left, and the hall fell into an awkward silence. Wulfhere could see the looks of triumph on the faces of those in the Norman camp. He knew that Alfgar had noticed them, too, for he was trembling.

The Earl of East Anglia's eyes raked the hall. "What are you all looking at?" he bellowed.

"My Lord Tostig will make a fine Earl of Northymbralond, do you not think so, Malet?" de Mantes was asking provocatively.

"I hear that he is Edward's favourite these days," Malet agreed, sneering at his uncle like he was something nasty on the bottom of his shoe.

Alfgar's son, Burghred, put a steadying hand on his father's arm. "Father, let us dine in our lodgings. The company is not favourable here," he said, a voice of reason amongst Alfgar's goading men.

Alfgar shook his son's hand from his arm, spread his feet and crossed his arms as if to stand his ground. He glared at de Mantes and Malet. Wulfhere did, too, wondering if they had contrived the situation. If they had, Alfgar had played into their hands with such ease that even they could not have wished for a better outcome. Well, if he was going to sink down further into the mire, he might as well do it with finesse.

"I think I know my uncle well," de Mantes continued, speaking as if Alfgar were not there at all. "And I know that Tostig Godwinson is a man much to his liking."

"Enough to make him an earl?" Malet asked, a sardonic smile upon his lips.

"Some say that the choice has already been made and it is just a matter for the king's announcement."

"Come, Father," urged Burghred again. "They only seek to provoke you. You are playing into their hands." But Alfgar seemed not to hear him; only his own fury.

De Mantes gave Alfgar a derisive smile as if inviting him to retaliate, like a mischievous child aggravating a playmate.

Alfgar was like a snarling wolf backed into a corner.

"The king is too fond of that avaricious Godwin family," he said with a wave of his arm, and launched into a diatribe, "They are nothing but traitors and thieving curs. When they came with an army against the king there were few who spoke against them, but one of them was me. Even my father gave into Godwin and advised the king to make peace with him…" Wulfhere thought that he was trying to contain himself so as not to use language he would later regret, but suddenly, the words burst forth from Alfgar's mouth, unchecked, "'Tis no surprise that men wonder which one of the Godwins is first in the king's bed at night, Tostig, Harold, or the queen!"

The shock of his outburst caused a murmuring of dissent amongst the crowds. There were cries of, 'shame on you', and, 'treason'. Ralph's huscarles stood around their lord in anticipation and many others were beginning to rise to their feet. There was an air of expectancy and everyone felt a need to be on their guard. Alfgar's own men stood loyally beside him too, their fortunes tied to his. At that moment, they were with him, and the tension in the hall was such that only the sharpest of knives could have cut it.

Wulfhere's stomach tightened and his heart began to pound. Like a sniffing, hunting dog, he could smell the danger in the air. Every man knew it would be breaking the king's peace should there be a fight, but all were steeling themselves just in case, disregarding any thoughts of what the consequences might be. This was what Wulfhere poetically called the *niðdraca*, the hostile malicious creature that hovers unseen, just before a battle. It fills the atmosphere with hatred and inserts the desire to fight in the hearts of men; this was *andbīdian*, the waiting.

Wulfhere eyed Alfgar. He could see the man was annoyed with himself for allowing his tongue to run away with him. He would be too proud to back down now. It would do no good anyway since the damage was done. Once Edward heard what he had said, there would be no pardon and Wulfhere was sure that Alfgar was not going to grovel. Humility was not one of his traits.

"Is there no one here who would stand with me against the Godwins for Northymbralond?" Alfgar demanded in a last attempt to gain support and save his skin. His gaze moved around the hall. Still Wulfhere's *niðdraca* hovered and blew smoking tendrils of fear and contempt into the atmosphere.

"Looks much like a vote of no confidence to me, my Lord Alfgar." Ralph's voice was the only one heard.

Alfgar's eyes bulged. He was isolated now; even his father had deserted him. "Then by Satan's blistered bollocks I hope you all rot in hell! And fuck all of you!" he yelled, as he turned on his heel and pushed his way through the crowds with his followers in tow.

The doors of the hall crashed open as he shouldered his way through, knocking the door thegns off their feet as they failed to avoid the impact.

"I say good riddance to bad rubbish, would you not agree, Will?" Ralph exclaimed in mock outrage.

"Agreed, my Lord Ralph. At least there is no longer a bad smell in this hall."

His companions laughed in agreement as an angry Alfgar and his men could be heard leaving the compound. There seemed to be a mutual agreement that at last men could go about their business without fear of falling foul of the churlish and unpleasant Alfgar, Lord of East Anglia.

Wulfhere's *niðdraca* dissolved; there had been no need for it to fulfil its purpose this time. Alfgar's hubris had been his downfall.

Edith Godwinsdottir, Queen of Englalond, held up the elegant new robe she had commissioned. She observed it critically in the light that filtered through an open shutter. Fine lilac silk, imported from the East; the embroidery, her own work, was the best she had ever executed in gold and silver thread. It had cost no little fortune, indeed. She was extremely pleased with it, and gave a contented murmur of pleasure as she fingered the intricate detail. Since her return to stately affairs, Edith had taken an active role in ensuring her husband was suitably attired for the office of king. She made it her business to see that he also possessed the expensive and elaborate trappings necessary for a man of his status. The thrones that she and Edward sat upon were decorated with beautiful hangings, embroidered with colourful designs at Edith's instruction. The king's golden staff was encrusted with bright gems and precious stones, and in the halls and great chambers, finely woven carpets from Spain adorned the walls, imported, and bought at her own expense.

Edward thought these items unnecessary and costly, but her frivolous nature no longer infuriated him as it used to. He seemed content enough to allow her to spend what she liked if she gave regularly to church funds and various good causes. Her life as queen had not always glittered with stardust as now. She had been hoping for a man who would adore her, hold her in exultation and value her as his most cherished wife; a man who would look upon her with desire; and a man who would be able to carry out his husbandly obligations to her in their marriage bed. She had hoped that the marriage would be fruitful; that she would beget a line of sons and daughters to bring great things to the world. Unfortunately, Edward's interest in her as a wife had been purely political, and he rarely shared her bed nowadays. How could she have known that his dislike of women had developed long before Edith had entered his life? Unfortunately, she had failed to bring about any change in his attitude.

At thirty-four, Edith's rank in life meant that she had not been subjected to the same stresses that women of lower status had to endure. Therefore, she still retained her good looks and clear milk-white skin. A few wrinkles and a sprinkling of grey in her hair were the only signs of aging. But this did nothing to attract Edward or arouse him in any way. The act of bedding each other had been like an endurance test for both of them, and Edith had not found the experience to be the exciting occasion she had anticipated. As far as her husband was concerned, God had determined that the divine right to produce an *atheling* was not their destiny. God had greater things for Edward other than procreation, it would seem, and Edith had long accepted that she would have to be content with being the wife of a king rather than a mother of kings.

Nevertheless, it was a manifold improvement on the state of affairs that had existed before her return to favour. Edward had treated her with nothing short of contempt, and had publicly humiliated her on many occasions during the years leading up to the Godwinsons' banishment. When her father and brothers had fled into exile, she had chosen to remain loyal to her husband, but somehow that interfering little creature, Robert Champart, had turned him against her. Thanks to him, she had been unceremoniously stripped of her finery and sent packing to a nunnery with no escort apart from her maid. So perhaps it was out of guilt that Edward allowed her to indulge herself with expensive tastes. At least if he had to put up with her, he could do so with some equanimity.

"I think this colour will suit my husband, *vous ne pensez pas,* Mathilde?" she asked, speaking the language of her maid. It was spoken often at court, Frencisc being the tongue Edward had grown up with.

"*Mais oui, certainement, Madame.* His Grace, the king, will be resplendent in this tunic," replied her servant, ingratiatingly.

Edith nodded agreeably. "His Grace the king must look his best when he holds court. It will be a very important day as it always is when a new earl is brought to office. And tomorrow will be a very important day *pour ma famille* when the rest of those *racaille impies*, that ungodly rabble, learn, once and for all, just who the leading family in this kingdom is!" She handed Edward's garment to Mathilde who placed it over a clothing pole. "Never again will those imbeciles be able to insult my family when my brother Tostig is promoted to the Earldom of Northymbralond. Now that Earl Siward has gone and that old goat Leofric is all but dead, too, we Godwins will control the whole of the kingdom. We will be the most powerful family in the land, Mathilde!"

"Oh, but I overheard some of the men speaking and they were saying that Lord Leofric's son, Alfgar, will be chosen for Northymbralond," Mathilde replied, pouring her mistress a goblet of red wine from a pewter jug.

"Not if I have anything to do with it," Edith replied scornfully. "Why, it is perfectly ridiculous that Edward would choose that slavering, rabid animal to be oversee one of the most important earldoms in Englalond... *c'est tellement ridicule!"*

Just then there was a knock on the door and Edith's butler requested permission to enter. "My Lady?"

"Yes, Harding, come in. What is it?" Edith asked impatiently.

A tall, dark-haired, bearded man entered the room and gave a curt bow. "My Lady, your mother the Countess of Wessex and your brothers are here to escort you to the council chamber."

"Tostig!" Edith clapped her hands gleefully, her impatience turning to girlish pleasure. Tostig was her favourite brother. Her older brother, Swegn, now deceased, had been his predecessor, despite his wayward and, some would say, villainous ways. She found Tostig far more pliant than her brother, Harold, who was apt to dig his heels in and resist her attempts to interfere in his life. Edith had desisted, trying to convince him he needed to formalise an important marriage with the daughter of a foreign count or noble. Flanders was full of eligible women, waiting to be swooped up and tossed into a marriage bed. Tostig had made a fine alliance for himself in marrying Judith, the daughter of Duke Baldwin of Flanders. Why should he not follow his example? It infuriated her the way that Harold had left a trail of heartbroken females, stubbornly clinging to that low-born temptress, Eadgyth, and her brood of spoilt brats.

Edith had not seen Tostig for some time and was excited about seeing him again, especially under such promising circumstances. It was her plan that Tostig would be invested with the honour of Northymbralond this very day, and then her world would begin to take on a much more powerful dimension. With the two most powerful earldoms safe in the hands of her brothers, Edith need never worry for she would then be well entrenched upon the throne alongside her husband. With the might and strength of her brothers behind her, and the absence of that malicious old bastard, Champart, she would be the most powerful woman in the land. She'd be a driving force in ruling the most enviable kingdoms in Christendom. Men would bow to her, defer to her wisdom, and offer her respect and admiration. She and Edward would be equal in all things; divine rulers in a divine kingdom.

"Mathilde, hand me that mirror. Harding, tell them to wait. I will instruct you when I am ready to see them."

Harding disappeared, and the queen removed her wimple and had her maid brush and re-braid her hair. No one was permitted to see her well-groomed tresses, but it gave Edith satisfaction to know that her hair was perfect beneath the undulating layers of rich yellow silk that floated about her shoulders and crowned by a jewel-encrusted gold circlet. She plucked at a few hairs on her eyebrows and top lip, and attempted to straighten the creases in her skirts before she decided she was acceptable to be seen.

Her mother and brothers were admitted after at least a half-hour wait. The brothers were accustomed to their sister's idiosyncrasies and had waited patiently in the antechamber, making jokes about, *who the hell* she thought she was to keep them waiting; the Queen of Englalond?

Edith flashed her mother and brothers the charming Godwin smile and embraced first her favourite, Tostig.

"'Tis good to have you back at court, dear brother. I trust all is well with Lady Judith? Is she not in your company?" Edith gushed.

Tostig was smiling at her fondly, his arms about her waist. "I am glad to be here once more in your presence, dear sister. And yes, thank you, all is well with Judith. More than well actually, dear sister, for the reason she could not be here is because she is with child. Alas the sickness is upon her so terribly in the mornings that it was not thought wise for her to travel."

If the queen, because of her childless state, felt envious at the news of her sister-in-law's pregnancy, she did not show it. She simply smiled and shared her brother's joy at becoming a father, telling him that when Judith was well enough she must come to court so she could look after her. She then turned to her mother, and kissed her on both cheeks, and gave the same welcome to her other brothers, who had been watching her obvious display of favouritism toward Tostig with interest.

"Isn't it wonderful that Tostig is to be a father in the autumn?" Edith clasped hold of his hand fondly. "What a wonderful way to start office, with a new child, a son or daughter to fill all our lives with joy!"

"Harold's Eadgyth is also with child again," the Lady Gytha remarked matter-of-factly as Edith gazed fondly at Tostig, imagining him regaled in the trappings of an earl. "She will give birth in midsummer," Lady Gytha continued, but Edith was doing her best to ignore her mother. She and Tostig were too busy exchanging pleasantries, absorbed in each other.

"She is absolutely blossoming," added Harold.

Edith huffed and turned briefly to him, saying disinterestedly, "How nice, Harold," before turning back to Tostig. "Tostig, I have a marvellous idea, instead of Judith coming here to London, Edward and I must visit you in Jorvik. Yes, of course, after all it would be improper for the heavily pregnant Lady of Northymbralond to travel south at such a time. And Edward and I have never travelled north before. It would be a wonderful experience for all of us!"

Edith's mania was such that even Tostig yawned at her incessant chatter. But it was Lady Gytha who poured water on the flames of Edith's imagination.

"The office of Northymbralond is not a foregone conclusion, daughter. We have yet to hear what the king's thoughts are upon the matter," Gytha interrupted.

"Mother, have you no faith at all? Of course, Tostig is a certainty for the post. I have Edward's ear on such matters. I thought you would know that by now. Edward is very fond of Tostig and has every intention of investing him with the office of Northymbralond." Edith looked indignantly at her mother as if it were a terrible crime that anyone would dare to question it.

"I have faith in Tostig as I have in all my children, but your husband, the king, is another matter. We must not forget that Edward has a will of his own, and cannot always be made to do the bidding of the Godwins... as we all know from past experience."

"Mother is right," put in Harold. "If Edward gave Northymbralond to Alfgar, he would be balancing out the power in the land. If he gives it to Tostig, he tips it back into the hands of we Godwins, and that is something he surely fears."

"Don't be absurd, Harold," Edith exclaimed. "Do you not think that I have no influence over my own husband? Gracious! What do you think I have been doing all week if not trying to persuade him to choose Tostig?"

"Persuade him? You cannot even persuade him to help us find Wulfnoth and Hakon," Harold declared with some annoyance. "How you think that he is remotely influenced by you, I have no idea."

Edith's face grew scarlet. She had to admit secretly that she had failed on that score. Edward cut her off every time she mentioned the boys, and she had given up trying now for fear of permanently displeasing him. The experience of being cast out into the road with nothing but the clothes she stood up in was still raw, and not an experience she wanted to repeat, nor was she willing to imperil her new found favour with her husband.

"Dear Brother, the boys are not lost, they are simply... abroad. Yes, they are abroad – in the safe hands of the Duke of Normandy. But this is not the time to be discussing such difficult matters," Edith replied. "My husband, the king, has much to contend with in his realm and has not had the time to deal with that yet."

"Yes, I suppose, *your husband, the king*, has many more important things to consider, like hunting, or spending hours praying, or playing *tafl*, or organising a boat race for his young male friends. I can see why he has not had time to give thought to the return of two young boys torn from their family, when he has much more pressing matters to deal with," Harold said, raising an irritated gaze to the ceiling.

"How dare you speak of the king in such a disparaging manner, Brother? Heavens, but I do not know what has gotten into you that you must bring up the subject of Wulfnoth and that chit of Swegn's, just now, when we should be concentrating on Tostig's promotion. Why, it's not as if they are not safe where they are. I am sure they will come to no harm in Normandy," Edith retorted. "In fact, perhaps that little horror, Hakon, will be learning how to conduct himself more appropriately these days. They know how to bring children up with decorum and proper manners in Normandy."

Harold opened his mouth to reply but his mother cut in. "That 'little horror' as you call him, daughter, is *my* grandson and I want him home as much as I want Wulfnoth. But it serves us nought to fight amongst ourselves. Harold, please leave the matter be for now."

"I meant only to say that now was not the right time, but Harold seemed intent on haranguing me about the subject when he knows full well it is not my fault," Edith said defensively.

"And I was merely pointing out that my sister's so-called influence over her husband is not as effective as she would like us to believe," was Harold's reply.

"Harold is right, and Mother has already pointed out that Edward is in possession of a mind of his own, as we all found out four years ago," added Gyrth. "Or have we already forgotten the events of that summer, four years since?"

"You think that I could forget such a time so easily, Gyrth? It is because of that, that I am loath to approach him just yet. The dust has yet to settle on that unhappy time," Edith said, her eyes glinting with terror at the memory of her incarceration.

"Surely there has been long enough for the dust to have settled, dear Sister? Just when would be the right time, could you tell me that?" Harold demanded.

For a moment, brother and sister glared at each other defiantly until finally Edith took a deep breath and said, "And just what have you done to secure their release, Harold? Do I have to do everything for this family? What of that boy, Ranulf? Did you not send him back to his father with a letter of appeal?"

"There has been no word since he left," Harold answered. "But, for heaven's sake, Edith, you are the queen – the boys' sister and aunt. Surely that must count for something."

"It obviously counts for nothing where you are concerned, Harold," Edith returned arrogantly. "You would do well to remember just exactly who I am, *dear brother*."

"How could I possibly forget who you are?"

"Please, let us leave the bickering for another day. Today we must concentrate on the matter in hand," Gytha interrupted. "Must it always be so with my children, always fighting amongst themselves? We need to be united more than ever now. Surely if we can show Edward that we are not here to pressure him or threaten his authority as king in any way, then he may be willing to choose Tostig over Alfgar. And then…" she broke off wearily, "maybe we can use our increasing influence to bring our boys back home." Tears welled in her old grey-blue eyes and Tostig, who had remained silent throughout the argument, put a hand on her shoulder to comfort her.

"Well, now that matter is sorted, let us proceed to the council chamber," Edith said rubbing her hands. She glanced over to the hour candle that had been burning in a sconce on the wall. "Goodness, the hour is well and truly here. We shall be late if we do not gather ourselves and make haste. And it would not do for the new Earl of Northymbralond to keep the *Witan* waiting, would it now."

She held out her arm to Tostig, and as he took it obediently, a feeling of excited anticipation overwhelmed her. As they walked ahead of the others, Edith whispered to her brother, "Are you well, brother? Have you heard any news?"

Tostig gave her a perceptive smile. "Hopefully the competition will be well and truly out of the running by now, dear sister," he replied. "If the fellows to whom a purse of silver was promised have done their job well, by now Lord Alfgar will be well into his own grave."

Edith raised an eyebrow and smiled happily at this. She was having second thoughts about the new robes for her husband. *They would look much finer at this evening's feasting on the new Earl of Northymbralond,* she thought to herself with a great sense of satisfaction.

Edward was outraged when he had heard about Alfgar's lunchtime display in the mead hall, but it was nothing to the anger he displayed when he demanded that the earl be brought to answer for his behaviour, and was told that the insubordinate, Alfgar, had fled from court with all his retainers. He paced up and down, ranting that he would, "have his eyes for this!" and other such torturous punishments that he could possibly think of. It was rare that Edward lost his reserve so publicly, but Alfgar's outrageous exhibit of contempt toward him and those close to him was something that he could not countenance with composure. Only in exceptional circumstances did Edward allow himself the luxury of a public outburst, but when he did, it was a glorious sight indeed. He gesticulated wildly, thrashing his arms in the air and spitting saliva, as he gave vent to all the curses and oaths that were waiting to burst from his tongue. He was like a spoilt child losing a game; hardly the pious and devout man he endeavoured to portray himself as.

Of course Edith was on hand to restore her disquieted husband to calm, directing him to sit and fanning him with the end of her wimple. When he was sufficiently calm, he summoned the members of the *Witan* to the council chamber and there he announced, before all his nobles and royal thegns, that Tostig Godwinson be invested with the office of earl for Northymbralond, and Alfgar to be exiled for his treasonous behaviour, meaning that he was now an outlaw, with three days to leave the kingdom, and should he be found to still be here after that, he could be lawfully made extinct by any free man who happened to come across him. In shame, the noble Lord Leofric was forced to listen as his son's reputation was lambasted in the council chamber. If some had thought that Alfgar had been maligned unfairly, and that maybe provocation had played a part in his downfall, they kept it to themselves, for to have him skulking openly as Earl of Northymbralond was a far greater evil than to have him uncontained as an outlaw.

That evening, there was a feast in honour of Earl Tostig in the Great Hall. Wulfhere sat amongst his friends, enjoying the food, and discussing the day's events, while court musicians entertained in the background. He observed with amusement that food was being shovelled into throats as if it was the last supper, and ale quaffed as though there was about to be a drought. At the top table, the king and queen sat attired in their best robes. With them were the king's in-laws, including the new Earl of Northymbralond, resplendent in new silk robes of lilac colour, interwoven with gold thread. Also with them were the king's nephew Ralph, his wife Gytha and the Archbishop of Jorvik, Cynesige, the ecclesiastic representative at the high table, who had a special interest in the election of the Northymbralond earldom as it was within his diocese.

"Tostig Godwinson is looking magnificent in his new situation," remarked Wulfhere to the others, looking up at the dais at the royal table.

"He positively radiates with happiness," Aelmer added, taking a bite of roasted meat, and chewing it savagely.

"Absolutely, like a smitten lover," laughed Leofnoth, who had been unusually quiet since his altercation with Alfgar.

Wulfhere looked at the two men curiously. "In fact, he looks much like a naughty boy who has played some trick and managed to get his playmate the blame," he commented. His companions' smug demeanour, coupled with their knowing glances, left him with a strange feeling. "Much like you two," he added with obvious sarcasm.

"Do you know what he is talking about, Leofnoth?" Aelmer responded, looking at Leofnoth with outrage, and then back at Wulfhere indignantly. "Wulfhere, what are you talking about?"

"Humph, I have definitely no idea what he is implying," Leofnoth said, shaking his head, and tearing into a piece of meat.

"Lords Tostig and Ralph are looking very friendly these days. I had no idea they were so close," Wulfhere said, after eating silently for a moment, hoping that he would prompt either Leofnoth or Aelmer into a confession which would satisfy his own suspicions that they had, indeed, something to do with Alfgar's downfall.

"Then you don't know very much, do you," Aelmer grunted, with a mouth full of roasted boar.

"Maybe not, but I think that you and Leofnoth are also *good friends* with the earls," Wulfhere said, swirling the last mouthful of mead in his cup before swallowing it down in one. He placed the empty cup directly before Leofnoth, who had the pewter jug in his possession and was pouring it into his own cup. The older thegn replenished Wulfhere's cup and grinned impudently, showing his vast empty gums.

"Come on, men. Tell me, did you two fellows have something to do with that fracas today?" Wulfhere asked directly, a smile emerging on his lips.

But Leofnoth and Aelmer ignored the implication and carried on stuffing their faces, gluttonously.

Wulfhere glared at them, with a frown and narrowed eyes, frustrated that they were not being very obliging. "*Horningsuna*, you know you did!" He swallowed his mead and thumped the table with the empty cup.

Aelmer shrugged. "He needed an excuse to leave court… didn't really want to be here… hates being at court, doesn't he? I hate to see the poor man suffer with such needless tedium."

"So what if we helped him get away on a bit of a sojourn," Leofnoth added, finishing his mouthful of food, and gulping noisily. He smiled his ugly grin.

"You nefarious old goats, the pair of you. They paid you, didn't they," Wulfhere exclaimed.

"Ssh! My confessor is over there!" Leofnoth exclaimed, trying to sound serious. Aelmer simply smiled as he chewed on another piece of crust.

Cana, who had been listening to their conversation, joined in. "What I want to know is; how did you know where Alfgar would want to sit?"

Aelmer put his finger to his lips to hush them, then spoke only loud enough for them to hear. "Some of Alfgar's men didn't want to be here either…"

"And they were a bit short of money too," added Leofnoth, showing them his pouch of silver coins.

Wulfhere shook his head. "You got them to make sure the confrontation happened. So, it was a conspiracy. A clever one at that!"

"Apparently Alfgar and Ragnald are well known for pushing men out of their way when spaces are short in the hall. We weren't sure if it would work, but with Alfgar's temperament and the enlistment of a couple of his avaricious old brutes, it worked well enough."

"Bastards," Wulfhere cried.

"Alfgar is a rogue; he doesn't deserve to be an earl," Leofnoth replied wryly.

"No, you are both bastards for not letting me in on it," Wulfhere said.

"You? You are too honest. Us? Well, we are already corrupt. We would not want you to compromise your innocent nature."

The men laughed and Wulfhere, although he wasn't exactly in agreement with their methods, had to hand it to them for the shrewd way in which they engineered the whole thing. With Ralph goading Alfgar into losing his temper and Tostig absent from the hall to avoid suspicion, between them all a thorough job had been done on the sorry, quarrelsome, Alfgar.

"At any rate, Alfgar was bound to do something outrageous before long and he didn't really need much help from them," Cana put in, nodding his head at Leofnoth and Aelmer.

"Did you know about it too, Cana?" Wulfhere asked.

"No, but I wish I did. I shat myself when he went for Leofnoth. Praise the Saints, that table was in the way!"

"And so you think that Tostig Godwinson will make a better earl?" Wulfhere was cynical.

"He is a Súþseaxan and a Godwin, isn't he? That's good enough for me. Our loyalty lies with him," Aelmer replied. "We owe it to his father. We were all Godwin's men once."

"And besides, Tostig is better looking than Alfgar! See how pretty he looks in his lilac robes?" Leofnoth roared as he threw back his head in laughter at his own jest.

Wulfhere laughed with the others, but wondered what might have happened if the plan had not worked. Tostig was not everyone's cup of mead, but they all seemed to think he was more palatable than Alfgar. But the plotters had been more successful than they had ever meant to be, for they had not only kept Northymbralond out of Alfgar's hands, but they had also succeeded in ousting him altogether. One way or another, there was a new lord in the north and the time was nearing for Wulfhere to return home again, in time for the spring sowing. He had been away two months, now, and would be glad to be going home to the comfort of his wife and the delights of his children. There would be time to spend working around the homestead and playing with his offspring.

Then the time would follow for the annual fyrd mustering; perhaps there may be another battle looming on the horizon. Wulfhere gave a shudder and hoped that there would be no battles for him to fight again this year, for the horror of Dunsinane Hill still haunted him at night. But summer was some way off yet and for the time being he need only worry about mending fences, bridges and breeding his mares… and perhaps breeding his wife too.

The fear of war could be put on hold for the time being. He thought that he must be getting old, for there was a time, once, when he would have welcomed the challenges and exhilaration that fighting in the shieldwall brought. The thrill and anticipation of putting your training to test was something that every new recruit looked forward to. But not now. Not anymore. After Dunsinane, he had become weary of it, and longed only for the time he could spend at home with his family, his horses, hawks, and hounds… the best time of all.

Chapter Eleven

Sons of Loki

April 1055

Ealdgytha sat by the hearth in the longhall, assiduously working on a rip in one of Wulfhere's tunics. The evening's supper weaved a delicious aroma through the air, as it simmered in the cauldron, above the smouldering flames. The younger of her children, Gerda and Drusilda, played beside her on sheepskins. Drusilda was walking now and becoming quite a handful, but four-year-old Gerda held her sister's attention as they played with the little woollen dolls that Ealdgytha had made for them. Upstairs in the bedchamber, Wulfhere was resting after his journey home from his court duties. He had travelled home with Leofnoth and Aemund, and Ealdgytha had insisted that they stayed awhile before continuing home.

Ealdgytha was pleased to have her husband back home and had truly missed him both in and out of her bed. It seemed that their marriage had found some new peace at last. As she sewed, she reflected on the positive changes that had taken place in their marriage, and compared them to the way things had been previously; but although she smiled when she thought about their lovemaking, she could not help but wonder how long the changes would last. Still, for now, she was happy and determined that previous recriminations should stay in the past.

Even their tenants had noticed that the atmosphere around the home was more pleasant than it had been since their master's dalliance with the Lady of Waldron some years before. The ever frank Sigfrith, always the voice, eyes, and ears of the people of Horstede, had confirmed it to her in one of their conversations. Although Ealdgytha would never admit it, she valued Sigfrith's opinions, and, if Sigfrith thought it was so, then she was certain it was.

"Many married men have such liaisons with other women. Heaven knows, there are as many loose women in the nearby villages as there are tomcats. But I believe, mistress, that Lord Wulfhere has been true and faithful these past years," Sigfrith had said, oblivious of Ealdgytha's unease at her servant's allusion to Wulfhere's past indiscretion.

"Sigfrith, it really is neither your business nor your place to speak of such things," Ealdgytha had replied curtly.

Those who knew Wulfhere well, also knew that his relationship with the woman Alfgyva was more than just some passing whim. He had often left the homestead for days to spend time with her when he should have been at home with his wife and family, carrying out the duties of a husband and father. It was not for nothing that Ealdgytha had reacted with such vehemence toward her husband for his infidelity. The two women had once been such good friends. Alfgyva had shared many wonderful times with Ealdgytha, teaching her much about herbs and potions. It had been Alfgyva who had taught Ealdgytha how to concoct the things that enhanced a woman's beauty: powders to redden the cheeks, lotions that would deepen the natural tones of hair, and gels that would darken and plump out the lips.

But there were still moments when Ealdgytha, recalling a tender moment with Wulfhere, could not help but think at the same time of the dark-haired enchantress. She had always been a presence, even though the affair was long over, shadowing them like a persistent dark cloud. She would never go away. Wulfhere's obvious devotion to her was the thing that had hurt Ealdgytha more than anything, and when she had learned that Wulfhere had fathered a child with her, the knife, already deep inside her, thrusted further, until it seemed that she would die of so great a wound. Ealdgytha made it clear to him that if there was to be any peace between them, he could no longer see Alfgyva, or the child. She had been relieved when he agreed, although she knew it was with a heavy heart that he did so. She turned a blind eye to his sending her and the child money, but some years after the little girl had been born, Alfgyva had refused to accept any more, sending word that she was to be married to a wealthy merchant who had promised to take the child, Rowena was her name, as his own.

Ealdgytha knew that it had been hard for Wulfhere to forget Alfgyva, especially when it seemed that she would never find it in her heart to forgive him. Ealdgytha had punished him by withdrawing herself from the bedchamber. She had just discovered herself to be pregnant with her sixth child, Gerda, when the affair came to her attention. At first, her pregnancy had been a good excuse. Many women found themselves unable to make love during this time. However, even after the birth of another daughter, they slept separately for some time until Ealdgytha relented for fear that tongues would wag amongst the villagers. They eventually began to share their bed again but it had only been on a few rare occasions as husband and wife. It was during one of these unusual moments that Ealdgytha had given into his demands and found herself pregnant again with Drusilda. But it was not until last year, when Wulfhere had returned home from the great battle, lucky to be alive, that Ealdgytha was able to bring herself to rekindle the love she once felt for him.

"My lady, the fire is going out. Should I fetch more tinder?"

Ealdgytha's thoughts were broken. She looked up from her sewing and glared disdainfully at her maid's rotund belly. The servant girl's growing paunch emphasised her illicit pregnancy. Sigfrith had divulged the name of the father after Herewulf had threatened to beat it out of her. It turned out to be, not surprisingly, the yellow-haired reeve, Tigfi. The truth had come out whilst Wulfhere had been away at court, and Ealdgytha knew at some point she was going to have to tell her husband that the young huscarle had seduced their maid. He would have to approach the earl about it. It was right and proper that Tigfi should pay some compensation for seducing a man's servant, and take some responsibility for the child.

"Yes, Sigfrith, and get the girls to help you," replied Ealdgytha as she watched her maid disappear, shaking her head disapprovingly as the young woman waddled awkwardly out of the door.

She stirred the pot of stew and tasted it; then offered some to Gerda who'd jumped up and hungrily pulled at her mother's skirts for a taste. Ealdgytha looked at her second youngest child anxiously as the little girl gave her a wide-eyed smile. This one could hardly say two words to anyone, and it was beginning to be evident that she was simple of mind. Despite being normal in every other way, Gerda was definitely underdeveloped when it came to communicating. The cute little smile that showed perfect kitten-like teeth and sparkling blue eyes, seemed to be her only means of communicating apart from the odd badly pronounced word or two. Poor child, Ealdgytha thought to herself, as she bent down to kiss her little girl's smiling face; a face that was so endearing. It was going to be hard to find her a decent husband; perhaps a nunnery would be the best thing for her if things did not improve.

Ealdgytha was startled, when she heard a cry over in the doorway as her maid, upon re-entering the hall with a bundle of tinder, was knocked sideways by a worried-faced Winflaed hurtling past her into the hall.

Kindling scattered over the floor as the little girl cried, "Mother, come quick!"

"Winflaed, what on earth?" Ealdgytha gasped in irritation at the sight of her daughter, her face red and perspiring, her hair a mass of tangled braids. No matter how hard she tried, thought Ealdgytha, the girl could never seem to keep herself clean or tidy.

She sighed in exasperation. "What has gotten into you, girl? Look at you! Can you not see what you have done to poor Sigfrith?"

"Mother, they are going to kill Tovi!" Winflaed wailed, ignoring her mother's rebuke.

"Who is going to kill Tovi?" Ealdgytha asked disbelievingly. Her hands went to her hips as they always did when she was irritated.

"Wulfric and Wulfwin! They are going to put him in the well!" Winflaed's frog-like eyes were wide with terror.

Ealdgytha breathed the frustrated sigh of a mother who had heard it all before. The twins were always up to mischief. Tovi was just going to have to learn to stand up for himself. *Kill him indeed; as if they would!*

"Winflaed, I have no time for silliness!" Ealdgytha said sharply. "Tell the boys that I said to leave him alone, and come inside and get ready for supper."

"But, Mother, they are going to *kill him*," Winflaed cried, dancing with agitation.

"Don't be absurd, child. Of course they are not going to kill Tovi. They're just playing with him. Can you not see that I am busy? You children need to learn how to behave. Now go and tell them what I have said, but before you do that, you can help Sigfrith pick up the kindling for the hearth, since you made her to throw it all over the floor."

"But…" Winflaed looked at Ealdgytha with pleading eyes but her mother was not giving in.

"Stop this nonsense now, Winflaed. I cannot be called every time you children have a spat or a falling out. Such a fuss over nothing. I am sure they are just pretending. You know what those two are like."

"Come, child, your mother is busy. Help me pick up this wood and then we shall see what is going on outside with your brothers," Sigfrith said to her in a calming voice.

Winflaed worked quickly to assist Sigfrith to pick up the wood.

"Father calls them *Sons of Loki*," Winflaed told her, then asked in a curious voice, "Does that mean that they are not really my brothers? And who is Loki?"

Sigfrith laughed as she gathered the tinder that Winflaed handed to her. "Loki is a devil who brought mischief to the old gods of our ancestors in the time before Christ. I think your father jests, little one," she replied then lowered her voice. "But it would not do to speak of the old gods in front of your mother. She would have me whipped in the stocks if she heard me utter such things."

Tovi was terror-stricken as he dangled halfway down the well shaft with the rope, that would normally hold the bucket, tethered under his arms. He was swearing and shouting in a language that would have embarrassed the bawdiest of men; arms flailing and legs kicking the sides of the shaft in futile attempts to climb his way out. He looked down into the darkness of the well, the murky dampness assailing his nostrils as his brothers lowered him further into the shaft. Frightened, he began to whimper tearfully and looked up at the devilish faces of his brothers as they grinned at him over the lip of the well. The shaft rang ominously with the sound of their mirth as they revelled in his plight.

"Beg for mercy, toad!" shouted Wulfwin, lowering his brother further into the well by about a foot.

Tovi obliged, "Mercy!" He was ashamed of his cowardice, but he did not want them to drown him.

"Sorry, I cannot hear you, little toad!" Wulfwin turned the crank and Tovi felt himself slip further down the well. He felt the cool, damp air rise from the bottom of the well, and hover around his bare feet.

"Please, Wulfwin, pull me back up. I'm sorry. I'll die down here," he sobbed.

Wulfwin smiled and looked at his brother. "What did he say, Wulfric? I can't hear him."

Wulfric gave an evil chuckle. "I think he said that he was sorry for breaking your fine bow made of yew, the one that Father gave you."

"Is that what he said? I didn't hear him, Wulfric."

Tovi thought he heard the rope creak as it strained to take his weight. He stopped wriggling for fear that it might cause it to snap. Trying to keep as still as possible but unable to stop the rope from swaying, he stared up at his brothers with wide, terrified eyes. The thought of being slowly let down into the depths of the well and left to drown in the dark was a terrifying notion. Of all the things they had done to him, this had to be the worst. They were going to kill him; of that he was certain now. They were going to let him drown and then tell everyone it was an accident. They would not have dared to do this if Ranulf were here... but he was not; and they were.

"I don't think I hear him, Wulfric," repeated Wulfwin, shouting into the well.

"I am sorry for breaking your fine bow made of yew, the one that Father gave you," Tovi replied breathlessly, hoping that if he did as he was told they would not let him drown after all. It never occurred to him that they would not do it, that they did not really want to kill him, or cause him any harm. Or that they would be too scared to do such a thing for fear of reprisal. To him, the threat of harm or death at their hands was very real, and very frightening.

"Did he say he was sorry for breaking your fine yew bow that Father gave you?" Wulfwin asked his twin brother. "The one that he brought back for you from the north?"

"I don't know, Wulfwin, did he?"

"Yes, I did!" Tovi shouted as loudly as he could without causing too much movement on the rope.

"He says he did... I think." Wulfwin cupped a hand to his ear as he leaned over the mouth of the well.

Tovi heard them laughing and in those moments, he whispered the *Paternoster*, that Father Paul had taught him, hoping that God would hear and come to his aid.

"Think that we should pull him out now, Wulfric?"

"Is he sorry?" Wulfwin asked.

"Sorry that he broke my fine bow, made from yew...the one that Father brought home for me from the war in the North, you mean?" Wulfric replied.

"Are you sorry that you broke Wulfric's bow that Father brought him back from the war in the North?"

"I am sorry that I broke your fine bow, made from yew, that Father brought you from the war in the North, Wulfric!" Tovi shouted desperately.

"I think that he said he is sorry, Wulfric."

"Then shall we pull him out, Wulfwin?"

Tovi dangled helplessly while he waited anxiously for the inevitable end, closing his eyes, and praying that they would pull him up soon.

"God's bones, what do you two hell hounds think you are doing?"

Tovi heard his father's voice and gave a sigh of relief. "Father!" he called.

By the time he had been pulled out of the well, bedraggled, tears staining his cheeks, a crowd had gathered.

"Tovi, look what you have done to your best tunic!" Ealdgytha exclaimed. She grabbed him and slapped the dirt off his tunic. "Why on earth could the good Lord not have given me children that behaved themselves? Not even the cottars' children are this troublesome."

"Good God, woman. Is that all you can say?" Wulfhere exclaimed. "Can you not assert any control over this household when I am not here?"

"So, it is my fault that our children run wild, is it?" Ealdgytha retaliated. "Do you not think that I have enough to do around the home while you are away, with the cooking, sewing, weaving, *and* spinning; not mentioning all the other endless tasks that I have to oversee?"

"Is it not also a woman's work to see that her children are brought up properly, with decorum?" Wulfhere hit back, frowning angrily.

"Perhaps if you chastised them just a little, they would not behave like such savages. Is that not a father's duty?" she retorted. "It's about time you realised that a good talking to is not what they need. They need their hides whipped!"

Tovi hated it when his parents fought. Frustrated, Ealdgytha grabbed her daughters by their hands. "Come, girls, let us women see to the supper and leave your father to punish the boys for trying to kill each other. That's if he sees fit to!" She turned indignantly, stomping haughtily in the direction of the hall.

Tovi took the opportunity of his parents' bickering to pick up a long stick from the ground and threw himself at the twins who were still laughing at him. Rage crackled in his throat as he rammed the stick with all his might across both their chests, as they stood side by side, a two-headed dragon, flaring nostrils that burst forth fire.

The scaly monster fought back, and the stick became a great sword. The creature's talons slashed across his face and neck. Again, he lunged at the monster, hacking at its two heads with his sword, knowing that if he cut their heads from its body, it would die.

"Stop this now, Tovi. Leave it!" Wulfhere bellowed as he broke up the fight, pulling Tovi away from them. One of the twins had disarmed him and both were setting about him with punches. They made to run away, but Wulfhere stalled them. "Not so fast, you two hounds of Loki. Where do you think you are going? Get you both over here now! God's teeth, is this what I have to come home to every time; to find you two mischief-makers trying to kill your own brother?"

"Tovi had fallen in the well and we were just trying to pull him out, Father," Wulfwin said meekly as he and his brother shuffled shamefacedly before their father.

"Aye, it was an unfortunate mishap. He fell in and we were saving him from drowning," Wulfric added in support.

For a moment Wulfhere wanted to believe them, but he was not convinced. He could see the humiliation on Tovi's bruised face and felt him shake with repressed anger as he held his shoulders.

"I don't believe either of you," Wulfhere said, eying them suspiciously. "Tell me the truth of it."

"He broke my bow," Wulfric said, tentatively, and after a long pause. "The fine yew one you bought back for me from the north, Father."

Wulfhere looked thoughtful for a moment and then said, "So, for a broken bow you would drown him?"

"We weren't trying to kill him; we just wanted to punish him," Wulfwin replied.

"You could have killed him!"

"We didn't mean to," Wulfric said apologetically.

"What if the rope had broken and he fell into the well?" Wulfhere was angry. The boys stared back at their father mutely. Wulfhere threw his arms up in frustration at their silence. "Well?"

"He attacked first!" Wulfwin retorted.

"I did not!" Tovi said. He had been staring at the ground and breathing hard.

"Liar! He is lying, Father," Wulfric said. "He ran me to the ground and pushed me over. He took my bow and snapped it."

"H-he was trying to shoot arrows at Winflaed. Th-they tied her t-to a t-tree!" Tovi stammered.

"Is that so, Wulfwin…Wulfric?"

"We used the blunted tips," replied Wulfric, with an air of innocence.

"And we weren't really aiming for her," Wulfwin added petulantly.

"And blunted tips don't hurt? God's teeth! I cannot believe you are the sons of my loins! May the Holy Cross curse me if I don't call you sons of that devil, Loki, for nothing?" Wulfhere's hands went to his hips, and he rolled his eyes to the sky. "And since when have I brought you boys up to pick on little girls? Or are you going to tell me, a little lass beat you to the ground, and danced on your head."

"She wasn't hurt." Wulfwin pouted.

Wulfhere looked from Tovi to the two boys. Wulfric's head was hung in shame, and even Wulfwin's usual self-assured arrogance was greatly diminished. Now nearing their thirteenth birthday, his sons had grown taller, and they were fast approaching his own height. Wulfhere had always enjoyed their exuberant mischievousness, their passion for prankish behaviour and good-humoured teasing. He knew that sometimes they went too far and were over fond of picking on their younger siblings, but at that moment he was angry at their foolhardiness, and the casual way they had endangered their younger siblings' safety. Wulfhere's father's fondness for leather strap beatings had negated the desire to use it on his own offspring; however, he was seriously fighting the urge. Nonetheless, he managed to control his anger. He ordered the twins to get out of his sight, telling them that he would deal with them later. They scurried away without protest but not without a vengeful glare at Tovi.

"Come, boy, you are safe now. I don't think those two will bother you again for a while," Wulfhere said comfortingly. He gave his son a reassuring pat on the back and bent down to wipe away a tear from his face. "What would you say if we took the new black colt out for his first ride, eh?"

Tovi's tearful, miserable face lit up in excited animation. "The one with the white nose and forelock?" he asked hopefully.

Wulfhere grinned and nodded. "Aye, I had it in mind that you might need a mount of your own soon, and thought that Blackie could be the one for you."

Tovi beamed. "Can I call him Grendl, Father? After Beowulf's monster?" he asked as they walked to the stables.

"A monster is a strange name for a horse, but if that is your wish. Personally, I would prefer Beowulf." Wulfhere shrugged.

"But he looks like a Grendl," Tovi argued, stroking the nose of his new friend.

"Then Grendl, he shall be," Wulfhere concurred as the horse whinnied and nodded in agreement.

That evening, the household were sat in their usual places having their evening meal. It was the sixth day of the week, the day when most of the villagers would come to feast with their lord. As usual, Ealdgytha and her sister-in-law, Gunnhild, exchanged disguised insults whilst her pock-faced son, Leofric, leered at Sigfrith and Freyda whenever he had the chance.

When everyone had their fill, the men sat around the stone hearth while Freyda entertained with her harp, and the women tidied the supper things away and put the children to bed.

"She is enchanting, your daughter," Leofnoth said to his host.

"She is," Wulfhere replied, a note of cynicism in his voice. He had still not come to terms with her betrothal to Edgar. Sometimes, he found it difficult to look at her without a tide of bile filling his throat – not for her, but for what she had brought upon them.

"Look at my son, Wulfhere. See how he is smitten with her." Leofnoth nodded over at his son who was indeed gazing at her as if under a spell.

The air was filled with her sweet lilting voice, accompanied by the resonating harp strings as her fingers plucked out the melody. Wulfhere was shrewd enough to note that his daughter appeared to be enjoying the attention. She had the look and ways of her mother, well versed in the art of womanly guile. He was sure that Freyda was aware of Aemund's interest in her; the coy, innocent expression did not convince him she employed, to portray disinterest in him.

"So, how binding exactly is this betrothal to Helghi of Gorde's son?" Leofnoth asked.

"Very. The earl decreed it, and they are to be married next autumn," Wulfhere replied with regret. "Providing there is no reason for it to not go ahead."

"What if it was found that this match would not be suitable?"

Wulfhere gave Leofnoth a cynical look. "It would have to be a good excuse."

"Does the earl not know that the lad is lame?"

Wulfhere nodded, smiling wryly. "Not lame enough, it would seem."

"Come on, Wulfhere, many betrothals are renounced on one pretext or another."

Wulfhere shook his head in frustration. He would have liked nothing better than to have had Aemund as a son-in-law. "Earl Harold desires a union between our families so that there will be no more feuding."

"So, you think he would still make you go ahead if there was a good enough reason?"

"He did suggest that, if, in a year or so, Edgar proved to be an unbefitting suitor we could withdraw from the contract. It would have to be inexcusable though, whatever it was."

Leofnoth leaned toward him furtively. "What if he were…" and he drew an invisible line across his throat.

Wulfhere looked at him in horror and shook his head. "Out of the question. I am not a murderer, Leofnoth, and the boy does not deserve it, even if his father does."

"Not even an unfortunate accident?"

Wulfhere shook his head again firmly. "Such a sin I could not live with."

"Well, maybe there would be another way. Look at my son, my friend. Can you not see how he longs to have your daughter?"

"I have another daughter, Winflaed."

"Too skinny and a little on the plain side, if you don't mind me speaking frankly," replied Leofnoth, shaking his head. "And too young."

"She will grow. As for her plainness, little cygnets grow into beautiful swans."

"No offence, Wulfhere, but it is Freyda that Aemund would have. His heart is set on it."

"You have had too much mead, Leofnoth."

"Pah, you are too pompous at times, Wulfhere. I only have one son and he will get everything when I die. He already has the lands of his late mother. Your daughter will be provided with much more than that crippled mule could give her."

"The Earl of Wessex has promised to give her thirty acres when she and Edgar are wed."

"She will have hundreds of acres with Aemund."

"I am sorry, my friend, but there is nothing I can do… unless…" Wulfhere's eyes suddenly came alight with an idea, like the glow of the fire.

"Yes?"

"…Unless – unless we can find an acceptable excuse as to why they should not marry."

"It may be done. We have more than a year. We managed to get rid of Alfgar. Helghi and his son should be no great problem," Leofnoth grinned.

"You toothless old goat," Wulfhere said, and smiled. "I believe you could do this – but I want you to leave it to me. I don't trust you not to lead us into the fires of hell and damnation!"

"Well, if you don't need my help…"

"However, I will want you to do something for me in return for my daughter."

"It could be a deal."

"I would be honoured if you would take my twins into your household, and teach them to be good warriors; to behave with honour and dignity. I would see that you are paid well for their keep. They need to start practising their skills on things other than their brother and sister, before they despatch one of them to an early death with their foolish pranks."

"I will teach them well, my friend. This is excellent, but don't wait too long in sorting out Helghi's runt. My son is a much sought-after catch."

"I don't doubt he is fighting them off by the dozen."

Wulfhere put his arms about his wife's waist and brushed his lips gently against her neck as she was getting herself ready for bed. The act made her feel warm with longing, but she was still not without anger at his hurtful words earlier that day, and so she gave him no response.

"I am sorry, dear heart," he whispered in her ear. "Do you not forgive me?"

"Should I?"

"Yes."

Her spine tingled as he probed her ear with his tongue. "Tell me what it is you have done wrong first?" she replied teasingly as she fought off the desire that was growing within her.

"I am sorry for blaming you for our children's terrible behaviour." He continued to nuzzle her neck.

"And what are we going to do about these terrible children of ours?"

"Can we not discuss them later?" Sensing her arousal, Wulfhere breathed gently into her ear.

"No, Wulfhere, we need to discuss them now. Tovi is a weakling, and spends far too much time with Winflaed, who runs wild in the forest instead of carrying out her chores; Gerda can hardly string two words together; Freyda keeps asking to marry Edgar now; and the twins do nothing but torment the others. Oh, and you know that Sigfrith is with child by that yellow-haired youth in the Earl's service?"

"The hundred reeve?"

She nodded. "You will need to inform the earl that his man has a duty to our servant girl and her child."

Wulfhere sighed and let go of her before walking over to the bed. "I thought we had problems with the twins, not the others, and certainly not Sigfrith." He scratched his head. He sat down on the bed and began to remove his hose and braies. Ealdgytha came and sat next to him, handing him a cup of warmed honey-flavoured mead that she had been heating on the brazier.

"It is not just the twins I am worried about. Edgar comes here and lounges around the homestead, watching Freyda all the time. Whenever I look for her, there he is in the weaving shed when she is weaving, or the dairy watching her churn butter, or peeling vegetables for the supper... or... or helping her hang out the laundry. It is too much, Wulfhere. I have tried to tell her that he is not to come here, but there he always is, no matter what I say. And they are always telling each other the rudest of riddles. It's disgusting!"

Wulfhere gulped down the contents of the cup. "Can you not just shout at him or something?"

"He is always bringing gifts. Today it was a basket of berries and herbs, and yesterday it was honey cakes; the day before that he chopped wood for the hearth. What can I say to him, 'Thank you, Edgar, for chopping the wood; now get out of my house'?"

"You could try telling him to go *swive* himself!"

"Wulfhere, this is no time to be flippant. What are we going to do? Leofnoth's boy Aemund is such a decent lad, and he is already a thegn with his own landholding. I've seen the way he looks at Freyda. I had always imagined that we would find a successful family for Freyda to marry into, and Aemund is just such a match."

Wulfhere leaned over to kiss her but she was not finished speaking and she pulled away from him. "Wulfric and Wulfwin need some discipline and should be sent somewhere to learn how to behave," she continued.

"Those two *Sons of Loki!*" Wulfhere exclaimed, scratching his head in frustration.

"Wulfhere, do not always refer to them as *Sons of Loki*. Such names are blasphemous, not to mention dangerous. You don't know what wild spirits you could be invoking."

Wulfhere burst into peals of laughter.

"I know you think it is amusing but it is not." Once more she brushed away his attempts to be playful. "And as for Tovi and Winflaed, it is not natural that they spend so much time together. Tovi should be with the boys, not cavorting in the woods with his sister."

"Ealdgytha, will you let me speak? God's teeth, woman. A man can hardly get in a word!"

"What then?" Ealdgytha demanded. "Say what you have to say, if it's worth saying."

"It will be taken care of, sweeting, trust me. Wulfwin and Wulfric are to go to Leofnoth to complete their warrior training. Leave Edgar and Freyda to me. I will stop this marriage if I have to lose a limb doing it."

"Leofnoth has agreed to take them?"

Wulfhere removed his tunic so he was now completely naked. He pulled her round onto the bed with him and burrowed close against her.

"Well, has he?" she asked him, seizing hold of his hand as he pulled at her nightshift.

Wulfhere sighed with frustration. "Leofnoth has promised to take the boys in return for my own promise that I will do what I can to revoke the contract with Helghi and Edgar. He wants Freyda, just as you do, for Aemund."

"I knew it!" Ealdgytha laughed and sat up joyfully. "I knew he wanted her too. Wulfhere, this is truly marvellous, I am so proud of you. But how are we going to achieve this?"

"I will think of something, my love. Now, can you stop this incessant chat about the children and welcome me home in the manner of a true wife?"

Ealdgytha smiled and then lay onto her back in a position of submission. Now that she was satisfied that Wulfhere was going to do something at last about the situation with Edgar and Freyda, she could willingly give herself wholeheartedly to him. She felt a twinge of pleasure as he pulled off her shift and laid his naked torso onto hers. His warm frame rippled against her and she felt content once more that her man was home.

Chapter Twelve

Alfgyva

Somewhere on the edge of the great forest of Andredeswald, a few miles east of Horstede, stood a settlement of modest proportions that housed the Lady of Waldron and two other even smaller households that belonged to her tenants. The warm spring day in the month of May was coming to an end, and although the sun still cast its rays weakly about the homestead, the cool evening air was beginning to herald the approaching dusk. Inside Alfgyva's house, a great sadness filled the air for her child was gravely ill, and hope was all but gone.

Alfgyva held the cup to the little girl's lips and gently bade her drink. It had been three days since the fever had come upon her, and she was showing no signs of recovery. The only time Alfgyva had left her daughter's side was to pray to the Holy Mother and make offerings to her in the ways of the old people. Alfgyva had been taught these ways by her mother, who had interwoven known ancient traditions with those taught her by the Christ worshippers. The Great Mother Rhiannon, nurturer and goddess of fertility and the Holy Mary, Mother of the Lord Jesus, were both one and the same to her. There were those who would pour scorn on her beliefs, but they were also the same people who dared not offend the woodland spirits whose names they brought to life in their ancient invocations. Alfgyva would smile at their hypocrisy, especially when they came to her for a potion or salve to help cure a sick relative. Sadly, it seemed that her healing skills were failing her just when she needed them most. Her little one was sorely ill and not responding to her treatment, despite the incantations and prayers offered to Brid, the goddess of healing.

Little Rowena shut her lips tight against the frothy liquid that her mother was desperate to have her swallow.

"Please, little flower," Alfgyva whispered to her daughter as she mopped the sweat from her forehead. She was as fair as her mother was dark. Her pale skin was now flushed with fever.

The little girl shivered and turned her head away from the cup. Her mother let her head fall back gently against the feathered pillow. It was no use, she thought with despair.

"She is cold," came a voice from behind her. "See how her teeth chatter. You should cover her."

"No, she is ablaze with fever and must be kept cool," replied Alfgyva firmly, shaking her head. "If she is not kept cool, the fire will burn inside her and she will die." She mopped her daughter's forehead, and said irritably, "Must you always creep up behind me like that, Fritha?"

"'Tis not fire but elves that have invaded her, tormenting her, and making her cold," said Fritha, ignoring the younger woman's irritation.

"I know what I am doing. Thank you for your advice, Mistress Fritha," Alfgyva replied sternly, but with control.

"If you say so, my Lady," Fritha conceded. "I have brought you some supper. There is stew and some cornbread. Eat, my Lady. You need your strength, for the sake of the child."

"I thank you again, Fritha."

"You are welcome, my Lady," Fritha replied somewhat stiffly. She breathed a heavy sigh. "You know best," she added.

Her tenant deposited the food on the little wooden trestle and left. When she had gone, Alfgyva burst into a flood of tears. She wept uncontrollably for the first time since the little girl had fallen ill. Her daughter had suffered with the usual childhood illnesses, but had always made a full recovery. Alfgyva had never before seen a fever like this one. It had taken hold so rapidly, purple blemishes appearing all over her body. She knew it was more than just a childhood ailment, and she now feared for the life of her precious little one.

As she wept, she wondered how she would cope without her child. Rowena had been a gift from the Holy Mother and had been her life these past seven years, her sole companion, apart from Welan, the nearby woodcutter, who brought her fuel for her hearth, and did odd jobs around her farm in return for clothing and food. She had been left just over a hide of land and two tenant holdings in her mother's will, which had in turn been given to her mother by King Harold Harefoot, more than fifteen years since.

Alfgyva remembered little of the land that she and her mother had been taken from all those years long ago. They had been sold into slavery, and both had been made to endure the most disgusting acts of inhumanity before they were cruelly separated. Years later, her mother found herself in Harold Harefoot's household. The coarse nature of this older son of Cnut's had probably been inherited from his bitter mother, but in a moment of rare compassion, Harold took pity upon

Alfgyva's mother, whose name had been Rhiannon, like the goddess, and promised to help her find her daughter. He kept his word, and Alfgyva was finally reunited with her mother. Alfgyva had still been a small girl, but she remembered a tall strong man with long brown hair and a rugged face, bending down to take her in strong arms, and throw her, laughing, in the air. She also remembered that he seemed to be very fond of her mother, and had memories of waking up on her pallet by her mother's bed to find him winking at her as he lay by her mother's side. She had blocked out the terrible memories of her abuse before being re-joined with her mother, but she held a sense of grimness, somewhere in her mind, that was born from the trauma of those terrible years.

Her memories of the land she had been wrenched from were of a mountainous country, dark and shadowy, with cave-like dwellings. Her mother had told her that it was a land where people had once been free to practise the old religion, and that their ancestors had been priests and shamans, highly revered amongst their people. They had long since been driven out by the *Romano* invaders who had come before the Angles and the Seaxans. There had been those amongst their descendants who'd wanted to keep their old gods alive, and when the men of Christ came to convert them, they were forced to go into the caves and the darker places, where they could practise their beliefs amongst their own, in secret. Hundreds of years later, they were betrayed, hunted down, and forced into slavery. In their new home, Alfgyva and her mother had been given a new language and new names. It was as if everything from their old lives had been erased... everything but that which was in their hearts and would remind them that once they had been free; the spirits of their ancestors.

Alfgyva had only Welan and the peasants who worked her land to offer her any sort of security. Though many of her neighbours thought of her as an enchantress, her dark, mysterious beauty brought her many suitors. Because she would have none of them, they turned on her and declared that she had cast spells upon them.

One day, she was threatened with a forced marriage by Helghi of Gorde, who claimed that he had been 'enchanted' by her. In desperation, she turned to Wulfhere, the husband of the one friend she had who did not think her a pagan witch. In doing so, she found herself unwillingly attracted to him, as he rescued her from Helghi's clutches. But Wulfhere was a married man and she had had to let him go. She would have been content to have been his mistress, but Wulfhere was a man of conscience, and although she knew it broke him to leave her, she had struggled with his loss ever since.

Then one day she was to marry a rich widower, a merchant from a nearby town. At first, he seemed to accept the child that Wulfhere had fathered upon her. Later, he came to her and told her, if she wanted to be his wife, she was to be rid of Rowena and that he would find a place in a nunnery for her. Alfgyva had refused to abandon the little girl she had named for her mother, and so she had remained unwed ever since.

Life had been hard for her as a husbandless woman with a bastard child, but Welan was like a father to both her and Rowena, and since he had lost his wife, and had no children of his own, Welan was happy to look after their interests in any way he humbly could. Welan was kind and Alfgyva welcomed him into her home to share her hearth and food. However, none but Rowena had ever filled the hole that Wulfhere had left in her heart.

Welan had been bringing in some firewood when he found her, unresponsive, on the floor beside Rowena's cot. He picked her up in his arms and laid her on her bed, covering her with a blanket. He saw that Rowena lay uncovered on her cot and knew that Alfgyva had insisted on her being left that way, but she seemed to have lost the fever and was sleeping deeply now, so he pulled the coverlet over her, sat down by the hearth and kindled the fire. It was dark outside and time for him to be setting out for his hut in the forest, but he could not bring himself to leave them. So he made himself a makeshift bed on the clay-packed floor by the hearth. He would stay, he thought to himself, for his lady might have need of him through the night.

Bright sunshine was filtering through the cracks of the wood-built walls of her house as Alfgyva awoke the next morning. Her head felt heavy and her eyes were swollen from crying. She lay there on her bed, staring at the rafters as the fuzziness of sleep cleared from her head. Suddenly she threw back the blanket, leapt up and went to kneel at her daughter's bedside. She had been so exhausted; she had not realised it was Welan who put her to bed. Thus, she was surprised when he entered the room with a bowl of warm buttermilk for her. After seeing that her daughter was in a deep sleep, she turned to him and thanked him for the drink and for staying with her.

"She has lost the fever," she said, feeling her daughter's skin, "but she is not out of danger yet."

"But it must be a good sign?" Welan asked hopefully.

Alfgyva looked up fondly at the man's wizened face. He was much younger than he looked, but the harshness of a forest dweller's life had left him looking much older than his forty years.

"Yes," Alfgyva nodded. She looked back at Rowena's face. She was pale now, the fevered redness had gone, but her breathing was still deep and rasping.

"You must eat, my Lady. I can warm up the stew that Fritha left, if you would like."

Alfgyva glanced up at him with a distant trance-like look in her eyes. She said nothing in reply, simply returned her gaze to her sleeping daughter as if she had not heard him. *I must comb her hair*, she thought as she ran her fingers through the little girl's tresses. The sweat had dried it in string-like strands that clung to her forehead and the sides of her face. *She had such beautiful hair*, Alfgyva thought to herself. *Now it is lifeless...just like she.*

"I will warm up the pot," Welan said and set about it.

Alfgyva picked up her daughter's comb. It had once been a fine piece of work made of bone with a carved pattern and tiny, pretty stones embedded in it. Wulfhere had sent it to her as a gift for his daughter in Rowena's early years. Rowena grew up never meeting Wulfhere, but she had cherished the comb above all her possessions, because she knew it was from the man who was her father. Even when some of the teeth became broken, she would not be parted from it. Alfgyva thought of the times she'd told her daughter that her father had to travel to a land faraway, to fight in the king's service, but would someday come home to her, and they would all be together again.

It was a lie that even Alfgyva sometimes liked to believe, fanciful though it was. Occasionally, in the evening when Rowena was abed, she would sit and sew and dream that he was with them, the three of them living blissfully, unaffected by the outside world.

She began to comb Rowena's hair gently, and as she did so, the little girl opened her eyes. They were no longer bright with fever as she gazed at her mother. Alfgyva was startled. She had been concentrating on the combing, when she heard her daughter speak in a frail, tiny voice, "Mother, is Father coming home to see me today?"

Alfgyva felt the tears well in her eyes. What could she say to her? Another lie? Would it make much difference? She had told her so many over the years.

"I hope so, my little flower," Alfgyva said.

"I do too, Mother, because if he doesn't... I fear I will never see him at all..." and she closed her eyes once more, and slept as if she had never opened them in the first place.

The tears flowed silently down Alfgyva's cheeks, touched deeply by her daughter's insight into the fact that she was dying.

"My Lady, what can I do?" Welan asked.

Alfgyva went into a deep thought, as if her mind had drifted off to another time and place. *"If ever you are in danger or in need of me, then I will come,"* Wulfhere had said the day he came to tell her it was over. *"I may not be able to be with you always, but I am with you, in here."* And she remembered how he had closed his hand over his heart.

"How will you know that we have need of you?" she had questioned him sadly.

"Send me a lock of your hair," he'd replied, and then, he had gone from her life for the last time.

Alfgyva took a pair of snips from her pouch and cut a lock from her hair, and then a lock from her daughter's. She wrapped the hair with the comb in a strip of linen and sealed it with candle wax. She handed the little parcel to Welan who looked at it curiously.

"Welan, you have always been of so much help to us. Will you do something more for me?" she asked the woodcutter, her dark eyes pleading.

"Anything, my Lady."

"Then take this to the thegn of Horstede as quickly as you might. You can take my horse."

"It shall be done, my Lady," Welan replied, with a nod of his head.

"But do not give it to his wife," Alfgyva said earnestly. "It is for the thegn, and the thegn alone."

Chapter Thirteen

A Lock of Hair

Sunday was always a day of rest for everybody in the village. After early morning Mass, people were free to put away their tools, their broom or sickle. Though it was Father Paul's duty to fine anyone who dared to disobey the rules of the Church and work on the Lord's Day of rest, it was not in his nature to be so harsh. He would often turn a blind eye if a woman needed to attend to some sewing, or if someone had a mind to catch fish for supper. Other recreational pursuits were allowed, although drinking to intoxication and dicing were frowned upon. There again, Father Paul was not such a hard taskmaster.

Sometimes the children would go into the forest to hunt voles and game birds, or if it was a hot day, they would go down to the rock pool to swim and play on the swing. It was on a day such as this that Winflaed and Tovi and a handful of the village children were running home after an afternoon in the forest. As she ran, Winflaed proudly swung a pheasant tied to her wrist, whilst Tovi carried the bow used to catch it clutched in his hand. In front of her, the quarrel full of arrows, strapped to her brother's back, bobbed as he overtook her in the race. The dogs barked excitedly, weaving in and out of them as they snaked through the trees. The forest rang with the laughter of children, their joy partly to do with the fact that Wulfric and Wulfwin's reign of terror was now over. They had been packed off with Leofnoth to learn how to be decent, honourable young men. Now that they were gone, all the children could enjoy their freedom without fearing the twins' next deadly prank.

As Tovi ran before her, Winflaed tried to take the lead, but he was too fast for her. She gained pace as they rounded a bend where the track forked, and as she drew closer to him, she deliberately put out her foot and caught his shin. Her brother was propelled forward, tripping over roots, and stumbling into potholes, but he managed to remain on his feet. She laughed loudly, finding this amusing, and he turned, still running, to make a defiant face at her.

"Nice try, Frog Spawn," he called to her.

Suddenly there was a sound of a horse neighing and a man yelled. Winflaed squealed and called out her brother's name in warning. Tovi turned, nearly colliding with the rearing horse, hooves flailing as the boy zigzagged out of its way. There was a sudden pile-up of children as they careered into each other, crashing in a heap behind him amid yells and peals of laughter.

"Whoa, whoa, girl!" shouted the man riding the horse, trying to gain control of her. Matters were made worse for him as the dogs began to dance and bark round the horse's hooves. Welan was thrown to the ground and the nervous mare charged off up another path.

"Damn, you little rascals," he groaned as he lay prostrate in the dirt. "You've broken my back and lost me my Lady's horse!"

"I-I am s-sorry, sir, I-I will c-catch it for you!" Tovi stammered and raced off after it.

"Horses don't stray too far from their masters." Winflaed bent down to the injured man and helped him to sit up.

"I'll wager this one does." Welan groaned painfully as he sat up and clutched his back.

"Can you move?" Winflaed asked, kneeling beside him. Her hound Elf, a big friendly canine with huge floppy ears, licked Welan's face.

"What do you think I am doing? Get off, mangy mutt," Welan cried sharply, trying to fight off the hound.

"Stop that, Elf," Winflaed told him, pushing the dog away from Welan.

"You call that thing Elf?" he asked in surprise.

"Tovi wanted to call him Pixie but I thought Elf was a better name," Winflaed replied with a cheeky grin.

"You little rascals are the pesky pixies, if anything. Confound you all. You could have killed me!"

"I am truly sorry for any hurt you have suffered, sir," Winflaed said. She and her young companions tried to help him up, but he shook them off, and used his hands to lever himself up off the ground.

"Damn it," he moaned, finding that when he stood, one of his ankles was badly sprained. "How am I going to fulfil my promise to her now?" he muttered.

Tovi returned without the horse, but with him were the charcoal people, Inewulf, his wife Eanflaed and their two sons. "I could not find the horse but I have brought help."

"Sir, you are hurt," Inewulf said as he knelt to Welan and examined his swollen ankle.

"So it would seem," replied Welan.

"If you can walk between me and my wife, our dwelling is not far. We are charcoal burners and people of the forest."

"Like myself, I am *wuduhéawere*." Welan put his arms on their shoulders.

"A carpenter?" asked Eanflaed.

Welan shook his head. "No, I am a hewer of trees."

"Then you must be a rich one for I know few folk who can afford a horse… unless you stole it."

"The horse is my Lady's," Welan told them indignantly. "She bade me take her and ride to Horstede. I have something to give to the thegn from her. It is urgent."

"And which lady might that be?" asked Eanflaed curiously.

"Alfgyva, the Lady of Waldron," Welan replied. "I have to get it to him urgently."

"Lady Alfgyva?" Eanflaed asked. Winflaed thought that she detected a strange look on the charcoal wife's face when the name was mentioned.

Welan nodded. "She is my mistress."

"She has magic in her, that one. She is a temptress," Eanflaed said fearfully and crossed herself.

"She is a good woman," Welan said, somewhat indignantly, "and I need to deliver this package for her."

"Well, you won't be going anywhere on that foot," said Inewulf.

"My father is the thegn," Winflaed said. "I can deliver it for you."

Welan looked at her. "You are the thegn's child?"

"They both are," Inewulf said, pointing in turn at the brother and sister. He was smiling. "Aye, they might blend in very well with these cottar's children, but they are, indeed, two of the thegn's brood."

Welan was looking at Winflaed and her brother in disbelief. Their faces were smeared in the dirt from the forest, their hair in tangles, and their clothing muddy and damp.

"These two creatures?" Welan asked incredulously. "Does your father know that you are running about the forest like wild things, scaring riders off their horses and half killing them?"

"I am not a creature, I am a thegn's daughter," Winflaed replied indignantly. "Do you want us to deliver your package or not?"

"You might just as well, sir, for you cannot walk and your horse is gone. They might be little rascals, but they are the thegn's children. I can vouch for that."

Welan looked at Winflaed and her brother pensively, and then, as if he had decided that she and Tovi were trustworthy, produced the linen parcel from his pouch. He waved it at them and said, "I am trusting you to deliver this safely. It is very important that your father – and your father alone – receives it."

"You can trust us; we are very dependable," Tovi said sincerely. "I have a seax from the Earl. He gave it to me for saving his daughter from drowning. He said I was someone he would always trust."

"The earl said that, did he? Well then, I must rely upon you," Welan said. He handed the parcel to Tovi and turned to the charcoalers. "I will accept your offer of hospitality whilst my foot heals." Turning back to Winflaed and Tovi, looking at the parcel with great interest, he said, "Hurry up, you two! There must be no delay!"

Wulfhere sat at his workbench, feeling the fading sunshine still warm upon his forehead. The plane in his hand was smoothing down a wooden practice sword he'd been working on for Tovi. He knew that he should not, for it could be seen as 'work', and only the sinful worked on the Lord's holy day. But he cared not, for woodworking was just as much an enjoyment for him as lying in the sun with a horn of good ale and talking nonsense with his friends. Besides, Sunday was often a good day to get done those little jobs that there was never any time to do during the week – and Father Paul would no doubt be too busy dicing and filling himself with ale at the nearest ale-wife's house to notice. *Hardly a fitting example of the Church*, Wulfhere sighed, though he knew he shouldn't complain, and often thanked the Lord for sending them Father Paul, and not some other brimstone and fire clergyman.

Wulfhere's concentration was suddenly disturbed as his little daughter, Gerda, jumped up on his lap. He felt his stomach rumble as Ealdgytha placed some welcome food, oat bread and hard cheese, and a pitcher of ale, before him. Drusilda, now toddling, jealously grabbed at his tunic.

"What is this? Two beautiful nymphs come to kidnap me?" he said with a laugh as his daughters fought for supremacy of their father. He lifted Drusilda up onto the bench beside him while Gerda sat firmly in his lap. "This one isn't about to give up her place to share her father with her little sister, is she?" He smiled and looking up into Ealdgytha's face, he saw with pleasure, she was smiling too.

"Don't you mean *three* beautiful nymphs?" she replied.

"Of course; you are the third, *min lufestre*," Wulfhere replied as she bent down and kissed his forehead.

"I hope that you are scheming of a way to get Freyda away from Edgar's clutches while you're sitting out here," she said. "Who is that for?" she added, meaning the wooden sword.

"For Tovi. He has split his old one in two."

"Tovi? I was hoping he would have no need for a sword. I fancy seeing him in the Church. He is not the fighting kind." She drew up a stool to sit.

"What makes you say that?" asked Wulfhere. None of his family had ever entered the Church, although it was not an uncommon thing to have a least one son or daughter devote their lives to God. It meant that they would be well cared for, educated, and they would not be a burden on the rest of the family. And, they would speak, first-hand to God, for the souls of their parents.

"He is not the warrior kind. 'Tis not in his nature to fight. He could never hold his own."

"And you know what of these things?" Wulfhere remarked with a little irony.

"You only have to look at how he is with his brothers. Remember the incident in the well…"

"That was not his fault. He didn't stand a chance against those two –" He checked himself from referring to the twins as the sons of Loki.

"Perhaps that is so, but if he had been more confident and given them as good as they gave him, they would not have done it to him."

"He shows good potential in practice. He may be of a more temperate nature than the twins but that does not mean he should follow the priesthood."

"Well, I am of the opinion that he would make a good monk or priest. Father Paul has confided that he does well in his reading lessons. He may even rise to become a bishop one day. It would be no bad thing to have a bishop in our family."

"My forefathers were warriors. We have always followed the ways of thegns."

"Well, I think it's time we changed that just a little. There is no great shame in having a son in the Church."

Wulfhere was about to reply that he did not agree, when they were distracted by Tovi and Winflaed running toward them through the long grass with the dogs barking in tow.

"Father!" cried Tovi, breathlessly. He thrust the small linen package onto the table in front of him. "This is for you!"

"What is it?" Ealdgytha asked curiously, staring at the package. Her attention was quickly diverted as she spied their unkempt demeanours. "Look at the two of you! Like as not, you've both been running wild in the forest as usual."

"Father, a man gave us this. He said to give it to you and only you," Tovi said, with a satisfied smile that he had carried out his important task.

"What man is this? And why did he not come himself?" Wulfhere said, suspicion raising an eyebrow.

"He had an accident. He tumbled from his horse in the forest and could not go any further. He is with the charcoal family, recovering," Tovi informed them.

Wulfhere took the package and examined it curiously before breaking the seal and unravelling the linen. The contents inside, took a few moments to register. There were two locks of hair, one black and one gold… and with it was a comb. He knew at once to whom it belonged. Tears pooled in his eyes and his stomach lurched as if he were riding a horse that had just stumbled. As if he were suddenly lost in a dream, a memory forged long ago, transported him to another time and place, where a raven-haired beauty, tears rolling down her cheeks, stood weeping before him. He heard the words he had told her…

"If ever you are in danger, or in need of me, then I will come…"

He could hear her ask as if it was yesterday, *"How will you know?"*

"Send me a lock of your hair," he replied.

As if hit by a bolt of lightning, Wulfhere sprang from his workbench. "Did the man say from whence he had come?"

"He said that the Lady of Waldron had sent him, Father," Tovi replied.

In a moment Wulfhere was gone, running across the yard toward the stables. He was saddling his horse when she burst through the stable door; her face blanched, beads of sweat gathering on her forehead.

Hwitegast was puffing and hoofing the ground with his foreleg in excitement at the prospect of a ride.

Wulfhere's eyes could not meet hers, as he tacked the saddle strap around Hwitegast's girth. He wanted to get away quickly, without hindrance. And he knew that's what Ealdgytha would do; hinder him.

"You're going to *her*, aren't you?" she spat at him venomously, grasping at his arm.

"I'll be back quickly, Ealdgytha," was all he could say. He continued to get Hwitegast ready for the ride.

"Why must you go, Wulfhere?" she cried, bitterly.

"She has need of me."

"And I do not?"

"She has a child, Ealdgytha... *my child*."

Ealdgytha opened her mouth to speak but no words came. Instead she said, "You went once to her before when she needed you... and I lost you." Her voice resonated with misery, and her eyes brimmed with unspent tears.

"I promise that will not happen again. I will see what has to be done, and then I will be back," Wulfhere said, adjusting the stirrups. His words were cold and matter-of-fact.

"It took me many years to forgive you, Wulfhere, and now... I cannot believe that after all this time she beckons – and – and you go running, like a little puppy – and yet, you do not for me!"

"She is in trouble, Ealdgytha. She would not call for me if that were not so." He turned and faced her, holding out his hands, imploring her.

"What trouble can she have, but that of her own making?" Ealdgytha protested.

Wulfhere grabbed the reins and ran his hand along them to grasp them at the right length and hauled himself up, placing his left foot in the stirrup and swinging his right over the saddle. She made a grab for the reins. "If you go to that woman, Wulfhere, it will be the end for us."

He put his hand gently to her flushed cheek. "I have to go, Ealdgytha. I stopped seeing her because you are my wife and it was you that I wanted... but she has my child, and I owe them both. I promised her that I would help her if ever she was in trouble."

"So, you are as you always are, so righteous!" she cried.

"Ealdgytha, please! I will be back as soon as all is well," he said, snatching the reins from her. "Can you not understand?"

"No!" She stood defiantly before him, blocking his way. "I cannot!"

When she realised he was not going to stay, she lifted her head, and moved silently aside to let him pass. She hesitated for a moment, and words seemed to be hanging on the tip of her tongue.

"I will be back, Ealdgytha; you know… I always come back," were his last words to her.

Alfgyva stroked her daughter's forehead. She was becoming weaker by the hour. Every so often, she would call out for her mother, even though she had hardly left her side. Alfgyva wondered whether Welan would make it to Horstede in time. She wondered whether Wulfhere would even be there at all. What if he was away on some official duty, or at court in attendance on the king? She was certain he would come if he received the message. He had promised all those years before that he would, if she had need of him. She realised later, that those were the only words she could trust. Yet, what if his feelings had changed? What if Ealdgytha prevented him? And why had not Welan returned? He had been gone for some time.

Thoughts and questions, what ifs and whys, echoed in her mind until it nearly drove her mad. She did not want to contemplate his not coming, for the thought of seeing him was like a light in the darkness consuming her. Yet this hopefulness filled her with guilt that at a time like this, she could think only how much she longed to see him, and not how much it meant to her dying daughter.

Every so often the little girl would ask in a faint voice, "Mother, is Father coming home now?" Alfgyva would bite back the tears and reply, "He is on his way, precious. He is on his way…" And Rowena's smile would become fainter and fainter each time she asked.

It was late afternoon by the time Wulfhere had reached Alfgyva's homestead. He threw himself from his horse, and called her name as he burst open the door of the porch. Entering the house, he was beset by the smell of sickness. Then he saw her, behind the drawn curtain, a sobbing heap of loose black hair, sprawled over the body of her child, wailing painfully like a wounded animal.

"Alfgyva!"

She rose to greet him, slowly; a movement that seemed painful.

He stood, watching her – frozen with anticipation. He said her name again, softly this time: "Alfgyva."

As he walked towards her, she mumbled; her voice, like a whisper, transported across time. "You are too late." Then louder, "You are too late... too late!"

He continued toward her and she screamed the words at him again followed by a high-pitched howl of pain. "Too late! Always too late!" she cried and beat at his chest with clenched fists.

He let her hammer at him, looking past her at the little bundle on the cot. The realisation that his daughter must have gone, just before he had arrived, hit him like a shield blow to his heart. He managed to push her gently aside, and went to her, the child, who had been no more than a babe the last time he saw her. He gazed at her lifeless face, pale and serene as if in a contented sleep. He kissed her lips, still warm, and stroked her hair.

"I am so sorry!" he sobbed, gathering her in his arms. "I am so sorry…"

"She waited for you," Alfgyva told him, and her bitterness cut through him like a knife.

He looked around at her, and drew a breath, as his gaze took her in. She still looked the same, just a little older. Beautiful, dark, and exotic. A glossy mane of the darkest hair covered her shoulders like charcoal. He remembered how it had felt in his hands and on his body. Alfgyva had been so proud of it, hating to cover it. Her tall, dark gracefulness greatly contrasted with Ealdgytha who was small and golden-haired. They were like a contradiction, these two women, and it was the differences of Alfgyva which had attracted him to her. To Wulfhere, they were like night and day: Ealdgytha was bright, burning sunshine; Alfgyva, mysterious and forbidding, like the night.

"She is beautiful," he said, looking back at his child.

"She was like you. Every day I looked at her, I saw your face in hers."

Wulfhere studied the child again and her words suddenly hit home. *She was gone.* Hair that had once been the colour of ripened corn was now lank, bereft of its wholesome lustre. He thought that it must have once shone like gold, just like his other daughters'. The little face with perfect features, held an expression of peace and contentment in a way that was strangely familiar to him. It was as if he were looking upon a face that he had known for years. Winflaed, that was it… she resembled Winflaed.

"I would have liked to have known her," he said softly, his fingers brushed her hand; so tiny compared to his.

"She knew you very well."

"She did?"

"She kept your comb all these years. Every day she asked to comb her hair with Papa's comb."

He pulled the comb from his pouch, and showed it to her. "I recognised it. You told her about me?"

"She had a right to know that she had a father."

"Did you tell her who I really was, or did you make me into something better than I am?" he asked, full of self-loathing and shame.

"I told her that you were a very important man who was away on king's business."

He smiled. "'Tis almost the truth."

"Which part – the part about being on king's business? Or the 'very important' bit?" she asked, one side of her mouth curled into a cynical smile.

"Perhaps neither after all," he said solemnly.

They were silent for a few moments. Then she spoke. "Will you pray with me, Wulfhere; for her soul?" Alfgyva asked him earnestly.

"I will stay as long as you need me. We must send for the priest. Was she…" he broke off, afraid to ask if the priest had come to see that she was shriven.

"The priest came early this morning," Alfgyva replied, but Wulfhere could not be sure that she did not lie. "But I do not want him to bury her. I want to do that myself. I want to bury her in the ways of my people. She will still go to heaven – and to God."

Wulfhere went to protest but then he thought that perhaps he did not have the right. After all, what harm could it do as long as she had been shriven? There was an ancient old stone cross just outside the homestead where the local priest came to deliver his sermon to the parish; surely that meant that the ground was consecrated. He also knew that Alfgyva had her own ideas about spiritual matters, based on her early childhood, in that strange place that even Alfgyva could not recall where it was she had come from. Perhaps her beliefs are not so unlike his. She was a good person, whatever she believed in, and would not have wanted her daughter to die unblessed.

Later, Alfgyva cleansed her daughter's body so that she would be clean when the angels came to take her. Wulfhere watched emotionally as she kissed her daughter's forehead. Then she led him to a corner of the room where she lit some candles and poured some incense oil into a burner, and they knelt in silent prayer. Both of them prayed in their own way, together, side by side. After some time, Alfgyva stoked the hearth and bade him sit with her in silent vigil together throughout the night, until they both fell asleep on the sheepskins that she had laid out for them on opposite sides of the room.

When morning came, they arose to a sun-filled day, ate a meagre breakfast of dry bread and cheese, and drank weak ale. Then Wulfhere watched as Alfgyva prepared the little girl for her burial, wrapping her in plain linen. All the time she cried silently, barely an audible sob left her lips, only the tears that fell from her eyes gave away her grief.

They buried her underneath an old oak that sat lonely in a nearby meadow. Alfgyva told Wulfhere how Rowena used to play amongst the ancient gnarled roots that splayed out of its trunk, and for a moment, a smile flickered across her tortured face. Wulfhere made a little wooden cross to mark the grave, so she would always know which side of the tree her daughter was buried.

"You are very thoughtful, but I will always know where my daughter lies." She smiled faintly.

Once upon a time, he had sworn her dark eyes could see into his soul, and he wondered if that was still so. If the answer was yes, then they would have seen the deep remorse and sorrow that lay within them; and that he was sorely bereft and aggrieved, to have lost a child, without ever having seen her.

"You should be going now," Alfgyva said as they sat to her table to share the midday meal of leftover bread and cheese.

Outside, the sun burst in through the open windows and door. The smell of death still lay within the house, but Alfgyva burned incense to refresh the air and keep the buzzards at bay. She felt him gazing at her silently, knowing that he saw the distance in her dark eyes as she saw the pain in his.

"My need for you is no more," she said dispassionately. "You are free to go now. Home to your family, and to your wife. Thank you for coming. I shall not have need of you again."

He nodded slowly and stood to his feet. She rose from the table. For a moment, they stared at each other, neither of them moving or saying a word. She felt his gaze explore her face, his eyes wandering over the long straight nose that curved slightly at the nostrils, the fullness of her lips and the high cheekbones. The olive hue of her skin was now pale from grief and her long, black eyelashes, swept down seemingly to avoid his eyes.

"I can't..."

Suddenly, he took hold of her face and kissed her feverishly, his tongue probing inside her mouth, seeking hers, twisting and entwining it in his own. For a moment, she did not resist and returned the kiss with mutual passion. As he moved his head away from her lips to her neck, caressing the smoothness of her skin with lips that were as light and gentle as a feather, she began to tremble with desire for him, but she realised that to give in to him would mean more pain.

"No, stop!" she protested. But he carried on, ignoring her pleas. "Haven't I suffered enough?" she groaned, managing to push him away.

He said her name softly, "Alfgyva," and attempted to pull her back.

She fought him, demanding that he stop. When he did not, she hit him full across the face so hard that he drew back, shocked, and ashamed.

"Do you know how long I waited for you?" she asked with such bitterness in her voice that it shook.

"I am so sorry," he told her, holding her eyes with his own.

"I waited – and I waited. Oh, I know you said that it had to end, but I really thought that you would come back. I thought that you had spoken the truth when you confessed your undying love for me, and that you thought of me above all others. When you said that it broke your heart to leave me, I thought you would not be able to stand it – that you would have to come back... eventually. Now I know that you meant none of it."

"I – I did love you, Alfgyva; in God's name, I did!" He put his arm out to her but she slapped it away.

"Don't touch me, Wulfhere. Your words mean nothing. If you had really loved me, you would not have abandoned us. You would have come back."

"And what of your husband? You sent word that you were to be married – that you no longer required my help."

"Husband? Where?" she laughed caustically. "Do you see him? Do you think he has just gone off hunting for the day and left me to tend to my dying child?"

She saw that he looked at her with a puzzled expression.

"No, Wulfhere. I have no husband."

"But you sent word…"

"He changed his mind, wanted no part of Rowena. It was either Rowena or him and I chose my daughter. Do you really expect me to believe that after all these years you had not heard?"

"I would have taken her to live with me."

Alfgyva's pained expression at once turned to anger. "How dare you! You never wanted her, just as you never wanted me. I was just some whore, a poor slave woman to take advantage of."

"You were never a whore to me, nor were you a slave, and you knew I wanted you… you and the child. If I had not been already wed…"

"She was my daughter, mine! And no man could have taken her from me. Not you or that bastard who thought himself such a great catch that I would give up my own flesh and blood to be his wife. He thought that I should be honoured that he wanted to marry me. Neither of you had anything but what was between your legs to offer me, and yours was even less than his!"

Her words must have stung him, for he slapped her face, hard. As she went down, he grabbed her arms and pulled her up from her knees. Her hair fell across her face as she sobbed desperately.

He was holding her by her arms, a look of horror on his face at what he had done. She saw it, and felt gladdened by the tears that were streaming down his flushed cheeks. She hoped he was in as much torment as she had been when he had left her. She hoped that the pain that burned in his eyes was as deep as that which had plagued her heart.

"Seven years ago, you left me in the most unimaginable loneliness," she began, speaking bitterly through her tears. "Seven years, Wulfhere; as if my love and my devotion to you meant nothing to you – nothing! If it had not been for my daughter, my beautiful flower, I would have died of a broken heart. And now all I have is grief – and despair – at losing the only thing I had in my life that had given it any meaning!" She paused momentarily. He was still holding her arms, crying. "I hate you," she sobbed. "I hate you!"

He pulled her to him. "You could not hate me as much as I hate myself," he cried and sniffed loudly.

"Why didn't you come?" she asked, feeling his heart pound as her head lay against his chest.

"I have… I am here," he said, brushing away her hair so he could whisper words of endearment softly into her ear. He caressed her hair; she felt his tears fall on her neck, and did not object as he held her close.

He sought her lips tenderly and she found herself wanting to respond. Her lips parted welcomingly, and as his tongue sank into the moistness inside her mouth, she felt an old desire stirring within her. As she melted into his arms, her mind whirled with mixed thoughts of the danger and the pleasure that lay ahead. Within seconds, she had yielded to his kiss, and found herself consumed by the need for more of him.

They revelled in the passion that had lain dormant for so many years, and spent the rest of the afternoon entwined in each other's bodies, fingers and tongues caressing and probing, revisiting the secret places that lay within each other and had once known so well. They loved each other in many ways, rekindling the spark that had once burned and any thoughts Wulfhere may have had of Ealdgytha, or his family, were left back in Horstede. For the time being he was in Waldron, with Alfgyva, and with no desire to go home.

Chapter Fourteen

Betrayal

In a daze, Ealdgytha returned to the hall from the stable-yard, having watched Wulfhere ride out of the gates. She felt numb, detached, as though in a dream. She carried on as if nothing had changed, seeing to the preparation of the evening's supper, and ensuring that the children were washed before they attended the evening Mass. But she was not entirely there. Part of her was missing. Somewhere in her mind she had closed a door, locking in the thoughts she did not want to think, and the feelings she could not bear to feel. Evening Mass came and went, and she sat through supper with such a strangeness about her, that none could fail to notice. Then, at hearth time, she sat by the fire, animated; chatting away to Gunnhild about her new pregnancy.

"Where is Wulfhere this eve?" Gunnhild asked her curiously. "It's not like him to miss Mass and supper."

"Why, he is on king's business, of course," Ealdgytha replied. She smiled and focused her attention on one of the village lads who was reciting a tale of bravery and magic.

"Mother, have you forgotten? Father had a package from the Lady of Waldron and has gone there to attend to something," Winflaed reminded her.

Ealdgytha felt jolted, as her daughter's innocent remark thrust her mind back through the swirling torrents of fantasy to the horror of reality. "Sweet Jesus," Ealdgytha whispered and felt an overwhelming feeling of despair that hit her like a blow to the gut. A sob escaped from her throat and she clasped at her stomach.

"Mother?"

Ealdgytha, stood and felt her knees tremble beneath her. She grabbed a table for support as a sharp twinge stabbed at her back. She steadied herself and breathed deeply against the rising pain.

"Ealdgytha, what is wrong? Are you ill?" Gunnhild asked. She was looking at Ealdgytha with concern.

Ealdgytha's features transformed, wincing in agony. Then, to her horror, she felt a trickle of warm fluid run down her legs.

"Ealdgytha, is it the babe?" Gunnhild asked anxiously.

Ealdgytha nodded. A dark red patch appeared on her skirt and she let out an agonised scream.

Winflaed cried, "Mama, what is happening to you?"

"It is your precious father's fault!" Ealdgytha shouted, directing her rancour at the sobbing child. She sank to her knees, clutching her abdomen. She was beside herself and as the words spat from her mouth, it felt as if some angry, vicious spirit possessed her.

Tovi rushed to her side. "Mother, what is wrong?" He attempted to help her to her feet.

"Your beloved father has done this to me!" she screamed, staring at her son with rage. "He has killed me!" She shook his hands from her. Her face was contorted with sheer poison as she clutched at her blood-soaked abdomen.

All around her, the longhall was abuzz with curious murmuring. Esegar and Gunnhild rushed to their mistress' aid and tried to get her to her feet, but every time they tried to move her, she let out a scream of pain. She was like a dead weight in their arms, and around her were the helpless eyes of her community. She threw herself to the ground sobbing as the blood poured from her, repeating over and over that Wulfhere had 'killed her', until Esegar gathered her up and carried her out of the hall.

Tovi stood watching. His confused mind raced as he tried to piece the bits of that day together. He knew it had something to do with the package they had brought him and the woman who had sent it, yet somehow, he felt that he must be to blame. If only he had never given his father that package. He would never forget the look on her face as she shouted, *"Your beloved father has done this to me! He has killed me!"* Her eyes had looked right through his soul and said; *but 'tis you who have caused it.*

*

Wulfhere felt warm, moist lips brush against his and he opened his eyes to the radiance of Alfgyva's smile. He had spent the night in her bed, and they had made love into the night. Later they had fallen exhausted into a deep sleep, and now she had woken him with a kiss and a cup of morning ale.

"Drink this, my love," she whispered. "'Tis time that you must go. Your family will be..." she faltered "...your wife...she will be looking for you."

Wulfhere took the cup in one hand and touched her face with the other. She looked so tempting, her soft naked body swathed by the beauty of her luscious black hair, leaving only the tantalising glimpse of a nipple that he longed to stroke.

"It is as if I have been woken by an angel," he said softly, pulling her to him, ignoring the cup as it spilled its contents over them. She laughed as she fell into his arms and he threw her underneath him, pushing her legs apart with his own. Laughing, she fought him playfully, and he recalled how her laughter was like the sound of water trickling through rocks.

Lost in their lovemaking, Wulfhere did not hear the hinges creak as someone threw open the door and peeled open the curtain that covered the sleeping booth. Nor did he hear the intruder gasp until a young voice, filled with horror, cried out, "Father?"

Wulfhere turned in surprise. He caught sight of a familiar figure; his son, Tovi.

Wulfhere was suddenly filled with dread, as Tovi exclaimed, "Father? What are you doing?" He paused, looked puzzled then, as if realisation had dawned, he cried out, "You bastard! You bastard!"

Feeling his face redden, Wulfhere withdrew from Ælfgyva and rolled onto his back. Tovi growled and picked up an empty wooden jug from a table nearby, threw it at them, and swore as it smashed off the wooden bedframe. The boy stood there, a shadow in the sunlight that poured into the room from the open door. Wulfhere's stomach rolled as he sensed the bewilderment and repugnance that Tovi was feeling.

"Tovi!" His mind raced to find appropriate words, but what could he say? His son had caught him. He was like an animal in a trap.

The boy turned to run from the dwelling, and Wulfhere saw him push past another figure who came in through the doorway to join them. He saw it was Freyda. The girl, too, was as horrified as her brother had been.

Wulfhere reached down the side of the bed and aimlessly groped around on the floor for his clothes.

Freyda threw them at him in disgust. "Are these what you are looking for?" she asked coldly.

Wulfhere shuddered. He was dumbstruck. He had taken the moral high ground with his daughter on many occasions, and now his holier-than-thou posturing and lecturing, seemed nothing but hypocritical. He was completely compromised – and he knew it.

"Freyda, what are you doing here?" He made a half-hearted attempt at sounding indignant, but felt completely ashamed of himself.

"We brought back the lady's horse, though it seems you could have done that yourself. We also came to fetch you, for Mother has taken ill, yet it appears that there is more than one lady in these parts that needs you." She threw Alfgyva, who had been cowering under the blanket beside him, a noxious glare.

"Freyda, it is not –"

"What? Not what I think?" She smiled sardonically. "I am not a little girl, Father. I know what it is to *swive*." She threw back her head scornfully. "But at least I can say it is with one love only." She turned on her heel and went, blown by her own storm of ire. Wulfhere swore, and leapt naked from the bed, calling after her.

Alfgyva grabbed his arm and held him back. "Wulfhere, you cannot go after them like that. At least put your clothes on."

As Wulfhere grabbed his clothes, Freyda's defiant words rang in his ears like the clanging of a great church bell.

"So, you must leave me again," Alfgyva said. Her voice held no malice, but he sensed her bitterness. The softness of her face, which had earlier been etched in grief and resentment, had now returned, and her sorrow had temporarily subsided with him beside her.

"You knew that I could not stay forever," he said, sadly, and held a hand to her cheek.

She nodded and he allowed her to help him do up the belt that held his hose in place. Then, as his head emerged through the neck of his tunic, she brushed his lips softly with her own.

"Will you come back to me?" she asked.

"I cannot say – but I want to. It's just that… I promise – only that I shall try."

"Then that is good enough for me, if that is all I can hope for."

"I do not regret what has gone between us today, just that I wish they had not seen us." He kissed her face before bending down to fasten his shoes.

"What will you say to them?"

"What can I say?" he replied matter-of-factly. "They knew nothing of you, nor Rowena. Perhaps it is time that they learn that there is more than one type of itch a man has to scratch."

"Is that what I am; an itch to be scratched?" Alfgyva asked him, an alluring smile formed upon her lips.

"Alfgyva, I am sorry. I did not mean…" He pulled her to him. "You have always been much more than that. I have always loved you."

"And your wife?" Alfgyva extricated herself from his embrace.

"She is exactly that: my wife, the mother of my children. I have a duty to her and to them."

"And do you love her as you say you love me?"

"Alfgyva, do not ask that of me. I will not lie; there has been enough lying over the years."

"Did she not know about Rowena?"

"Aye, she knows…"

"Then what are these, 'lies'?"

"That hardly a day goes by that I do not think of you and my daughter. That sometimes when I hold Ealdgytha in my arms, it is you that I want. And that if only I had met you first…"

Alfgyva held out her arms to him and kissed his head gently.

"Go now, my love. I will not make demands on you that you cannot keep. You need to be with your son and daughter, and I need to grieve for my child."

"But you will be alone. It is hard for me to bear that you are alone in your grief here."

"I have my tenants. They will comfort me."

He kissed her reluctantly. "I will try to come, but I will not give you false hope. It may be impossible."

"I know."

She watched him ride off on his ghostly white horse in the growing warmth of midday. He only turned once to wave goodbye, but she had gone inside her house. Later, as she sat at her table alone to eat an evening meal, she rubbed her belly and wondered hopefully if he had given her another child. At least if she was pregnant, she would not need to be alone and he would have another bond that this time, perhaps, he would not want to loosen. That night, before going to bed, she prayed at Rowena's grave, and asked the Great Mother to fertilise Wulfhere's seed inside her so that she may grow plump with child once more.

Wulfhere arrived back at Horstede later that day, unsaddled his horse and led him to his booth. Hwitegast gave him a knowing look and a nod of his head as he stroked his nose. "Thanks for the good luck, my friend. I think I'll need it," Wulfhere murmured with a cautious chuckle. He sighed as he closed the stable door. "You are a fool, Wulfhere," he whispered to himself as he stored away Hwitegast's gear.

"My Lord." Wulfhere turned and saw that it was Aelfstan. He was leading a young chestnut stallion. His face, though blackened by the dirt of his trade, was noticeably grave.

Wulfhere nodded to his smith and rubbed the nose of the chestnut. Hygethrymm gave an appreciative whinny. He had not long been broken in and was still quite a spirited animal.

"So he is now shod?" Wulfhere asked Aelfstan, sensing his blacksmith's disapproving gaze. He bent down to lift one of the horse's front hooves and checked it over. He nodded approvingly and raised himself back up. "Don't look at me like that, for God's sake, man," he moaned, seeing the look on Aelfstan's face. "Am I the only man in the world to have slept with a woman that was not his wife?"

Aelfstan moved past him with the chestnut, remarking casually as he led the horse into his stall, "'Tis not for me to judge, Lord. Your business is your business."

"Then why do you give me that – that reproving face?" Wulfhere demanded; a hint of anger in his voice.

"'Tis not *my face* you should be worried about, Lord. Your wife's perhaps..."

Wulfhere and Aelfstan had shared their childhood, growing up in Horstede together. Aelfstan's father, before him, had also plied his craft for Wulfhere's father. There were not many men with whom Wulfhere would allow to speak to him so candidly, but Aelfstan was one.

Hands on his hips, Wulfhere sighed audibly. "Oh, come now, Aelfstan. Dispense with the moral high ground thing. She is not the first woman to – What? What is it?" Wulfhere observed the gravity in Aelfstan's eyes as the stocky smith shook his head. He was suddenly filled with dread. "What's amiss then? Tell me, for Christ's sake, man!"

"The Lady Ealdgytha took to her bed last night, gravely ill. You should go to her... now that you are back," Aelfstan replied, the last with bleak sarcasm.

"Is she so ill that you must look at me with such blame?" he asked, his face growing hot with anxiety.

"She says you have killed her."

Chapter Fifteen

The Itch

Winflaed heaved the bucket out of the well and onto the ground. Trying not to spill its contents, she lugged it back into the hall and placed it by the hearth where Sigfrith poured it into a cauldron that hung from a chain over the flames. She saw her father sitting morosely on a bench in the corner of the hall where he kept all his weapons, the tools of his trade. In one hand was the whetstone he was using to sharpen the blade of his seax, held gently on his knee as he worked on it. Elsewhere around her, the hall was abuzz with activity. Freyda and some of the village girls spun in a corner, giggling at some girlish gossip, whilst the formidable Gunnhild led a team of women, sweeping the hall in preparation for the new rushes to be laid. Tovi, she knew, was out in the fields with the village children, scaring birds away from the newly lain seeds. He seemed to do anything these days to stay away from the hall.

It was mid-morning and the shutters of the high windows were yet to be opened but, nonetheless, light entered the hall through the open doors. The familiar odour of burning wood hung in the air as the living space was filled with smoke.

"Good morning, Papa," Winflaed said, approaching him.

"Morning, *min lyttel Fléogenda*," he answered softly, calling her by his pet name for her, his little bird.

He was wearing his riding-out boots; and his cloak and leather satchel lay on the trestle beside him. He looked as if he was getting ready to go on some journey and a feeling of dread swamped her. He often went away, but for some reason, his going at this time filled her with anxiety. This past week had not been very pleasant since the day that Father had received the mysterious linen-wrapped package and had disappeared for a while. Then Mother had fainted in the hall that same evening, screaming obscenities, like a crazed beast, at everyone. Father had come home from wherever he had been, as distant as if he were a stranger. Tovi had fallen into a mood so black it was as if a cloud of blackness had enveloped him and he refused to speak or play with her. Freyda was wandering about with an ever-increasing air of self-righteousness, and both Father and Mother seemed to want nothing to do with any of them – nor each other. Mother had taken to

218

her bed for days in a deep melancholic state, and the only sense that Winflaed could make of it all was that it was something to do with that package.

She looked at her father with a worried expression. "You are going away again?"

He nodded and smiled at her. "As I always do this time of year."

"Why, Father?"

She gave a little sob and he reached out for her. "Nay, child, don't cry. Why all these tears?"

She went to him and sat on his lap. He cradled her as she sobbed gently. "I am afraid you will not come back," she told him.

"Why, little *Fléogenda*? What makes you think that?" He kissed her forehead.

"I don't know, I just do."

"But you know that your father is a very important man and that he has the king's work to do?"

She nodded but then she threw her arms around his neck and cried, "I don't want you to go."

"I must, but I will be home for the harvest. I always am."

"Where do you go, Papa?" she asked after she had dried her tears. She was no more reassured, but accepted that she could not dissuade him from leaving.

"Well, you see, your father is so good at making horses that he must take them to the king's nephew in a place called Hereford." He shifted her off his lap and picked up his seax from the floor, where it had fallen from his knees. He slid it into its sheath.

"What will the king's nephew do with the horses?" Winflaed asked curiously.

"He is teaching men how to ride and fight on them," replied Wulfhere, bending down to fasten the buckle on his boots.

Winflaed looked thoughtful, imagining what fun it would be to fight on horseback. "Are you going to fight a war again, Papa?"

"I hope not, little *Fléogenda*." he answered, smiling as he stood to his feet.

She followed him out to the stables with an irritated Sigfrith calling after her to fetch more water.

"Aren't you going to say good bye to Mother?" she asked as she hurried alongside him.

Wulfhere turned; a sheepish look on his face. "Mother and I have said our farewell, daughter." She did not know that he was lying.

Esegar and Aelfstan were waiting for him by the stables. Four horses had been made ready to journey; two of them were the stud horses he had sold to Ralph for his new mounted army, and the other two were to be the journey horses for the way back.

The two stallions had been bred from Hwitegast and a mare that Father had once purchased from a Norman horse merchant, Seaxa. "You are going to give Earl Ralph those two?" Winflaed asked, sad to see the beautiful creatures leave her father's stud.

"Not give, my little *Fléogenda*, but sell," Wulfhere replied.

"Why?"

"The earl wants them to make more steeds of the type that are used for warfare on the Continent. Besides, that is how I make my fortune."

"What's the Continent, and what is so special about these horses? Will they get killed in battle, Father?" Winflaed looked at her father with worried eyes.

"They have Barb and Arabian blood in them, so I am had told. I was never sure whether, or not, to trust those horse merchants, but judging by the distinctive curve in Hwitegast and Seaxa's necks, and their greater height than our native breeds, this was one horse merchant that was, perhaps, honest." He led her to the horses and pointed out their attributes to her. "See their powerful front legs? Those legs and their stamina enable them to gallop at great speed; and their wide girth gives them strength to carry men with their heavy armour."

"But what if they get hurt?"

"Do not worry your pretty head, daughter, they will be safe."

She watched her father greet his fyrdsman with a nod. Aelfstan was helping Esegar saddle and gear up the two riderless horses.

Wulfhere checked the horses over and made sure that they were properly saddled and bridled. He checked all their hooves, ensuring that they were properly shod for the long journey on which they were about to embark. As he ran his fingers over the copper shoe rims, checking that the six nails hammered into the insensitive part of the hoof were correctly placed, Winflaed's hovered near him, observing closely what he was doing.

"What do you think, *Fléogenda*?" he asked.

"Perfect," Winflaed replied. "Are you going now, Father?"

He stood up and patted her head. "Aye, but do not fret. Esegar and I will be home soon."

"I wish I could come with you," she whispered, sadly.

He bent down to embrace her. "I need you here to look after your mother."

She nodded. "I will look after her. *Faran þe wel*, Father. Goodbye."

A tear descended from her eye. She nodded and he gave her another squeeze before mounting Hwitegast as Aelfstan steadied him. Once Esegar was ready, they ambled to the gatehouse, each of them leading one of Ralph's stallions. It was going to be a long and arduous journey, but one that he must make if he was to collect the fees for the horses. Being an accomplished horseman, Wulfhere had been commissioned by Edward to assist Earl Ralph as one of his mounted soldiers. Ralph had been counteracting the yearly raiding parties that came from across the great earthen dyke in the country of the Wéalas. He and his Norman friends had been building timber motte and bailey castles along the border marches. For some time now, the earl had been endeavouring to augment his Norman defences with a successful mounted army that would see off the raiders once and for all. For Wulfhere, this style of warfare would be a challenge. Fighting on horses was not unknown amongst the Englisc, but it was not often used as a discipline for the fyrd as a whole. Only the elite owned horses, and some thegns were not used to fighting in any other way than on foot. Wulfhere was looking forward to the change, and felt enthused by the prospect of fighting as part of a mounted force.

Winflaed ran ahead of them to help Yrmenlaf open the gates for them. As they passed through them, Wulfhere turned in the saddle and gave them a wave. There was no farewell party to see him off. He didn't blame them. Since his return from Waldron, his guilt had weighed on him heavily. It was irresponsible of him to have behaved so faithlessly, but what could he do? He'd had to act on the promise that he'd made to Alfgyva all those years ago, but in acting nobly, he had dishonoured his wife, and himself. Now he was plagued with sleepless nights spent shut out of their bedchamber. And the loss of their child, not yet fully formed in her womb, had been a double blow to exacerbate his guilt, forcing him to take the blame for causing the heartache that had induced Ealdgytha's miscarriage.

When the gates closed behind them, he resolved not to think any more about what he had done. At least for a while. He needed to give his conscience a rest. As he rode with Esegar along the track that journeyed northwards, Wulfhere steered his mind to the events ahead of him. He engaged Esegar in conversation about Ralph's mounted riders, and they discussed the possible tactics that the earl might use.

They came to a fork in the road that Wulfhere knew would take him to Waldron. As they rode past the leafy track, an image of Alfgyva invaded his mind; uninvited.

"Wait!" Wulfhere said, suddenly halting. "There is something I need to do first."

"No, lord, don't go," Esegar protested.

"I have to, Esegar. Take the horses and go on without me. I promise I will catch up with you before the sun sets."

He threw the reins at Esegar and wheeled his horse around.

"But, lord," called Esegar after him.

"I have to."

Wulfhere ignored Esegar's cries and clipped Hwitegast's flanks with his heels. He took the left fork in the road and spurred the horse into a canter, then a gallop, so that he would no longer hear Esegar's frantic calls. He did not want to be deterred from his mission. He had to see her again before he went. He knew he was being reckless, but he did not care. All that he could think of at that moment was the need for the relief that only Alfgyva could provide.

Alfgyva pulled opened the door of her house and gave the cat a gentle tap to its back legs to encourage it to go out into the yard. "Go on, puss," she said softly. "Off you go about your business."

She was distracted by the sound of trotting and the rustling of tree branches. She peered out of the doorway and then she saw him emerging from the darkness into the clearing that was her yard.

"Wulfhere!" she cried, overwhelmed with joy at seeing him.

He slid from his saddle and hurried to her open arms.

"How long do you have?" she dared herself to ask.

"Not long, for I must go away," he said. "Ah, but I have missed you so much."

Wulfhere pinned her to him and for a minute or two they embraced before she pulled away from him and led him inside. She was elated to have him back; even if it was but for only a short while, it would be worth it. She led him to her bed and they lay down together. They made love, tenderly and passionately, and for now he was hers... and they could forget the world around them, forget that he belonged to another woman... For now, there was just the two of them… and the child that would blossom inside her.

Chapter Sixteen

The Outlaw and the King

Rhuddlan, June 1055

The young girl lay back against the wooden strakes of the floating vessel, her tired eyes considering the evening sky. The vast expanse was ablaze with the flames of a dying sun; an elaborate weaving of red and gold glory, against a deep blue background. *How beautiful it looks,* she thought, as the boat glided gently up the river carrying her and her family along the lush, green marshy banks of yet another alien valley. Beautiful, yet cold and harsh, it left her with a sense of foreboding. Behind her, at the helm, sat her father, silent and morose, heading for a place she knew not, nor for what purpose. Resting in her lap were the little heads of her younger brothers Edwin and Morcar, one dark and one fair, and in front of her, rowing tirelessly with a handful of her father's household men, was her elder brother, strong dependable, Burghred.

Aldith shivered involuntarily as she felt the cool misty air envelop her, and she instinctively drew her cloak closer to her. She was only twelve years old and had known only contentment and security in her short life until a few months ago, when her father had returned home from court in a mighty rage that burned with a fury that was, even for him, the hottest anyone had seen before. There had been no time to lose as they were told to pack their belongings without delay. They sailed to Iralond where they had lived nomadically, journeying from settlement to settlement of any Norse colonists that would welcome their father's gold.

It had been futile for Aldith to ask questions, for no one had time for the inquisitiveness of a young girl. Even her older brother, Burghred, always ready with a smile and a kind word for her, answered her queries with grim ambiguity. There had been a lot of meetings between her father and the Irish-Norse, and a lot more of travelling to more places for more meetings. Aldith had not liked the company of these coarse, hairy giants who spat and swore like demonic heathens, and were disgracefully drunk every night. They would eye her lasciviously, leer at her and say disgusting things, she imagined, in their own tongues... and no one seemed to care, they were more concerned with their meetings and talking.

One day, she and her little brothers, who were just seven and eight, had been herded onto a vessel again. This time they were accompanied by a flotilla of seventeen ships, filled with at least a thousand or so of these vulgar *Norþmenn*, in total. They sailed across the sea again and Aldith had hoped that they were returning home to Englalond, but the place that they came to was unfamiliar. They left the fleet and its crews in the harbour where the mouth of the river met the sea; and she and her little brothers began their lonely journey into this new unknown territory. She had no idea why her life had changed so much, and it was with great sadness and uncertainty, that she again found herself ferried up another river, dreaming of her home and those that she had been forced to leave behind: her horse, her puppy, and the warm comforting smile of her nursemaid.

"Here it is, Rhuddlan, home to King Gruffudd of Gwynedd," she heard the gruff voice of her father's captain, Ragnald, informing them, as they manoeuvred through Gruffudd's own splendid fleet of ships to dock the boat at the wharf. Ragnald helped her father alight from the craft, and when the rest of the crew had jumped ashore, Burghred lifted her and her brothers to stand with him and Alfgar as they surveyed the Wéalisc leader's fortress in the darkness. The towers blazed with torches making an impressive sight. It was as large a structure as it well might have been for the stronghold of a king. There was a high palisade fence around a deep ditch with a rampart and towers at each corner. Around the palisade were the peasants' huts, and lying adjacent was a little church built of stone. As a party of men rode out from the tower gate on horseback to greet them, Aldith surveyed this strange place and wondered what fortune lay beyond those high walls.

Aldith and her little brothers were cold and weary as they followed their father and older brother into Rhuddlan's vast enclosure. The warmth of the summer months had yet to come to this northern outpost of the country that was known to the Englisc as the land of the Wéalas. For the past few months, rain had fallen like the tears of a thousand angels, and the green of the surrounding hilltops glistened like undulating rows of emeralds. Aldith gave a small sigh of appreciation as they were ushered into the noisy Great Hall, crowded with the clamour of people enjoying the gaiety of the atmosphere. Those who could not find places at the tables either stood or sat on the floor without a care, blithely partaking in the evening supper. Gruffudd's court musicians played amongst the crowded dining area, and in the middle of the hall, the hearth smouldered from a lower floor level below, sending fronds of smoke up through the rafters. Over it was the biggest cauldron pot that Aldith had ever seen, the contents of which were bubbling fiercely. A tasty aroma suffused the air and her nostrils were tantalised. At one end of the hall, people were sitting high on a raised dais and appeared to be watching them as they moved into the hall.

Her stomach rumbled hungrily as a stocky, young man left the dais and approached her father with an agreeable face.

"I am Rhys the Saes," the man said in perfect Englisc, and gave a quick bow of the head and smiled.

Alfgar cocked his head at him. "The *Saes*?" he replied, curiously.

Rhys nodded, still smiling pleasantly. "Aye, my mother's family come from the western scīra and I was raised in my uncle's household in Hereford. Now I am back amongst my father's people in the service of my lord of Gwynedd, King Gruffudd ap Llywellyn."

Aldith stood behind them, her tired legs aching. As the pleasant-faced interpreter conversed with her father, she looked up to stare at the people on the dais. She had no idea who any of them were, but was aware of their importance, for she knew enough to know that only people of high status would sit at such a lavish table.

Her youngest brother, Morcar, who, like his brother, Edwin, was holding Aldith's hand, had begun to whimper and complain. Aldith tried to quieten him, but he was not interested in being compliant. He was hungry and tired, and was not able to contain his distress any longer. He began to wail loudly; their father looked around at them with a scornful glare, clearly furious at the distraction.

"See, you have made your papa angry," Aldith whispered harshly to her brother.

"I want to go home," whimpered Morcar, tugging on her hand.

She put her fingers to her lips and hunkered down to his level. "Ssh! You see that man up there on the dais? He is the king and will cut out your tongue if you don't stop crying."

It had the desired effect. Morcar bit his lip and cried quietly.

Aldith turned her attention to the dais again. A woman caught her with a sympathetic eye and Aldith saw her whisper to the man next to her. She noticed, with interest, that the noble Wéalisc lady wore no wimple to cover her hair like Englisc women. Her long, dark red braids were intertwined with delicate strips of fine silk and the crown of her head was covered by a short, simple, silk veil; the whole arrangement held in place by a gold circlet. Aldith next studied the man seated next to the lady. She presumed that he was the king, for he too was wearing a gold circlet. He had strong features with dark receding hair that was clipped closely to his head. He leaned toward the woman as she spoke to him and then appeared to pat her arm indulgently.

"My lord Alfgar, you and your retinue may approach the dais," he called out to them in thickly accented English.

Her father was in the middle of explaining to Gruffudd's interpreter the purpose of their visit, when the Wéalisc lord spoke. Immediately the conversation stopped, and Alfgar made his way through the people to the foot of the dais. He turned and nodded to his children to follow. Aldith and her elder brother came, dragging the little ones with them. Morcar began to cry again, and Edwin with him.

"He is going to cut out my tongue," wailed Edwin.

"Hush, be still," urged Aldith. She turned to her elder brother and touched his arm saying, "Who are these people?"

"He is Gruffudd, ruler of Gwynedd. The lady is his sister," Burghred informed her.

"My lord of Gwynedd," Alfgar said with a bow. He indicated to the rest of his family to follow suit, also giving the boys a look that bade them cease their snivelling or all would not be well with them.

"I am the lord of *all* the Wéalas," Gruffudd corrected indignantly.

"My lord, forgive me for I beg to differ," Alfgar began, and Aldith bit her lip at her father's outspokenness, and was mildly confused as to why the king needed an interpreter when he could speak Englisc himself. "Strictly speaking that is not true, for your rival Gruffudd ap Rhydderch of the Deheubarth in the south, still lives, and as I understand it, is an obstacle to your ambitions of supremacy."

If Gruffudd felt any anger at her father's boldness, Aldith thought he hid it well. The king smirked as if amused. "Very astute of you, Mercian," was his reply. "It seems we may have much in common, for I hear you also have enemies of your own that are keeping you out in the cold."

Aldith fought to stay alert despite her fatigue. Her father had enemies? Was this why they had left in such a hurry to get away? She suddenly felt very anxious, for their words spelt doom and intimated that she might never see her home again.

"So, what brings you to my court?" continued Gruffudd. "It must be something of great importance for a Mercian to visit the stronghold of an ancient enemy."

"I think we may be of some assistance to each other. We have, after all, a common need." Aldith sensed that her father spoke through gritted teeth. It was not in his nature to grovel, and she was not fooled by his fake, courteous manner.

"What can you offer me, that I should help *you* in return, Mercian?" Gruffudd replied tersely. He looked as if he were enjoying having the Englisc man grovel at his feet. "'Tis not the first time that a *Saeson* prince has washed up on my shores like a bad penny, begging for an alliance. Remember that ill-begotten bastard, Swegn ap Godwin? He was another rogue, always at odds with the Englisc court. I helped him for a while, but it came to nought. He is dead now."

Alfgar nodded. "I lose no sleep over the death of a Godwin. Nor do I beg for alliances, Lord Gruffudd."

"Then what do you do here, Mercian, if not to seek refuge in my fortress?"

"I come to offer my assistance. I have eighteen ships full of *Norþmenn*, from Dyfflin and the coast of Iralond, waiting in the harbour. You help me get my lands back, and justice against those who have cheated me, and in return, I help you get rid of Rhydderch, and the Deheubarth will be yours."

Gruffudd was pensive. The lady leaned toward him and spoke to her brother in their own tongue. He smiled at her and patted her arm again, reassuringly. Aldith saw the woman smiling at her warmly.

"My dear sister, the Lady Angharad requests that she be able to offer your children some rest and supper in her private apartments," Gruffudd said with a smile for his sister. "She is concerned that the little ones are in need of a soft bed and a woman's tenderness. She sees that they bring no mother with them."

"Your good lady sister is very kind and observant. My children do indeed have need of a woman's tenderness, for their own mother passed away some years ago, and they had to leave behind their nurse in our lands in East Anglia. My daughter, Aldith, has been like a mother to her brothers ever since."

Gruffudd nodded, and his sister left her place at the table coming to collect the children with a couple of male servants, who took the two sleepy boys into their arms and carried them off. She took Aldith kindly by her hand, smiling at her in a reassuring manner. Aldith felt her fear melt as she allowed herself to be led away by the lady with the beautiful hair. She saw that she had a mature, but benevolent, face. Aldith felt safe at last.

"Now, my lord Alfgar," Aldith heard Gruffudd say as they were leaving. "Let us get down to business."

Aldith was shaken awake; as she looked up sleepily into the face of a maidservant, lit by the candle she was holding, prattling away in a language Aldith did not understand. Aldith tried to focus, remembering that she had been taken to the Lady Angharad's apartments, given some food and a soft pallet to rest on. She had felt relieved to lay her head on the pillow. Now she was groaning at having her slumber disturbed.

The woman, upon seeing that Aldith was confused, gesticulated for her to get out of her bed and as Aldith did so, she grabbed the girl's hand and roughly pulled her out of the curtained area in which Aldith had been sleeping. She looked about the chamber for the Lady Angharad, but she was nowhere to be seen. The maid servant spoke to her in the Wéalisc tongue again, as if she was supposed to understand. She didn't seem to be bothered whether Aldith could comprehend or not. Without waiting for an answer, she grabbed Aldith's arm and led her to the door.

Cold, damp air filled the illuminated courtyard, and the torches ensconced around the inner palisade flickered in the night wind. Aldith was led, almost dragged, hastily across the yard to Gruffudd's chambers. The maid led her up an outside wooden staircase and a door was flung open. She felt herself pushed through the doorway and into a sparsely furnished room. An iron latticed charcoal brazier burned in a corner, warming the darkened room with a reddish glow. Her father and brother were sitting at a wooden trestle with Gruffudd and Llyward, his *ynad*, or *seneschal*, as some might refer to him, and Rhys the Saes. On the table, there was an empty jug of honey-sweetened mead to share between them. They all appeared to be a little intoxicated; the rosy glow on their cheeks had not only come from the heat of the brazier. In the corner of the chamber, Gruffudd's younger brothers, Bleddyn and Rhiwallon, sat quietly, looking somewhat bored. The maid ushered Aldith further into the room, and she stood trembling and confused before them. Her father and brother were obviously having another 'meeting', but what her part in it was to be, she had no idea. What did they want with her? And what could be so important that they had to drag her from her much-needed slumber?

"So here is the little lass you would have me take as my wife," Gruffudd said.

She felt the drowsiness leave her and observed this formidable Wéalas king. She liked the lightness in his voice, the gentility of which belied his harsh, cold demeanour.

Gruffudd looked at her with interest and smiled. She blushed as he looked her up and down, stroking his chin. He turned to Llyward and said something in Wéalisc and they both laughed. Aldith thought it exceedingly rude, seeing that neither she nor her father spoke their language. Her father joined them with a grin, and Aldith imagined it was only to ingratiate himself with the king, and not because he was sharing their camaraderie.

Aldith glanced at Burghred, and was alarmed to see the contempt plainly written on his face. It occurred to her that her brother was not very comfortable at being in their company, though she was uncertain why.

"Come here, daughter, and let lord Gruffudd get a closer look at you," Alfgar said encouragingly.

Aldith stepped forward timidly. Alfgar grasped her arm clumsily and drew her closer to them. She looked downwards to conceal the terror in her eyes. She was tired, tearful, and bewildered, hardly knowing what to make of it all, but she knew she would be beaten if she cried, and so she held back the tears. Holding a candle up to her face, Gruffudd lifted her chin and held it level with his. Aldith noticed that he was not an unpleasant looking man. He looked much younger than his forty-four years; but his cold eyes made her shiver inwardly as they probed her; as if she was an inanimate object worthy of inspection.

He was gazing at her youthful features, the smoothness of her skin and her high cheekbones that gave symmetry to her face. Her soft brown eyes resembled those of a sad puppy, and her lips were dark and pleasantly shaped. He pushed the cap back off her head, grabbed hold of her braid and held it to the candlelight to check its colour, seeing that it was brown like her eyes, but tinged with coppery-red strands. All the time he was examining her, Aldith felt painfully discomforted and sensed that Burghred did too. Then Gruffudd put his hands to her small budding breasts and cupped them momentarily. She gasped in disbelief at the intrusion. Burghred shifted in his seat. He looked anxious, but her father put a warning arm across his stomach to keep him in check should he wish to object.

"She is pretty enough," Gruffudd said in his strongly accented Englisc. He looked at Llyward and spoke again in Wéalisc. His seneschal shrugged and replied in the same tongue.

"How old are you, lass?" Gruffudd asked.

Surprised at being directly spoken to, Aldith replied, "I am in my twelfth year, sir."

Gruffudd looked at his seneschal and they conversed again in their own tongue; then he looked back at Aldith and spoke to her again.

"What would you say if you were to become my wife, little one… when you are grown a year or so more?"

Aldith was startled. She looked at Alfgar who nodded his approval, then glanced at Burghred who was looking away in revulsion. She did not like her brother's discomfort, but knew it was her father that she should worry about.

"If my father does wish it," she replied, bowing her head. She began to feel anxious beads of sweat break out across her forehead.

"He does, do you not, my lord Alfgar." Gruffudd smiled, handsomely. Aldith felt his eyes boring, dark and penetrating, into her soul.

"Indeed. A marriage tie between our people would be most beneficial and definitely to my liking. I would be proud to be the father of the Queen of *Cymru*. Imagine, daughter, you will be a queen and wear a crown."

"Queen, sir?" Aldith asked wondrously.

"Aye, it will not be long before I am king of all the *Cymru*. And you, my pretty, will indeed rule with me."

Aldith gasped.

"What say you then, daughter?" Alfgar demanded in his gruff manner.

She looked bewildered, too stunned to speak. The idea that she would be a queen both thrilled and frightened her.

"I fear she is too overwhelmed with joy to speak." Alfgar laughed, and patted her backside.

"A mixing of *Cymry* and Saeson blood would be a challenge to my subjects, but it is a contract I am willing to accept, and, if I am satisfied, then so will my people be. But before your daughter can become a queen, we must attend to the business of ensuring that I am king of all *Cymru*... which means ridding ourselves of a certain lord of the South."

"And in return you will help me sort out my business with the King of Englalond... and his insufferable cronies, those avaricious Godwinsons and his lapdog, de Mantes."

Aldith raised her head apprehensively and saw that they were all smiling, except for her brother Burghred, who was looking decidedly unnerved at the arrangement. Her father patted her backside again, and signalled that the maid could now return his daughter to her bed. Aldith allowed the maid to take her hand once more, relieved that their need to poke and prod her was fulfilled. As she was hurried out of the door, she gave a backward glance at her brother who caught her eye with a look of sadness; changed swiftly to a smile and a wink for her. Then the man, Rhys the Saes, also smiled at her, and she felt comforted by both.

With Aldith gone, the men carried on with their bargaining, discussing plans to attack the castles of Ralph de Mantes, bordering the lands of Herefordscīr, and those of the Wéalas. Gruffudd insisted that, firstly, his Englisc ally and Alfgar's army of Irish-Norse fighters, assist him in the removal of his rival, Gruffudd ap Rhydderch, King of the Deheubarth, in the south, ensuring his ascendancy to the overlordship of what, to the Wéalas, was called the Cymru.

Although Alfgar, was eager to attack Hereford first and as soon as possible, frustratingly for him, Gruffudd had a different strategy. He knew, from experience, that waiting until late autumn meant they could attack Hereford when the fyrd was disbanded. This meant that they could retreat, unhindered, with booty, and quickly if need be, back into the mountains of *Eryri*, before the snows came in time to act as a natural defence blockade from any Englisc army.

"My men will not wish to tarry too long here, for they will want to return to their homes and families, in time for the winter months," Alfgar told Gruffudd, irritably.

Gruffudd shook his head. "Trust me, Lord Alfgar, experience has taught me over the years that the mountains which surround us, offer us the best fortress we could have; all the better when the snows of winter come."

"I don't intend to be retreating after we fight de Mantes," Alfgar said defiantly. "When we meet Edward's army, I shall not be running back over the mountains to hide, my friend. We meet them head-on and I will take back what is mine – or die!"

Gruffudd chuckled and sneered at Alfgar. "Lord Alfgar, it is as well that your lack of military judgement is not a shortcoming of mine." Suddenly he leaned forward, thrusting his face close to the Mercian. "Sacking Hereford will be like taking food from a baby. Ralph's horsemen will fall easily before our armies, but Edward's forces, led by this Godwin earl, will not. If you think that I would risk all by going into battle against the whole of Wessex, then think again."

"Then what use is any of this? What use are you to me if you will not fight now?" Alfgar demanded sourly.

Gruffudd sat back in his chair and breathed deeply. The Englisc man was beginning to annoy him. When he had been young, his sister, Angharad, had plagued him for his irritating lassitude. One day, when she had thrown him out of the home for lying abed for too long, he stood outside the kitchen wondering what to do next, when he heard a maidservant complaining about a piece of beef that would not stay at the bottom of the boiling pan. It kept rising to the top, and no matter how many times she pushed it back down, back up it came. It was then that he made his mind up to never be pushed down again, and back he went into the house. From that day on, he was never indolent again, nor would he do any man or woman's bidding again. If Alfgar did not like to take orders from him, then so be it. He was no one's hireling, certainly not this uncouth Saes.

"If you want my help, then we do it my way," Gruffudd said matter-of-factly. "If not then you are free to go."

Alfgar stroked his beard. "I want my lands back."

"Good." Gruffudd nodded. "I, too, desire my lands back, the lost lands, *y Lloegyr*, as we call them in Cymru. The lands that my ancestors were forced to relinquish to you Saeson. Many of my fellow *Cymry* have tried to claw back the lost territories, but none have made any real difference. I, Gruffudd ap Llywellyn, a Prince of House Mathrafal, will be the one who will. So, you see, we have much in common with each other."

Alfgar nodded his head slowly. "Then you will fight with me?"

"If you will fight with me?" Gruffudd grinned.

"We go south first?" Alfgar asked and Gruffudd nodded. "And then we go to Hereford?"

"We go to the Deheubarth and rid us of ap Rhydderch, then to Hereford, in the autumn, ravage and burn the strongholds of de Mantes. We show them what will happen if they do not treat with us. We goad the king and Godwinson into a peace treaty. I get my lands, so do you."

Silence sat between them whilst Alfgar perused what Gruffudd had put to him. In a few moments, the Wéalas king said, "Do we have a bargain then, Mercian?" He leant forward and offered Alfgar his hand.

Alfgar took Gruffudd's hand and said heartily, "Aye, we do!" And they sealed their deal with a handshake.

"You are at a loss for words," Burghred heard his father say, as he lowered himself down onto his sleeping pallet and began removing his clothing for bed. "Are you not pleased with the plans we have made?"

Burghred tightened his lips and removed his boots and leather hose. Alfgar was watching him bemusedly, as he kicked a boot across the room in a surly manner. Underneath his earlier composure, he was seething with anger at the path his father had made for them. He was loyal to his father, always had been. Throughout his life, he had endured being part of his father's petty squabbles, and off times the butt of his anger, sometimes with patience and sometimes without, but this quarrel had far-reaching consequences. His life, and that of his siblings, was never going to be the same.

"Speak to me, for God's sake, lad. I cannot stand your brooding." Alfgar said, with irritation.

"And what plans might those be, Father? The plan to murder the King of Deheubarth? Or, the plan to ruin de Mantes and devastate Hereford? Or, is it the one in which we parade my sister, like a slave at the market, to marry her to a foreigner more than four times her age; a man who has the audacity to prod her like a prize cow without so much as a —"

"Good God, lad!" Alfgar exclaimed. "We have just allied ourselves with a king!" He poured himself the remains of the mead from the jug and sat on his mattress. "What ails you? I cannot understand what your objections are. Your sister is to be a queen. Do you think we should worry about a bit of prodding? Think of how powerful that will make us. I should never have left you with your grandmother. She taught you to be soft."

"Does it not matter to you that, whilst that bastard touches your daughter like an old letch, you sit by and watch him? Aldith is barely out of childhood, for Christ's sake." Burghred fumed. "How do you think it felt for her to be pawed at by that disgusting piece of *scite*?"

"Pah! You are soft like an old woman's tits. What does it matter what she felt? She will get a crown out of it soon enough. Besides, I married her mother when she was of the same age. Aldith is far from being a child anymore."

"Have you forgotten who this man is?" Burghred asked, angrily. "This is the man who killed your uncle."

Alfgar shrugged nonchalantly. A battle between Mercian and Gruffudd's forces had taken place fifteen years ago, when his father's brother had lost his life. "Things have changed much since then, son. Men get killed all the time. You make enemies; then you make allies, sometimes with the very men you were enemies with the year before. They may have raped your women and buggered your children, but you still do it if there is a means to an end. When all is said, and done, it is all the same, as long as you are on the winning side."

Burghred shook his head as his father blew out the candles.

"In the end, it is all the same…" Alfgar repeated, yawning as he lay back on the pallet, wrapping his cloak round him snugly.

Burghred listened to him fall into a deep sleep, and lay there wondering what on earth was going to happen next. The situation saddened him and he wished he had not followed his father into exile. He should have stayed with his grandfather. As a boy, he had worshipped Alfgar. He was not an affectionate man, rarely giving praise when it was deserved, but, nonetheless, Burghred had conjured up the image of Alfgar as a great warrior, courageous, wise, and just. As he grew older, he saw the real Alfgar, a man full of spite and ire. Despite the reality, Burghred remained steadfast in his loyalty.

Back in March, when his father had stepped right into a plot to oust him, he found those amongst his men who'd betrayed him for a bag of silver, and slit their throats as they counted their money. Burghred knew that his father would not let any man cross him and get away with it. Ralph de Mantes and his own nephew, William Malet, were now on his revenge list, and, so too, Tostig Godwinson. Retribution had been all that he'd talked about from the plains of East Anglia to the wilds of Iralond.

Burghred had tried to encourage his father to return and ask for the king's pardon, but Alfgar was having none of it. He would get his lands back, he told his worried son, but on his terms only, and in doing so, he planned to rout the Godwins and turn the tide of fortune back firmly in his direction. When Burghred had questioned the reality of doing so, he had replied gruffly that, if he did not attempt it, there would be no opportunities for Burghred and his brothers, nor anyone else for that matter, because the Godwins would have everything.

Listening to his father's mead-induced snoring, Burghred lay there with these thoughts, and images of home, revolving around in his head. He wondered if he would ever be able to visit his grandfather's longhall ever again, or hear Englisc spoken with the dialect of the Midlands. He thought of his little brothers having to be dragged off wherever and whenever his father saw fit, perhaps being held as hostage should the king's supporters ever catch up with them. He thought fondly of his gentle little sister, left behind with strangers who spoke a foreign tongue, and sharing the bed of a man much older than herself. He imagined he would be declared by the *Witan*, an outlaw, a man without status, lands or integrity, and a tear rolled down his cheek.

If only he could send word to his grandfather, explain the situation, and beg him to petition Edward to pardon him. But it was impossible. If he left of his own accord, he would never make it out of the Wéalas lands alive, and if he did, he would probably be taken by his father's enemies. It was too late now. Burghred had thrown his lot in with his father. The blood bond was too strong to break, and he would have to remain loyally at his father's side, no matter the right or wrong of it, or whether his exile was justified or not.

He wiped away the tear and stifled a sob, closed his eyes, and welcomed sleep. Tomorrow would be another day in exile, but for now, he could rest and dream of what his heart ached for… home.

Chapter Seventeen

The Wolf Banner

Horstede, August1055

Freyda skipped along with the other village youngsters who were following the last cartload of grain. It trundled slowly along the tree-lined cartways that ran alongside the plough-fields and back up to the village. Their voices rang out in song, reminding everyone of the enjoyable prospects of imbibing, feasting, and general merrymaking, due to come later that evening in their thegn's hall. It was the last day of *Haerfest* and the celebrations would, at long last, culminate with prayers said over the very last sheaf of corn. Then it would be left in the field to preside over the fertility of the ground for next year's ploughing. It was believed that if it was to be cut down with the other clusters, the *Hærfest ælfen*, the little spirit who dwelt within it, would bring bad luck in the future and wrought famine upon the village.

It was a pleasantly mild, breezy afternoon. White puffs of cloud dotted the light blue sky against the warm, hazy sunshine. Freyda smiled to herself as some of the girls chatted amongst themselves about which lad they hoped to dance with that evening. She thought of Edgar, and hoped that she would be more than dancing with him. She gave a little chuckle and a sensation of pleasure coursed through her body at the thought of him touching her. It was not always easy to find time to meet with him under the watchful eyes of her mother and Gunnhild. Sometimes she would bribe her brother, Tovi, and he would send word to Edgar to meet her in the forest. With the promise of some reward, Tovi would create a diversion, and she would steal out of the homestead through a broken panel in the fencing. Sometimes, Edgar would sneak in through the fence, and they would hide in the weaving shed. Occasionally, he would use the conventional method of entering through the gatehouse, bringing baskets of various foodstuffs or gifts for her mother, and successfully gaining access by appealing to Ealdgytha's softer nature.

"So, my love, here I find you." Freyda felt a masculine arm around her and her heart leapt when she saw that it was Edgar. He was limping adeptly beside her, a roguish smile lighting up his face. She loved the way his dark-grey eyes danced and twinkled when he laughed.

"Edgar, what are you doing here? Shouldn't you be helping your father?"

"Are you not pleased to see me? I have come to share the harvest feast with my soon to be father-in-law," he replied with a mischievous look in his eyes. "And my love, of course."

"But what about Helghi? Will he not be looking for you?"

"By now he will be so full of mead, he won't even realise that I'm not there. Besides, he cares not. He prefers my brother, Eadnoth, to me. He is not a cripple."

"Nor you, Edgar. You are not a cripple, either." She stopped and kissed his cheek.

"I do limp, though," he said matter-of-factly.

"Aye, but you are very good at it!"

They both laughed and held hands, swinging them as they went.

"How did you know where to find me?" she asked.

"I went to your father's hall and he scowled when he saw me, but Sigfrith told me you had gone to help in the fields."

"I came to get away from the misery within our household. My father and mother are not on speaking terms at the moment; nothing unusual there. Well, Father tries his best to speak to Mother, but she will not have any of him. And so she shouldn't after what he has done."

Edgar nodded. He had heard of Wulfhere's recent misdemeanour through Freyda. "My father constantly beds other women. Sometimes against their wishes... in fact, mostly against their wishes. His cousins are all the same." Edgar looked away shamefacedly.

"But you are not." Freyda touched his face, tenderly.

"Nor is your father, Freyda. He is not such a bad man."

She gave him an incredulous look. "Only a man would say such a thing. That woman is a sorceress, I tell you."

"I remember her. She caused great trouble… in our family," Edgar recalled.

"I was too young to remember it, but I do remember that for some time my mother hated my father. I'd always believed it to be her fault, and would always take his side. Now I am not so sure, especially when I found him with this woman, doing it in her bed. But I am not stupid enough to know that men cannot keep their cock to themselves."

"So, what did you do when you found them together, you never told me?"

"I told him exactly what I thought, that he was a self-righteous hypocrite! How dare he lecture me on chastity when he does not even know the meaning of the word?"

"You told him he was a hypocrite?" Edgar asked in surprise.

"Not in so many words, but I think he understood." Freyda laughed.

"That was brave, my love."

"Perhaps it was, but at least now he cannot try to keep us apart. He can play the self-righteous old fart as much as he likes. I shall pay no heed."

They both laughed.

"I do believe you would shame the devil sometimes!" Edgar declared.

Freyda smacked him playfully and skipped round him as he tried to catch her. "Catch me if you can!" she cried, and made a run for it.

Inside the longhall, preparations were being made for the *bendfeorm*, the harvest celebratory feast. Winflaed was helping her mother decorate the hall, and they were about to open an ancient chest the Lady Gerda had bequeathed to Ealdgytha in her will. Gerda had kept the coffer hidden for years, often enigmatically referring to it as her 'treasure trove'. It was believed to hold many lush furnishings such as curtains, bedding, and old wall hangings, but Lady Gerda's allusion to treasure had instigated a new theory that it contained something else of great value. Ealdgytha had all but forgotten about the chest, until that day when she was trying to think of what she could do to enhance her old hall furnishings, and Winflaed reminded her of its existence.

Curious to know what mysteries lay hidden inside it, Winflaed was eagerly awaiting the revelation of its contents. Once the thick layer of dust had been removed, she could see that it was a beautiful piece of furniture, made of solid chestnut. The animations, skilfully carved on its fine surface, were of particular interest to Winflaed. Depictions of forest animals, otters, badgers, squirrels, hares, wolves, and trees, adorned the lid and the side panels, but it was the main wolf which caught Winflaed's eye. Beautifully hand-carved with such intricate detail, the engraver had captured the slenderness of the wolf's body and the piercing, feral eyes. All the figures were beautifully done, but for some reason the wolf stood out more than the others.

Winflaed ran her fingers over the carving of the wolf and then along the other images. "'Tis beautiful, Mother. Look at the wolves. See how sleek they are."

"Hideous creatures," Ealdgytha bridled.

Winflaed felt her mother shiver beside her.

"Open it, Ealdgytha," urged Gunnhild tersely. Winflaed knew that her aunt had been somewhat piqued that the chest had been left to Ealdgytha, and not she, in Gerda's will. She had been pressing Ealdgytha to open it all morning.

Ealdgytha took a key from her belt and unlocked the chest. The lid was heavy as she and Winflaed opened the box together. Inside was full with materials of different colours and textures. Winflaed poked her head into the box and was rummaging through it, when she drew Ealdgytha's attention to a large folded piece of thickly woven linen. Even folded, it promised to be something of great magnificence. Winflaed gave a little gasp at its beauty, as together they unravelled it while the others waited expectantly. It was a wall hanging, too long to be set out in its entirety. Although slightly faded with age, the embroidery would not have looked out of place in the great hall of the king's palace at Westminster. It was a beautiful piece of work, made with extreme skill. Dust flew from it as they laid it out on the floor so that they could all view it properly.

"Such workmanship," Gunnhild declared in awe, fingering the material and embroidery appreciatively.

Everyone studied the images intensely. Like the coffer, it seemed to be dominated by various images of wolves. Some were mysterious outlines cast in the background; others loomed larger in the fore.

"'Tis almost large enough to stretch across one side of the hall," Godgyva, Esegar's wife, stated in disbelief. "I have never seen a piece of work on such a scale before."

"What is it?" Sigfrith asked curiously, bending over the work to study it more closely.

"Well, of course it is a wall embroidery, made to portray some past event of great importance," Gunnhild told them, huffing as if she were the only person with any sense.

"It is the work of the *hæðencynn*, idol worshippers who went before the Christ-worshipers came to these lands," Ealdgytha remarked hoarsely.

Winflaed noticed a look of dread in her mother's eyes. She stared at it, trying to see what it was about it that had made her mother seem afraid. Silently, she attempted to interpret the story the embroidered images were telling her. Hills and trees on one side and on the other a coastal shoreline on which a half-dozen or so sea vessels floated, created in richly coloured wool, all possessing sails crested with the head of a wolf. In one corner of the tapestry was the summit of a hill, or a mountain, that sloped down into woodland. Along the rising gradient, wolves appeared to be running upwards out of the forest, with the largest of the creatures at the hill's pinnacle, standing on a promontory, its dark grey-blue shape howling at a perfectly round moon against a darkened sky. This was clearly the leader, Winflaed decided, for it was the largest and most clearly represented. Behind it, the others looked small and insignificant against its majesty. Interestingly, there were no images of humans. It was as if the wolves themselves had sailed and alighted ashore from the boats and were running freely across a depicted land.

"It is beautiful," Winflaed said, dreamily.

"Aye," agreed Gunnhild approvingly.

Ealdgytha shook her head dismissively. "There is something frightening about it," she whispered gloomily. "It is like a... like a portent of doom."

"Nonsense," declared Gunnhild. *Nothing frightened her*, thought Winflaed. "They are *Brimwulfas*," she said with certainty. "The Sea Wolves. That is what the people whose land we took, called our ancestors."

"Why did they call them that?" Winflaed asked.

"Because, my dear child, they came wearing wolf skins. And the wolves were the most fearsome of battle creatures, familiars of the old gods. Our ancestors considered themselves to be born of the wolf and mated with humans."

"*Werwulf*," Winflaed said with a shiver, thinking about the chilling tales that were spoken of on cold wintry nights at hearth time; stories of the half-man, half-wolf creature, stalking the forest at night. The wind would be whistling eerily outside and sometimes, if you listened hard enough, you could hear the wolves' plaintive howl, its þeótan, conjured by the words that spoke their names.

"Don't speak of such things!" Ealdgytha snapped. "We are Christians, and it is blasphemous and ungodly to talk of them!"

"I am just explaining to the child about our ancestors. We cannot help our forefathers' beliefs. What harm is there to tell her of our past?" Gunnhild replied, looking affronted.

"That we are descended from wolves?" Ealdgytha retorted angrily; her bad temper had grown worse over the last few days. "I won't have such idolatrous drivel spoken of in my house. Now, Sigfrith, you and Winflaed can put the damn thing away. In fact, tomorrow, after the harvest feast, I am going to burn the monstrosity."

Winflaed saw that Gunnhild was horrified. Her round face glowed with indignation. "You shall do no such thing!" her aunt replied in her loud, robust voice. "That piece of work belonged to our ancestors. How can you think of destroying such a thing? I will not let you!"

"How dare you tell me what I can and cannot do in my household!" Ealdgytha retorted, raising her voice so that it competed with Gunnhild's. "You are only here because I pity you! Otherwise you would be no use to —" Her rant was suddenly put to an end as Gunnhild's hand connected with her face in a sickening slapping sound.

Winflaed gasped. Her aunt hit her mother so hard that it unpinned her wimple.

"No wonder your husband sought the arms of another woman!" Gunnhild snapped. "He obviously could not stand your tempers and your high and mighty airs!"

Ealdgytha clasped her hand to her face and stared open-mouthed at her sister-in-law. Winflaed felt her face prick with horror. If Ealdgytha were to retaliate, Gunnhild would sweep the floor with her. Winflaed had once seen Gunnhild fell a man with one punch when he'd dared insult her. She held onto her mother's arm protectively. But Mother must have known that she would not win against her sister-in-law, built like an ox, that she was, with the strength of ten men.

"Do what you all damned well like! I cannot be around *any* of you at the moment!" Ealdgytha yelled as she fled the hall sobbing.

Sigfrith went to follow.

"Leave her be, girl. She needs to be alone to calm down. A rest will do her good and help her to gather her wits. She will need them for tonight," Gunnhild said, unsympathetically.

"But you've just hit her... and she has just lost her babe!" Sigfrith protested.

"I had to. She was hysterical. You think she is the only woman whose husband has strayed, the only woman to lose a babe?" Gunnhild said cuttingly.

Sigfrith gave Gunnhild a scowl and went nonetheless. Winflaed went to follow her, but Gunnhild held her fast by her collar. "Now, young lady, let's get on with the preparations. It looks like it's just you and I, and that lot," she said, cocking her head at the women standing by in stony-faced silence.

"Get on with your work," she called to them gruffly. "There's still much to do and only a short while to go. They'll all be piling in here soon from the fields, their disgusting tongues hanging out and their fool eyes popping out on stalks, expecting to be fed and watered!"

She beckoned to Winflaed, who came somewhat reluctantly. Her aunt bent down to her and said, "You and I are going to hang this embroidery up and everyone will see what fine ancestors we had. *And*, as we do it, I am going to tell you a tale of a wolf king and how he came with his sons to this land from across the sea. And how they defeated and drove out the folk who were here before, because they would not leave them in peace."

"But my mother is upset. I should go to her," Winflaed replied meekly.

"Such nonsense, girl," her aunt declared coldly. "There is nothing wrong with your mother that a good reasoning with wouldn't go amiss. She is lucky to have such beautiful children and a husband who provides well for her. What is more, she will be able to go on to have more children, and no doubt will; a pleasure that some of us will never know again."

Winflaed guessed that Gunnhild was referring to the fact that she was a widow and would not be able to have any more children. She felt a moment of sympathy for her fearsome aunt, but it was hard to hold it in light of what she had just done to her mother. Still, she was intrigued to hear about her ancestors, and since Gunnhild was not going to let her go, she decided she might as well get on with it.

Gunnhild was a good organiser and set about preparing the hall for the feast, delegating the work to the helpers in a precise and orderly manner. Winflaed had to agree that she did this with aplomb, unlike her mother whose anxieties about the outcome sent everyone into a state of confusion. Winflaed observed, with secret admiration, how her aunt seemed to facilitate the task with confidence and without disorder, seeming to know exactly what to do and how to do it.

When it came to the wall hanging, she commandeered some men to help them lift it and hook it onto the iron poles that projected from the walls. As she and Winflaed helped to straighten and buffet the dust off it, she told her about the *Wulfcynn*, who were the followers of, Aelle, leader of the Súþseaxa. More than five hundred and fifty years ago, they had followed him to these shores across the sea from the continent. Their own chieftain had been a man called, Wulfgar, who was the forefather of many of the families that now lived in those parts; hence the name prefix *Wulf* that had traditionally remained prevalent thereabouts. Winflaed forgot her fear of her aunt and found herself entranced by the story. There was something quite exciting about hearing tales of one's ancestors.

Once the hanging had been positioned to her aunt's satisfaction, they stood back from the wall to study it in its entirety. Winflaed marvelled at the magnificence of the work. It stretched along most of one side of the wall. It was a little tattered in places, but nothing that could not be repaired. Winflaed's eyes rolled over it from one side to another before they alighted on the scenes near the end.

"Look, Aunt Gunnhild, there is a scene here with a bishop and a church... and people instead of the wolves."

"Aye, it seems that those scenes were added later, to depict the baptism of the wolf people," Gunnhild informed her, joining her at the end.

"What is this?" Winflaed turned and saw it was her father who had come to admire the new wall hanging. "Have we acquired new décor for the hall?"

"It came from Grandmother's treasure chest, Father," Winflaed replied proudly.

"Yes indeed. I am surprised it has not seen the light of day for so long," Gunnhild agreed haughtily. "Your daughter and I have saved it from your wife's clutches. She wanted to burn it."

Wulfhere studied it intently. "I can see why, wolves howling at the moon. Not the sort of thing that should be hanging in a Christian household." He observed it closer. "I remember this from when I was a small child," he said animatedly. "It once hung here in the very same place it is hung now. But Grandmother Gerda, did not like it. She tried to make it seem more Christian by adding that scene at the end, but she always said it did nothing to dispel the pagan magic from it, and brought them nothing but bad fortune whilst it hung there, so she made my father take it down. He did it for her, though, in truth, I believe he loved it."

"I remember as children your father used to tell us stories of wolves and the coming of the end of days when there would be the *Vargold*, the Age of the Wolf. How I loved to listen to him," Gunnhild said. There was a wistful look in her eye and momentarily, Gunnhild was once more that young girl again, recalling happier times from her past.

Wulfhere nodded. "When chaos would come to this earth, and brothers would battle to the very end, and there would be betrayal and confusion in the lands," he reminisced. He smiled and shook his head. "But we must not talk of such things in these Christian times."

"'Tis harmless enough. Nobody in their right minds would believe the tales anyway," Gunnhild said.

Wulfhere cocked an eyebrow and chuckled. "So, our ancestors were mad, is that what you're implying, Gunnhild?" Then he turned to Winflaed. "What else was in this chest you spoke of, daughter?"

"I'll show you, Papa." They left Gunnhild to get on with her work and she took him to where the chest stood. "We had not thought to look for anything else." Wulfhere studied it and Winflaed could tell he was admiring its beauty.

"Open it, Papa," she said and he lifted the lid. She reached in and pulled out a small piece of folded linen. It was a much smaller piece than the wall hanging, shaped like that of a standard; the type one took into battle. It was rectangular in shape, with a long body that graded to a tip. The background colour was a shade of amber. At the centre, someone had sewn the emblem, a running wolf, its head shaded with brown and amber threads. Skilful hands had obviously produced it with loving care, but the years had not been kind to it and it was torn, battered and threadbare in places.

"Is it the wolf-king, Papa?" Winflaed questioned admiringly.

"Indeed, I do think it is," Wulfhere agreed, fingering the broken stitching with a distant look in his eyes. "'Tis your grandfather's old war banner. He used to ride into battle with it held high, proudly fluttering in the wind above men's heads."

He studied it fondly as if he were reminiscing.

"What is it for, Father?" Winflaed asked him softly, sensitive to the poignant look in his eyes.

"It is a war banner, sweeting. Something that a lord takes into battle..." He took a spear down from the wall and hooked the banner onto it, "... and raises it high so that his men will recognise it and rally to him. Just like this," he said, raising the end of the spear above his head and waving it.

"Does Earl Harold have one?"

"Oh yes, he has the Golden Warrior."

"And the king?"

He nodded. "The Dragon of Wessex."

"Who makes it for them?"

"Why, most likely their womenfolk do."

"Do you have one, Father?"

"Not anymore."

"Why don't you use this one?"

"It is in need of repair now."

Winflaed climbed into his lap as he slunk down onto the floor by the open chest. Around them, Gunnhild and her team of workers carried on with their jobs, whilst father and daughter were oblivious to their clamour. Winflaed held the banner in her lap. "So, the earl has a warrior, the king, a dragon. What is so special about a wolf?" she asked curiously, looking up at her father, her eyes round.

"Haven't you listened to anything your aunt told you about our ancestors being wolves?" Wulfhere said, pretending to rebuke her.

"But that is just legend, is it not, Father?" She looked up at him with her huge, innocent blue eyes.

"Legend? Good heavens, no! All of it is true! Soon you will have your own wolf hair and then you will see."

"No, Father, I don't believe you." She laughed.

"You mean you have not grown your wolf hair yet?" She laughed as he took her arm and pretended to search it for hairs. "See, here look at these. They are starting to grow already!"

Playfully, she retrieved her arm. "No, they are not!" she declared. "You haven't told me why the wolf is so important."

"Because, of all the gods' creatures, the wolf was considered the most fearsome of beasts," he replied in an ominous tone. "A wolf meant slaughter was afoot, it is an eater of carrion on the battlefield. No matter who won the battle, it was always the wolf who was the true winner. You see, the wolf need not exert himself...for men show their respect, by providing him with their enemies, dead, on the field, for them to feast on."

She looked at him intently. "Such a fearsome creature!" she said with childlike awe. "Is that why men hate him so much?"

Wulfhere shook his head. "No, little *Fléogenda*. We do not hate the wolf. He is a creature to be feared and respected, but not hated... And they eat little girls just as easily as they would eat warriors on a field of slaughter!" He playfully attacked her, making wolf noises, and nibbling at her neck. She squealed, and her girlish laughter rang out across the hall.

Suddenly she leapt into his arms and covered his face with kisses. "Oh, Father, I love you so! Please don't ever go away and leave us again!" she begged.

"Daughter, what troubles you that you should say such a thing?" He held her back from him and studied her.

"You and Mother... you fight terribly and I fear that it is my fault." She began to cry.

"'Tis no fault of yours, sweeting."

"But we brought you the package, Tovi and I."

"'Tis not your fault. You weren't to know the mischief that package would bring. Now dry your tears. Tonight, we will have fun and there will be storytelling and riddles and –"

"Father?" Wulfhere looked up. It was Tovi. "Mother wishes that you attend to her upstairs." There was a look of jealousy in Tovi's eyes.

Her father patted Winflaed's back and urged her to her feet. "I will go to her," he said awkwardly, standing up slowly, nodding at his son.

Winflaed watched their interaction. Wulfhere was attempting to make her sullen brother smile, ruffling his hair; but the boy dodged him and slunk away. Their discomfort made her feel anxious, and she felt her heart palpitate.

Her father looked at her knowing eyes and shrugged. "At least *you* are talking to me, little *Fléogenda*." He bent down and kissed her forehead. "I must go to your mother. I have my orders!" He smiled and walked away.

"Father," Winflaed called after him. He turned to her. "I would like to fix it for you." She held the ruined banner up. "So, you can have a banner to take into battle."

"I should like that," he replied.

Wulfhere found Ealdgytha in their chamber above the hall. She was dressed in her usual summer wear of a linen underdress and an overtunic made of light wool fabric, decorated with pretty embroidered cuffs and collar. Her hair was covered and it seemed to Wulfhere that, by wearing the full wimple, she was making herself utterly unavailable to him. Standing defensively with her hands on her hips, her demeanour was one of glaring obstinacy. His heart sank when he saw her, wondering what his misconduct had been this time. At first, he had taken her reproofs with humility, but now that humility was fast beginning to wear thin. He had reproached himself often, had done penance after penance as instructed by Father Paul. But when should he cease paying for his crime? How much more would he be able to stand the emotional exile Ealdgytha imposed upon him?

"You summoned me my love?" he said flatly.

"You have allowed that awful embroidery to be hung in my hall, and I clearly forbade that woman to do so!" Ealdgytha said scornfully, her beauty contorted by malice.

Wulfhere was about to respond submissively but then changed his stance. "So what?" he replied. "'Tis just an old wall hanging."

"So what? It is an abomination of God! I will have no such thing in this house," she retorted angrily.

"It is no such thing. Yes, it is true that it depicts an old legend, but we still remember the old tales from long ago. They are harmless enough and do not cause offence to God, I am sure. Besides, a Christian element has been added to it."

Ealdgytha did not appear to be listening to him. "It is wrong to hang on to such beliefs. The Christian church does not allow it. And I will not have your sister-in-law filling my children's heads with stories that they are descended from wolves!"

Wulfhere let a smile creep across his face, but he held back the temptation to burst into laughter. "Ealdgytha, calm yourself, it is but a lifeless object, that is all. It makes us no less Christians to have it hanging in our hall. And it is a thing of beauty; the craftsmanship that has gone into it–"

"You sound just like that onerously stupid Gunnhild! Both of you have no idea of what is good and proper!"

"What has Gunnhild done to you, woman? You have been like a bear with a sore head this past week! You have hardly had a good word for anyone, not even your own children!"

"Did you know that that woman hit me?" Ealdgytha demanded indignantly.

Wulfhere was not surprised. He imagined that Gunnhild would have retaliated at some point. She and Ealdgytha had never got along well, and his forthright sister-in-law had never had a mind to hold her tongue when she felt the need. Nor would she allow herself to be bullied by anyone, thegn's lady or no.

"Well husband? What do you say of your precious sister-in-law now?"

Wulfhere sighed with weariness. He was tired of the animosity; tired of having to eat humble pie, and tired of having to hide his feelings of longing. He wanted to be loved like any man should be. Ealdgytha's coldness toward him had been understandable, for he knew how much she had suffered with his unfaithfulness and the miscarriage. But he was heartsick of it all.

"Ealdgytha," he said in a gentler voice. "This is not about the damned wall hanging, nor is it about Gunnhild. This is about you and me. Since I went to Waldron, you have been beside yourself with anger, and that I can understand, but just how long do I have to pay? How can we live like this?"

"Pay? You ask *me* such a question? 'Tis not you that pays for your sins, but I!"

He grabbed her by her forearms in desperation. "I am sorry for the hurt I have caused you again. For the love of God, I ask that you forgive me and let us live in peace once more."

"Forgive you? It took me years to forgive you last time. We were just beginning to put our lives together again and *she* comes back into it with a click of her fingers. Or perhaps it was witchcraft that lured you back to her."

The tears that streamed down her face were unstoppable. She tried to free herself but he held her secure in his grasp. "It was not because of her that I went, but because of the child," he said, knowing that it was only a half-truth.

"The children saw you together," she said impassively. "How do you think that feels, knowing that my own children saw their father with another woman in her bed?"

"I am so sorry—"

"You were sorry before, but it never seems to stop you. How do I know that you have not been with her, often, in the last six years?"

"I swear to you that I have not, and that last time was the first time since I last saw her, all those years ago."

For a moment, she dropped her defences. "I can see that you are earnest, but you cannot expect me to just go back to the way it was… just like that."

"So, will I always be at your mercy, Ealdgytha? For I swear that I cannot stomach this any longer. Many a man has strayed beyond their wives' beds and God's bones… they would not put up with this."

"That may be so, Wulfhere, but it is the love that you gave to her that I cannot forgive. That is what makes it so hard, that she has your love… you love her, don't you?"

He released her from his grip and bowed his head, knowing that he could not answer truthfully without hurting her. "But I have love for you too, Ealdgytha. If you only knew how it pains me to—"

An almost maniacal laugh burst forth from Ealdgytha's lips. "Oh, spare me your pain, Wulfhere. You know nothing of pain, nor hurt, nor what it is like to be humiliated in front of your family and those who look up to you. To be writhing in torment at their feet, screaming like a wounded animal. Spare me, Wulfhere, from your pain; it is nothing compared to mine."

He seized her by her wrists. "You tell me I know nothing of suffering? Let me tell you I have seen suffering on the battlefield that you could never imagine."

"I lost a child!"

"And so did I!"

He let go of her and they stood facing each other in silent defiance. Tears continued to flow down her cheeks, silently. Horns could be heard blowing outside in the yard. Below them, the noise of the people coming in from the fields was filling the hall. It would soon be time for the harvest feast, and they would have to take on their roles as the lord and lady of the manor presiding over the festivities.

"We need to go and take our places in the hall," Ealdgytha said, wiping her eyes with her sleeve.

Wulfhere breathed out heavily. He turned, feeling as if the energy had drained from him, and left their chamber, hurrying down the stairs. Opening the door to the porch, he was greeted by the sight of Freyda and Edgar huddled together in an embrace. Inside the hall, he could hear music and the clamour of people enjoying themselves.

When he saw his daughter and Edgar together he was suddenly filled with envy. Edgar was loved, something he longed for himself, and he suddenly recalled what Freyda had said to him that day in Alfgyva's house and it filled him with rage.

"You!" he shouted at Edgar. "Get your filthy *ceorl's* hands off my daughter and get you gone from my home!"

Edgar and Freyda leapt out of their embrace, wide-eyed with fear. Wulfhere grabbed Edgar by the cuff of his tunic and pushed him so hard that he fell out through the porch opening and onto the ground outside. He rolled in the dust before scrambling to his feet, humiliated. Wulfhere was like a wild man who had murder on his mind. Freyda pushed her way in front of him to rush to her lover.

"Edgar, are you hurt?" she asked him in a voice filled with shock.

Edgar shook his head. "'Tis nothing. I had better go, sweetheart," he said nervously.

"No, you are staying, Edgar. You are my betrothed and you have a right to be here." Freyda looked up at her father with the same defiant look her mother had given him just minutes before.

"Betrothed? How can you give yourself to this worthless cripple, who has nothing to give you but the prick in his braies?" Wulfhere spat.

"He respects me, Father... not that you would know the meaning of the word," Freyda retorted with a tremor in her voice.

"I love your daughter, Lord Wulfhere. We are to be wed, after all," Edgar ventured to say.

Wulfhere threw back his head and laughed as if he had just heard some hysterical joke.

"If he goes, Father, then I am going with him," Freyda declared.

Wulfhere came out of the porch like a hurricane. "Go to hell, the pair of you!" he raged, as he shoved them both aside, roughly.

They watched him storm his way over to the stables. It was as if the ground shook in his wake, so strong was his anger. "Where is he going in such a rage?" Edgar asked Freyda.

"To *her*," she whispered.

Part Three

Demons

Chapter Eighteen

The Exiles

Winceaster, September 1055

With his youngest son in his arms, Harold stooped to enter the room his sister, the queen, had allocated for their stay. Looking swiftly around, he was pleased to see that there was adequate space for all of them. The room was well furnished with a large wood-framed bed, smaller cots for the children, and a table, chairs, and wooden clothing posts. All the furnishings were brightly coloured, and there were furs and rugs spread over the rush mats for their comfort.

"Well, my love, I think we should be comfortable here. See, there is even a tiny cot for the little one," Harold said as Eadgyth followed him in, cradling their latest addition, baby Gunhildr, in her arms. "Edith has been thoughtful, after all."

"Yes, indeed," she replied walking around surveying the furnishings, a smile of pleasure on her lips. "I might be too comfortable to leave the apartment," she added, fingering one of the wall hangings appreciatively. "Perhaps that is what the queen is hoping for, and why she has provided all this luxury." Eadgyth gave him one of her elegant smiles and he returned it with a raised eyebrow.

"Now, now, my love. You promised me you would accompany me to all the banquets, and you promised me you would be gracious," Harold said in a serious tone, although the corners of his mouth were raised slightly.

"Of course I will be gracious, Harold. Your sister and I will get along fine... just as we always do. Even if I do have to endure it as she reminds you, again, how disappointed she is that you haven't made as important a match as Tostig has." Eadgyth smiled at him and laid the baby, who was sleeping soundly, into the little crib provided.

It had taken Harold a great *deal* of persuasion to get Eadgyth to come to Winceaster for the end of September *Witanagemot*. He was sympathetic to the overwhelming tiredness that came with a new babe, but he longed to have her and the children with him when he could. Moreover, he was aware that she would rather not have to be in the company of his sister who seemed to greatly enjoy slighting her at any opportunity. Edith, Harold told her, was jealous of her, for not only did she possess great beauty, but she had been able to produce a bundle of healthy children, something that his sister longed for, but could not achieve.

He let Magnus slip from his arms, and he and the other children made themselves comfortable amongst the rugs and furs with their nurse, Hild.

"Will we see the king, Father?" demanded Magnus, now five years old and becoming more articulate as he grew.

"That depends," Harold replied with a serious face.

"On what?" asked Magnus, curiously.

"On how you conduct yourself," Harold replied, laughing. "Aye, and if all you children are badly behaved, the king might want to have you all served up for dinner!"

"Oh no, Father!" Magnus gasped with the innocent uncertainty of a child.

"Oh yes, *Father*!" Harold laughed again, and joined the children on the floor, engaging them in a play-fight. Eadgyth laughed as, swamped by his buoyant offspring, he rolled from one side to another to escape the deluge. They continued to leap up and down on him, squealing with delight as he made mock groaning noises.

"Come now, children, leave your poor father alone. He cannot go before the king all black and blue now, can he?" Eadgyth laughed.

"But he's wearing blue already," Edmund declared, giving his father one last kick as he lay on the floor curled up in a ball to protect himself.

"Why can't he wear black and blue?" asked Gytha curiously.

"She means covered in bruises," Godwin cried, in an exasperated tone, which led Harold to believe that his eldest, fast growing in his intellectual skills, was revelling in his newfound superiority of mind. Godwin continued with an air of authority that made Harold chuckle, "Father is a very important man, and he must look respectable when he goes before the king and his council."

Eadgyth bent down to the children, smiling, and said, "Godwin is right. It would not do for your papa to look as though he has been in a brawl!"

"Is he as important as the king?" Magnus, red-faced and panting from the fight, asked his mother. He threw his little arms around her neck as she readjusted his clothes.

"Of course I am!" Harold declared, beaming from ear to ear, as he picked himself up off the floor. "Well almost, for in truth I am sure I work harder than the king, fighting such fierce dragons such as these." He growled, and pretended to lash out at them, laughing as they squealed and ran away.

"Harold, you should not say such things." Eadgyth smiled. She was straightening and brushing off his clothing as if he were one of her children. "Even if they are true!"

"Do you really work harder than the king?" Gytha asked.

"Of course, Father works harder than the king," interjected Godwin.

"And who told you that, my son?" Harold questioned.

"You just said so, Father. And Mother says that the king is lazy, and that all he does is sleep or go hunting while his earls and thegns do all the hard work in the kingdom," Godwin replied.

"Does she now?" Harold looked sternly at Eadgyth and then gave her a sly wink.

"Godwin, how can you say that? I have never told you any such thing," Eadgyth exclaimed.

"No, but I heard you telling Grandmother Gytha once," Godwin replied confidently.

Eadgyth felt her face glow. "Well," she shrugged, looking at Harold, "I cannot help it if he has big ears."

"Who, the king, or our son?" Harold laughed, enclosing his arms about her waist. "Now *there* is something you cannot say about the king! He has the most delicate little ears I have ever seen in the whole of *eardom*!"

"It is *you* who have the biggest ears! And your son too! Just like his father!" Eadgyth laughed as he held her close to him.

Harold gazed, lovingly, into her pale blue eyes, and a thrill whistled through him at the attractive way they shone with her laughter. From the moment he had laid eyes on her, he had been stricken with love and desire for her. He had wanted to marry her, but his parents had advised him that he should not, and to take her as his handfasted wife only. With Swegn constantly out of favour, Harold would be the first amongst the Godwin brothers, and, therefore, would most likely need to make an important marriage alliance someday.

Gazing at her innocent beauty now, he wondered how his sister could treat her so badly. There was not a bad bone in Eadgyth's body. "I know how it pains you to come to court," he whispered to her as he held her. "I know how much you would prefer to be home in Waltham, supervising the building of our new church and bossing the masons around." Like Edward, Harold had wanted to build a church of stone, dedicated in thanksgiving for his full recovery from a severe paralysis sickness. His mother had prayed for his life in the little timber church at Waltham, and he had promised himself one day that he would rebuild it in magnificent stone. Eadgyth had taken it upon herself to manage the progress of it when he was not there, and she had endeared herself to the workers, ensuring that they were fed and well looked after. There, in the home that Harold had built with her, Eadgyth was full of confidence, holding sway as lady of the manor, but, at court, Harold knew she was out of her depth, thanks to his sister's arrogance. His Eadgyth was an affluent woman in her own right, having inherited an abundance of wealth and lands from her parents, but she was not noble enough for his sister, and this angered him greatly.

She drew back from him. "I like to be with you also, Harold, and if you would have me and the children with you, then I will go where you bid me," she replied modestly. "I promise you I shall endure your sister's derision without any animosity. I shall even humble myself before her, should she deign to acknowledge me."

"You are wicked, my Lady Eadgyth," Harold said softly, nuzzling her neck. "But also, very beautiful, and I want nothing more right now than to make love to you. Can we not put the children to bed and—"

"Harold, it's just after midday!" Eadgyth laughed. "Shh! The children will hear you."

"Oh yes, they all have big ears like their father!" He swept her into his arms and kissed her. "I am so glad you have come to court, Eadgyth. I know that you did not desire it, but it is good to have you here with me; you and the children."

"All of us are glad to be here with you, my love."

Apart from Wilton, where Queen Edith had spent her childhood years being educated, Winceaster was her favourite residence. She much preferred it to Lundenburgh, which she believed to be far less cultured than Winceaster. Despite the smells from the discarded waste one often had to sidestep, Edith enjoyed trailing through the streets, visiting the booths and workshops of the fine metal workers, jewellers, and weavers. Here she could accompany Edward to the ecclesiastical quarter where they could view the illuminated manuscripts, and beautiful embroidered works produced by the skilled hands of the nuns of the Minster.

Since the death of the old Dowager, Queen Emma, three years ago, Edith had been commended with her properties in Winceaster, and the protection of the treasury was her right. The trust she had been invested with, and the reality that now she was fully ensconced as Edward's queen, filled her with an immense sense of greatness. The days when she was ignored, belittled, and scorned upon, were now nothing more than an unpleasant, distant memory.

The royal couple had arrived at their palace only a few days ago, and Edith had complained, vociferously, at what she considered to be an inefficient effort to make the place clean and comfortable for His Lordship's arrival. Upon her orders, the palace had been duly scrubbed and swept from top to bottom, and fresh rush mats infused with scented herbs, were scattered about the floors. The old linen had been replaced with new, and the decorative hangings had been taken down, and the dirt beaten from them until they were completely dust free.

For Edith, this was all part of what she considered to be her queenly duty, ensuring that the Great Hall and its surroundings, were fit to welcome the guests that would be arriving for the Witenagemot. Like the one that had been held in the early spring, this meeting was to discuss matters of importance as well as to compile the king's dues, which had been collected by the earls' scīr-reeves and their officials.

She was in the upper-storey rooms of the palace, combing the long, greying curls of her husband the king. She had trimmed his beard, and rubbed him with scented powder before assisting him into the outfit she had specifically picked out for him to wear at the gemot. She insisted on carrying out these duties instead of Edward's chief chamberlain, Hugolin, who often found himself vying with the queen for Edward's attention.

As for Edward, he found that he was getting too long in the tooth now to protest who did what to him. All he wanted was to get his courtly duties over and done with, so that he could go hunting in the West Country as he did every autumn, when the leaves withered from their branches and lay upon the forest floor. The weather outside had been turning cool and damp for the time of year, but that day it was developing into a sunny afternoon, which just took the edge off the morning chill. It was unquestionably the sort of afternoon that would be perfect for the hunt, and Edward had some newly matured hounds that he was longing to bring to their first chase. *Oh, the joy of the hunt!* He was glad that his brother-in-law, Tostig, would be here to share in the excitement this year. He had missed the good and noble Lord Tostig, full of scintillating conversation and piety, like himself. Now that he was beginning to recover from the news that his old friend, Robert Champart, had sadly expired in Normandy, he was able to focus his attention on a new favourite.

Tostig swelled with pride as he entered the Council Chamber, revelling in his newfound fame as Earl of Northymbralond. Like a jealous child, he knew his brother, Harold, would be there to see him, walking sedately between the king and queen, arm in arm. It gave him great satisfaction to know that, at last, he could rival Harold. For years, he had been compelled to wait in the background whilst his older brothers, Harold and Swegn, grabbed the limelight. Tostig still resented the fact that he had been made to wait until he was thirty to get some recognition, whereas Harold and Swegn, had been some years younger than he, when they came to the fore. He smiled at his sister as she patted his arm encouragingly when they passed by their brothers and mother. Thank God, he had Edith to confide in. She knew how he felt about Harold, and had offered him succour when he had been left out in the cold.

Tostig felt his heart race as he caught Harold's eye. He imagined for a moment, that Harold had let his usual nonchalance slip, exposing a flicker of envy. *In time, good brother,* he thought to himself, *you will see who is the most powerful of we two... all in good time.*

"A strange *ménage à trois,* don't you think, brother?" whispered Harold to Gyrth, as the threesome passed them in the passageway. They were a curious sight, Edith, the king and Tostig, as they walked together through the chambers, nodding, and smiling as people stood aside in deference to let them pass.

"Aye, anyone would think that our dear brother, Tostig, was king instead of Edward," replied Gyrth.

"I am surprised that Edith hasn't placed the crown on his head by mistake," joked Harold when the group was out of earshot. He was grinning amusedly.

"Perhaps one day she will," said Gyrth, more soberly than his brother had spoken.

Bishop Ealdred of Worcester walked with much vigour for an old man who had not long returned from travelling almost the length and breadth of Europe and back. His increasing age was contradicted by the tireless energy that made him such a useful servant of the Crown. He was recently returned to Englalond from the Continent, having been sent on a mission to Cologne with a request that Emperor Henry assist the king in locating his nephew, Edward the Exile.

The room was filling up with members of the *Witan*, as he proceeded to approach the dais. In front of him, on the raised platform, he could see a bored looking Edward sitting on his throne, his exultant queen next to him. Next to the dais, Archbishop Stigand sat in his own high-backed chair. His clerics were seated nearby at a writing table to record the day's transactions. Around them sat Edward's closest advisors, the Earl of Wessex among them. As Ealdred came closer, he thought how smugly the queen sat and how arrogantly her brother, the Earl of Northymbralond, stood; perched to one side of the dais on a lower step, one knee raised on the platform, his arms crossed. Tostig wore a delicately embroidered, ankle-length silken robe; his fingers were heavily ringed in gold, and a dazzling jewelled cross hung about his neck. Such attire which rivalled the king's, could only have been acquired for him by his sister, the queen. And, after all, she had the key to the treasury to purchase such expensive items. The late afternoon sun shone through the high windows and glistened in the strands of Tostig's collar-length hair. He stood there, assuming a regal stance; arms folded as if he were an impenetrable fortress, waiting for someone to attack. Ealdred smiled inwardly as he observed that Tostig appeared more royal than the man sitting on the throne. There certainly had been some changes since he had left for the Continent.

"My Lord Ealdred, I happily welcome you home… with good news of my brother's son, I do hope," Edward said in his quiet, thin voice, as the bishop knelt before him.

The king indicated with his hand for the bishop to rise to his feet.

"My Lord King, I do indeed have news that Edward the Exile is alive and well, praise the Lord God in Heaven," Ealdred replied, rising from one knee. He was speaking loudly so that everyone in the chamber could hear.

There was a murmuring of approval from those around them. It was now evident to most, that Edward and Edith would not be providing the kingdom with an heir of their own. Duke William, Edward's Norman cousin, was a possible contender, but he was a foreigner, and not favourable to most Englisc men. There was also Ralph de Mantes, the king's nephew, who sat on the dais with Edward; but he had not even been considered as a candidate, not even by Edward, who loved him dearly. He was too 'Norman', some thought. But there was another with a stronger claim: Edward, the exiled son of Edmund Ironside, the king's older brother.

Edward Edmundson, was a true prince of the great royal line of Wessex. Many still remembered his father, who had been king for a short while. It was Edmund's courage and valour that had earned him the name *Ironside*; a better title than his father, Ethelred, known as the *Unraed* whose name mostly evoked his ineptness and inability to do anything about the Danish invaders.

Ealdred waited for the murmuring to cease before continuing. "He resides at the court of King Andrew of Hungary, and is married to the king's niece, Lady Agatha. They have three children, one of whom is a son, your great nephew, my lord."

Edward smiled delightedly, and there were more interested murmurings. In contrast, Edith looked on impassively, as did Tostig. Ealdred interpreted their lack of enthusiasm as disapproval, and wondered if they had been harbouring hopes of their own. Did Edith still hope to produce a child? Surely not? Before he had left, her mother, Countess Gytha, had confided to him that her daughter had confessed that her marriage to the king was now sexless, so there was not even a possibility of a bastard being foisted upon them; not that Edith would ever stoop to such a sin. For the ruse to be successful there would have to be *some* sexual intercourse between a man and woman, even if it were only very occasional. He wondered if there was any significance in the looks that passed between Earl Tostig and his sister, as he reported the news of the Exile. Tostig's closeness to the king was evident. And Tostig had long been a favourite of Edith's. Perhaps, he thought, the brother and sister had a scheme of their own.

"So, you have seen my dear nephew for yourself?" Edward asked curiously.

"Alas, my lord, it was not possible for me to meet with the Exile in person, due to the hostilities between my host, His Grace, the Emperor and the King of Hungary. I was prevented from travelling into the country, but I have letters to prove his existence from King Andrew himself. I am sure that, when the situation there is resolved, we will be able to send for him and his family."

"It is regrettable that your mission was hampered by forces beyond your control, Lord Ealdred. I commend you for your hard work, even though you have been gone almost a year," Edward commented. He pointed an accusatory finger at the Bishop. "It is a shame that you could not have brought my nephew Edward home with you. Still, I understand that there are problems abroad which must have prevented you."

Ealdred sensed that the ever-frugal Edward, would be quite perturbed about the potential cost of another embassy to locate the *atheling* and ship him home. "My lord, the Emperor Henry has given me his assurance that he will assist in any way possible in the achievement of our goal, but the current hostilities between he and the King of Hungary, prevent him from giving the matter his full attention for the time being. As soon as this is resolved, he assures me he will do all that he can to help us bring the Exile back to these shores."

The bishop's voice was controlled, but King Edward's snipe at his failure to bring home the prince, stung him. He particularly disliked the king's insinuation that he had been away longer than necessary. What did he think he had been doing so far away from home all this time? True, he had visited the courts of other lands whilst abroad, but much of the hospitality he had received had been offered to him at no expense, leaving him more than able to purchase many holy relics as gifts for Edward with which to endow his churches and monasteries. It was no fault of his that he was stopped from going to Hungary. He might as well take advantage of the offers of hospitality he received from various quarters. Was he supposed to sit around the palace at Cologne doing little else but twiddle his thumbs? After all, it had been the Emperor himself who had refused to let him go further. Any fool would know that it was not in Henry's interest to allow negotiations between his enemy and an envoy from Englalond.

"Then it is good news, my Lord Bishop of Worcester," Edward replied approvingly, after appearing to give it much thought. "At least we know that my brother's son and his family are alive and safe. I take it that my loyal subjects are in agreement, and as soon as the situation between the two countries has improved, we will send for my dear brother's son and his family. If indeed this is possible."

Humming sounds of approval echoed around the Chamber, accompanied by the sound of voices in unison saying, "Aye."

"Sire," Harold said, standing to his feet. "I would request that I be the one to accompany my Lord Ealdred to the Continent to seek out the Exile and bring him home."

Ealdred saw the queen's eyes flash resentfully as her brother spoke, and was certain that Tostig had shifted uncomfortably, a cloud of disapproval on his face. He wondered if Harold had noticed it too; then, curiously, he observed that Harold had turned his head so that his eyes locked with Edith's as if he were engaging her in a psychic battle of wills. Ealdred had known the Godwin siblings since they were children. They had always been at loggerheads with each other. Nothing had changed as they had grown into adulthood.

"I am sure that Lord Ealdred will welcome your presence should he wish to return to Germany to collect the *atheling*," Edward replied graciously.

"Indeed, my Lord King, I would be most grateful for Earl Harold's assistance," Ealdred said with a smile for Harold.

Harold had wanted to use this opportunity to broach the subject of the Godwin hostages in the presence of the *Witan* but his mother, pre-empting his thoughts, put a restraining hand on his arm, and whispered in his ear that it was not the best time. The king, she had told him, became as prickly as a hedgehog whenever the hostages were mentioned, and to do so in public would be disastrous. If they wanted to get Edward on side, she added, they would have to be patient and speak to him in private.

This was a source of frustration to Harold, but he respected his mother's counsel and heeded her advice. Perhaps it was best to wait for a more opportune moment. When the meeting had ended, he would seek a private audience with Edward to discuss plans for the return of his brother and nephew. He had hoped that Tostig would be more supportive, but he and Edith seemed too engrossed in their own machinations to be concerned about the plight of their own kin. Harold found it difficult to understand that the two members of the family, most best placed to secure Edward's support, were about as useful as a cooking pot in a famine.

Harold was intrigued to see how the pair of them seemed to bridle when he spoke of going abroad with Ealdred to seek out the Exile. Was there some other undisclosed plan or objective regarding the succession known only to them? He felt Edith's eyes burning into him as he stood before the king, stating his intention. He flicked his eyes in her direction and saw the look of malice that she gazed at him with. But Tostig's face was even more interesting, for he gave away nothing in his passive expression.

Now, with the matter of the succession ended for the time being, and other business such as taxation levels and revision of laws concluded, court was disbanded for the day. The Chamber began to empty, and people filed out of the room chatting amongst themselves about the day's proceedings.

Harold bade his younger brothers and Bishop Ealdred to stay behind with him. He then took the opportunity to approach the dais. "My Lord King, we would ask permission to speak with you in private," he said, politely.

"Brother, our king is weary after this afternoon's work," Edith interposed. She was looking at Harold sharply. "It is time for his afternoon nap."

Harold inclined his head to one side to meet her gaze. "It shall not take long, good sister. I wish to speak about our brother and nephew who are in Normandy." He glanced behind him at his mother as if seeking her approval. The Countess indicated with a nod that he should continue.

"Oh, that little matter," Edward said as if it were of no importance, patting Edith's hand gently. "What is it you wish to know?"

"My sister informed us recently that you had agreed to write to the Duke of Normandy requesting our relatives' return. My mother and I would like to hear if there has been any correspondence from Duke William in reply."

Tostig stepped off the dais to approach Harold, and touched his brother's elbow as if he wanted him to leave. "Come, brother, the king is tired. We should not plague him with matters that can wait for another time." His smile was patronising.

Harold was wryly amused at his siblings' efforts to hinder his audience with the king. Were they privy to something that he was not? Edith had always been closer to Swegn and Tostig than he, not that he cared much. His sister had always been self-obsessed and full of her own importance. Swegn had been a wolf in sheep's clothing, and as for Tostig, he was never satisfied with anything he was given and was jealous of Harold in every way. Tostig and Gyrth had once been close; they had shared their exile together with their father and mother in St Omer, whilst Leofwin had gone to Iralond with Harold to help him drum up support for their cause. Thus, the brothers had been divided with Leofwin on Harold's side and Gyrth on Tostig's. But since Tostig had been created Earl of Northymbralond, and had become the king's favourite, Gyrth had drifted toward Harold, and Harold suspected Tostig was jealous of that, too.

Harold shook Tostig's hand from his arm. There was a threatening demeanour about him that made Harold prickle at his touch. "I acknowledge your concern for the king, brother. It is an admirable quality. Would that you had the same concern about the welfare of your kinsmen rotting somewhere in Norman chains for all we know."

"How dare you speak to me with such contempt in the presence of our king," Tostig exclaimed angrily.

Harold squared himself. "It is with the same daring that I ask, why you and my dear sister, seem to want to obstruct any debate with the king about Wulfnoth and Hakon."

Edith stood up, framed by her throne. Her eyes were full of fire. "What are you inferring, Harold?" she demanded.

Harold ignored her. He and his brother stood stock still, facing each other with fists clenched by their sides. Once, when they were youths, the two brothers had fought a bitter fight at court. It had been Swegn who had been the instigator, but somehow, he'd kept out of it. Harold, being the elder, had the advantage and won the fight. Harold wondered if Tostig thought about that fight, too, all those years ago, as they stood before the king now.

"Lords, this is not the behaviour expected of the two most prominent earls of the land. Cease this posturing now, I implore you," Ealdred pleaded with them.

"I will, if my dear brother, Tostig, will stop his infernal interfering," Harold replied through gritted teeth.

"My dear lords Tostig and Harold," Edward interrupted, an amused smile broadening his face as if he were enjoying the division he had created amongst the Godwins. "There is no need to quarrel. I am able to respond to Harold's enquiry about his brothers without all this bickering."

Harold turned to the dais. Edith had sat back down, and Edward was patting her hand again, to still her temper, as she clenched the carved arm of her throne.

"My lord, I am pleased that you should divulge what you know," Harold said eagerly.

"Your boys are well, and are living under the care of my cousin the Duke."

Harold heard his mother gasp. "Sir, you have word of them? This is good news," she said happily, stepping forward and clapping her hands together.

"Of course, why should I not? Do you think that I would not make enquiries about the welfare of my wife's kin? After the sad demise of my good friend, Robert Champart, they are now in the care of Duke William. His scribe has written me on behalf of Lord William. He tells me they flourish. Wulfnoth is being schooled amongst the abbots in Jumièges, where dear Robert was once abbot, and young Hakon is a page in the household of the Duchess. It would seem a shame to interrupt their education and wrench them home. Many men would give their eye teeth to have their sons educated at such a noble court." Edward was smiling and there was a glint in his eye.

...in the care of Duke William... Harold flinched at the thought. So, with Champart dead, the boys' care had been transferred to the confounded duke. He was their patron, their benefactor. In essence, they belonged to him. *Oh, damn them, Father, not even in death are you free of Edward's malice,* Harold thought, woefully.

There was no more to say. Hakon and Wulfnoth were to remain at the king's behest in Normandy. It had not been expressly confirmed that they were part of a bargain between the king, Champart and the duke, but it did not have to be said. It was obvious; Harold knew it. The Godwinsons left the Council Chamber deflated. The king had played his pieces well. Edward had written to the duke, he claimed, and he was happy to let the boys stay as hostages. They were being well treated and educated. What would be the point in disrupting their lives now? Had not he, the king, had a good Norman education?

Harold locked himself in conversation with Bishop Ealdred as they walked along the open passageway to the Godwinsons' apartments. His mother walked with them, her arm linked through her eldest son's. Behind them walked Gyrth and Leofwin.

"What I do not understand is what Edward gains from this," Harold was saying to Ealdred. He had come to view the older man like a father. He had missed his wisdom and good judgement this past year when he had been abroad, and was grateful the Bishop was now here for him to confide in.

"Apart from revenge on your father?" Ealdred replied. "A promise from Normandy not to harbour pirates and allow them to use their ports to raid our shores?"

"There has to be more."

"That he would consider William as his heir?" Ealdred continued, as if he were making a statement rather than a question.

"Then why send you abroad to find the Exile and his family? Why agree to allow me to go with you to the Holy Roman Emperor's court to fetch another contender for the throne, when he has already promised his crown to William?"

Ealdred shrugged his sturdy shoulders as they turned into the Godwins' apartments. The room was furnished with cushioned stools and chairs and a latticed iron brazier in case heat was needed. A wicker partition divided off the sleeping areas. Like Harold and Eadgyth's apartment, it was lavishly furnished.

"I have a theory," Ealdred began. "I don't believe that Edward ever really meant to make a serious offer to the Duke. I believe it was a whim, come to him, when the tide had turned against your father; that, and the influence of Champart. I trust he regrets it now, and would prefer to steer clear of any discussions with the duke about the return of the boys, for fear of reopening the dialogue about the succession. I don't think that Edward is so stupid to believe that William of Normandy would be a popular choice for king here in Englalond, but at the same time, he would not want to risk angering him by reneging on the bargain. He likes to keep his cousin, the duke, sweet. Since his meeting with William three years ago, our coastlines have been safe from the seafaring incursions of the Wícinga. All that could start again if William found out that he was being replaced as heir, and decided to retaliate by allowing those pirates to use his ports to attack our coasts again. Remember how Edward shudders at the very name, Wícinga?"

"And so, rather than open a jar of worms, our secretive monarch prefers to ignore the situation and hope that it will go away," Harold said pensively. His eyebrows were furrowed as he tried to think of a way around the conundrum.

"But unfortunately, it will not go away and that could put our boys at risk," Countess Gytha added emotionally. "Oh, Lord in Heaven, why did that devil, Champart, take them away from us!" She looked as if she was going to collapse, and her maid directed her to a cushioned chair. She sank down and clasped her head in her hands, her maid kneeling beside her to offer her comfort.

"I'm worried about my mother's health in all this," Harold said to Ealdred as the other brothers fussed around Gytha, offering her wine to steady her nerves.

Ealdred nodded and placed a fatherly hand on Harold's arm. "There is nothing anyone can do. Edward would rather play along with the duke by saying nothing. There are some things that we just cannot get Edward to do. He is a stubborn old fool."

"I wouldn't put it past him to have not written to Normandy at all, and that he has fabricated the whole tale into the bargain!" Harold kicked the plastered wall in frustration. "God, but this is such a mess! Damn them all; Edward, the duke, my sister... Champart!"

Gyrth threw his hands up in frustration. "This is beyond any logic; the king *must* do something. These boys are his wife's family. Edith shows more concern for the wards in her care, yet not a jot about her own brother and nephew! And what of Tostig? Is he not the king's current favourite? I cannot believe he is not able to influence the king in any way."

They were surprised when, without knocking, Tostig opened the door to the chamber just as Gyrth shouted his name.

"Talking about me, dear brothers? Well, here I am in person. You can say it to my face… whatever it was." Tostig stepped in haughtily, closing the door behind him.

"Don't you have your own rooms to go to, or do you sleep in between the royal couple? Perhaps Alfgar was right after all," said Gyrth, sourly.

"I should be careful, brother. That Mercian ball-bag wasn't that difficult to get rid of, nor should you be, brother or no."

"*Horningsunu!*" Gyrth shouted as he lunged forward and grabbed Tostig by the throat, slamming him into the wall behind him. "Do you only care about yourself? What about your younger brother? And Hakon? Do they not deserve some bloody consideration?"

"Get your hands off me, you stupid fool!" Tostig slammed his palms into Gyrth's chest. "I could have you outlawed, just like -"

"Just like? Alfgar?" Gyrth spat as he wrestled with him. He lashed out, but Tostig caught his arm and thrust his fist into his stomach, forcing him to double up. In a swift movement, Tostig grabbed him in a headlock.

Harold shouted at them to stop. The Countess was crying and pleading for them to desist. "Why must it always be so with my children?" she cried.

Harold and Leofwin tried to separate them, Harold grasping Tostig by his shoulders and heaving him away, constraining him so that he was forced to release his grip on Gyrth. As they were pulled apart, Gyrth managed to free his arm from Leofwin's grasp and swung one last punch at Tostig. Harold pre-empted it, catching the blow with the palm of his hand, and holding Tostig back, firmly, with his other hand.

"What are we, animals? Or men?" shouted Harold. He pushed Tostig out of Gyrth's reach and Leofwin caught and held Gyrth with the help of the bishop.

"You men are not fit to be earls! If your poor father, God rest his soul, could see you all now, he would certainly be turning in his grave." Gytha had risen to her feet and was wringing her hands in anguish.

Harold grabbed Tostig and dragged him behind the partition and into the sleeping area.

"What the hell are you doing?" he shouted. He saw that Tostig was shaking. In the other room, they could hear their mother berating Gyrth in between her sobbing.

"Mother is upset -I did not come here for this," Tostig said, and tried to leave.

Harold stopped him, placing his hand on his chest. "What did you come here for then?" he asked, coldly.

"I came to join my family. We are still family, are we not; or so I thought. Now, I realise that you are all against me."

"And what makes you think that, brother?" Harold found himself shaking with anger. He paced before Tostig, gesticulating furiously. "Why on earth would you think we are all against you? Tell me what leads you to that conclusion? Could it be your lack of interest in helping our boys? Could it be your obstruction of any conversation with the king about the matter of Wulfnoth and Hakon? Or is it the way you put yourself before all others?"

"I cannot for the life of me know, Harold, what it is that I am supposed to have done to make all of you behave toward me with such suspicion and disdain. I came here to tell you I promise that, when the time is right, I will speak for Wulfnoth and Hakon. Just now, before the king, when you spoke to me with such rancour, I was trying to tell you that it was not a good time to speak of the matter. Edith tried to tell you as well. The trouble with you, Harold, is you never listen to anyone but yourself."

Harold was astounded. "You manipulative bastard! You think I'm fooled by your pathetic deception? Don't think that I don't know what all this sucking up to Edward is all about. You intervened because you want to ingratiate yourself with him, not because you care about the king being tired, or our brother and nephew, languishing somewhere – alone – without their family. And another thing, don't even try to think that I have not noticed the looks that go between you and Edith." He paced the room, then stopped, and folded his arms, glaring hotly at his brother. "I've suspected for a long time that you're both up to something…"

Tostig looked wounded. "Why is it so difficult for you to believe me, Harold? We are brothers. Does that not count for anything? I can't help it if Edward enjoys my company and has taken me into his confidence," he said in an imploring voice, throwing Harold a beseeching look. "What has happened to you, brother, that you are so filled with suspicion and animosity?"

"*What has happened to me?* Nay, Tostig, 'tis you who are the changed one!" Harold threw his head back as if he were seeking aid from the heavens. There were words on the tip of his tongue that he did not want to let loose, lest he should forever regret them. Instead he breathed in deeply. He knew Tostig was lying, for he had turned his face and would not allow his eyes to meet his directly.

"The boys are safe, Harold. I do not know what all the fuss is about. They are receiving a good education in Normandy; you heard what Edward said." Still Tostig refused to look at him.

"And what will happen to them when William finds out that Edward is dangling his crown in front of another?"

"They say that William is a devout man; they will come to no harm. They will be treated well. William is an honourable man, this much I do know."

"Just how do you know?" Harold shifted his stance and stiffened as he refolded his arms across his chest. "Look me in the eye, Tostig, and tell me they will be safe." He paused as he saw Tostig flinch. "You can't – can you?"

"Are you forgetting his wife is my Judith's own kin? Besides, it would be futile for William to harm them if he is to get his hands on the crown. They are his surety, after all." He sat down on a coffer and folded his arms defensively. "Whatever you think of me, Harold, I do care about our brother... and Swegn's boy. I am not so ambitious that I would put myself before their welfare."

Harold stood with his back against the partition. He sighed heavily. He wanted to believe him, but when a man did not look you consistently in the eye, the chances were that he was feigning. He gazed at Tostig. His brother was looking at the floor. In their silence, their mother could be heard still arguing with Gyrth who was fuming about Tostig's 'selfishness'. Harold had not realised how much of a hothead his younger brother could be. As the thought came to mind, he remembered what Gyrth had said earlier when he had been fighting with Tostig: *Just like Alfgar!*

"What did you do?" Harold asked, as the significance of what the brothers had said about Alfgar, suddenly dawned upon him.

"What?"

"Alfgar. You set him up, didn't you? You said, 'That Mercian ball-bag was easily got rid of!' What did you mean by that?"

"Come on, brother, it would only have been a matter of time before Alfgar got himself exiled. He has always been an arrogant, dishonourable bastard. He was not fit to wear the office of an earl; even you could not deny that."

Harold shook his head, shifting uncomfortably. "So, I was right in my suspicions… Your conceit is deplorable, brother; you contrived the whole thing, didn't you? It was you and Ralph, wasn't it? God knows I had not wanted to believe it! I wanted to believe that you had been given the earldom on your own merit, and not because you had anything to do with ousting Alfgar."

"And so what? We did Edward a favour! Everyone knows that Edward dislikes Alfgar, and, well, the man showed his true colours!

Do you think there is one person, in the whole of Englalond, who cares?" Tostig rose to his feet; his expression, dark.

"Do not be so sure that there isn't, Tostig. Can you not see what this now means for the kingdom?"

"Aye, I see a brighter future!" Tostig smirked.

"Jesus, Tostig, do you think that Alfgar will be idly twiddling his thumbs somewhere on an island, living his days out quietly in peaceful retirement?"

Tostig shrugged and sat back down. He was still smirking, and that riled Harold even more. "Bloody hell, Tostig, your arrogance offends me. Get out of my sight before I do something to you that I will regret."

Tostig stood to his feet again. "I did Englalond a favour, Harold, if you would but see it. Do not worry, I am leaving. I would not want to sully your presence with mine."

As Tostig moved to leave, Harold caught his arm. "Alfgar went with a band of followers, Tostig... and money. I have heard that he went to Iralond to gather forces. There are plenty of willing mercenaries there, just waiting for the opportunity to fill their coffers with Englisc booty. What do you think will happen if he succeeds?"

"Then we will fight him, brother, and rid ourselves of him finally."

"What if he allies himself with Gruffudd? It would not be the first time a rebellious earl has done that, as we know."

"Then we kill two birds with one stone!"

Tostig pushed past the partition, and Harold let him go. When Gyrth saw him, he leapt to his feet with his fists at the ready. Harold and Leofwin had to restrain him again.

"No, Gyrth, leave him be. He is not worth it," Harold muttered. He waited for Tostig to leave the chamber before he released Gyrth.

"I cannot believe how close we once were," Gyrth said bitterly, when Tostig had gone. "What has happened to him to make him like this?"

"Edith happened to him," Leofwin replied.

Ealdred laid gentle hands on Harold and Gyrth's shoulders. "My sons, we should pray for him."

Dinner was a lavish affair as usual. Eadgyth sat at the very end of the high table, next to her mother-in-law and Ealdred, Gytha's lifelong friend. She cynically considered herself lucky to be there at all, for although the queen had managed to seat as many of the important guests as possible, Eadgyth had originally been left off the seating plan. It had been Edith's intention that she sat amongst the lesser nobles but, when the Countess of Wessex had seen that there was no place for Eadgyth, she insisted that one be set for her next to herself.

Gytha had been pointing out to Eadgyth who everyone was. Some she had met before; others were new to her. The king and queen sat in their customary places in the middle of the table on their extravagantly furnished high-back thrones. Tostig was sitting as guest of honour to the left of the king, without his heavily pregnant wife, who was in her final month and had stayed in Jorvik rather than risk the journey south. Seated next to him was Lord Cynsige, the Archbishop of Jorvik, who had travelled with him. Also at the king's table was his nephew, de Mantes, and his wife, another Gytha, followed by William Malet and another favourite of Edward's, Robert FitzWimarc, his standard bearer. There were also other leading nobles such as the Archbishop of Cantwarabyrig, Stigand. Gytha explained to Eadgyth that he should have been sitting closer to the king than the Archbishop of Jorvik, because Cantwarabyrig had precedence over Jorvik. However, he had been a friend and supporter of Edward's mother, and had replaced Champart, making him the devil incarnate in Edward's ever resentful eyes.

Eadgyth was disappointed that she could not sit next to Harold. He had been forced to sit next to his sister. She imagined that he was not finding it a pleasurable experience. She knew that he and Edith merely tolerated each other. The queen, she knew, loathed the way he resisted her domineering nature, unlike Tostig, and in return, Harold detested her efforts to control him. Gyrth and Leofwin also had places at the royal table. Eadgyth liked the younger Godwin brothers, for they were affable and good-natured like her Harold.

"I do not see Earl Leofric," Eadgyth mentioned to the Countess, her eyes searching the hall.

"Yes, he is notable by his absence, isn't he? It seems he has sent a representative who informed the court that he is ailing; most likely the cause of it is the stress brought by that braggart son of his, Lord Alfgar."

"So sad that a son should cause so much heartache for his father," Eadgyth remarked. Immediately she felt her face redden, when she realised the effect her statement might have on the Countess.

"Never a truer thing was said, my dear," Gytha said, patting her hand.

"My Lady, it was thoughtless of me to say," Eadgyth replied shamefully.

"Nonsense, when you have many apples in a basket, it is bound that you will find at least one or two bad ones."

Gytha chuckled, and Eadgyth was glad that her husband's mother was as good-natured as he. Eadgyth thought about her own basket of fruit. So far, she had five children. She momentarily prayed that none of them would become rotten.

"Never fear, my darling, for I am sure that none of your apples will go bad," Gytha said intuitively, "as long as you look after them with all your heart."

The two women smiled at each other. How glad she was that Harold's mother was here with her. She could not have endured the evening otherwise. She had caught Harold's sister's eye on more than one occasion. She was sure that Edith was irritated by her presence, judging by the prickly stare she gave her. She was not surprised that she had tried to leave her out, for it seemed that it was the queen's lifelong ambition to convince everyone of her non-existence. Danish-style love marriages were not uncommon in Englisc society, and considered just as legal as marriages blessed by priests; yet Edith had always found it difficult to accept Eadgyth was her brother's wife. In truth, Eadgyth Swannehaels was no lowborn harlot, as the queen liked to make her out to be. She was the daughter of a wealthy and high-standing thegn, and should always be treated as any other highborn lady. This, Eadgyth knew, Harold had tried to reason with his sister at length, but to no avail. She would always be a 'mistress' in Edith's eyes, she had told him, and as the brother-in-law of the king, he should keep his harlot hidden away and not flaunt her at court.

After the symbels of the feast had been performed, people were free to move from one table to another or move their seats. Eadgyth was pleased when Harold came and sat next to her.

"Are you enjoying the evening, sweetheart?" Harold whispered to Eadgyth.

Eadgyth smiled. The court musicians were playing and there was the constant drone of voices locked in conversation. She knew she could say what she felt without being overheard. "In truth, I am hating every minute of it, my love," she replied with a grin. She was fiddling with the ends of her wimple, a habit that she had when she felt restless or uncomfortable.

"I know, but it is just Edith. No one else is bothered by your presence."

"I can't help but wonder, Harold. It is almost as if the other women are afraid to talk to me in case they become tainted in some way," she said sadly, smiling as if it were of little importance to her.

"I concede that Edith does have that power."

"Harold, you know that I am out of my depth here. It is late and, although your mother has been so gracious to me, I would that you would escort me back to our chamber."

"Ah, Eadgyth, I am truly sorry," Harold said regretfully. "Of course I will accompany you back, sweetheart."

She nodded, relieved. "I am tired, and the babe will be wanting her feed."

"Then I am at your service, my love."

Harold knew it would be a good chance for them to spend a few moments together as he walked her to their apartment. He began to tell Eadgyth what had gone before in the day between him and Tostig, when they saw a group of men marching towards them along the passageway, the noise of their boots resounding as they hit the floor in unison.

"Good God, is that the Earl of Mercia?" Harold said to Eadgyth in surprise. Then he reaffirmed, "I think it is."

"I thought he was unwell?" Eadgyth said, surprised.

"So did I."

As they neared them, Harold and Eadgyth saw that it was indeed Earl Leofric. His strong, stout body was unmistakeable, even from a distance.

"So, he has recovered suddenly," Harold remarked to Eadgyth, but there was something about the group of men that made her feel uneasy. They were dressed in their mail and their swords hung by their sides. They came to a halt in front of them.

"Lord Leofric, it pleases me that you have made the journey to court after all," Harold said.

Leofric nodded grimly, unable to even force a smile out of politeness. There was no great love between the Houses of Godwin and Mercia.

"I come with news for the king's ears only," Leofric said in his usual proud voice. "It is about my son, Alfgar. My grandson here has much to report." Harold realised that no matter how far Alfgar dragged him, Leofric would never humble himself before a Godwinson.

Eadgyth and Harold looked at the young man beside him whose half-starved face bore the scars of a soul in torment.

The younger man stepped forward. "Lord Harold," Burghred said, with humility, "I come to beg the king's pardon, and have news that will be of great importance to him and Lord Ralph. My father has allied himself with Gruffudd, King of Gwynedd, and now of all Wales. He has raised an army with the intention of attacking the Earl Ralph's stronghold in Hereford. Soon his armies will be gathering in the hills of the *scīra*."

Harold stared open-mouthed at both Burghred and Leofric. Then he smiled, and said, "Well, I'll be damned."

Chapter Nineteen

Demons

September 1055

Freyda carried out her chores with her usual lack of enthusiasm. She hated having to churn butter, but her mother's ever watchful eye meant there was no getting out of it. She stopped for a moment to wipe the sweat from her brow and then continued, ramming the handle down into the small wooden bucket with great ferocity as if it were to blame for her irritation. The morning had started as it usually did: with the sound of the cock's crowing. After a light breakfast of yesterday's bread, cheese, and light ale, Freyda began her work in the dairy, and everyone else went about their own business. The weather was turning. The long searing months of summer were tapering into autumn, blended with frosty mornings and cooler evenings. It had been a good harvest, and the orchards had yielded a decent crop of various succulent fruits. But there was no compensation for the darkening gloom that had caught the thegn's household in its grasp, influencing every action or word that anyone said.

Father had whisked back home from Hereford and then, before two days were up, he was gone again; attending to other duties, he had informed them, mostly collecting the revenues that were due for the king and the earl. Freyda had wondered about these duties and mused on whether they included visiting a certain lady over at Waldron.

During the times when he was at home, Freyda had noticed that there was an air of acceptance between her parents. They rarely spoke, but when they did, there was a cold civility between them. Although they once again shared their bedchamber, Freyda doubted that they made love. She knew that her mother would only have allowed him back in their chamber to create a smokescreen, so that people would think that there was no disharmony between them. Perceptively, Freyda knew that her mother's pride would force her to bury her head under a cloak of pretence in the belief that, if they carried on the deception of normality, no one would know what truly went on in their household.

As Freyda toiled, she began to hum a favourite song. She was thinking of ways of escaping the depressing atmosphere of Horstede Hall. She longed to go rollicking in the forest with Edgar and smiled at the thought of him. He had not been to the homestead much since her father's angry outburst. They met mostly in the forest after dark, using Tovi to pass messages between them. Her younger brother seemed to enjoy the intrigue.

As Freyda's mind drifted, remembering fondly her meetings with her lover, she suddenly felt a presence behind her and a voice that said softly, "*A man comes walking to where he knew…*"

"Edgar…" she whispered wistfully as she felt him close his arms around her and kiss her neck softly. She leaned into him and allowed herself to sink into his arms. "Someone may see you."

"*And came upon a maiden…*" Ignoring her warning, he placed his hand over hers on the handle of the churn, helping her turn it, and she felt his moustache nuzzling her neck. "*Reached beneath his skirt and drew…*" Edgar continued. He grabbed her other hand and placed it underneath his tunic and against his groin "*…something stiff and brazen.*" She laughed and Edgar sighed with pleasure at the sensation of her hand rubbing his cock through his clothing.

He pushed himself closer to her and, teasingly, she held on to him and took over the recitation. "*Beneath her belt he worked his will… they –*"

"*Both began to wiggle…*" they said in unison and Edgar whirled her round to face him, pulling her close. "*And wiggle,*" they repeated, laughing. Their lips locked and Freyda felt him push against her, his breathing growing heavier in her ear.

"*…Weary of the work and tired, his handy helper bidden,*" he whispered. Freyda shivered as he breathed against her ear, sensing the lust in his voice.

"*Less strong now than she at last…*" Freyda continued, pushing him away with a playful laugh and ignoring Edgar's moans of frustration. "Not here. Someone may come in!" she protested.

"You have to finish it! There's more yet!" he cried, making a grab for her.

Freyda darted out of his way. She ran out of the hut and into the yard outside. Edgar chased her under the washing line, much to Sigfrith's annoyance. They became entangled in newly washed linen, tossing it to the grass as they fought their way out of it. Edgar caught Freyda, and in a whirl of hysterical giggling, dragged her back into the dairy leaving Sigfrith muttering obscenities as she retrieved her spoilt washing.

Inside the hut, Freyda screamed with delight as he threw her onto the floor and tried to pin her down. She fought him off as best she could, but was incapacitated by her hysterical laughter as she squirmed beneath him. The prospect of getting caught added to the excitement even though she knew it was risky.

"No, Edgar!" she cried out.

Edgar held her arms firmly and finally she gave up the fight. She closed her eyes in the full knowledge of what was about to come. Feeling the wetness of his tongue as he ran it up her face, she squealed. Peels of her laughter rang out of the hut.

"Edgar, if my mother catches us we will be done for!"

"And what will she do?"

"She will stop us from being together."

"She can't. We are betrothed on the Earl of Wessex's orders," Edgar ignored her pleas, continuing his assault on her.

"Please, Edgar, no more…I don't want us to get caught like this," she entreated him. "If my father should catch us..."

"Then meet me tonight? Say 'yes' or I will lick you to death!"

"Yes, yes, all right, I will meet you tonight. I will meet you!" she yelled and their lips met in a languorous kiss.

Wulfhere scratched his head, pondering on what could be done about the rotting timber posts on one of the burgh houses. He and Esegar had been checking the buildings around the homestead to see what needed fixing before the dampness of winter set in. They would have to fix it temporarily but, looking at the deterioration in the wood, Wulfhere knew that the building would eventually be ruined, and the whole structure would have to be rebuilt. In the meantime, they would be fine for one more winter with some patching up. He and Esegar had cut some wooden planks, and were banging them along the bottom of the structure to reinforce the rotting timbers. Esegar held the wood in place while his master banged the nails in. Normally they would be deep in conversation, sharing little anecdotes about their wives or children. Sometimes, Wulfhere would regale Esegar with tales of life at Edward's court, but today he was quiet and somewhat morose, though that did not deter Esegar from chatting to him regardless, even if there was a dearth of enthusiasm in Wulfhere's responses.

"That child has the yellow hair of his father for sure," Esegar observed.

Wulfhere was about to bang in another nail. "What child?" he asked indifferently. His mood was such that he could barely make the effort to sound interested.

"Why, your serving maid, Sigfrith's child," Esegar replied. "He has exactly the same colour hair as Tigfi's. And they don't call him *The Yellow* for nothing. There'll be no denying he's the father."

Wulfhere looked up and saw Sigfrith walk across the yard to where the newly washed bed-linen hung out to dry. A yellow tuft of hair poked out of the baby swaddle strapped to her back. Dammit! He had forgotten that he was supposed to speak to the earl about his huscarle getting the girl pregnant. What with all that had happened recently, and having been away in Hereford, he had not even realised that the child had been born.

He spoke grimly. "Thank you for reminding me, Esegar. I need to speak to the earl about the child. Tigfi will have to compensate the girl. Lord Harold should have a care that his men do not take liberties with their host's servants."

"Well, it could have been worse, lord. The child's father was nearly Helghi!" Esegar said. He shook his head and laughed.

At the mention of Helghi's name, Wulfhere banged the hammer against his thumb and cried out in pain. "What's that about Helghi?" he asked when his breath returned.

"Oh nothing, my lord, I was jesting of course. Perhaps in bad taste," Esegar replied, turning bright red.

"You said something about Helghi. Did you say 'it could have been Helghi's?" Wulfhere asked, sucking his throbbing thumb. He noticed the sheepish expression on his fyrdsman's face and knew that he had heard right. "What makes you say that, Esegar?"

"No reason, I just said the first name that came into my head, my lord. Nothing more." Esegar was looking around him, as if hunting for the next piece of wood, but Wulfhere knew he was avoiding his eyes.

"Why is it that I don't believe you, Esegar? You have turned the colour of your tunic. Tell me what you meant by, 'it could have been Helghi'."

"Lord, it was said in jest, nothing more."

"If I find out there is more to this Esegar, then –"

"My lord, I-I am s-sorry," Esegar stammered. He took a deep breath, readying himself to confess and continued warily, "Tigfi and I caught Helghi trying to force himself on Sigfrith the night of your daughter's betrothal."

"God's bones! Why did you keep this from me?" Wulfhere threw down a plank of wood, leaned back on his heels and then jumped quickly to his feet, still clutching the hammer.

Esegar stood to his feet, worriedly. "Because if you knew," he reasoned, "there would be more feuding 'tween you and Helghi, lord – and that would not please Earl Harold," Esegar said, exasperatedly. "I'm sorry I kept it from you, but it was not my idea."

Wulfhere saw him glance at the hammer in his hand. It had a heavy iron head on it and could easily smash a skull into pieces. "Whose idea was it?" he demanded, the hammer shook in his hand, ominously.

"Tigfi's," Esegar murmured, grudgingly.

"Damn Tigfi!" Wulfhere swore. "So, he rescues Sigfrith from Helghi's clutches and then humps her himself! How very gallant!" He glanced over to where he'd seen Sigfrith walking, and suddenly baulked at the scene that met his eyes. Edgar was chasing Freyda through washing, whilst an enraged Sigfrith was swearing and cursing at them. He heard them laughing, and the sight of them fuelled his rage; already boiling.

"My Lord!" Esegar cried. He clutched his forehead momentarily as Wulfhere strode toward the dairy. "Please, put down the hammer, lord!"

Wulfhere barely heard Esegar's plea. His ears were filled with a ringing, like that of bells. He grasped the hammer threateningly, driven by murderous intent. If Freyda marries Edgar, Helghi, will have her in his clutches to pass between those fat kinsmen of his, like a joint of succulent meat. *Well, I am damned if I am going to let that happen!* he thought, as he stormed toward them.

Wulfhere caught sight of Sigfrith, her face filled with horror, as she turned on her heel and ran to warn the young couple. He followed her, intent on his mission, thrust her aside and stormed his way into the dairy. Before Edgar could do anything to defend himself, Wulfhere slammed him up against the wall by his throat.

"No, lord!" Esegar his grabbed Wulfhere's arm, as he drew the hammer back in his fist.

"Stay away from my daughter!" Wulfhere snarled.

"Lord, the lad is not to blame," Esegar pleaded, hanging onto his lord's arm.

Wulfhere retracted his arm from Esegar's grip and pushed him gently away from him. "Step away, Esegar, or I will do to you what I am about to do to him!"

Not wanting to experience the hammer crashing against his face, Esegar did as he was told.

Wulfhere was holding the hammerhead against a frightened Edgar's face. "If you don't, you stinking *swinescite*, this is what I will do! And not even your own mother will recognise you!" Wulfhere smashed the hammer into the wall, breaking the plaster, an inch away from Edgar's face. Edgar let out a howl as he felt the hammer thud into the wall.

"Father, leave him! He has done nothing wrong!" Freyda screamed, grabbing at Wulfhere's tunic.

He pushed her aside. "Esegar, take her out of my way!" he ordered. If Edgar had not had his eyes closed, he would have seen the burning rage in Wulfhere's dilated pupils as he pulled him forward, swung him round by his collar, and propelled him into the yard outside. As he lay quivering in the dirt, Wulfhere lunged at him and Freyda flew past him, having escaped Esegar, and threw herself over Edgar's prone body.

"No, I won't let you hurt him!" she shouted. Her tear-stained face peered up at him defiantly.

Wulfhere grabbed her, and threw her to one side, as if she was nothing more than a piece of rag. She kicked him, calling him a 'brute'. He felt a sharp pain in his calf, and instantly, without thought, his arm flew out and caught her on the side of her face. It was an involuntary reaction, and he regretted it instantly; but the deed was done.

She fell to the ground with a cry of pain just as her mother, alerted to the disturbance, came running to the scene.

"What are you doing, Wulfhere?" Ealdgytha cried, as Freyda sank to her knees, holding her injured cheek.

Wulfhere's shock gave Edgar time to react. Whilst Wulfhere stood stunned, Edgar leapt to his feet and barged against Wulfhere, with as much force as his strength would allow. The thegn staggered, surprised at Edgar's sudden burst of energy.

"What are you going to do, whelp?" Wulfhere taunted. "Look at you, you can hardly stand. You're just a boy. Think you can fight me, cripple boy?"

"You think it makes you a man to beat a girl? Your own daughter?" Edgar retorted, his fists clenched and his eyes bright with anger.

"She is *my* daughter!" Wulfhere replied. He had not wanted to hurt her, but he was damned if he was going to let the lad lecture him.

"And she is to be *my* wife."

"Do you honestly believe I am really going to let you marry her?"

"We have a contract!" Edgar shouted. He stood before Wulfhere with his head held high.

"There *is* no contract now!" Wulfhere grabbed Edgar by his collar, but this time the youth fought back, landing Wulfhere an almighty punch, connecting with his nose.

Immediately, the shock caused Wulfhere to loosen his grip on Edgar, forcing him to absorb what had just happened. Wulfhere felt a wetness around his left nostril and put his fingers to his nose. He wiped the trickle of blood from his moustache.

Edgar, buoyed on by his sudden burst of courage, swung back his fist to hit him again, but Wulfhere was recovered. He caught Edgar's arm and twisted him off balance. Edgar's crippled leg could not support him, and Wulfhere kicked his legs from under him, forcing him facedown into the dirt. He felt a feeling of satisfaction as Edgar's face hit the dust with a cry of pain. It was Helghi's pain. Years of anger at the wounds Helghi had inflicted upon him, glinted in his narrowed eyes.

Then, an anguished cry interrupted his thoughts. "Edgar!" shouted Freyda. It was a heart-wrenching sound, chilling his soul, bringing home that she loved this boy, who he had just put to the ground. He felt his heart sink as he stood there, drowning in the tears of his daughter.

"Wulfhere, leave him be," Ealdgytha implored, she was helping Freyda to her feet and comforting her. "Have you lost your wits completely?"

Deafened by the storm of anger that was raging inside his head, he closed his ears to their voices; Esegar's attempts to reason with him, Ealdgytha's admonishments, and Freyda's cries for mercy. He did not want to hear them, for he was afraid that it would make him stop and he did not want to stop. He did not want to let anything stand in his way of revenge. He bent down and rolled Edgar onto his back. He had Edgar's collar in his grasp as he swung back his fist and rammed it into his face. Behind him, Freyda was hysterical and Ealdgytha shouted at him to stop.

But the only words he heard as he drew back his fist to bear down, once more, on Edgar's bloodied face, were Esegar's. "Lord, don't do this! The lad is not Helghi!"

He was just about to hit him again, when Esegar's words stayed his hand. "He is not Helghi!" *God Damn them all.* He was looking into Edgar's frightened eyes and felt ashamed. He let go of him and Edgar fell back on the ground. The boy's lips were swollen and bleeding, a cut and swelling were developing on his right cheek, and blood poured from his nose and another cut over his eye.

Wulfhere put a hand to his forehead, his fingers gnawing at his temple. Esegar was right: Edgar was not the true cause of his anger. It was longing for Alfgyva, the loss of the child, Ealdgytha's coldness, Helghi's scheming, his guilt... nothing of which was Edgar's doing. He was angry with himself because, like the greatest of fools, he lacked the temerity to put any of it right, no matter how hard he tried. But his conscience stabbed at him and his pride was hurt. He had tried to bury his shame deep within and it had turned in on him, waiting for the opportunity to rear its ugly head.

Quite unexpectedly, Tovi appeared beside him, grasping the edge of his sleeve. "Father, don't hurt Edgar anymore." Wulfhere looked over his shoulder at his son. *Why are you doing this?* said the tearful young eyes.

"I am not responsible," Wulfhere replied. But still Tovi's eyes stared at him with condemnation.

Wulfhere felt confused. Was this his fault after all?

He was suddenly aware of all those around him. They were all there; everyone who had always looked up to him. He looked at all their faces and knew what they were thinking. They would expect him to behave honourably, like a king's thegn.

Father Paul approached him, and spoke to him gently, "Come, Lord Wulfhere, it is over. Let it go now. Let God deal with this in his own way."

Wulfhere looked around at all their worried faces. He knew they would all be thinking that the feud would begin again now. He could feel their staring eyes. It unnerved him. He dared not look at any of them. Instead he held his hand out to Edgar who took it reluctantly.

Wulfhere helped Edgar to his feet; his hand still enclosed around the boy's, tightly. He pulled him toward him and spoke quietly into his ear, "I want you gone from here, and if you ever come back, I will finish this."

Edgar's desperation glowed from him, but he made no move to fight again. He simply bowed his head in defeat.

"Why, Father? What has he done wrong?" Tovi asked, his voice pitted with sadness.

"Yes... why, Father? What has he done wrong?" Freyda cried. She stood by Edgar's side, her arms around him protectively. "You cannot do this. We are betrothed."

"No longer, daughter. I will not have you marry the son of a man who would force himself on a maid in the house of his host. I know it is not the fault of Edgar's. However, I cannot allow you to marry into such a family."

Freyda looked stunned. Edgar's face flushed and his chin quivered.

"I do not believe you!" Freyda replied defiantly. "You're clutching at straws, Father!"

"Clutching at straws, am I?" Wulfhere cried; then walked to Sigfrith and grabbed hold of her by her shoulders. "Tell them, girl! Tell them what that animal tried to do to you."

"Sigfrith?" Freyda looked at the girl questioningly.

Sigfrith, who had been ruefully averting her eyes, looked up at Freyda and nodded. "But Esegar and Tigfi... they stopped it."

Freyda turned to Esegar, her voice filled with disbelief. "Esegar, is this true?"

"Esegar, tell her." Wulfhere looked grimly at his right-hand man.

"'Tis true. I am sorry, Lady Freyda," Esegar replied with a deep sigh.

"Did you know about this, Edgar?" Freyda demanded, looking at him fiercely.

"No, Freyda, I swear I did not."

She stared at him with a look of disgust; her open mouth was trying to find the right words, but she was unable to speak. She started to back away from him. He called to her, but she had already gone, running to the hall, her mother hurrying after her. He called out to her again and made to follow her, but Esegar held him back. "If you know what is good for you, lad, you will leave here and never come back," he said to him firmly.

Edgar looked to Wulfhere. "Lord Wulfhere, I swear I did not know," he implored, hands held out palms upwards in a gesture of incredulity.

Wulfhere suddenly felt pity for the boy. "I believe you... but you have to go. It is over, Edgar. She will not want you now. Now leave my land... whilst you still can." Wulfhere turned and began to walk away.

"No, Father, don't make Edgar go," Tovi beseeched him, grasping at his sleeve. "I don't want him to go." Wulfhere shook him off and continued to stride, unwaveringly, toward the hall. "Father!" Tovi ran in front of him, but Wulfhere pushed him aside, ignoring his pleas as if the boy were a fly to be swatted away.

As Wulfhere entered the hall, he did not see the sadness etched on his son's eyes as he stood, confused, watching with Father Paul. Nor did he see the look of gloom on the priest's face, as he placed a comforting arm around Tovi's shoulders.

Wulfhere stared at his daughter with tired eyes; she, tracing the contours of the table with a fingertip. Her own eyes, cold and harsh, were following the unseen patterns that her finger drew. Ealdgytha sat on the bench next to him, his partner in judgement as their daughter, as sullen as a dog that has had its bone confiscated, waited for them to begin the sermon.

"I am sorry, Freyda, that you had to hear of it in this manner," Wulfhere began. "I admit I have never wanted this marriage for you, but nonetheless, it was not my desire to have you hurt in anyway." Annoyingly, she did not acknowledge his words and continued to worm her finger around the table, sourly.

Wulfhere allowed her to remain silent. In some ways, he was glad that she refused to speak. It made it all the easier if she did not.

Instead, Ealdgytha spoke. "Well, daughter, I do not necessarily approve of the manner in which it was done," she glared at Wulfhere before returning her gaze back to her daughter, "but now you have your chance to extricate yourself from this betrothal contract. Lord Leofnoth's son, Aemund, is keen to have you as his bride. It will be a good match for you, far better than the one that you had made with Edgar Helghison." She paused, as if she was waiting for an acknowledgement from her daughter. When none came, she continued, reaching out across the table's surface, stilling Freyda's hand. "I know you were fond of Edgar, but when you are wed to Aemund, you will realise that he was not the one for you."

Freyda stared at her hand as if it had been replaced by some terrible creature's. She looked up at her parents, obstinately. "You planned this, Father, didn't you?" Her voice was shaking as she spoke.

Wulfhere shifted in his seat and faced her. "If you mean that I fabricated the story about Helghi just to get you out of the marriage then, no, of course I did not. Sigfrith and Esegar confirmed the truth of it. You heard them, did you not?" He recoiled inwardly as he noticed the red swelling on her cheek where he had hit her. She was glaring at him as if he had slapped her again.

"But you had already talked with Lord Leofnoth and had come to an agreement," Freyda replied, her voice dark with bitterness.

"Freyda, it was only a matter of time before Edgar proved himself unworthy," Ealdgytha interjected. "He has bad blood."

Freyda, her eyes beaming her anger like shards of fire in her mother's direction, spoke with determination. "Edgar *is* worthy. It is his father who is at fault. But whatever manner of man Helghi is, at least he is not a trickster like the thegn of Horstede!" Freyda pushed back her stool and rose angrily. "I will decide whether or not I marry Edgar!"

"Freyda, sit down. We have not yet finished with you," Ealdgytha ordered.

"But *I* have finished with *you!*" She began to walk away then checked herself and turned to glare at them. "How can you still share your bed with him, Mother, after all he has done to you? *He*, who dares to sit there in judgement of others!"

"*Freyda!*" exclaimed her mother. "Would you shame your own father?"

"It is *he* who shames himself. And you too, Mother. Have you no pride? Or perhaps you have too much –"

During Freyda's diatribe, Ealdgytha had stood to her feet and was about to slap her daughter's face, when Wulfhere stayed her hand. "No, wife, leave her be. She has had enough for one day." He turned to his daughter. "Go about your business, Freyda. We will talk more on this later."

She ran to the door, and turning before she exited, yelled, "I *will* marry Edgar!" Then was gone from their sight.

"Well, you got what you wanted, wife." Wulfhere sat back down as if, despite his victory, he had somehow been defeated.

"And you wanted her to marry Edgar, did you?" Ealdgytha replied with hoarse terseness. She began to stride the hall, her agitation pervading the air like the smoke from the hearth, stinging him with a viciousness of its own.

"You know that I did not, woman." Wulfhere remained seated, as if he were cowering in the wake of her anger. He took a flask of mead and poured some into his horn. "But I cannot help but be stung by her unhappiness. At least the boy loved her enough to want to fight for her."

"So now you want to get sentimental? Love! What could she possibly know about it?"

"A lot it would seem," Wulfhere replied and he drank deeply from the horn.

"What's that supposed to mean?"

"Forget it." Wulfhere sighed and took another mouthful of mead. Ealdgytha stopped pacing and sat before him. He passed the flask to her, but she waved it away.

"Love belongs to the *skalds* and *scops*. It has nothing to do with the real world," she said.

"Try not to sound too bitter, *wife*," Wulfhere replied, acerbically.

"Why, of course I have nothing to be bitter about, do I, *husband*?" Ealdgytha ripped the horn from him and drank thirstily from it.

Wulfhere sighed. She was looking more tired of late, and there seemed to be lines on her face where there had been none before. She rarely smiled, and a discontented frown threatened to permanently furrow her brow. Her beauty was fading, not with age, but with the strain of a relationship that was once again in tatters. Pity stabbed at his heart and he reached for her hand. She instantly recoiled from him and took another swig from the horn.

"Ealdgytha, how long must we live like this? For another five years?"

Her pain spewed forth from her mouth. "Bitterness knows no timescale."

"Just what exactly are you bitter about, Ealdgytha? Is it because people might be gossiping about us? What are they saying? That the thegn's lady is such a *scréawa*? A bad-tempered scold? That he must look elsewhere for satisfaction? Is that what you are so bitter about?"

he retorted with an anger of his own that he soon regretted when he saw her eyes. "I am sorry, *min deor*." He reached for her hand again, and once more she pulled away.

"So, am I such a *scréawa*, then?" Ealdgytha asked sadly.

"I should not have said that."

They were silent for a moment. Wulfhere felt the guilt gnawing at his stomach, ravenously. If only he could cast it aside forever. *Why does it always haunt me?* But there was a voice in his head telling him that he was the engineer of his own shortcomings, and only he had the power to rid himself of it.

For a time, their eyes locked, though it was Wulfhere who eventually drifted his gaze, downwards, to escape her biting glare.

"Why, Wulfhere? What qualities does she possess that I do not?" Ealdgytha demanded. What takes you from my bed to hers?"

He took the horn from her and noticed that she had drunk it all. As he reached for the flask to replenish it, he felt her eyes searching for his again. "Please, Wulfhere. I often ask myself, *what did I not do that he should need to stray from me?* I need to know." The malice was gone from her voice, and he was cast off into the sea of her deep despair. He wanted to close his ears to her pain, but she would not let him.

He sighed and shook his head. "I cannot say it to you." He hung his head in shame.

"Why?"

"I do not wish to cause you further hurt."

"You could not hurt me more than you have already."

He paused again and then, seeing that she was determined to unlock the answer, he replied. Taking a deep breath, he began, "She... she... she took me as I am... never criticised or – or tried to change me… She loved me, content just to be with me. With her, I was myself, no more, no less. Just me… just me."

Ealdgytha's eyes glistened and her face was flushed from drinking too quickly. Her arm wobbled as she rested her chin in her hand, looking away for a moment, as if taking in his words. Then she faced him again with deep bitterness. For Wulfhere, the pain in her eyes was almost unbearable.

"I only wanted the best for you... for us, and the children. I only wanted better… for all of us."

"But *nothing* is ever enough for you." He demonstrated his frustration by throwing his arms up.

She laughed. "You were always content to be a thegn with just five hides of land, a church and a mill, and a few horses to breed."

"What is wrong in that?"

"You could have been so much more, Wulfhere. *We* could have had so much more."

"And just what was I supposed to do about that? Grovel at men's feet? Lick their backsides clean? You know that is not me."

"The way to get more is to ask for it. Offer favours. Loyalty is never enough; you have to buy your way sometimes. You could have done more for the king's favour. Sent him an extra horse from your stable, gifts... God knows it worked for the Godwins! And the Earl, he likes you. You could have gotten more out of him if you'd tried hard enough. But you wouldn't try, would you, Wulfhere? Your damned stupid pride is more important than the advancement of your family."

"You think I have ships that I can send the King as Godwin did, with golden prows and men to sail them?" He stared at her wide-eyed. "So, I am right. I am not enough for you am I, Ealdgytha? You should have been born first, then you would have married that rich thegn that your older sister got. Perhaps then you would have been happier."

"I was happy with you, Wulfhere. I just wanted more for our children, more for us. What you mistook for criticism was encouragement."

"You wanted more for no one but yourself – granddaughter of Tovi the Proud – always flaunting your great bloodline at me." Wulfhere rose to his feet and threw the drinking horn across the hall so that it fell onto the floor. It cracked on impact, and bounced into the fire pit. "And just when did you ever encourage me? You put me down at every opportunity, and thought nothing of belittling me. I put up with it in the early years because I was a bedazzled youth. But I grew up and became a man... and that's when I started to fight back. And you resented me for it."

Ealdgytha stood to her feet to meet his eyes with a defiant glare. "If you had been a worthy man, you would never have given me call to make you feel belittled!" she retorted, her eyes wide with anger.

Wulfhere was unable to quell the rising rage within him. He grabbed at her, and caught by her wimple as she tried to dodge him. There was a scuffle between them and Wulfhere pushed her to the ground. Tovi, having kept a watchful eye over his warring parents from the doorway, came running into the hall, seeing his cue to intervene. He stood on the table, jumped onto his father's back, just as Wulfhere was about to strike Ealdgytha as she knelt on the floor. Tovi clung to his father by his legs and pounded him with clenched fists; obscenities and cries of, 'leave her alone!' pouring from his lips. Wulfhere grabbed hold of his assailant's arm, spun him around and threw him down as if he were a playful puppy.

"Leave my mother alone, you bastard!" Tovi was crying as he picked himself up.

His son's words cut him. "Get out! This is no place for you, boy! Get out before I teach you not to come between your mother and me again!"

Ealdgytha stood to her feet with the help of Sigfrith, who'd been hovering in the sewing corner just in case she would be needed.

"You threw her on the ground," Tovi sobbed as he ignored his father's order, and beat at his father's frame with pathetic fists that were clearly useless.

Wulfhere held the boy's arms as he squirmed, trying to hit out at him, either kicking or ramming his knees into Wulfhere's legs.

"Tovi that is enough! How dare you treat your father with such disrespect," Ealdgytha shouted. She grabbed the boy, and landed a slap across the side of his head so hard that his ear glowed.

The boy was stunned. He looked at his mother, as he clasped a hand to his smarting ear, horror-struck. Even Ealdgytha appeared shocked at her own temper.

"What is wrong with you all?" The angry sound of Sigfrith's voice echoed around the hall.

Wulfhere and his wife watched helplessly as Sigfrith took charge, grabbing Tovi by his hand and pulling him aside. "Is it not enough that you fight each other, that you have to hurt the children as well?" Sigfrith chastised them with a sudden air of self-righteousness. As usual, she was the voice of reason. Her baby who was strapped to her back was, remarkably, sleeping contentedly, despite the uproar. Gerda and Drusilda clung to her skirts crying. Wulfhere heard a little sob from over by the doorway, and looked up to see Winflaed, watching the scene in dismay, tears running down her face.

"Come, children. Leave your parents to discuss their problems with each other. You can help me with the supper, since your mother has so much to sort out with your father." They left the hall amid sobs and tears.

Wulfhere turned to Ealdgytha. Tears were streaking her face. He stepped toward her and she moved away, straightening her wimple.

"A fine example we are for the children," she muttered, bitterly.

"Ealdgytha, I am truly sorry…"

"Forget it, Wulfhere." She pushed him away as he tried to take her shoulders.

"How can I make amends if you never let me?"

"I am not ready, Wulfhere," she said, turning away from him. She walked toward the ante chamber, looked back at him before stepping through the open door. "I don't even know if I want your amends."

Wulfhere slumped down on the bench and held his head in his hands, his elbows resting on the table. What a day it had been. He could not have felt more exhausted after an afternoon of battle training. Perhaps that was what he needed: a good session with Esegar… with sword and shield he could thrash out his frustration. But he would probably kill Esegar the way he was feeling. Or he could ride over to Alfgyva and take comfort in her bed. But that would only cause more trouble. He reached for the mead flask and drained it.

"Esegar!" he called, beginning to feel quite inebriated. "Esegar!"

"Yes, lord!" Esegar came running into the hall nervously.

"Get our horses!" Wulfhere said, rising to his feet. He grabbed his cloak from its hook. "We are going dicing!"

"Where, lord?"

"The Ale house by the river!"

"I have not my purse, lord."

"Don't worry, I have mine. And bring that old fool, Aelfstan and his boy, whatever his name is," Wulfhere ordered as he left the hall. "I feel like doing some merry-making for there is little of *that* round here these days!"

Edgar sat waiting nervously, his horse, Wolf, his only companion, as around him the sunset was transforming the forest into bright colours of autumnal gold, breaking through the branches to light up the woodland like a torch. At the water's edge, the bulrushes rustled in the cool breeze, and wild fowl and toads made their respective noises.

Earlier, Tovi had sought him out with a message from Freyda to meet her at the usual place by the pond. Edgar had not returned home yesterday after his fight with Wulfhere. He had been hiding in the forest since then, afraid to go home and face his father and the others. If Helghi was sober, he would be infuriated; enraged if he was drunk. His uncles and cousins would taunt him; his brother would have laughed at him. Mildrith would have offered him sympathy, and it would have been her pity that would hurt the most. No, the forest and all its demons were far less an evil than Gorde was.

He had bathed his face in the water and rested his leg, and talked to Wolf about Freyda, and his hopes that they might still have a chance. If only Wulfhere would give him that chance, to prove that he was not like his father. He had slept fitfully with only his cloak for comfort. When he awoke in the morning, he still could not bring himself to go home. Then, as luck would have it, Freyda had sent Tovi to Gorde with a message for him, but Edgar had waylaid him from his hiding place. He was filled with hope when he heard that she was coming.

"Edgar?" She came, rustling through the undergrowth.

He turned and his heart leapt when he saw her. "You came!"

"Yes, Edgar, I have come. I am sorry it took so long. Mother and Father were watching me like hawks." She touched his face noting the injuries. Her eyes glistened with tears. She was wearing her grey woollen tunic and red cloak. Her hair was wrapped in a white linen scarf covered by a brown linen hood. "You were wonderful yesterday. It was like Beowulf fighting that monster, Grendl."

"Except Beowulf usually wins." He would have laughed, but it was painful to do so because of his swollen cut lip and the bruising to his jaw, right where it met his cheekbones. A bruise and a graze had also developed on the left side of his forehead, when his face had rubbed against the dirt.

She embraced him tightly. "I am so sorry that you endure this for my sake."

He shook his head as if it were nothing. "What about your father?"

"He says I am to marry Aemund, Leofnoth of Stochingham's son. I cannot stand him. He is a conceited little peacock, strutting around as if he were God's gift to all women!"

"But you belong to me! They cannot do this. We had a contract. We must appeal to the Earl. It was his wish after all." Edgar took her face in his hands. "I will appeal to the hundred moot!"

"Nay, Edgar. What good will the hundred moot do? We must run away. My father is certain that the earl will rescind the betrothal because of what your father has done."

"Damn Helghi! Why wasn't I blessed with a father like yours?" Edgar said bitterly.

"Even after what he has done to you, you still have the grace to look up to him, though I cannot think why," she said, shaking her head. "But you are mistaken. He is no honourable man. He is as bad as your father. He has the morals of a tomcat."

"At least he does not try to force himself on his women," Edgar replied. "But enough, we will not run. I will appeal to the moot and then the earl if necessary; then the king and God himself if I must. I will not lose you, and I will act honourably."

"Can you be sure that they will take our side?" Freyda buried herself in his arms. "I cannot bear to live without you."

"I promise I will not lose you. As sure as the sun rises and sets over this land, I will not."

Ealdgytha reached out worried fingers, searching for the flickering candle that danced and fluttered beside her bedside table. She shone it over at the floor where Wulfhere lay on his feathered pallet; his place of exile. He was having another nightmare; his shouting and calling disturbing her ever more these last few nights, which had seen him tossing and turning, and muttering unintelligibly, his unsettled slumber not aided by the amount of drinking he had been doing in the nearby ale house. She saw that he was sitting up, his legs bent toward his chest and his head resting on his knees. His arms encircled his head and he breathed heavily as he rocked, gently.

"Wulfhere, what is it? Are you ill?"

He neither replied nor acknowledged her. She remembered when he had first come home from Scotland and had been plagued by bad dreams. Now, it appeared, his demons had returned. *Demons of his own making*, she thought, self-righteously.

She called out to him again. He lay back down, muttering that nothing was wrong and that she should go back to sleep. She wanted to, but felt compelled to ask, "Is it the nightmares again?"

"No. Go back to sleep," he replied, tersely.

She saw that he had lay back down and turned his back to her, facing the wall.

"You were shouting so loudly…"

"I will try not to."

The sadness in his voice touched her. That evening he had missed supper. Esegar and Aelfstan had returned home from the tavern carrying their master between them for the third night running. She had never seen him so drunk before. They put him straight to bed, and to her shame, Ealdgytha realised that they would have noted the separation. She enjoyed punishing him, enjoyed the humiliation he would feel by her neglect of him. But she was certain his torment was nothing to the degradation she had felt that day in the hall, when she had broken down in front of everyone. Her pride was shattered and her heart broken into pieces. Broken again… for a second time... and for the same reason.

But now, as she watched him lying there, trying to hide his tears, she felt a sudden wave of pity, and although she tried to suppress it, it poured itself into her heart, and she could do nothing but let it warm through her veins like the strongest wine. Almost involuntarily, she went to him and climbed onto the mattress beside him. Pulling herself against his back, she tentatively put her arm around his waist. It was a cold night and the chamber was freezing. It was comforting to feel the familiar warmth of his body again.

She sensed his surprise at her unexpected presence next to him. He sniffed and stifled a sob as he put his hand on hers which rested on his stomach.

"I am s-so s-sorry, Ealdgytha," he stammered piteously. "I am nothing but a fool."

"Yes, you are. So am I – if I forgive you."

He shuffled his body round to face her. In the darkness, he could not read her expression. "Will you forgive me?"

"You have to choose, Wulfhere. Who is it that you want? Me? Or her?"

"You are my wife, Ealdgytha."

"Men have wives but they don't necessarily want them."

"I always wanted you, Ealdgytha. Always…"

Ealdgytha hated the things he had done. She despised his lack of ambition and drive. But she could not hate him. And she could not deny that the depth of her hurt had sprung from her love for him. She wanted him back, but this time it would have to be on her terms and not his. "Well, is it me or her?"

There was a silent moment between them and Ealdgytha half expected him to say that he refused to choose.

"I will not share you with that woman, Wulfhere," Her tone was resolute.

"I want *you*, Ealdgytha."

"Then you must never see that woman again, Wulfhere, for if you do, it will be over this time."

"I will not see her again, I promise," he replied. He kissed her lips and found them willing and they made love for the first time in months.

Afterwards, he lay there with her head resting on his chest. Contentedly, he stroked her golden hair as she slept and let their newfound peace envelop them. He contemplated what had just passed between them and the promise he had just made. As much as it would hurt, he could never see Alfgyva again. Except perhaps once, just to tell her it was over… and to say goodbye. There had to be an ending. He owed her that much.

Chapter Twenty

Whispers in the Wind

Hiding in the hayloft, Freyda smirked to herself as she hunkered down amongst the piles of silage. They would never think of looking here for her. Most likely her parents would assume she had gone to hide in the forest. They wanted her to marry that arrogant toad, Aemund, Leofnoth's woolly-headed son, but she was not going to. She had seen him a few times on visits with his father. She swore that he just came to leer at her. Whenever he tried to catch her attention, her nose went in the air and off she would flounce, but to her annoyance, he never gave up trying. She had heard that he had been sent abroad to study when he was younger, but he was back now, and her parents' plot to have them married only served to make her dislike him even more. She decided that, if she could hide just long enough to make good her escape, she would flee to be with Edgar.

"So, you don't want to speak with me then?" came a voice from below the loft.

Bollocks! She thought to herself. How did he know she was there? Could he see her through the cracks in the wooden boards? She could see him, so most likely he saw her, and as she squinted through the planked floor, he appeared to be looking upwards at her, but she could not be certain.

"I don't blame you. I am not as handsome as Edgar of Gorde… but I do have a certain appeal," he was saying. Although she tried not to, she could not help but like the soothing tone in his voice. "Most girls are fascinated by me, especially by my humble charisma. But if you're not the sort of girl who gets taken in by a fellow's charm, then I can understand your reluctance."

Freyda stifled a giggle. She edged closer to where the floor ended and peered at him. She had, of course been familiar with his appearance, but she was tempted to study him in detail, for the first time, to see what manner of creature her parents wanted her to marry.

She saw that he was not unattractive. He had sandy-coloured hair, was stocky but not fat, not particularly tall, but not short, either. He was a young man, nothing more, nothing less. Even though she had met him before, he seemed different somehow, more grown-up perhaps.

"We could speak like this if you like. I would be quite content to converse with you whilst you carry out your business up there in the loft…whatever it is girls do in such places." Freyda released a little giggle. "Or… perhaps you would prefer it if I came up there?" He paused, and Freyda felt the hair on the back of her neck bristle anxiously under her headscarf. "So, what do you say, my Lady Freyda?"

She remained silent. She liked the way he said her name and was intrigued by him, but Edgar was still firmly set in her heart, and she was determined not to give into the charms of this affable young man.

"Oh well, you won't be needing the gift I have for you, then. I had been saving it for our wedding night, but I thought you might have liked to have an early viewing. I was rather hoping that it might compare favourably to my rival's. I have it here, right now, if you'd like to come down and see."

He moved underneath the loft and out of sight, so that Freyda could no longer see him without leaning further forward. She felt a hint of curiosity, and wondering what the gift could be, shuffled backwards, lying flat on her stomach so that she could peer at him through the cracks in the flooring. But she was not able to see him well enough, and when she saw his shape move back to where he'd stood before, she slid herself to the edge once more, and peered over the edge.

Upon seeing him, and the gift that he wanted her to see, she drew in her breath, cupped her hand over her mouth, and withdrew from sight, desperately restraining the desire to laugh out loud. She'd seen him standing, hands arrogantly placed on his hips, his trousers round his ankles, brazenly displaying his cock as if it were his prize possession. Her head appeared over the edge once more and she continued to suppress her laughter. He was looking up at her with a grin. *The conceited earsling, thinking he can impress me with his cock!* she thought, amused at his impudence.

Sitting back away from the edge, she reflected for a minute or two and then a mischievous thought came to her, accompanied by an equally mischievous smile. She began to climb slowly down from the loft, being careful not to lose her footing on the rungs of the ladder, and stood before him with an expression of wry amusement. She surveyed him with an air of self-confidence, as he stood there with a somewhat dumbfounded expression, as if he was completely taken aback by her.

Her eyes rested on his face. His features were pleasant enough despite a few adolescent spots. His brown eyes were fringed with long dark lashes, giving them an almost feminine look, and his dimpled cheeks still bore the roundness of youth. His lips were pink and full, and he was possessed with a set of good, strong white teeth. Slowly, her eyes travelled down his torso and rested on his loins. She noted with interest that, what he lacked in looks, he made up for in the crotch department. Edgar may have been fairer of face but Aemund was better endowed.

Under her unabashed gaze, Aemund's haughtiness began to diminish. She felt a hint of pleasure in his unease. Did he expect her to be coy and avert her eyes in embarrassment? *Ha, that will teach him to be so brazen! He has found his match in this girl!*

"Well, are you not impressed, Lady Freyda?" he asked. "Most ladies are when they see it. Some, like you, are speechless; others, well, they just have to make a grab for it!"

Freyda remained silent. A growing confidence began to overwhelm her. She was about to do something that would surprise even herself. Still staring at him mutely, she began to remove her headscarf. Throwing it on the floor, she uncoiled her hair to let it fall about her shoulders in an array of gold. Her mother had insisted that she cover her hair, especially since the onset of her womanhood. *A woman's hair is her crowning beauty*, Mother had always said, and if men were to see it, it would drive them wild with lust. But Aemund's response was quite different to what she had expected.

"I stand here with my most precious asset on display and all you show me is your hair?" he replied in an offended tone. "Is that *all* I am to be given in return?"

Freyda stared at him defiantly. Her eyes narrowed like a scheming cat's. After a moment's pause, she began to remove her woollen tunic and then her linen underdress until she was completely naked. She threw her hair behind her shoulders so that he could see the pertness of her small, but rounded breasts. His jaw dropped and his eyes gawped, ogling her body with a look of admiration and astonishment.

She gave him an alluring smile and allowed him to look over the milky white smoothness of her thighs, her neatly trimmed mound, and the pinkness of her nipples. She saw that he was aroused and she liked it. He was under her spell, and she basked in the power it gave her.

Then, after a few moments, with a wicked laugh, she pulled on her clothes and rushed to escape.

"Don't leave me here like this!" Aemund called after her, pulling his trousers up as she reached the door. "What am I going to do with this?"

She looked back at him with one foot in and one foot out of the byre. She laughed; even his clothes could not hide his risen manhood.

"I cannot go back into your father's hall wearing this – this clothes hook, can I?"

She shrugged, still smiling, and turned to go.

"Hold on! I understand that you might want to wait until we are wed, but can you not take me to somewhere I can resume to normal, and be fit to go before your parents again?"

Freyda smiled and thought for a moment. "Come with me," she said. "But don't think that I am going to touch your *thing*!"

"She speaks! The lady has a voice! Does this mean you'll marry me now?" he said with a boyish shrug and a widening of his arms.

She sighed and smiled broadly at him. All of a sudden, she liked him; he amused her. It was as if all her negative thoughts of him had melted away, and left her with a feeling that she had always liked him. Somehow, she felt drawn to him, wanted to know him better. Most of all, she enjoyed the feeling of control she had over him.

"What? Why is it so funny?" he asked.

Freyda continued to laugh helplessly.

"Come, my Lady, this is serious. Do you think I can go back into the hall with this? How will I explain this," he pointed both his index fingers at his groin, "to your parents?"

"Forgive me, but I was just imagining you sitting in the hall trying to hide it from my parents. They will think that you are very impressed with me."

"I could say that you have bewitched me."

Freyda's hands went to her hips. She looked at him thoughtfully. "Come, we can walk in the woods. At least until that thing goes down."

"Come then, show me your woods. I hear the Horstede children are very fond of them."

She took the arm that he held out to her, and still giggling girlishly, led him around the back of the barn to where one of the palisaded fence panels was broken and they climbed through it. This was her secret way out at the northern end of her father's enclosure, where the ditch that surrounded the homestead had not been properly maintained over the years. It had been purposely filled in with earth so that it was easy to cross. Just beyond the village perimeter fence was the track that led to the rock pool. Staring at it with anticipation, she sensed that her life was about to change.

As they walked through the shadows of the forest, it felt strange to feel and smell another beside her where Edgar had been, and she was aware of the many subtle differences between them. They walked and talked. Aemund did most of the talking, speaking of his boyhood home, and the lands left to him by his mother in her will, which he was to inherit upon his marriage. He talked about his love for his dogs, his longing to ride through the pastures and meadowlands that surround his home, when the time comes for him to settle there – with his new wife. He has a passion for archery and hawking, he told her, and books on many subjects.

"I love to read," he wittered on. "Father Goronwy, my father's priest, has many books in his scriptorium. Goronwy is from the lands of the Wéalas and they have many beautiful manuscripts there. He has a great library of books. He taught me to speak the Wéalisc language, Latin too, and, Frencisc."

Freyda was in awe of him. "You should be a bishop, or even an archbishop," she suggested. "I cannot read much. Father insists that we learn, but Father Paul has had a hard task to teach me to read. I hear the queen is very well educated. They say she speaks many languages, and sings beautifully."

Aemund flattered her. "You have a wonderful singing voice. And you play the harp as well as any *scop* I have ever heard."

Freyda enjoyed the compliments. Strangely, she was becoming increasingly drawn to him as each moment passed. She searched her mind for something to boast about. "I know many riddles!"

Aemund pulled a face and replied, "How nauseating! I have heard them so many times I think I know them all by heart." She laughed at his reply, not at all insulted by his dismissal of her penchant for riddles. He continued. "When I was a small boy, my mother had a dream that I would one day sit in the highest church in the land, and she convinced my father to send me to Rome for my education, but after a while they sent me back."

"Rome! I have heard that the city of Rome is beautiful, and that the pope wears cloth of gold. Why did they send you home?"

"Apparently, I was not as industrious as the other boys, and I was a troublemaker, and a reprobate."

She burst into laughter. "How terrible for your mother!"

"Fortunately for my dear mother, she passed away before my return and was spared the shame," Aemund replied, matter-of-factly.

"I am sorry for your mother, but... how silly am I for even thinking you would make a good bishop!"

"Me? A bishop? Bishops are old and ugly! I am far too handsome to waste my good looks on things holy!" Aemund laughed and skipped in front of her. "Besides, I do not think that God would approve of me doing His business on earth."

Freyda laughed. She had never met anyone like him. There was a vibrant, charismatic air about him; his zest for life, the way he talked about himself, and the things in his life he liked the most. He was so different from Edgar, who was much like many of the young men of their hundred. They were neither educated nor witty, and not one amongst them had ever heard of Rome, let alone been there.

"I am a good catch, you know. They are lining up all over the country to be my wife."

She giggled as he did a funny sort of dance in front of her. "You? A good catch? No, Lord Aemund – though I don't doubt that you think that you are. However, it is I who am the catch!" She pushed past him and shouted as she ran up the path, "See if you can run as fast as me, for all your learning and letters!"

She ran through the woods and he followed closely behind, until she led him to the rock pool. He caught up with her as she threw herself down on the grassy bank.

"Caught you!" he cried. He rested his hands lightly on her shoulders, sitting snugly behind her. "So, this is your secret place?"

His breath tickled her neck and her spine tingled. "Not just mine; nearly all the village children come here to play in the summer, but I come here always, whatever the season. It is my favourite place." Just then a kingfisher dived into the water, skimming it with its beak. It must have missed its meal, for it swooped back up again and settled back on its perch, an overhanging branch of a willow, which caught the rope-swing, making it swing gently back and forth. "See, there is where the Earl's daughter fell, and would have drowned if not for my little brother."

Aemund looked over at the swinging rope. "I am conjuring up a picture of children laughing as they fly high above the pool, splashing as they swim in the sunlit waters."

"Aye, that is just how it is," Freyda said, her voice, light and happy.

"Is this where you meet him? Edgar, I mean," Aemund asked, softly.

Freyda turned surprised eyes to him. His expression was one of curiosity rather than disapproval.

"You know about him?" she asked.

"Of course! Half of Súþ Seaxa knows the story about how you burned down his father's hall. I know that you were betrothed to him, but now your father does not approve, and wishes you to marry me. Good choice, I'd say!"

"You do not care that I have been betrothed to someone else?"

They sat in contemplative silence for a moment. There was no sound, apart from the rippling of the water, and the wind rustling in the reeds as frogs and other pond life went about their business.

After a while, Aemund said, "I've had many lovers myself; the girls just cannot keep their hands off me."

Freyda gave him a disbelieving look.

"No, 'tis true! They all want me... all the thegns' daughters... except perhaps one..." There was a yearning in his eyes, and a sudden earnest.

"And who is this thegn's daughter?" she asked, wistfully.

He turned to look at her, directly; his eyes piercing hers with a look of longing. "She is the thegn of Horstede's daughter."

She felt her heart jump, and a feeling mixed with excitement and dread came over her. Her face flushed and she looked away, remembering that she was promised to Edgar. "If you have had so many females, why do you want me?" she replied, trying to sound offended.

"I haven't said that I want you... but Lord Alfgar might."

"Lord Alfgar?" she asked, giving him a stupefied look. "Who is Lord Alfgar?"

He glanced at his lap before taking her hand and placing it over his manhood. Through his clothes, she felt his arousal, and it excited her.

"You call your – your *thing*, Lord Alfgar?" She giggled and pulled her hand away.

He nodded.

"Why?" She laughed again.

"Because like the real Lord Alfgar, he is a rogue and a womaniser. When all the girls see him, they just cannot wait to get their hands on him."

"Then he should be sent into exile!" she exclaimed, continuing to giggle girlishly.

He jerked with mock offence. "No, please, my Lady, do not banish him! Give him a chance!"

She allowed him to stare at her with hungry eyes. They ingested her ravenously, and she felt as if he had turned her soul to fire. The force of his stare made her feel uncomfortable, as though she was sitting on a bed of thorns. She wished that he would look away, but at the same time she wished that he would never stop.

She pushed him playfully and he pushed her back. Their eyes met once more, and she saw her reflection in his. He leant forward and drew her to him like a magnet. She felt their lips lock; and Freyda felt a sensation that not even Edgar had stirred within her before. As Aemund kissed her, she sank into his embrace; her soul joined with his, she was transported from the familiarity of her life, and Edgar... and everything she knew. Even in this place, where she had shared so much with Edgar, it was strange and yet familiar, and her head reeled with confusion.

"Did you and Edgar...?" Aemund asked, at last releasing her.

The question awakened her from her reverie and she was no longer within him. Disappointment rose inside her and she looked downcast. She could lie but he would know the story eventually, so she said nothing.

"I don't mind that you have."

"You don't?" She looked surprised. How did you know?"

He laughed. "How many virgins would stand naked before a fellow they'd never met before? Besides, who doesn't poke their betrothed? Everyone does it where I come from. What is passed is passed for both of us, yes?"

She nodded.

"Just as long as you are not with child."

"I have had my last flux. I was always careful not to…"

"No need to say any more, Freyda."

"Aemund, why do you want me? You know that I am no blushing virgin bride."

"I want you because our parents wish it, and when parents wish things, it is inevitable it's going to happen. Besides..." he looked reflective, "you are the most beautiful girl I have ever laid eyes on; and I have loved you since the day I first heard you singing in your father's hall."

He touched her hair which she had left uncovered. Her heart leapt and her whole body stirred in a way not known to her before. ... *you are the most beautiful girl I have ever laid eyes on...* His words sent a shiver down her spine... *and I have loved you since the day I first heard you singing in your father's hall.*

They kissed again. She closed her eyes, and thoughts of Edgar paled into a distant memory, as though he never existed. Sensing that Aemund wanted her too, her hand felt for his groin... but he pulled it away.

"No, my lovely Freyda. I want our wedding night to be our first. It shall not be long."

She smiled and wiped away a tear.

"Have I offended you?" he asked earnestly.

"No, Aemund, you have not. It's just that I... I – well, Edgar – he didn't..."

"Edgar never gave you that courtesy, did he?"

She shook her head.

"I thought as much," he replied kindly. "You shall have it from me, though, my Lady."

Freyda barely heard his reply as she felt her initial resistance to him dissipate. In the short time it took her to descend the ladder from the loft and fall prey to his charms, so much had happened within her heart. It is not that she sees this boy as the answer to all her dreams, she certainly has not fallen in love with him; it is more to do with what she and Edgar have not, and the clarity with which she now saw things. Edgar was a symbol of her need to reject her parent's authority. He was, and always would be, nothing more than a vessel for her adolescent rebellious nature.

Aemund's words cut into her thoughts. "I talk like a great lover, but I am a gentleman at heart. Is that not right, Lord Alfgar? Down boy, and shame on you for such outrageous behaviour in front of the lady."

He was speaking to his lap, which caused amused laughter from Freyda. "He makes his apologies, my Lady."

She was still laughing when he leapt to his feet and offered her his hand. Together they walked back to the homestead and for once there was a lightness in her heart; something that she had lost with all the hiding and the lying she had been forced to endure with Edgar. But, as they drew nearer home, a feeling of dread washed over her as she was thrust back to reality.

What was she going to say to Edgar?

Edgar sat in their usual place in the forest waiting for Freyda to come. It was way past sundown, their usual time for meeting. She was late. Or perhaps she had not been able to slip away. It was the second consecutive night that she had not turned up. Sometimes, she sent Tovi, if she was unable to get away, but last night neither Freyda nor Tovi had come.

He waited for what seemed like an age and was about to give up and go home when he heard a rustling in the trees. His heart leapt with excitement. "Is that you, Freyda? Over here by the…"

Tovi emerged from a thicket. "No, it is me, Tovi."

"So, your sister was unable to come?" Edgar asked despondently, dismounting the large rock he had been sitting on by the pond. Frustration rushed through him like wind rushing through the trees. He had missed her last night and now she had not come again.

Tovi approached him tentatively. He was carrying an oil lantern and in his other hand he carried a small woollen pouch.

"She sent me to give you this," Tovi said, and Edgar was very aware of the solemnity of his tone.

At once, Edgar intuitively felt that something was very wrong. He took the pouch, undid the strings, and peered into it. He reached inside and pulled out a pretty gem-studded brooch. He studied it for a moment, dropping the pouch and grabbing the lantern from Tovi so he could better see the item. Then he reached down and picked out some more small pieces of jewellery from the bag.

"No!" he moaned, realising that she had returned the betrothal gifts. He threw the bag and its contents.

"She says to tell you that she is sorry –"

Anger rose within him, unchecked. He dropped the lantern and grabbed Tovi by his shoulders.

"Is she to marry Aemund?" he demanded.

"I did not want to be the one to tell you, but she made me." Tovi sniffed at a tear and reached up a hand to touch Edgar's shoulder.

"Just tell me, boy! Is she to marry Aemund?" Edgar's fingers dug into Tovi's arms and the boy winced. He stammered, struggling to answer. Edgar let him go and swung round ramming his fist into the trunk of a beech tree.

"I'm sorry, Edgar!" Tovi cried, his hands clenched in anguish.

Edgar turned around clasping his bleeding knuckles.

"Sorry? Why are *you* sorry, boy? It is your sister who has betrayed me, not you. Is it not enough that I have been beaten and humiliated by your damn father… and now to be spurned like this for another?"

"It is because they are making her."

"Then why could she not come herself and tell me?" Edgar said bitterly, hardly believing that she would be so cruel as to send her brother to bear the news. "She has shown herself to be nothing but a *hore*, a *galdricge* – evil temptress! No doubt she has already opened her legs for that *horningsunu*!"

"No, my sister would not do that," Tovi protested.

Edgar grabbed Tovi by his cloak and shook him violently. His eyes brimmed with hate. "Poor Tovi, you have such a childish view of the world. Because your parents have let you down, you look to your sister and I, to create your perfect world. Well, I am sorry to tell you, dear Tovi, that your sister is a hore, who could not wait to lie with me in a pile of straw. Aemund is welcome to her. I would not wish a harlot for my wife."

"Edgar, don't say that! Please!"

"You need to grow up, boy. Look at you! Snivelling like a girl at someone else's misfortune. Life is not perfect. Men and women are fickle! Why do you care so much about me, anyway, eh? I am the son of your father's enemy!" Edgar let him go, and bent down to retrieve the betrothal gifts.

"Because you are my friend, Edgar. You were kind to me – like a brother."

"I am not your brother, Tovi. And I was only kind to you for Freyda's sake. I want nothing to do with your family, ever again." He waved the bag of betrothal gifts in his face, and said, "You can thank your goddamned sister for these… and, you can give her this in return!"

Without any warning, he punched the boy, and felled him to the ground. He turned, and left Tovi, clutching his face, sobbing, without any regret, and limped away into the thickness of the trees. The pain and humiliation of losing Freyda was raw, and where there had once been love, there was now deep bitterness and hatred. He had come so close to having her... then fate had snatched her away like a falcon seizes its prey. Any hope he'd had of marrying her was now gone. He should have known that it was too good to be true. Hadn't his father always told him that he would never amount to anything? Almost as bad as losing Freyda was the fact that his father would be proved right, and that was the deepest cut of all.

Freyda hugged the slop bucket between both her arms, trying hard not to splash the contents over the sides as she hurried through the early morning dew to the midden pit. She threw the filthy stew-like waste into the pit, tipping the bucket right up and shaking out the last of its contents. Careful not to slip on the muddy bank, she stepped back to avoid the inevitable splash. She had done this a thousand times, but no matter how hard she tried, some of it always caught her. It was the task that she hated the most; more than the butter churn, or sweeping up the dog mess from the rushes in the hall. It had once been Sigfrith's task, but ever since her betrothal to Edgar, she had been consigned to it as a punishment, so Freyda believed.

She hoped that there were no stains on her clothes, for she would hate it if Aemund saw her looking anything but perfect. Buoyed by the prospect of being Aemund's wife, her head was full of how her life was going to greatly progress, away from the oppressive dominance of her mother and the disapproving glances of her father. Wulfhere still barely spoke to her, even though she had accepted their decision to marry her to Aemund. However, never mind that, Aemund excited her and stirred her heart with a new sense of exhilaration. Edgar now seemed like a far-off memory, like a childhood dream relegated to the distant corners of her mind.

"Pssst, Freyda!"

The hoarse whisper startled her, causing her to drop the bucket into the pit as she tried to steady herself. Stumbling backwards, she fell onto her bottom with a painful thud as her feet slipped in the mud. Lying at the edge of the ditch, she looked toward her father's orchard. There was Edgar, calling to her from behind an old apple tree. He looked dishevelled, as if he had not slept all night and even from where she stood, she could see the look of black sorrow in his grey eyes.

"Freyda!" he called again, his voice rasping in his throat.

She struggled to her feet. She'd wished that she would never have to face him again. She had seen the black eye that Tovi had received and hoped her brother had told the truth when he said that he'd walked into a tree in the darkness. In her heart of hearts she'd guessed that Edgar had done it out of hurt and spite for her rejection of him.

"Edgar, please go! My father will kill you if he sees you here!" she cried out, her voice failing to hide her desperation.

"Please let me talk to you." He came towards her and stopped halfway, baulking at her fear of him. "Freyda, please…"

"No, Edgar, I cannot talk to you now – not ever! I am to marry Aemund."

"But you are promised to me…. You cannot marry him."

"It is my father's wish that I do. I cannot… we cannot fight it anymore, Edgar. 'Tis over. The *norns* are spinning a different fate for us."

"But he cannot go against the earl."

"He says the earl will not oppose it when he tells him what your father did."

"It is just an excuse. Your father never wanted us to marry and would have done anything to prevent it."

Stricken with guilt, she could not bear the sound of desperation in his voice. With a heavy heart, she closed her ears to his pain.

"I am tired of all the hiding and the deceit, Edgar," she replied in a weary voice.

He made towards her again and stopped as she stepped backwards.

"How can you run from me? Only a few days ago, you would have gone anywhere with me? What a fool I was to have thought that our chances lay within the courts. If I had listened to you then, we would be gone from here, together, and you would not be marrying Aemund. Come with me, Freyda, -- it's not too late…" He took another step nearer.

She hated to see him like this, fraught with desperation and pleading. For a fleeting moment, she tried to remember how his grey eyes danced when a smile lit up his face. He had always smiled when he was with her. The smiling, laughing Edgar was gone, and the man that stood before her now filled her with a mixture of both remorse and repugnance. His weakness disturbed her, and she knew it was Aemund's strength that she wanted.

She shook her head. "It is useless, Edgar."

"But we could run away…"

"Run where? Where could we go that they would not find us?"

"Anywhere. I have my father's kin in the town of Lewes. Burgesses. They would help us fight our case. Or perhaps we could go north," he replied fervently.

"No, Edgar, it would not work. We would be fugitives with nothing. Would you want that for us? For our children?"

"What would it matter? We would have each other… and our love."

"But I do not love you anymore, Edgar." She tried not to sound heartless.

He hung his head and a few moments later replied bitterly, "You want to marry him, don't you."

Freyda did not reply, but looked down at her feet, clenching her hands.

"You do, don't you?" he shouted. "Look at me, Freyda!" He lunged toward her and grabbed her arms. She flinched and turned her head away from him. "Look me in the eye and tell me that you desire this marriage with Aemund."

Refusing to look at him, she squirmed in his grasp, but he would not release her. At last she turned her face to him, daring to meet his gaze with hers. He was so filled with fire that she felt herself burn under his gaze.

"I desire it," she replied, staring at him with steely determination.

He let her go, almost pushing her away. "Will he still want you when he knows it was I who had you first?" he muttered sourly.

"He knows it already," she replied, and gave a wry smile of triumph.

"I do not believe you, Freyda… but perhaps he has already had you as I have, since you care not for your modesty. How many others have you promised yourself to?"

He caught her wrist as she poised to slap his face.

"So, you would add violence to your list of insults. Is it not enough to have endured beatings from your father that you must strike me too?" Red-hot shame stung in her cheeks and eyes as he clung to her. "Freyda... I never thought that your name would slip so painfully from my lips. You have ripped my heart from me..."

"I would have let him have me, Edgar, but he is not like you, he wants to wait for our wedding night – you gave me no choice. I was but an innocent maid, and you took advantage of that."

He was still holding her wrist and staring at her with venomous eyes. He threw her arm down, letting it go. His eyes pricked with tears, and Freyda wondered at the change in this gentle soul she had once known, unable to acknowledge her part in it.

Suddenly they heard a voice calling, "Freyda!" A youth came running toward them from the back of the hall. "Take your hands off her, you bastard!"

Aemund. He ran toward them like a whirlwind making its way across the earth. Unsheathing his seax, he leapt like a hound after its quarry.

"No, Aemund, please don't fight him! He has suffered enough!"

Aemund looked confused. "He was attacking you!" Pushing her aside, he thrust forward as Edgar pulled out his own seax. Freyda stepped back and watched helplessly as her two suitors turned on each other.

"No!" she screamed as Edgar lashed out with his blade, but Aemund deftly caught the hand that held the blade and thrust it away. About to drive the point of his seax into Edgar's gut, he stopped as Freyda cried out, "Don't hurt him!"

Instead, Aemund threw his seax away and felled Edgar with a punch to the midriff. He said, as he stood over Edgar, "If it were not for the lady's compassion, I would kill you right now. Get you gone from Horstede and never return!"

Edgar scrambled to his feet. "You…" He looked at Aemund with pure hatred. His eyes wavered between his rival and Freyda. "You will both be sorry for this. I pray to God that you will never be happy!" he spat.

Aemund went to hit him again, but Freyda held him. "Let him go, Aemund. He has had enough," she implored.

"Are you hurt?" Aemund asked as they watched Edgar disappear, limping through the grove. He touched her cheek with affection. "Did that whoreson touch you? If he comes back, I will –"

She shook her head. "No, he shall not return. It is over."

Aemund tenderly lifted her chin. "You are fond of him?" he asked and she lowered her gaze. "'Tis no shame that you are, Freyda. I am glad that your heart is not made of stone. I would not have a cold-hearted witch for a wife."

"My heart feels as if it is made of stone right now," she said tearfully. "It was hard to see him so heartbroken."

"His heart will mend, Freyda. And I will help to soften yours again." Soothingly, he took her hand and, kissing it, said, "In time we are all just whispers in the wind... you will see... just a whisper in time is all he will be to you."

"Whispers in the wind..." she repeated thoughtfully, and wiped away a tear. *Yes, that is all that any of us are.*

Wulfhere and Leofnoth had been coming out of the hall, and spied the young couple in their embrace.

"I told you he would endear himself to her," Leofnoth chuckled. "My son's allure could charm flies off a decaying carcass! Soon, she will forget Edgar Helghison."

"I will take that as a compliment, Leofnoth, although Freyda may think otherwise," Wulfhere replied with a smile. "I fear Helghi will make trouble though. I do not expect he will take the news that we are no longer to be in-laws, very calmly," Wulfhere said worriedly. "And the earl will be mightily displeased, also."

"Nonsense, he will understand. That is why the sooner they are wed the better. Anyway, Lord Harold has more important things to worry about. Leave him to me; he will see the sense in it." Leofnoth clapped a reassuring hand on his friend's shoulder. "We may have to pay a fine and Helghi some compensation, but I will take care of that. It is worth it to see my son happy."

Wulfhere looked up to see their children were hurrying toward them with their arms locked together. "Did you see that *Horningsunu*, Edgar? He has just run off into the forest after threatening us!" Aemund said, breathlessly.

Upon hearing this, Wulfhere made to go after Edgar, but Freyda pleaded with him not to.

"Did he hurt either of you?"

"Please, Father, it is over now. He knows that I am to be wed to Aemund," she said, taking Wulfhere's arm and leading him away so they could speak privately.

"Will you ever forget Edgar, Freyda? Can you be a good wife to Aemund?"

"Edgar?" She halted and looked toward whence he had gone. Wulfhere was troubled at the deeply pensive expression on her face. After a moment, she turned back to him, her eyes gazing at his, as if searching his thoughts, and said finally, "He is just a whisper in the wind now, Father."

Wulfhere took hold of her shoulders and rubbed them affectionately. "I wish only for your happiness. It is all I ever wanted for you."

"Yes, Father, I know. I'm sorry. I have behaved so badly," she said, throwing her arms around his waist and hanging onto him tightly. Together they walked back to the hall, arms encircling each other. "Oh Father, I have missed you so much. It has been terrible to fight with you," she declared.

"'Tis time to stop this war between us, daughter," he told her.

She nodded. "Yes, Father, I would like that."

At last Freyda had found a sense of peace. From now on, all that that had passed with Edgar, was to be exiled to the distant corners of her mind, and it was only *now* that counted. She thought she knew what she desired in life. She had planned it so carefully from the moment she met Edgar walking in the woods; when they had danced together at their betrothal, and the first time she had lain with him in the weaving shed. Now those memories seemed so distant that she felt they belonged only to the wind, to be blown like leaves to who knows where. Moments that were gone like whispers in the wind.

Chapter Twenty-one

The Battle of Hereford

Hereford, October 24th 1055

Ralph walked along the rampart of his palisaded defences, as the chilled late autumn morning swathed the burgh in a cloak of mist. He was proud of his strong timber and earth castle, built within the walls of Hereford not long after his uncle, Edward, had invested him with the office of earl, four years since. If he looked out over the parapet on a clear day, to the north, he would be sure to see any sign of the enemy coming.

This morning was like any other morning that had passed since, upon hearing Burghred's news, he had wasted no time in gathering his bodyguard, and raced across the ancient tracks to the West Country, sending out summonses to all the mounted men that Edward had commended to him. Looking out over the fog-laden hills, he contemplated another morning of watching and waiting. Down in the courtyard, his men would be on standby. He was proud of his accomplishments in Hereford, and fiercely proud of the mounted cavalry he had trained. Some of the Englisc looked upon his ideas with derision, but he would show them just what a mounted army could achieve. He had stubbornly refused Harold's offer to rally the Wessex fyrd to aid him, convincing everyone, except for Harold, that he had no need of them. This was not, he'd said, a matter of national emergency. His mounted soldiers would be match enough for Alfgar and Gruffudd, he'd guaranteed them.

"Another morning and still they do not come," muttered William Malet, joining him in leaning against the wooden barrier. Dressed and ready for battle, the men wore their armour of little metal links, skilfully welded together to form the hauberk, the tunic of mail that protected the length of their torso, arms, and legs. Under them they wore a padded shirt, which would stop the metal from chafing, adding to the protection that their armour already afforded them. "I am beginning to think that they never will."

"Oh, they will come all right; your cousin Burghred was sure of it. It seems your uncle has been collecting his forces all summer." Ralph looked sideways at Malet. "And when they do, Will, we shall be ready for them. Ha, we will soon have our chance to prove to Godwinson that we are quite capable of sorting out our own defences here in the west!"

"In hindsight, do you think it was wise not to accept his offer to call out the fyrd?" Malet asked, retrospectively.

"What? And have nice, golden, shiny Harold take all the glory? No, my friend, this one is for us. Besides, it would be a great waste of manpower. Costly, too. Our combination of cavalry, light infantry and bowmen is the right formula needed to win the battle against the Wéalas."

Malet looked a little sceptical, and Ralph looked at him scornfully. "You do not doubt that the victory will be ours, William?"

"No, Ralph, I do not. It is just that –"

"I know that perhaps it is hard for you to go to war against your uncle," Ralph suggested, without any empathy in his voice.

Will shook his head and replied firmly, "You know how I feel about that brainless idiot! He has the intellect of a newt, uncle or not. I am ashamed to say he is of my blood."

"Then why do you have that doubtful expression on your face?"

"I just thought that perhaps it would have been advantageous to have the Wessex fyrd here, just in case. After all, Harold is –"

"Harold is not here!" Ralph responded angrily. "And what's more, we do not need him!"

"But the men are untried and inexperienced, lord," Malet argued, gently.

"Do you doubt me, Will?" Ralph thrust a disturbed look in his friend's direction.

"No, lord. No…"

"You know how I have been waiting for this chance to ingratiate the *Witan*, Will? And why should I not? I have royal blood coursing through my veins. I am *throneworthy*! An *atheling*!" He thumped the edge of the wooden strakes in earnest. "Why should I work so hard all these years, only to have Harold Godwinson come along at the last minute and interfere in my command? This victory will gain me the accolade I deserve, and put an end to the threat that comes swamping over the marcher borders, year after year!"

"My lord, you are indeed throneworthy!" Malet said, supportively. He frowned slightly, and changed his cynical expression to one of fervent loyalty.

"If only the *Witan* would recognise me as so," Ralph said, regretfully. "*Mon Dieu!* They send out to lands afar, searching for long-lost Englisc princes, doing deals with that bastard in Normandy, dropping hints at Swein of Denmark, and, all the time, here I am, a prince with the blood of Alfred, right under their snotty noses! So what if I was born on the distaff side of the royal line? I am just as much a contender, if not more. The king, my uncle, loves me, does he not? And yet still I have to prove myself... and prove myself I will!"

"My lord, we will win this. If they come today, I swear we will win this!" Malet replied with genuine sincerity.

He was standing in front of Ralph as the earl leaned with his back against the parapet, the wind blowing his short dark hair forward. Ralph put a grateful hand on Malet's shoulder. "Thank you, Will. When I finally sit on the throne of this damned kingdom, I will see that you are rewarded for your loyal service."

"Good God!" Malet interrupted. "Look, my lord!"

"What?"

Ralph saw that Malet was surveying the valley behind him intently. He swung round and faced the view over the hills. He felt his stomach tighten as he realised what his friend had been staring at: the fast-moving shadow of a lone horseman, galloping amidst the thick morning haze drifting toward them across the plain.

"It's one of your scouts, my lord. Look, he holds your banner aloft. That means they are coming... At last they are..."

"Then we must see that the men are ready. Fitzscrob!" Ralph yelled loudly for his captain. He grabbed his helmet and shoved it onto his head.

"Yes, my lord?" A small, lithe Norman dressed in mail came running up the wooden rungs of the rampart to join them.

"See that the men are armoured and the horses ready," Ralph ordered. "Alfgar and Gruffudd are on their way. We will ride out to engage them." He felt a ripple of excitement in his veins, and a fluttering in his stomach. "*Maintenant! Now, Fitzscrob! Que vous attendez? What are you waiting for? Allez, allez!*"

"Yes, my lord," replied the little man, dutifully, as he turned and ran quickly down the parapet.

Ralph breathed in deeply as he secured the chinstrap of his helm. He had been waiting for this moment, and now it had arrived. At last he could show the world his worth, and that Edward and his Englisc subjects need not look to that far-off place, Hungary, for their next king. He pictured himself sitting on the throne in Edward's Palace of Westminster with his wife Gytha by his side. *Yes, now his chance had come...*

Freyda's wedding to Aemund had not taken place after all, for Wulfhere had received the summons which would take him away from Horstede again, soon after Edgar had come there to make trouble. Wulfhere's orders were to return to Hereford and give aid to the king's nephew. Gruffudd and Alfgar were planning an attack on Hereford, and Wulfhere would have to leave the safety of his family to Aemund and Leofnoth, for he did not trust Helghi not to try anything. Knowing that he could count on Leofnoth, he and Esegar set out once more, but not before Wulfhere had gone to Waldron to see Alfgyva one more time. He had to go, he had explained to a bemused Esegar, whose discerning expression obliged Wulfhere to justify himself. He was going to tell her that he must no longer see her, he told his fyrdsman. "I owe her that much."

"Lord, you must do what you must do," was Esegar's reply. "It is not for me to judge you."

Wulfhere had been desperate to return to the way things were before Alfgyva came back into his life again. He had promised Ealdgytha that the affair was over, and when he had gone to Alfgyva's place, he had done so with the full intention of telling her so. But it would never be over... not now. For before he could even begin to tell her why he had come, she had thrown her arms around him, and joyfully informed him of her good news... that she was with child again. *A child that would be born in the spring.* How could he tell her that he was never coming back?

When he finally left her to catch up with Esegar, it was as if nothing had changed. They had made love again, and, even now, he could picture her face, flushed with blissful happiness, unaware of Wulfhere's true reason for coming. She had waved him off with that enigmatic smile of hers; the very smile that had enchanted him right from the very first. No, nothing had changed... but he knew that he must never see her again, if he was to stay clear of her enchantment... if indeed, he could.

He had been both surprised and honoured to receive the charge of a mounted unit of twenty-five men. He had hoped it would help him take his mind off the deep troubles he had left behind him in Horstede. However, it did little to stave off the dreams of terror which came almost nightly. Would he never be rid of his guilt? Would he never be rid of the tangled web that the spinners were weaving for him?

Now, at the head of his unit, Wulfhere was staring at the large volume of men as they spewed over the crest of the hill before him, gradually making their way down into the fields below. They were a formidable sight, Gruffudd's army, as they formed their lines, some two thousand and more warriors, ten or so men deep. Hwitegast snorted and slammed his right hoof into the ground, scuffing the dirt to show his discontent. Wulfhere gave him a reassuring pat on his withers, and sighed deeply.

"*Scite!*" cried Esegar, mounted next to him. "There are so many of them."

Wulfhere puffed out his cheeks and wondered how six hundred mounted men, supported by one hundred or so bowmen, plus no more than three hundred and fifty infantry, were going to triumph over Gruffudd's vastly larger host.

"Aye, there are indeed," he agreed with a shudder, hoping that their cavalry would compensate for their lack of numbers.

"Lord, look to the left flank." Esegar's voice was shaking.

Wulfhere looked to where Esegar had indicated. "Hell has arrived," he muttered under his breath.

There were at least eighteen hundred more men, Wícinga, coming around the side of the foothills in the valley to join the main army as they marched toward them. Their steel helmets flashed as the mist cleared. Sharpened spear-tips bristled as they augmented the lines of Gruffudd's men, shouting, "*Odin! Odin!*" The noise was thunderous as they invoked their deity to make them triumphant, whilst the Wéalas called out, "*Llaith at y Saeson!*" "Death to the Englisc!"

Wulfhere felt his stomach bubbling. He heard Esegar's sharp intake of breath.

"Lord, we *were* greatly outnumbered. Now we are severely outnumbered," his fyrdsman said; a look of resignation on his horrified face.

As Wulfhere's eyes squinted out over the daunting scene of so many armoured men stamping their way across the green fields toward them, he felt his face prickle with fear, and despite the cold, started to sweat. He breathed deeply, trying not to remember the horrors of Dunsinane.

Gruffudd himself had a smaller mounted force, his *teulu*, but the amount of heavily armoured Norse foot soldiers, alone, far outnumbered the entirety of Ralph's force. Wulfhere gulped his nausea down into his gullet. They needed to charge soon, for if they didn't, the whole purpose of them as a mounted force would be pointless. Horses are rendered useless in a defensive formation.

Oh, my God, he thought to himself, *there is going to be slaughter unless we charge – now!*

Earl Ralph's enthusiasm was not dampened by the bleak weather, as he rode up and down along the lines of his men. Standards were snapping in the wind, as he delivered his battle speech with gusto, shouting out encouragements until his voice was hoarse. Ralph had seen to it that his Frencisc bards were present to take in all the details of his impending victory, so they could compose songs of his great achievement. He had imagined they would invent something akin to the popular, *Chanson de Roland*, to be sung in his name at the court of his uncle, and possibly find their way into the ears of that bastard cousin of his, the Duke of Normandy. Then that uneducated ignoramus from across the sea would know that the crown of Englalond would be Ralph's, and not his. This was going to be Ralph's moment of glory, and by God he was going to make sure it was as splendid a day as it could possibly be.

Ralph's forces had ridden out two miles north of Hereford, when they came across the amassing forces of Gruffudd and Alfgar. The earl sensed the unease spreading throughout his men, as the realisation that they were facing a far greater army than they had expected, began to unsettle them. The horses felt it too; their ears were splayed back and they bared their yellowed teeth. Their riders' anxiety flooded down through their trunks and their legs, seeping into the horse's spine and nervous system. Fear filled the air with its unmistakeable tension and aroma.

"My lord," William said to Ralph apprehensively. "There must be four thousand of them."

"But the scout said that there was half that number," Ralph replied, incredulously. "How can he have got it so wrong?"

"The sly vipers split up and concealed themselves behind the slope of the hill, then marched along the valley so that we would not know there were so many of them," Malet replied. "Who would have thought that Alfgar could be so cunning?"

"Not Alfgar; Gruffudd more like. Alfgar would not be so clever. Gruffudd is the brains behind this." Ralph shifted uneasily in his saddle. The enemy army was fast approaching. "We must send for reinforcements!"

William looked at him aghast. It was an absurd comment. "How can we? There's no time. They're bloody well upon us, Ralph!"

Fitzscrob, captain of the middle-guard, rode over to them. "My lord, the enemy are advancing. What should we do? We are overwhelmingly outnumbered!"

"What of it? We have the advantage. We have more cavalry than they. A man on a horse is worth two on foot. We can cut them down if we use the double circular formation, and feigned retreat to break their lines," Ralph replied. He knew that he was asking a lot from his inexperienced troops who were used to fighting in a shieldwall, but he had to save face... somehow. He looked out across the plain and saw the enemy vanguard advancing toward them, their pace quickening now as they got closer. The noise was thunderous. Trumpets were blaring and men were screaming obscenities at the "*Saes* bastards!" as they loomed toward them.

"My lord, we will be cut to pieces! The men are untried and full of fear!" Fitzscrob shouted. "We must retreat and defend the town. It's our only hope!"

Defend Hereford? This mob would overrun it in seconds, Ralph thought, his bravado beginning to wane. The enemy was thundering toward them now. Ralph's fear began to overwhelm him. He lost all control of his bladder and his bowels, as he sat quaking in his saddle. The 'great' army he had raised did not seem so great now.

Wulfhere couldn't stand it any longer. His mind roared; *why do they not give the order?* They must either charge forward to meet the onslaught, or retreat. He heard neither command. His heels gently nudged his horse's flanks, and Hwitegast dutifully cantered over to the Norman section behind the lines.

He called over to Ralph as he neared their position. "My lord, we must attack or retreat! We are like sitting ducks! If we stand here any longer, we will be cut down. Give the order!" Wulfhere pleaded. He smelt the fear, and saw the confusion on the earl's sweating, quivering features. *My God, the man's a coward!* Wulfhere thought in dismay.

Ralph's companions joined him, and Wulfhere noted the anxiety in their faces.

"If we are going to fight, you must give the order to charge, lord," Fitzscrob urged, and Malet echoed him.

Wulfhere saw to his relief that Ralph nodded, albeit without urgency, as if fear had dulled his senses. He pulled on Hwitegast's reins and he returned to his position.

"Foreweard hilderæs! Forward charge!" Wulfhere yelled, and his unit sped forth, their voices raised loudly in a thundering war cry, as they spurred their horses into a gallop. The earth pounded beneath their beasts' hooves, as they dug their stirrups into the horses' flanks to make them go faster. The Wéalas bowmen sent over a volley of arrows, and the commands of the Norse leaders followed as their men obeyed with precise discipline, to halt, and gather into a great shieldwall, knowing that the horses would baulk at their man-made blockade.

About a hundred bowmen from the enemy front ranks fired their arrows. Wulfhere was disheartened as some of his fellow soldiers were felled leaving the horses to scatter, riderless, in confused panic. Wulfhere expected Ralph's men to be engaging the bowmen in the centre, mowing them down with their javelins and sword strikes, but where the hell were they? Suddenly something did not feel right.

"Wulfhere!" He heard Esegar's anguished voice calling him. "The earl and his huscarles are leaving the field, lord!"

Wulfhere swivelled to his right. He reeled with shock and disbelief as Ralph and Malet were running from the field, the Normans in tow, like fleeing vermin. The right flank, too, had gone, and he saw that Gruffudd's rear-guard was charging after the soldiers in flight.

"What are they doing, sir?" Esegar asked, baffled.

Wulfhere's voice was pitched at an angry growl. "Saving their fucking Norman skins... leaving the rest of us to the wolves to die like sheep!"

Even before a single spear was thrown, the craven Normans had fled, leaving the earl's 'great' army of mounted men at the mercy of the crushing enemy.

Wulfhere looked across the mud-churned field, and gasped as the fleeing Englisc were struck down by javelins and arrows. The horses did not escape the vicious attack either. Their distressed whinnies fused with the howling of wounded men, so that the noise became like the sound of hell on earth. In the mayhem, the horses took flight in all directions, running into each other and throwing off their riders. The warriors were cut to ribbons as they lay helplessly on the ground. Whooping filled the air as the Wéalas leapt upon them with great savagery, slitting their throats and hacking at them in a frenzy of bloodlust.

All this happened within seconds, but as Wulfhere plundered his mind for what to do next, it seemed to him that an age had gone by. He fought his instincts to run and save his skin like Ralph, and twisting his head back round, he saw that the men of his left flank had no choice but to fight, as the Norse broke their ranks and charged into the horsemen, using their deadly spears and great axes to hack at them with terrible ferocity. Wulfhere's eyes captured some of his army fleeing the battle. His heightened sense of fear set off the mechanism needed for survival: battle lust. The overwhelming rush of blood and energy stormed through to his head. He wanted to run also, but his pride and anger at this debacle created by Ralph, would not allow it. Cowardice may have won the day for Ralph, but for Wulfhere, death in battle was preferable. He would sooner die than sully his name with the infamy of leaving his men to perish without him. His mind inadvertently took him to Dunsinane, and the memory ignited his anger as he visualised the terrible carnage of that battle.

He spat phlegm from a dry mouth before shouting, "Stand your ground! Do not flee! Are we cowards like the bastards who have left us to die? Retreat back, unto me!"

He rode amongst the chaos, roaring and screaming until his throat was hoarse. He derided those who tried to leave for being cowardly, calling them scum, worse than the droppings expelled from a dog's arse! Men began to heed his call to rally. They were disengaging from the mêlée to regroup the lines, swinging their horses' heads round and galloping back to gather around him.

The survivors of the left cavalry flank were organised once more, thanks to Wulfhere. Those whose mounts had been killed from under them, ran back on foot, or took charge of the horses that had lost their riders. Wulfhere searched for Esegar briefly, thought he saw him

323

amongst the chaos, and was relieved. He heard the bellowing of the Norse infantry as they, too, were regrouping their lines, and the ground shook with the thundering of Gruffudd and Alfgar's troops, as they pursued the fleeing Englisc into the distance. Wulfhere felt as if he was under water, and gazed up at the ravens circling in the sky above them, already waiting to swoop on the dead carcasses. *Not yet, you dark devils, I am not ready for you yet!*

Wulfhere stared at the faces of the snarling enemy. They were banging their weapons against their shields, chanting and calling out insults to them. Some of them were emulating horses by pretending to gallop up and down the field, accompanying their inane stupidity with neighing and whinnying. Their companions found their antics highly amusing. Wulfhere did not. They were heavily outnumbered and he was appalled. If he had to give his carcass up to the scavengers of the battlefield, he would die like a true warrior, valiantly, as they did in the old days.

He gave the order to charge; he knew his men were looking to him for his leadership. It filled him with both fear and excitement, but there *was* no time to think on that now, as he charged ahead of his lines into the cordon of *Norþmenn* who ran head-on into them like mad braying fools, some of whom wore the bearskins of the infamous Berserkers.

His sword arm swept down at the contorted faces of the *Wicinga* warriors, but for every man he felled, another took their place. He cut and slashed at them with animal-like ferocity. His kite-shaped shield in his other grasp, battered at any would-be assassins on his left side. A warrior on the right of him took a blow from him across his neck and shoulder, and the man's blood splattered across Wulfhere's face. He tasted the iron as it seeped into his mouth. The man staggered and clasped a hand over the wound, as thick blood poured through his fingers. Wulfhere lost him as Hwitegast lunged sideways with the impact. Another snarling *Wicinga* came at him with a great axe. Wulfhere saw him aim for Hwitegast's neck. Anger and panic filled his very being. *No, I am not going to let you kill my horse!* his mind screamed. He shortened the reins, pulled on them and Hwitegast responded by rearing away from the axe's deadly blade. He swung his sword arm downwards to smash into his assailant as he sidled his mount. The impact felled the axeman instantly, and the man lost his grip on the handle of his weapon, rendering him useless for another assault.

Wulfhere sensed the chaos around him as the men of the mounted unit courageously fended off Alfgar's crazed mercenaries. Some of the enemy were trampled under hooves, as they tried to unhorse the Englisc, slipping in the mire of blood and entrails lying on the ground. His vision filled with unlucky riders, whose horses succumbed to the vicious blades of the Norse axes. Their weapons sliced into the necks of the horses, almost decapitating them, sending out great jets of scarlet. Their masters were also cut down, and the stench of blood and bodily fluids swirled in Wulfhere's nostrils. Men were roaring and screaming, the clash of steel ringing in his ears. His own dread glowed hot through his veins, spurring him on with the determination that he would not die without fighting well.

A great collective cry of voices burst through the chaos as about one hundred or so foot soldiers, men of the local fyrd, ran into the havoc, snarling like angry wolves, and yelling a rallying call, "Hereford! Hereford!"

Wulfhere's heart leapt with hope, even though he knew they were still vastly outnumbered. Spotting the exposed flesh of a man occupied in a fight with one of the Englisc foot soldiers, he swung his faithful sword, *Hildbana*. Wulfhere grunted with the impact, satisfied that it met its mark, as his blade sank into the man's exposed neck. His victim's head bent forward and the wound at the top of his spine gaped, showing the white of a broken vertebra. Blood pumped slowly out onto his mail as he fell to his knees, dropping his sword. Wulfhere manoeuvred his mount closer to the fallen man so that he could strike him once more. *Hildbana* thundered down, but his aim was not good and he caught the man's helmet, thrusting him forward to the ground. Another warrior rode over the man unintentionally, the animal's hooves stamping on head and limbs, indiscriminately. There was no more Wulfhere could do to him, and he turned to his right just as an axe bit deeply into the horse next to him. The beautiful creature sank onto its front, a fountain of blood spurting from the wound and over Wulfhere, so that he was covered in a multitude of scarlet droplets. Wulfhere instantly recognised the stallion he had sold to Ralph, and a lump formed in his throat. Its rider screamed and hit the ground as the horse collapsed. The unfortunate man was then met with a spear to his back, skewering him like a spitted wild boar. Hwitegast reared and whinnied, a haunting eerie sound, as if he recognised the offspring that he had brought forth from his own loins.

As Wulfhere struggled to steady his distressed mount, he wondered if there was any point in carrying on. Men were dying and he felt like a dead man already. His eyes flashed round him. Horses were being cut from beneath their riders, and he was angry. Men dying, was one thing but, Christ on the Cross, not the horses...

He slid from Hwitegast and smacked his horse's rump; hard. His bewildered mount took off, but not before giving Wulfhere a questioning look as if his master was abandoning him. A blow barged into Wulfhere's shoulder. Thankfully his shield took the brunt of it. He reeled round, swinging his shield round from his back and lifted his sword to defend himself, hardly noticing as his assailant's sword slashed into his leg, close to where previously an arrow had hit him.

The man before him was, like him, drenched in blood. Wulfhere raised his shield to parry the sword blow descending upon him. He was filled with a terrible fury and retaliated with his sword, swinging it upwards and catching the man's shield with such a force it knocked him back a few paces. His rage gathered momentum and Wulfhere hacked at the man before he could recover, his sword blows bashing his shield aside, creating an opening for him to deliver a slash across the man's gut, knocking the Norþmann off his feet. He pinned him with his foot, and thrust his sword tip into the man's throat as the enemy lay prone in the morass of mud and guts beneath him. The man's eyes stared up at him, glasslike and questioning, as red spittle frothed from his mouth and trickled into his beard. Wulfhere wasted no time. Sensing danger to his rear, he whirled around to ward off a blow from some other warrior. Suddenly, he was surrounded and had to fight them off like a madman. His fury continued to enrage him. He battled on; hardly realising he was injured until he began to weaken. Legs buckling underneath him, he dropped into the bloody slough, and covered himself with his shield, waiting for the end. He knew his life was over.

Esegar stumbled from the mass of fighting men. His horse was gone, butchered from underneath him. He was injured, but where he couldn't tell. He thought it might be his leg, or his hip, or perhaps both. Blood spread through his mail, seeping like puss from a rancid boil. He was shaking and wanted to vomit. He had to get away before he was killed. He felt like a coward leaving his lord to die without him, but he was thinking of his wife and children, and what would happen to them if he did not return home.

He saw a grouping of trees before him, the promise of safety. He hurried to it, dragging his wounded body wracked with exhaustion. His shield was gone. All he had to protect him was his seax. His heart thumped in his chest and his sight was a blur. The ground moved beneath his feet, moving backward, not forward and it appeared as though he would never reach the copse. He heard running behind him and twisted his head to see two men with vicious faces shouting and coming for him with raised hand axes. He could not run anymore and collapsed onto his knees and prayed. He was done for. He closed his eyes and waited for death to loom. A horn blew and voices rang out, shouting what sounded like orders. He waited an age for them to kill him, but then, he realised that death had not arrived after all. He opened his eyes, looked behind him, amazed to see that his pursuers were nowhere to be seen. He gazed over to the battlefield. To his astonishment, Alfgar's forces were disappearing into the next valley, leaving the carcasses of his fellow soldiers scattered over the blood-soaked field. He figured that they were running toward Hereford to catch and cut down those who had fled. He did not want to think about the disaster that was about to befall Hereford. Instead, he allowed the relief to flow through his body, and the tears burst forth as he knelt in the long grass. *He was alive.*

Chapter Twenty-two

The Ravaging of Hereford

Father Tremerig threw open the large, newly hung church doors, and rushed along the nave to the altar, where the elderly, Bishop Athelstan, was kneeling with his canons, in prayer. Tremerig had just ran from the battlefield, where he had been sent by his master to carry out God's work, administering blessings and reassurance that God would be with them this day. Behind him, three men hurried. They were the church's men, commended to fight for Ralph by Athelstan. God, it seemed, had better things to do this day, than ensure the lives of this little community.

Tremerig, the bishop's deputy, wasted no time in shouting that Gruffudd's great army was approaching the town, and that soon they would be upon them, pouring their lust for blood into the very heart of Hereford. His blessings, it seemed, had been fruitless. It felt strange for him to be shouting that the Wéalas were coming, for he was born of that country himself. It had been many years now, thirteen in fact, since he had left his community in Glamorgan, to become the deputy of the old bishop. Since an illness had robbed Athelstan of his sight, Tremerig had been his eyes, rarely leaving his side. The longevity of his appointment made him feel as if he had been there all his life.

But he doubted that neither his race nor his holy office would keep him safe from Gruffudd's army. They were just as likely to cut his throat as they would his fellow clergymen. He had known Gruffudd when he was a lazy good-for-nothing youth. He was not a compassionate man, nor was he particularly devout. The only thing he had shown any passion for was the crown of Wales. With this in mind, Tremerig feared the worst.

At the sound of his deputy's terrified warning, the old bishop stood gingerly from prayer, but not before crossing himself and genuflecting to the gold-plated crucifix that hung above the altar. He turned to face them calmly, but Tremerig saw the indisputable fear in his old unseeing eyes. To be blind and facing the most horrific danger must be a terrible thing indeed, Tremerig thought.

"You men have just come from the battle?" Athelstan asked, his voice trembling anxiously. Had he not been blind he would not have needed to ask, for the soldier's blood-stained, dishevelled appearance would have told him that they had.

"What of the Earl?" Athelstan asked as the men affirmed.

"He has gone," replied one of the men bitterly.

"Gone?" The bishop crossed himself, aghast. "You mean he has been killed?"

The men looked at each other and laughed sardonically. A second man said, "No, Father, he did not stay for that pleasure. He ran like a squealing swine from a pack of hunting dogs! He was gone before even a spear was thrown or an arrow released!"

"He deserted?" the bishop asked incredulously. "I cannot believe it. Tremerig, my friend, is this true?" Tears welled in the old man's eyes as he reached for his deputy.

Father Tremerig took the old man's hands and said in a voice that was low and sorrowful, "I am afraid it is true, your lordship. The army he had raised was magnificently overwhelmed."

"Then where did he go? If he fled, surely he has returned to defend the burh?" Athelstan inquired in a voice that was naively hopeful.

"It seems that he has not, Lord Athelstan," Tremerig said gently. "He has left us to our fate. Our lives are in God's hands now."

The bishop rolled his cloudy eyes to the ceiling. "Heaven have mercy on us!" he cried. "What is going to become of this beloved church that we have only just finished restoring?"

"Father, we must flee from here," entreated one of the canons.

"Too late!" Tremerig cried. "Look!" As he spoke, the heavy wooden doors of the Saint Guthlac's Mynstre, once again flew open, and panic-stricken townsfolk poured through them.

"You have your swords?" Athelstan said to the three soldiers.

"Yes, Father."

"Tremerig, you and Father Eadnoth – fetch our gardening tools; anything will do. Spades, trowels, axes… oh, and get Father Gospatric to bring his meat cleaver – and our hunting bows. We will defend God's Holy Church ourselves!"

"But, my Lord Bishop, you cannot see!" Tremerig protested.

"Then you will be my eyes, Father Tremerig, just as you always have been!"

Thurkill was the captain of the garrison, left behind to guard the town whilst the main army sallied forth. Ralph had been so certain of victory, that he had not thought that Hereford would need any more than a dozen men. Any man or boy over the age of fourteen had gone with the army. From the tower at Ralph's castle, Thurkill could see the great foreign army pouring over the hills and down the valleys in pursuit of Ralph's fleeing men. Some were seen being pursued into the river, where they perished in waters soon to run deep with blood; others were wounded or killed, as they rushed toward the town walls.

Thurkill jumped down from the parapet, shouting for his men to close the castle gates as the townsfolk rushed through them. Old men and hysterical women came pouring in with their screaming children clinging to them. The air inside the bailey was filled with a tangible terror, emanating from the burh's frightened people.

"What about the town gates?" yelled a young thegn, Marleswein, as he helped to push closed the gates of the castle.

Thurkill looked at the lad wryly. "What gates? Hereford has no gates!" he replied. "Our illustrious earl was so intent on creating his magnificent mounted army and building a great castle for himself, he neglected to ensure that the marauders wouldn't be able to gain access into the burgh that surrounds it! What structures we do have do not shut properly, and the eastern gate is so rotted that it's a wonder it still stands."

Suddenly there came the terrifying noise of women screaming and babies crying outside the castle. Thurkill felt his blood curdle at the sound. It meant the invaders were in the streets. They would be killing, raping and looting. Soon, they would be pounding on the castle gates. The distress on the faces of those inside filled him with horror as they cried with fear, helpless to aid those on the other side of the gates.

"Open the gates, lord," begged Marleswein. "My wife and children are out there."

"As are mine!" Thurkill yelled. His voice was drowned out by a terrifying scream, rising through the air. He shook his head and held it in his hands, desperately trying to think what to do. "If we open them, we will be met with death, for sure. There are no more than twelve of us here, what can we do against thousands."

"We cannot leave them out there to be killed," Marleswein replied desperately.

"Do you think that I want to?" Thurkill shouted back at him, the spittle flying from his mouth as he spoke with desperation. "But if we open the gates now, we would only be letting the bastard enemy in, not our people!"

"We are dead anyway," shouted one of the garrison, in a voice filled with anguish. "Let them in and we'll take our chances."

The shouting and screaming outside the castle gates grew louder, and they could hear the crazed bloodlust of the invaders. Then came the pungent smell of smoke, and a hail of burning arrows flew over the wooden palisade. When they landed, they set fire to some of the thatched buildings. Soon the fire spread quickly and terrifyingly.

"We are going to die!" screamed a woman carrying two wailing children in her arms.

"Oh Christ preserve us! Where is the Godforsaken earl?" screamed Thurkill, as the gates were pounded and pushed in by the enemy on the other side. "Bowmen to the walls, others to the gates! To the gates!" the thegn cried.

Men and boys rushed to hold the gates, those who were too old or too young to fight in the fyrd. Women, too, joined them, but they were not enough to defend them, and soon the structures were broken down by Alfgar and his Irish-Norse, who poured in through the gaping breach. They triumphantly hacked and slashed at anyone who got in their way. They were indiscriminate, not caring if their victim be man, woman, or child. There was no sign of the earl or his cronies, nor his wife or son. He must have left them at court to ensure their safety.

Alfgar felt cheated of his revenge. He had hoped that Ralph and his nephew, Will Malet, would have run back to the burgh, when they fled from the battlefield like cowardly peasants, and now they would not even give him the satisfaction of hiding in the castle, so he could exact his revenge on them both.

It had been easy to take the castle; once through the gates, the small garrison of men gave no resistance. The surviving defenders were brought before him in the courtyard, as his comrades were rounding up the women and children, and any males who would be suitable as slaves. Those who were too frail were killed, their throats cut like sheep. Alfgar sneered at the garrison warriors. Many were young men in their twenties, and they were frightened, shaking with terror at what they imagined was about to come. He singled out one of them, whom he recognised.

"I know you; you are Marleswein Sweinson! Tell me where the earl is," Alfgar growled at him.

"I wish we knew. He has left us all to die, and fled to save himself," muttered Marleswein, bitterly.

Alfgar laughed. "Your precious earl has saved his own skin, then. And his precious Frencisc shits with him." He was laughing as if his sides would split. Oh, the irony of it! The Earl of Hereford, for all his boasting, was nothing but a coward! "Join me and my men then, Marleswein. You will find that I am a more loyal lord than de Mantes."

"I would rather take my chances here with the others," spat Marleswein, venomously.

Alfgar smiled and shrugged. "So be it then," he said casually.

He stood before the line of prisoners, thrown to their knees brutally by his men. Their hands were roped behind their backs. Only Marleswein and one other, held their heads high; the rest hung theirs in shame. Behind them, the heat scorched their backs as the flames that burned the castle's tower and ramparts, crackled.

Alfgar stared at the other, momentarily, with scornful eyes. The man's gaze followed him, as he walked along the line. He felt unnerved as the man's eyes bore into him as he stood in front of all the men, examining them one by one as if they were animals in a market. Alfgar came back to him, and studied him, looking him up and down. He was a man in his prime, about thirty, he would say, his hair was made browner by the dust and he'd a dark moustache, tinged with blood from damaged lips and broken teeth. He held himself like a leader.

"You – your name?" Alfgar demanded.

Thurkill continued to stare, defiantly. "Thurkill, my name is Thurkill."

"Address me as your lord, man! Do you not know who I am?" Alfgar raged, and he gave Thurkill's gut the pommel of his sword.

Thurkill was knocked back by the blow, but he was strong, his stomach muscles hardened by rigorous training. He managed to keep his balance. "Yes sir, I know who you are," he said calmly, and smiled. "You're a cunt."

His fellow captives held their breath as the insult slid easily from Thurkill's tongue, leaving them flinching and shaking with fear. Alfgar laughed inwardly, revelling in the cowards' fear, but Thurkill's defiance irritated him. He wanted to teach him a lesson.

"My lord," Ragnald said, pulling Thurkill's head back by his hair to expose his neck. "Shall I slit his filthy throat?"

Alfgar gazed at Thurkill's rebellious eyes, and marvelled at his bravery. The man had guts, he would give him that. "No, Ragnald. Killing them would be too easy."

Alfgar looked around him at the carnage within the compound. Some of his men were carrying off the prettier women to rape them inside the buildings. Some were more interested in booty and were ransacking the huts. It had occurred to him that perhaps the families of these defeated, humbled men were amongst this batch of screaming wenches and their brats. What greater punishment could a man suffer, than to see his womenfolk and *bearns* raped and slaughtered before his eyes. But perhaps he should hang the men in front of their women... He could not decide.

Ragnald still held Thurkill by his hair, looking at Alfgar with hopeful eyes that pleaded with him to be allowed to kill him. The captured thegn was unable to struggle, for Ragnald had a firm grip on him, but his defiant expression remained, like the light of a candle that refused to go out in the wind. Alfgar imagined Ralph de Mantes' face before him. He was angry that the earl had escaped. He would have made him beg for his life, had he been there. But instead, he was going to have to make do with who he had before him.

"Bind them together in the square," Alfgar ordered. "They can watch the town burn."

All the men were lined up, and were dragged together, through Hereford's streets of chaos to the open area of the town. A rope linked their bound hands together, and as they were forced to walk, their eyes met such scenes of horror they never would have believed imaginable. Men, women, and children were running everywhere, like frightened animals, desperate to escape whatever terrible fate awaited them, should they be caught by their pursuers. Those caught, were either rounded up to be taken into slavery, or slaughtered mercilessly if they tried to fight back.

Even the children were not spared. Thurkill saw one boy of about eleven skewered with by a javelin, as he tried to save his mother from being raped. He fought to keep down the vomit pooling in his throat, but, when he walked over the mutilated body of a dead baby lying in the mud, it spewed from his mouth unchecked. One of his tormenters kicked him in the back, and forced him forward. His eyes took stock of the man's face, locking his features away in his mind so that he would remember him always, and if he survived this, he could someday return the favour.

In the marketplace, they were herded into the centre. The atmosphere was searing, not only with the heat of the flames, but also with the terrified screams and moans of the distressed, echoing around the square, mingling with the sizzling, and crackling of buildings, destroyed by the fire... Although he struggled, Thurkill was not able to release himself from the ropes that bound him. They were made to sit in a circle, back to back around the stone cross that marked the square. Next to him, a young lad wept audibly.

"Courage, lad," Thurkill said to him compassionately. "We die as men, not as weeping women."

The boy, who was only sixteen, barely a hair on his chin, sniffed back his tears, and nodded.

"Thurkill!" screamed a woman and his eyes followed the voice.

She was being held by a tall *Wicinga* who was carrying her under his arm. Two small infants were hurrying beside them, their little arms reaching out to her.

"Osyth! For God's sake, let her go!" Thurkill shouted, straining forward against the rope that bound his chest. He bit his lip to see his lovely wife, her beautiful red-gold hair splayed loose, and her clothes awry, struggling robustly, to escape the man.

Alfgar looked pleased. "Bring that woman and her brats here."

The *Wicinga* warrior did not look pleased to hand her over to Alfgar, but he did so, reluctantly, before running off to find another prize. It was Ragnald who brought her before her husband. The children clung to her hands with quiet fear. Thurkill's heart sank; the tears stung in his eyes as he met her distraught gaze.

"Alfgar, let her go and I will join your war band," he cried.

"It's a little late for that now," Alfgar replied, ominously. "You had your chance."

Thurkill felt something cold touching his hand. Something sharp, pricking his palm. Marleswein was leaning against him. At first, he thought that his friend was trying to make himself more comfortable. Then he saw that Marleswein was looking at him, using his eyes and his head to gesture down at his hands. By the Saints, it was a knife! Marleswein was handing him a knife! When they had been caught,

334

their weapons were removed from them, including their seaxes. Marleswein must have secreted a smaller blade somewhere on himself.

Thurkill took the knife, and began to twist it in his hands so that the blade was touching the rope. His fingers caught the cutting edge, and he tried not to wince. If he could cut himself free, the others would be able to unwind the rope that entwined them all.

"Let her go, Lord Alfgar, and we will all join you," Thurkill demanded, his stomach nauseous again at the sight of his wife and children in Alfgar's merciless clutches.

"Can I fuck her before I kill her?" Ragnald asked, leering. His left arm was grasping Osyth across her breasts, while his right held a knife to her throat.

Alfgar held his hand up to Ragnald.

"You bastard! If you touch her, I swear I will bring down such a catastrophe upon you all, that you will never have seen before!" Thurkill raged. If only he could cut through the rope and not his own flesh.

"So, you want to join us now, Thurkill? Too late. I only give men one chance."

Suddenly, Thurkill felt his hands free. He shrugged and loosened the rest of the rope that bound him, taking the knife, and cutting through it. Then he lunged forward, and Alfgar looked more than surprised.

"Not too late for me to kill you!" he roared as he threw himself at the Mercian.

Marleswein followed him, jumping to wrestle with Ragnald.

It was a valiant attempt, but inevitably it failed dismally. They were soon overpowered. Thurkill had thought it better to die defending his family, than to watch them die in front of his eyes, but it was not to be. The thegns were bound once more, and forced to sit in the dirt and the rain, which had started to spit, whilst all around them, houses burned, and chaos ruled. It was as if the earth had opened, and hell had risen from its bowels.

Thurkill sustained more injuries in the fight, and Marleswein, too, was badly hurt, having taken a kicking, but the worst was yet to come. Thurkill was forced to watch his children, a boy of four and a daughter of three, breathe their last as their throats were cut, their little bodies falling limply into the mud, as their life's blood flowed from them.

Before they closed their eyes, he was sure they had looked at him accusingly. *How could you let them do this to us, Papa?*

Thurkill wanted to scream and roar with grief. Let the rage inside of him break through the wall he had built around his heart. But there was no way he would expose his anguish to them so nakedly. He would give them nothing. He heard his wife wailing as she too was forced to watch. If only she hadn't called to him, he thought. If only he had not tried to save them. If only he had agreed to join Alfgar. If only...

Then, Osyth was next. They stripped her, and raped her in front of them all, and when he tried to close his eyes, they stood behind him and forced his eyes open. It was then that Thurkill allowed himself to cry. Three or four took her before he lost count.

Alfgar had not touched her. He would not denigrate himself with such a sin. But he allowed his men to use her and then Ragnald, having had his turn also, drew his knife across her throat.

But Alfgar was just as culpable of her abuse and murder. God would see what he has done, and punish him. It was Thurkill's only consolation; and, if he lived through this, retribution would come; one day. He would kill him.

Gruffudd and his men attacked the cathedral, allowing Alfgar to take Ralph's castle. His men were crazed with the glory of the slaughter. For so long they had listened to the bards sing of their forefathers' glorious battles against the invading Saes. Stories like that of the *Gododdin*. Now it was time to return to those glory days.

"Burn it to the ground!" Gruffudd ordered, and his men gave great shouts of delight, as they prepared to set the place alight. "But first, take anything of worth. There will be plenty of booty for all of you!"

By sundown, word that Hereford was ablaze reached the king, waiting for news in Gleawecestre. He entrusted Earl Harold to summon the fyrd, and go against the invading army. His disgraced nephew, the Earl of Hereford, had retreated to Worcester, and conveniently, was too ill to answer any questions about his flight from Hereford. In fact, Ralph de Mantes was never to fully recover from his shattered dreams of ever being king.

Chapter Twenty-three

Into Hell

Smoke, death, and destruction filled his nostrils, as he stumbled through the smouldering wreckage of the once proud and ancient town of Hereford, his face caked in a crust of mud, blood, and gore. He surveyed, with grim intensity, the burning shells of the once well-maintained houses, made lurid by the flames, and the glow of twilight. His bloodshot eyes hardly took in the scene without flinching. He shivered involuntarily and crossed himself, stepping over the charred, and bloodied, remains of the townsfolk. Wulfhere surmised that they had been escaping from their burning homes, lit by the marauders' torches, and flaming arrows, only to meet their deaths in the streets. Of those corpses that were not blackened by fire, the sight was horrific. As if charred bodies were not bad enough, there was worse yet to come.

Little children, too, had been hacked down with their mothers, as they tried to protect them; limbs and entrails scattering the streets, manifesting into a slaughter farm. There were old men, young boys, women, girls, and babies. Some of the girls' corpses bore the signs of rape, their clothes torn from them, exposing their shame. Wulfhere was sickened by the sight, and thought of his own young daughters. He did his best to cover their exposed private parts, but his battered body was not able to bend without causing him unbearable pain. He felt guilty because he could not carry out, sufficiently, the one thing he could possibly do for them. No woman, child or beast should be butchered this way.

He had stumbled into hell…

He'd staggered from the battlefield, more surprised than grateful to be alive. Luckily for him, he had blacked out, wedged amongst the bodies of fallen warriors. The spinners were truly on his side that day, as they spun the threads, expressly made for him. Not so for most of his unit, and those of the others. He left the field – awash with scarlet pools of blood and entrails, alone – after the terrible task of releasing his dying comrades of their agony. One young horseman lay with his guts leaking out of his ripped belly, onto the grass in a congealed pile of gore. The man grasped Wulfhere's hand, begged him in a voice that

337

cracked with the distress of the dying, to tell his wife and children that he had fought valiantly, and that he loved them dearly. Wulfhere promised that, if he could find them, he would, before slitting the soldier's throat, and closing his eyes with his thumbs, to ease his suffering into the next world.

Now, as he limped back through the devastation, his eyes smarting with congealing blood – or sweat – he could not be sure which. He was badly wounded. His right shoulder throbbed, and his sword arm hung uselessly by his side, his hand unable to clasp his sword. From his upper right thigh, blood oozed where the arrow tip had pierced him, still buried in the wound. Close to that, blood seeped where a sword blade had slashed him. Such was the chaos that day, the injuries could easily have been inflicted by his own comrades, as well as the enemy. His left hand held his sword, for his scabbard had been broken in the mêlée, and his right hand was useless, could not even hold his prick if he needed to piss. *Hildbana* dripped with the blood of those he'd put out of misery, and a trail of crimson followed him, as he forced himself to walk the two miles back to Hereford, head hammering with monstrous pain under his dented helm, gripping his head like the pincers of a giant claw.

Suddenly he heard his name and looked up. He heard it, as if it were distant. "Lord Wulfhere, thank God! I never thought to see you alive again!"

Esegar emerged out of the smoke, miraculously and wonderfully alive, astride Hwitegast, his beloved animal. Wulfhere stopped in his tracks. He sighed with heartfelt relief. He could barely see as his vision grew increasingly blurred, and it hurt to raise his eyes. He hardly believed that he was hearing the sweet sound of his treasured stallion calling to him. Alive! Hwitegast was alive! Esegar was alive! He praised the Lord, and kissed the little iron cross hanging about his neck.

Through his tears, he tried to smile as they approached, but even to smile was to hurt. Although he winced, he was overjoyed. They were all alive. The last thing he was conscious of was the warm sound of Hwitegast's nicker as he nuzzled his face. Then Wulfhere collapsed into blessed darkness.

Wulfhere awoke under a makeshift shelter. It was dark, and the air was permeated with the sound of crackling wood fires, men groaning and women sobbing. He sat bolt upright, trying to gauge his location, and saw that he was lying on a pile of blood-stained straw, covered by a blanket of rough wool. His torn mail had been removed, and, as he investigated further, he felt bandages wrapping his thigh and torso. His head pounded as if he had suddenly been hit an almighty blow. Esegar was sitting opposite him, with his legs crossed, and the worried look of a man waiting for death to take his friend. Wulfhere looked at him with confused eyes. It took him some moments to recall what had happened, and where he might possibly be.

"My lord, you must rest. Here, take some of this and lie back upon your bed," Esegar urged him gently. He came to his side and put a clay flask to his lips.

"What the fuck is that?" Wulfhere asked, crumpling his face after he had taken in a mouthful of sour-tasting liquid.

"'Tis mixed with feverfew, cowslip and other herbs. It was prescribed by the good Father, Tremerig."

"Tastes like horse's piss and shite mixed together! Where are we?" Wulfhere grunted, laying back onto the straw. He put his left hand up to his forehead. "God's teeth and Satan's ears, I have the worst headache! My leg is... what's happened to my leg?"

"Lord, you had a gaping wound in your right thigh, which has now been stitched, and a spear hole in your right shoulder blade. Not to mention the arrow head the surgeon chiselled out of the same leg. You're lucky they didn't cut off the limb."

"Why does my arm ache so much?" Wulfhere demanded gruffly.

"Dislocated. You didn't half struggle when they pushed it back into the socket. And it took six of us to hold you down whilst they worked on your leg."

"I remember nothing of it."

"You were very feverish."

Wulfhere flinched as pain shot through him, all over his body.

"Take more of it," Esegar said, indicating the potion he still had in his hand. "It will help the pain and the fever."

Wulfhere sipped at the flask. "What of you? When I came to on the field, I thought you must have been killed." He handed back the flask, and lay back against the straw.

"I have some small wounds. They smart, but are not serious. Not like yours, anyway. I was lucky."

"Hwitegast! You found my horse. Where is he?"

"In the compound with the other horses, lord. He is safe. Though I don't know how it is that he lived. Most of the others had to be destroyed."

Wulfhere smiled proudly at the astuteness of his beloved steed. "I dismounted and sent him running. What of your mount, Hyhtgiefa?" In the shadows, Wulfhere could see the sadness in Esegar's eyes.

"I am sorry, my lord. He is gone." Esegar bowed his head. "I loved that horse, lord." The horse had been gifted to him by Wulfhere, for his service. "I am ashamed that I lost him... and I –"

"Ach, so many good steeds, as well as men, have lost their lives in such madness!" Wulfhere was thinking of Hygethrymm and the other horses he had supplied to de Mantes, and felt a wrench of anger at their loss. "You have not told me where we are."

"We are in the precinct of the old church... in Hereford. It is now a ruin. Some of the priests died defending the doors. But the old bishop, he still lives... and his deputy, Tremerig."

They were silent, and Wulfhere could see that his fyrdsman looked troubled. "What is it Esegar?" he asked. Esegar's lip started to tremble. "'Tis not your fault about the horse."

Esegar burst into tears. "I am ashamed, lord. Because of the horse, yes, but also, because I ran and left you – I left you to die!"

Esegar was sobbing. Wulfhere took great pains to sit up and face him. "I saw such terrible destruction. It was like Dunsinane all over again," Wulfhere said, hoarsely. He wanted to reach out to comfort him, but it hurt too much. "I do not blame you, Esegar, for that was your fate, to live and bring Hwitegast back to me."

It was agony to sit, and Esegar, let his tears fall on him, as he supported him to lie back down.

"It is not how we die that counts, but in what manner we live our lives, Esegar. We cannot escape our fate, but we do the best we can with the fate we have been given."

"Rest, Lord Wulfhere," Esegar encouraged. "You will need your strength to recover from your wounds."

Before Esegar could finish his words, Wulfhere had already drifted back to sleep.

The nightmare begins as it always does: Wulfhere stands alone and deserted on Dunsinane hill, searching for his fellows amongst the carnage around him. As usual, the scenes drift and change, and he finds himself walking through blood-soaked streets. He sees his hands are covered in sticky red fluid, and knows not whether it his blood or that of others. He is wearing mail; it slows him down. It feels as if a great hand is pushing against him, and he struggles to go forward. Around him, buildings burn, tortured souls howl, dark shadows fly past him, and ghostly horses are screaming.

He hears a child calling to him; Winflaed, or perhaps Freyda. But then he thinks it sounds like Tovi. Or perhaps it is all of them, calling out for him to save them. Then he sees them through the flames, hollow ghostly figures. Their faces illuminated by the fire-glow; their eyes, sorrowful and pleading. Freyda is there, looking mournful, with little Drusilda in her arms and Winflaed beside her, tears pouring down her cheeks. The twins are there also, standing on either side of their sisters; then Tovi and Gerda appear in front of them, as if by magic. There is another small figure, separate from them. A little girl with fair hair and familiar features looks out of a burning doorway. She holds up a comb, purposefully: Alfgyva's child, the daughter he had helped to bury. Her lips do not move, but he can hear her calling to him... *"Father, I am dying, please come..."* The child wears an expression of deep melancholy, and he absorbs her sadness into his own.

His heart beats fast as a prickling sensation runs through his veins. He does not know which way to run. He hears Rowena call him, her voice almost drowned out by the pleas of his other children. Which way first? *Why the hell can they not all be in the same place?*

The fire grows. Tongues of flame lash out at him, and the danger of the children being completely swallowed in the fire is acute. He rushes forward, stops halfway, turns to the left, then the right. Who should he save first? Rowena, or the others? Should he save one small lonely soul, and let seven other souls die? Or should he save the one that is already dead? What would be the purpose in that, other than to ease his guilt?

He imagines he hears Rowena's voice. "It's all right, Father. I am already passed, remember? Save the others." She has given him permission.

But the fire is too hot. It pushes him back. He calls out to his children, shouts for them to get out of the building. They do not move. They simply stare at him with tears flowing from their hollow eyes. He realises they are doomed, and they are crying for him, arms outstretched. He stands, powerless. The flames scorch him. Then their faces melt in the heat, like candle wax, and as their features distort, their mouths gape open, as if they are silently screaming. He calls out to them, shouting their names on by one as he runs toward them, but the more he runs, the further away he seems to be.

He tries to hurry, and finally, he gets there. Just as he is about to reach for the door, the building collapses, and tendrils of fire leap out at him, like the tongues of devils. The burning effigies of his children are standing lifeless amongst the roasting timber. A voice cries out in the darkness, a distressed and mournful resonance. Staring into the blackness, he suddenly realises that it is his own voice that he hears.

"Who is that?" The man leapt out of his blanket and jumped to his feet with his sword drawn, nervous, in case the Wéalas and their allies had returned to attack them in the dark of night.

"Satan's bollocks, are we being attacked?" another man yells. He, too, had drawn his sword, and his arm was raised high.

"He's just having a nightmare. Go back to sleep," Esegar told them gruffly. "Are you all right, lord?"

"Aye," Wulfhere replied. He felt stupid. Hardened men did not have nightmares. "Just a dream. Go back to sleep, I'm fine."

"You're sweating," the first man said.

"How can you see if he's sweating in this darkness?" someone else asked, impatiently.

"I can hear him."

"Leave him be. Go back to sleep, Leofgar," called out one of the other men. "For God's sake, let a man get his rest!"

Esegar patted Wulfhere on his shoulder, reassuringly, and snuggled back down under his blanket. Wulfhere lay back. He stared into the darkness, afraid to close his eyes, lest he should drift off into the nightmare again. Nightmares, his father had told him, were demons sent to torment a man when his conscience was disturbed. Was that really so? Or had the recent events left him scarred, both physically and mentally?

The pain in his leg had returned, and he bit his lip to stop himself from crying out in agony. He reached out and drew the medicine flask to him. He let the bitter, warm liquid, flow down into his gullet and through his veins. Then his head spun and he was gone again.

Chapter Twenty-four

Into the Shadows

Harold pitched his camp in a clearing at the foothills, away from the woods, lining the River Dore, in the Golden Valley. He had followed the trail of dead campfires along the paths running deep into the valley, bordering the large mountainous area the Wéalas called, *Y Mynyddoedd Duon*, the Black Mountains. After the fall of Hereford, he'd summoned a large proportion of the Wessex fyrd, coming out of Gleawecestre with a large body of men to hunt down the raiders, and ordering Robert FitzWimarc, the king's standard bearer, to remain behind in Hereford, to wait for the rest of the Wessex fyrd to arrive.

Harold had not stopped to view the devastation inflicted upon Hereford. There would be time enough later to stand and survey the wreckage; and to weep for what had been lost there. For now, he wanted to settle the score, but Gruffudd and Alfgar, had disappeared like wraiths in the night and their armies were nowhere to be seen. Here, the enemy tracks had suddenly gone cold, and they left no more of themselves than churned mud and smouldering timber, amongst the eerie stillness of the mountains.

Harold and his companions, sat under an awning with two large hares roasting on a spit over the campfire. Evening was falling over the misty valley, bringing with it a fine sprinkling of icy rain, which did not bode well for another night in the elements. The smoke from the other campfires wafted through the air, leaving them in a grey haze. They watched the evening's supper turning on the crackling spit until the roasted skin sizzled, eliciting a chorus of hungry rumblings from their stomachs.

"You seem deep in thought, Lord Harold," old Brihtric, a man of Gleawecestre, said as a young thegn filled his drinking horn before going on to the next man.

Harold gave him a lazy look. He shivered with the cold, tired after trekking through the muddied, waterlogged tracks. "I am wondering how the bastards managed to get across the ridge with all that booty... and then disappear into the mists, as if they had never set foot out of the mountains," he replied, tossing an apple core with which he had temporarily appeased his noisy stomach with, onto the fire.

It had been a difficult journey, especially for the horses. Those whose job it was to pull cartloads of gear, did so with great hardship. The wheels got stuck in the muddy furrows, and sometimes a horse lost its footing. Harold knew that it was going to be an impossible mission: to send heavily armoured, mounted troops through the misty mountains of South Wales. He had sent smaller skirmishing units and scouts on ahead to see where the Wéalas might be hiding, but the enemy knew the area so well, and they attacked with great ferocity, any pursuing bands sent by Harold. Quick as lightning, they pounced out of the trees, like mythical beasts in the wilderness; then, just as rapidly as they appeared, they evaporated into the ether.

"The Wéalas have been harrying the borderlands for years now, with lightning attacks, raiding the settlements along the Wye Valley... then disappearing into the mountains again. They are used to negotiating the old Mercian ditch and difficult terrain," Brihtric said, matter-of-factly. "*And* they have feet, nimble, like the paws of a polecat!"

"Nippy little bastards are the Wéalas. And the *Norþmenn* will be long on their way in their ships by now. Most likely they have gone northwards, to Caestre," said Esegar of Middeleseax, sniffing loudly, as droplets of mucus hung off the end of his frozen nose. "What I cannot understand is how did it all go so wrong for Lord Ralph? Why, not so long ago, he was boasting to anyone who would listen, about his 'well-trained, highly efficient, army of cavalrymen'."

"According to Ralph, they were faced with an enemy of overwhelming numbers, and were forced to flee when his right flank turned and ran," Harold replied, trying not to sound too sceptical.

"So much for his great army of mounted men!" laughed Eadnoth, in the West Country twang.

Harold gave the rugged thegn a warning look. He was furious with Ralph for refusing to accept extra men to help him defend Hereford. The Earl of Hereford's pride had caused him to underestimate the strength of the alliance against him, but he would not have the men badmouth the earl. Such talk might find its way back to the king, who was fond of his nephew, and Harold did not want to be associated with it. It was to his own close followers he had privately expressed his annoyance, stating that, if Ralph had not been so pig-headed, and Edward so willing to indulge him, perhaps they would not be there now pursuing an invisible enemy.

Harold had demanded that Ralph accompany him on the chase, since he was the creator of the disaster, but his wife pleaded that he was laid up, ill, with the stomach cramps and fever, which plagued him since Hereford had fallen. Ralph's own report of that day had seen him fighting valiantly. Once he had given his account to the king, he took to his bed with Edward's admiration for his bravery, sympathy for his travail, and good wishes for his recovery. No one other than the Lady Gytha had seen him since. The full extent of Ralph's cowardice was not yet known, but Harold sensed that there was more to the sorry tale.

William Malet, had graciously offered to go with Harold in Ralph's place, but Harold had made him stay behind with Richard Fitzscrob and Robert FitzWimarc, in Hereford, to oversee the town's repairs. Harold knew that Malet's presence during the campaign would only serve to irritate him, so he thought it wiser to have him to stay in Hereford. He knew William quite well, for he and Harold were both godparents to Ralph's son, also called Harold, but he had no liking for the man. He was an agitator. Where there was trouble, there was William, gloating in the background. Alfgar's nephew was undeniably Ralph's lapdog, and Harold was certain he had been as much privy to the plot to rid the kingdom of Alfgar, as Ralph and Tostig were. The Earl of Wessex was not greatly fond of Alfgar either, but the trio's scheming had resulted in far-reaching consequences, as Alfgar's vengeful deeds had shown.

Harold pushed his seat back so he could stand, and moved to the edge of the awning. He looked out into the foggy distance, scanning the horizon to see if there was any sign of the missing scouts he had sent out earlier, one of which was his brother, Leofwin. They had not yet arrived back at the camp with the others. He had not wanted to send his younger brother on such a dangerous mission, but Leofwin had insisted on going, and now only a handful of men had returned. The returning warriors informed him that a band of Wéalas fighters had attacked them, scattering them in the skirmish. The unfortunate dead were accounted for, but Leofwin, Tigfi and Skalpi, were missing.

Harold sighed, as he silently prayed for the men's return. *Leofwin, dear God not Leofwin...* His younger brother was eager and ambitious. Gyrth had just taken charge of Alfgar's lands, and was waiting to have the title of earl officially bestowed upon him. Now, Leofwin was champing at the bit, keen for advancement like his brother's, taking advantage of any opportunity to prove himself with enthusiasm... a little too much perhaps. Harold knew that his younger brother wanted to win his honours on merit alone, and not because he was a Godwin. With a sense of unease, he scanned the stony rise through the mist, looming in front of them. The darkening clouds were casting a shadow over the scene, and thick fog was hampering the receding light. The wind snapped at his eyes, but even so, through the spreading grimness, he thought that he could see dark shapes moving down the ravine towards them. He walked a few steps out from under the shelter, motioning to a couple of his huscarles to follow, just in case they were not friendly figures.

Shielding his eyes from the wind and rain that peppered his face, he squinted to see if there were three of them and if they were indeed human. Sometimes, out in the wilds, it was said that fiends in human form could be seen roaming. He was not a man given to such unchristian notions, but, nonetheless, the place did indeed have an eerie feel to it, and Harold could see how easy it was for a man's mind to conjure up such thoughts, when he was fearful and weary. Now, as the figures drew closer, he could make out a horse and two men on foot. He would not have wished to lose any of his men, but he had no desire to inform his mother that she had lost another of her beloved sons.

"Is that them, my lord?" inquired one of the men that Harold had motioned to his side. Gauti was a man of Harold's age, a Dane, like many of Harold's huscarles. "Looks like there are just two of them."

Harold felt a hot wave of fear rush over him. Could the one who was missing be his brother? Then his anxiety turned to relief, as he recognised the familiar and unmistakable long hair of his brother, billowing from underneath his conical helmet. He exhaled, puffing out cheeks, red from the cold, wet wind. But then he noticed that there was a third man after all, slumped forward onto the horse's neck, as Leofwin and his other companion, Skalpi, led it laboriously down the rocky pathway.

"My lord!" Skalpi called, and hurried toward them. As he came closer, Harold could see that he was pale and exhausted. His eyes and nose were streaming with cold, his scarred features ruddy from the wind. "The Wéalas are around us; they hide like elves and cannot be seen. They are here, there, and everywhere. If they do reveal themselves, it is not for long. Then they disappear into the shadows, like ghosts."

And wild, evil spirits, thought Harold grimly. He saw that it was young Tigfi the Yellow, lying prone over the horse's neck, injured. Harold grasped Skalpi's hand and nodded to his brother. "What happened?" he asked, indicating toward Tigfi.

"Watchful eyes were upon us. We heard them, but saw only the rustling of the trees and glimpses of an arm or a leg. They would not engage us, but then we were ambushed by about fifty of them. We found ourselves separated from our unit in a wooded area. Tigfi took an arrow in the shoulder. We fought them off; but only just."

Harold saw that the men were indeed badly battered, just like the others who had returned, but their ordeal appeared to have been worse, judging by their pitted shields. Leofwin's shield still had an arrow protruding from it.

"They came upon us without sound or movement, leaping out from their hiding places," continued Skalpi. His features were animated, and Harold could tell he was enjoying telling the tale, though his face grew grim when he informed his lord that they had lost two good horses in the foray.

Harold nodded, and went to examine his injured young huscarle, whose grimy, dust-covered face was feverish and sweating. He studied the injury with concern.

Tigfi raised his head sheepishly. "'Tis nothing but a pinprick. I have had worse from my sister's sewing needle." He struggled to smile, but the pain was etched, deeply, upon his face. Harold rubbed his back reassuringly. "We will have that out in a moment, lad, you'll see."

"We were cornered by about seven men, but most ran when I showed them my beauty." Skalpi grinned, referring to his Dane axe. "Unfortunately, I left it buried in the head of a Wéalas. But I am sorrier about losing my horse. He was a good ambler, and nimble with it, especially through mountain tracks. I shall not get another like him."

"I shall see that you are reimbursed with another from my own stables, my friend, and with another beauty" Harold said, clapping his man on his shoulder with genuine affection. "And you, my brother? Are you hurt?"

"I am fine, brother," Leofwin reassured him, shaking his head.

"He took a bash to the side of his head, but his helm took care that no serious hurt was caused to him. Good steel that helm! He'll live," Skalpi said. "Both of them fought well. Tigfi showed them the proper use of a sword, until the wound got the better of him, whilst your brother's archery skills proved better than theirs. They soon ran like children, screaming into the woods, when they saw what the blade of my beloved Dane could do."

Harold clasped the back of Leofwin's head, and drew him to him. "I am gladdened that you are in one piece, brother. I would not have wished to face our mother's tongue lashing if you had not returned safely!" he exclaimed. The relief in his voice was evident.

Leofwin was his favourite brother. Four years ago, when the whole family had been outlawed by the king and their enemies, it had been Leofwin, who had followed Harold to Ireland whilst the others fled to Flanders. And it was Leofwin, who had fought courageously by his side, when they burst back onto the shores of Porlock to regain their foothold. Harold saw that his brother's face reddened, and knew that Leofwin hated being treated like a young pup. "Well done, lad," he told him to compensate.

Leofwin smiled, and nodded to the injured huscarle. "It was Tigfi who showed the real courage. Even after he took the arrow, he kept on fighting."

Harold was worried about Tigfi. He knew that he would need the arrowhead removed soon if he was going to survive. Most likely the bowman who had delivered the shot had dipped the arrow tip in something unsavoury, making sure that the wound would fester. "Let us not stand here in the rain. Tigfi is in need of a surgeon. The arrow must be removed immediately. Gauti, fetch Ulfketil. Tell him we have a wounded man in need of his skill." Then Harold added more morosely, "'Tis no small wonder that they have returned alive."

They brought Tigfi into Harold's tent and made him as comfortable as they could. They laid him face down on a pile of sheepskins, and stripped him of his armour and mail. Whilst the surgeon and his assistant set to work, Harold and his men discussed the best course of action. Should they stay another night and follow the trail into the next valley, pursuing the enemy deeper into their heartland? It was unknown territory for them, and the logistics of manoeuvring a large force into unfamiliar country would be dangerous. Perhaps it would be better to try to draw them out of the hills and mountains onto open ground, where they could not hide. Or, should they return to Hereford tomorrow, and wait for a diplomatic resolution? Sooner or later, Alfgar would make himself known again. Perhaps, diplomacy would be the only solution. And Harold's view was better to compromise, than to lose good men in war.

Later, when Harold was to enter the charred ruins of the once proud and ancient burgh of Hereford, and see for himself the devastation and suffering that Alfgar and Gruffudd had wrought, he knew that it would be a bitter wine to swallow, when eventually he sat across the other side of the bargaining table.

A week after the battle, Wulfhere knelt before Earl Harold in the charred wreckage of Hereford's main street. The terrible smell of putrefying human flesh was everywhere, indiscernible from that of the decaying animal carcasses and indescribable filth. Not even the smoke from the fire pits could rid the air of it. The clean-up had only just begun, and there was much to do as well as refortifying the burgh.

The earl dismounted and brought Wulfhere to his feet, a kindness that Wulfhere was thankful for, as the wound in his leg made it excruciatingly painful to kneel. Harold embraced him warmly, and Wulfhere saw that his blue eyes watered with the smoke and stench, that he himself was already used to.

"Wulfhere, it gladdens me to know that you survived the terrible carnage here." Harold's eyes swept over him. "I see you are wounded," he added, sounding genuinely concerned and moulded his features into an expression of anguish.

"My lord, there are many who are in a worse state than I," Wulfhere replied, humbly. For the last week, he had lain in a fever, with a sickness in his stomach he thought would never dissipate. His wounds still throbbed; bad dreams still plagued his sleep. If it had not been for the care of the surviving priests of St Guthlac's, and Esegar's care, he did not think he would be able to stand on his feet. Home never strayed far from his thoughts, and he wanted nothing more than to be there, with his family. Some of the badly injured had been sent home already, but he knew there was still much to do here, and he would not forgo his duty, until everyone else did.

"Aye, I have seen the church and heard about the bravery of the canons who tried to defend it. The good Bishop Athelstan and his vicar live, though the Bishop himself knows not how the miracle has been wrought, when so many of his good servants have been slaughtered."

Wulfhere nodded, and indicated to the men who had been kneeling with him, their heads bowed. "Thurkill and Marleswein, here, were amongst those who survived the storming of the castle," he said. "Thurkill lost his wife and two children at the hands of the invaders. The children were killed on Alfgar's orders, in front of him, and then he was made to watch as his wife was raped, before also having her throat cut. Marleswein has yet to find his family. He knows not whether they are amongst the charred bodies, or have been carried off by *Wicinga* scum."

Harold bade the two men to stand and embraced both of them. Tears filled his eyes at the sight of them, but he did not flinch at their maimed faces. Thurkill and Marleswein were unrecognisable as the men who had been entrusted to man the castle. The space where their noses had once been, was now a bloody, congealed mess. Alfgar's men had mutilated them, the last indignity inflicted upon them, after they had beaten them, along with the other prisoners. They had been left to die – but they did not. Wulfhere had wondered if it would have been better if they had.

Thurkill was visibly traumatised. Patches of white had been spreading through his brown hair. Each day he awoke, there were more. He was a man, who, just a week ago, had a home, a wife, two children, and a reason for living. Now his reason for living was revenge. Wulfhere felt his guts churn. Yesterday he had watched men like Thurkill bury his family in a massive pit beside the ruined church, despite being ill from his wounds. Wulfhere felt for him then, and, as he gazed upon the man's grief, he longed to be sitting around his own hearth, far away from the stench and the visions of hell.

"I am deeply saddened by your loss, Thurkill," Harold said compassionately. The thegn lifted his head faintly, but there was no reply.

"My lord, this man bleeds," Father Tremerig said, stepping forward. Blood was seeping through Thurkill's torn clothing. "He must have his wounds seen to."

"Aye," Harold nodded, and touched the man's shoulder. "Go with the good Father, Thurkill, and have your wounds tended. You have served your king and country well. Your bravery will not go unrewarded."

"'Tis not reward that I desire, my lord, but revenge," Thurkill said through broken teeth and swollen lips. He gazed up at Harold with a steely look of determination.

"You will have it, good Thurkill. God in his state of grace will see to it. And you too, Marleswein, go with the holy canons. I pray that your family are found safe and well."

They watched the men being led away by Tremerig and the surviving priests, to the makeshift hospital they had set up. Harold muttered an oath in Danish to one of his huscarles and then turned back to Wulfhere.

"I would like you to give me an account of the battle, Wulfhere. I have heard many interpretations, but now I want to hear yours," he said, smiling wryly. "I know that you are an honest man, and would not embellish or under exaggerate."

Wulfhere's face suddenly blanched. He had spotted William Malet, amongst the earl's attendants. Wulfhere's reproachful eyes swivelled towards him. The Norman was sitting smugly in his saddle with a look of undeserved magnitude. *He has not even the good grace to dismount!* Wulfhere thought angrily, *and sits with the air of one who has not lost that which those he left to die, have!* His rancour swelled inside of him, threatening to become an irrepressible torrent of rage.

Malet had gone as red as his cloak. *He remembers me!* Wulfhere thought.

He sensed that Harold noticed the tension, but the earl said nothing, and Wulfhere began the tale, speaking grimly and through clenched teeth. His gaze remained on Malet, melting the man like candle wax in the heat of his stare. "We faced Gruffudd and Alfgar. Our numbers were much fewer than theirs... much fewer... nevertheless, we stayed our ground. We stayed loyal. Faced our enemy like men... and with courage! We were Earl Ralph's glorious mounted men, waiting... and waiting... waiting for the earl to give an order, as the enemy charged us in their droves." Wulfhere's voice trembled with bitterness, eyes glowing with abhorrence, as he gazed upon the Norman baron with great malice.

William shifted uncomfortably in his saddle. Wulfhere's resentment was like a knife piercing his soul's armour.

He continued, "Then, when the enemy were fast closing in on us, the earl at last gave the order we were waiting for... but by then, it was too late... too late! And then the bastards deserted us." Wulfhere pointed his finger directly at Malet. "He, there, and that spineless prick, de Mantes, ran from the field with their cowardly *cnihts* following them like foxes after chickens. He gave the order to attack,

351

and then they ran from the field, leaving us with Gruffudd's army swarming down on us. They betrayed us, those Godforsaken Norman dogs!"

Harold gave Malet a questioning look. Malet was sitting motionless on his mount. He mouthed something inaudible, as Wulfhere spewed forth more vitriol. "Where is the gutless Earl? He left us like lambs to the slaughter. Is he so ashamed that he dares not face us, here in the town he was supposed to defend? He left us all to die! He left the burgh-folk to die, and you followed him!" Then he thrust forward an accusing arm at Malet. "You, sir, do not deserve to be alive! You, Lord Malet, are a coward! A *níðing*!"

Wulfhere grabbed his seax, using his left hand, for his right was still damaged. He roared, and lunged towards the Norman. Malet's face was frozen with shame and fear. Esegar and another man held Wulfhere back as he struggled.

"Nay, lord, do not do this. He is not worth it," his fyrdsman whispered to him soothingly.

"Do you have anything to say for yourself, William?" Harold asked, looking at Malet disdainfully. "Ralph is not here to defend himself, but you are. How do you answer these charges?"

"The man is understandably half-crazed with grief. He knows not what he says, my lord." William tried to sound reasonable.

"We were a force of mighty mounted warriors, they said," Wulfhere spat bitterly. "*Chevaliers*, he called us. We were going to give battle, and there was going to be a great slaughter. Well, there was a slaughter, for certain!"

"My lord, I —" Malet protested, but the earl was in no mood to hear his excuses. Harold stopped him, raising his hand. "Shut up, Malet! I do not want to hear your pathetic justifications as to why you – and de Mantes – left your men to the mercy of Gruffudd's army and ran to save your own flesh."

"W-we were outnumbered, m-my lord. If-if we had not retreated – we thought the men would follow —" Malet stammered. "Besides, it was Ralph who gave the order too late! Not I!"

Harold looked at Malet with contempt. "Save it for those who will listen, Malet." He mounted his horse. "But I will give you this: at least you are here, which is more than can be said for bloody de Mantes!"

Just then a soft wind blew, and autumn leaves rustled amongst the rubble and the debris. Not so far away the plaintive cries of a child could be heard. Fresh smoke filtered through the air from cooking fires, but no one could mistake the acrid stench of death, nor the look of sorrow on the earl's face, as he gazed upon the carnage surrounding him.

Wulfhere sneered with the satisfaction of a child whose sibling has been forced to take the blame. The earl turned to Malet and said, "Say a prayer of thanks, William, that it is not you who has no family or home to go to today."

Chapter Twenty-five

The New Bargain

Hereford, November 1055

Laughter boomed around the smoke-filled building as ale and mead flowed in copious amounts. A company of those sweet-lipped women whose appearance was inevitable whenever the fyrd was on duty, joined the men in helping them spend their money. Neither the stench of stale sweat, nor the crudity of men so drunk they pissed where they stood, served to deter these lovely ladies from plying their trade. The carousing warriors were all full of strong liquor and good-natured banter, which meant they were easy customers. It had been two weeks since that fateful day when thousands of marauding men poured through the broken defences, driving their bloodlust into the hearts and souls of their victims. Whilst long days and nights of mourning encumbered the townsfolk, the fyrd welcomed the presence of the alewife and her women, as relief from the endless burying, clearing, repairing and building… and the boredom of waiting for a battle.

Wulfhere was as vociferous as the rest of them, howling with amusement, as Leofnoth slammed a young thegn's fist into a puddle of spilled ale on the table before him. The old thegn punched the air in victory, as the fifth opponent to fail the challenge was put down. Wulfhere was proud that his venerable old friend could still best most of the youths at an arm wrestle.

"Who is next then?" Leofnoth yelled, above the din.

Osward gave his friend a gentle shove forward out of the crowd. "Wulfward is next!"

With encouragement from his friends, Wulfward shouldered his way through the throng, the crowd chanting his name and stamping their feet.

"What are they playing for?" asked Aelmer. He'd just joined them. The men were leaning on each other, arms slung around one another's shoulders and gathered around Leofnoth's table.

"If Leofnoth beats them, they have to provide him with a flagon of the strongest ale. If they beat *him*, he has offered them a horn of mead," Wulfhere replied.

"Seems a fair deal. Let me guess though; Leofnoth is full to the bladder with ale." Aelmer laughed.

"You guessed right!" confirmed Cana, standing next to Wulfhere.

"I'd bet for the mead," Aelmer stated. "It has a slightly more refined nature."

"Who cares what it is, as long as it makes a man intoxicated!" Cana guffawed, sinking down his own horn full of the strong honeyed drink.

"He wins every time; even his own son cannot defeat him," Wulfhere said, glancing over at his prospective son-in-law, who had turned to the dicing table, where the losers migrated to comfort themselves with a wager and a pretty girl.

Once again, Leofnoth was the winner. There was more stomping and clapping, as the crowd acknowledged another victory, and Wulfward staggered off to purchase another jug of strong ale for Leofnoth.

"Next?" shouted Leofnoth. He was making a great show of his champion right arm, and flexing his muscles. The air was filled with nominations of names, but no one was willing to step forward. "Come on, lads! There must be at least one amongst you who can best an old man like me! There's a skin full of mead for anyone who can beat me!" There was much laughter and banter, but no takers. "Wulfhere, I challenge *you*!" Leofnoth shouted, looking round at his friend.

Wulfhere grinned and shook his head, indicating his injured shoulder which only two weeks previously, had been out of its socket. "I would love to beat you, old friend," he smiled, "but, alas, my arm is not yet fully recovered." He raised his drinking cup in salutation, and swigged its contents down.

"Ah, come now, Wulfhere, are you going to let a little scratch like that stop you?" Leofnoth grinned. "We'll make use of our left arms then."

Wulfhere gave him a cynical look. "I would not want to show you up, Leofnoth."

"You refuse? Are you scared of being beaten by an old devil like me?" Leofnoth grinned, and held out his left hand to him. "Come on, man, show these young whelps what real men can do. Or are you afraid I'll beat you quicker than I can beat them?"

Wulfhere had not wanted to wrestle Leofnoth that night. His body still felt weak after the wounds he had taken in battle, but he was drunk, and, when he was drunk, he was open to persuasion, especially if Leofnoth was goading him.

"You know I can wrestle you with one arm tied behind my back," he replied, his words beginning to slur.

"What should that matter? You only need one arm anyhow. Ha! Ha!" Leofnoth roared. His laughter was contagious, and soon echoed by their companions. "You think that you can best me with your left arm?"

"Come on, Wulfhere! Beat the old goat!" Osward called out.

Soon Wulfhere's name resounded about the hall. Feet stomped the ground and hands slammed rhythmically on wood. The building was filling up with the curious, who, hearing the commotion, came in from outside to satisfy their interest, cramming the building further. Wulfhere shrugged, and sat down on the bench. Word had got round about his bravery on the battlefield, being one of those who had stood his ground, and refused to flee. Now, as his name was chanted, some had begun to call out, "Hereford!" in respect for what he had done that day.

Wulfhere looked at Leofnoth sitting confidently before him, elbow resting on the table, his large ham-like hand open-palmed at the ready. Wulfhere stared into his watery bloodshot eyes as, mischievously, they dared him to take his hand.

"Are you afraid, Lord Wulfhere?" Leofnoth grinned mischievously, showing what few rotten teeth he had left. "You should be."

"Afraid? What, of a decrepit, toothless old wolf like you? What can you do against a man half your age, you pompous old bag of horse *scite*?" Wulfhere replied. He took the other man's hand firmly in his own left one. "Wulfward, you say, 'when'."

"Wait, we need a wager," Leofnoth said. "If I win, you give me that new brood mare you acquired last summer."

Wulfhere drew in his breath at the high stake proposed, but he gripped Leofnoth's hand determinedly. "And what do I get should I be the winner, which of course I will be."

"You get me as an in-law!" Leofnoth laughed heartily.

"As I will anyway." Wulfhere smiled back.

"Of course, what finer prize could you have?"

"Not good enough. What do I get?"

"Ask what you will, you won't get it anyway, for it is I who will win."

"A hide of land for my daughter's wedding gift, after she marries your son."

"Done! But your daughter will not have it, for I am going to win," Leofnoth said, and grasped his friend's hand, purposefully.

By now, as many men as possible had gathered around their table. Until then, the competition had been pretty one-sided, but now there was a new confidence in those who wanted to see Leofnoth knocked off his champion's perch. Wulfhere's standing as a man who had cheated death, with the courage and determination of a true hero, seemed to be gathering a great following, and men started waging their bets as to who would win, and in what time.

"Have you two finished your wager yet? Can we get on with the match?" yelled Aelmer, tiresomely.

"You ready to be milled into sawdust, Wulfhere? God help you if you let them down." Leofnoth grinned, absurdly, at him. The crowd's favouritism was not lost on the older man, but he showed no concern. The two men locked their left hands together.

"I am ready. Are you?" Wulfhere replied.

Leofnoth nodded. "Say, 'when', Wulfward."

Wulfward's fist hovered above the table. "Ready? On the count of three. One, two... three! Begin!"

As Wulfward slammed the table, the two thegns pushed their hands together and began the contest. Men began shouting the name of the man they wanted to win. Soon the whole building was filled with stomping feet, banging fists, and coarse language, as they watched the two men grapple with each other.

Wulfhere felt his face glow like an inferno, as he strained to push the older man's hand down. The shouts and sound of rhythmic stamping rang loudly through his ears like booming thunder, as he steeled himself to win the contest. The muscles in his upper arm and chest were tensed to the maximum, putting pressure on his wounded shoulder, as he pushed against the formidable strength of his opponent. But he was determined not to allow any pain to hinder him.

For a while, it seemed that neither man was going to give way. Wulfhere felt Leofnoth starting to get the better of him, as the throbbing pain in his right shoulder, weakened his resistance. But Wulfhere, hearing his name on everyone's lips, was determined to fight back. Summoning up as much willpower as possible, Wulfhere pushed back with his fist, spurred on by the shouting of his supporters. Pain ripped through his shoulder, but the inner force that resides in everyone's core, flew through his muscles, buoyed by the strong liquor that filled his veins.

Wulfhere's clenched left fist began to regain some ground, and he returned Leofnoth's hand to the starting point. Both of them pushed and strained, their faces glowing brightly, with the intensity. It had been fifteen seconds, and neither man appeared to be getting the better of the other. Wulfhere fought the desire to lift his elbow off the table, for to do so would be to forfeit the contest. He pushed even harder, and still Leofnoth could not be moved. Through bulging eyes, Wulfhere saw, with frustration, that his rival seemed to be showing no signs of caving in. He had surmised that Leofnoth's strength would have been weakened by now, considering he had spent most of the evening, wrestling already. But he had not counted on Leofnoth's relentless resilience. *Damn the old bastard!*

Wulfhere clenched his teeth and fought on. Leofnoth smiled. And winked at him. Wulfhere was sure the old goat could read his mind. Leofnoth's casual goading infuriated him, and he summoned all his power again, drawing on his strength from the depths of his soul. Images of the battlefield infiltrated his mind, and suddenly he was back there amongst the blood, the gore, and the screams of men and horses.

He grasped Leofnoth's ample hand with his own sweat-ridden, clammy palm, ignoring the pain that seared his shoulder, as he pushed down in a vice-like clamp. Leofnoth's eyes widened, as Wulfhere's grip seemed to squeeze the blood out of his hand.

Wulfhere's arm shuddered, as he mustered all his strength. For a moment, the two men wavered in a deadlock, then Wulfhere realised that his newfound strength had upped the ante, and Leofnoth's composure began to disintegrate. He looked at Wulfhere in disbelief, desperately trying to fight back. Leofnoth's smile had become a strained contortion of effort.

"I really wanted that brood mare," the older man spluttered, as Wulfhere slammed their hands against the table top.

Shouts of, "Wulfhere!" resonated around the room, and hands and feet stomped on the floor and furniture. Wulfhere leapt to his feet victoriously, pelted heartily by the men around him, marking his triumph. He thrust away his pain, to acknowledge their demonstrations of admiration.

"Looks like your daughter gets her hide," shouted Cana.

"Aye, and Leofnoth gets a hi-*ding!*" laughed Aelmer, which sparked more hoots of raucous laughter from the others.

Leofnoth took his defeat well, and congratulated his friend without animosity. They shook hands, and shared Leofnoth's drinking horn.

"My reign of terror had to end sometime." Leofnoth laughed, good-humouredly.

"Who is next to take on the champion?" Wulfward demanded drunkenly. "Who will challenge Wulfhere, Lord of... where are you from again?"

Wulfhere sighed impatiently. "I am Wulfhere of Horstede," he replied testily, sitting down, shaking his head at what he had let himself in for. His left arm felt weakened, and his right shoulder ached heavily. After that last scrap with Leofnoth, he had not anticipated another bout, but men around him were calling for a new challenger. The atmosphere was drowning in excitement. For so long now the men of the fyrd had tarried, waiting for a fight that never came. They had come for a battle, revenge for the bloody destruction of Hereford, and been denied it. An arm wrestling contest was no consolation prize for the anticipation of battle, but Wulfhere understood that at least it went some way towards addressing the boredom and pent-up frustration the men were feeling.

"I challenge Lord Wulfhere!" The noise in the room diminished, as Wulfhere's new challenger pushed aside a young warrior, and sat before Wulfhere, who was slugging back the winner's ale.

Wulfhere slammed down the cup and sighed. Reluctantly, he brought his left arm up ready for the fight. He was about to explain to the man that he was now left handed, when he realised, to his horror, that it was Helghi.

"You!" he exclaimed, snatching his hand away.

"We had an agreement!" Helghi snarled at Wulfhere. "You broke your oath!"

"You truly think I could let my daughter breed with your kind?" Wulfhere replied in disgust.

Helghi leaned forward, so that his fetid breath blew hot on Wulfhere's face. "You set such high store for your little *wyrmlic*, Wulfhere. What gives you the right to look down on me and my kind? Do you think that you are too noble for my family? My grandsire was a king's thegn." Helghi thumped his chest. "My family has the blood of nobles. Our bloodline stretches as far back as yours does to the mighty Aelle, first of our Súþseaxa kings."

"Your mother may have been the daughter of a thegn, but that does not make you one. Being born in a stable does not make you a horse! A *ceorl* you are, and a *ceorl* you will always be, because you do not have what it takes to be a thegn. Men do not look up to you; they scorn you!" Wulfhere's face was furrowed in anger. "And I will tell you more, Helghi. Were you indeed a thegn, or an earl, or an emperor, I would not give my daughter to your ilk."

Wulfhere had hoped to avoid a run-in with Helghi. He had not seen him, or Edgar, since he had run from Horstede with his tail between his legs. He stared into the hateful eyes of his enemy, and those of his other son Eadnoth, standing behind him like a shadow. He realised then that he could not have evaded them forever.

"You think you can disregard what the Earl of Wessex has decreed? Your dishonour proves your falseness. Hardly the act of a noble and honest thegn, as you claim to be."

"I have the Earl's confidence and friendship. He will understand why I have done what I have done."

"What will he understand?" Helghi snorted, looking at him fiercely. "That you are an oath breaker, a liar... and a disgrace to your rank? You beat my son and threw him out of your home!"

Wulfhere narrowed his eyes and said angrily, "My reasons are justified!"

"Your daughter had no qualms about being the whore of a *ceorl*, when she willingly spread her legs for my son," Helghi spat. An unpleasant grin grew across his face, masked with the spite of a thousand hatreds.

Wulfhere clenched his fists, shuddering at Helghi's words. He rose to his feet, threateningly. Helghi did the same.

"You think I refuse to wed my daughter to your cripple because of your status?" Wulfhere exclaimed angrily. His face was white with rage.

"What else would it be? Your kind has always looked down on mine!" Helghi snarled.

Wulfhere was enraged. He spat into the floor rushes nearby. "No, Helghi! The reason I broke the oath is because I would rather hang from the highest tree, than see Freyda married to your spawn. You disgust me, you ill-bred defiler of women! Ill-mannered, pig-brained covetous piece of scum, that you are! You are an abomination before God! And I would not, as God is my witness, allow my daughter to be taken into your home." The spittle flew from his mouth as he shouted.

"Lord, this is not the time. Not here," Esegar whispered to Wulfhere, standing behind him.

"You are right, Esegar. I will not degrade myself any longer in dialogue with this filth," Wulfhere replied, calmed momentarily by his man's words.

Helghi looked indignant. "Do not look so smug, Wulfhere. We will have your pretty little daughter. Do not think you will be getting away with this."

From the corner of his eye, Wulfhere saw Aemund lunge at Helghi, unable to keep his own rage in check. "I'll kill you before you lay a hand on my betrothed."

Thankfully, Wulfhere saw that Leofnoth held him back with the help of his friends.

"Leave well alone, Helghi! The girl is promised to my son now!" Leofnoth interrupted, pushing Aemund behind him.

Helghi turned to him and hissed, "Your son, eh? I wonder how many others the slut has been swived by!"

That was all the justification Wulfhere needed. He instinctively swung back his right arm, ignoring the excruciating pain. He ploughed his fist into Helghi's eye, catching the bridge of his nose, causing Helghi to stumble backward. Helghi grimaced, and held a hand over the injury, then turned to face Wulfhere, his bottom lip trembling like a child about to cry.

"Fight me," Wulfhere invited. His voice was venomous.

The two men stood, fists clenched, eyes locked in their mutual hatred of one another. The atmosphere was tense. The obvious animosity between the two enemies was absorbed by the men who looked on in envious silence. There was an air of expectancy. The *Niðdraca*, borne of their enmity, hovered. The monster thrived on their lust for revenge, their need for a reckoning, and the endless waiting.

Suddenly Helghi grabbed the wooden table that they stood across. Intoxication had slowed Wulfhere's reflexes, and he was unable to defend himself, as Helghi thrust it forward so that it was rammed into his wounded leg. Roaring with pain, his fighting-lust was triggered again. He heaved the table sideways, and smashed his fist once again into Helghi's bulbous nose. Stunned, Helghi stepped back onto the feet of a man who was standing behind him. The man responded by pushing Helghi back at Wulfhere, indignant at the trespass against his person. Wulfhere made to grab Helghi's neck and throw him to the ground, but this time Helghi was ready, and he drew back his fist and aimed a punch. Wulfhere ducked, and Helghi's fist slammed into a warrior who had unfortunately got in the way. The man went down with blood spurting from his mouth. For a fleeting moment, Wulfhere felt lucky to have avoided the blow, for the man's front teeth scattered, nauseatingly, onto the wooden floor.

Now the *Niðdraca* burst from its chains, and unleashed its own brand of hell, as the house erupted into chaos. Wulfhere lost sight of Helghi, as men found excuses to fight one another. One man bumped into another and was rewarded with a punch – and so it went on. Wulfhere searched in the mayhem for his enemy, trying to avoid the elbows and fists that flew around his head. Some broke up the trestles to use as weapons. Luckily, weapons had been left outside in the racks before entering the alehouse. However, the men still had their eating knives, a dangerous tool should they have a mind to use them. Eventually Wulfhere caught sight of Helghi on the other side of the hearth. He breathed in deeply as he spotted him, searching tentatively through the stormy sea of heaving men. Helghi was looking for him, just as he was looking for Helghi. He waded through the crowd, pushing, shoving, and plunging toward his target, finding what he was looking for. The two men grappled with each other. Wulfhere tried to get him to the floor, but the area was packed tight with men. A man fell on top of them, and Wulfhere lost him again somewhere in the upheaval.

Leofnoth surveyed the mass of brawling men half killing each other. He sighed deeply. Well, what could you expect when large numbers of drunken men were gathered together, frustrated and eager for a fight? Helghi was brandishing a table leg at someone, so he relieved a serving wench of her griddle, bashing him over the head with it, but not without unintentionally taking out a few others, as he did so. Helghi put his hand up to the back of his head and looked at the blood in his hand.

Leofnoth was surprised that he still stood. *He must have a head like an old tree trunk*, he thought, amusedly. Leofnoth stared at him, devilishly, and saw that there was surprise in Helghi's eyes. The other man was about to lunge at him, but one of the men who Leofnoth had accidentally caught with the griddle, threw himself at Leofnoth with fists flying for revenge.

Gradually, more men joined in the affray, entering from outside, where they were drinking, huddled around braziers. Before long, the whole building was a pulsing throng of fighting men. Some, like Helghi, may have had old insults or scores to settle, but for most, it was just an opportunity for a fight.

Wulfhere was panicking as the fight progressed. Up till then it has been a case of punch now, worry about the consequences later. If the earl got wind of it, and found out that he was at the centre of it, then Harold would also learn that he had gone back on his word with Helghi. Moments earlier, he had thought about sticking his knife into Helghi's heart. Who would know who was responsible in the rumpus? But the chance evaded him, and now that he had sobered up, he thought it best that it had. He did not need murder added to his already growing catalogue of sins. And Harold, he knew, did not need a bloodfeud to reckon with as well as Gruffudd and Alfgar.

He was starting to feel guilty, and he knew it would not be long before the huscarles were aware of the fighting. Harold despised bad conduct amongst his men whilst on campaign, and always demanded good behaviour. Whoring and wenching, he turned a blind eye to, but drunken behaviour, rape and fighting, was always disciplined. He would not be best pleased when he learned of tonight's episode.

Wulfhere thought that he had better do something to stop the fight. By now it was a veritable battleground. He stood on the periphery, battered, and bruised, having given up trying to catch his prey again. He surveyed the terrible scene. Smashed furniture was scattered on the floor, ale spilt everywhere, and angry serving women used their pots and pans to bash heads, in a futile effort to bring some order back to the place. The lanterns and braziers came close to setting the place alight, and some poor fool got knocked into the blazing hearth, and had to be doused in water. Not knowing where to start, Wulfhere roared out an order to stop fighting. If anyone heard him, they did not take any notice, for the chaos continued. He looked out for Esegar, Cana and Aelmer, to help him restore order, but could not see them amongst the confusion.

He pulled and pushed at the wrestling mass of men, the pain was numbed by the need to stop the fight. He roared until his throat was as dry as an empty well. The mission was pointless, and when he got in the way, his efforts were rewarded with blows. He looked over the heaving sea of men and saw Leofnoth amidst the chaos, struggling with the huge bulk that was Helghi. He was not certain, but it looked like Helghi was winning. Wulfhere heaved with his elbows, as he jostled through the throng to rescue Leofnoth. Suddenly, he felt an excruciating pain in the right temple. In a moment, brightness, like a flash of lightning, seared his eyes… and there was nothing but darkness.

Wulfhere took the stool that Harold had offered and accepted a horn of weak ale. His head pounded. He did not know what pained him more: the injury to his head, or the headache from the previous night's drinking.

"Another injury to add to your others, Wulfhere," Harold said, ironically, referring to the bloodied linen bandage, crudely wrapped around the other man's head. Harold's tent offered some warmth from the cold autumnal weather outside; however, there was no warmth in the earl's eyes. The moment Wulfhere had hoped to avoid had arrived, and he was not relishing having to explain himself.

"Do you want to tell me why you have broken your oath to Helghi – not to mention your pledge to me?" Harold asked sternly. Then, without waiting for Wulfhere's reply, he leaned forward and continued harshly, "Do you honestly think I need this right now, Wulfhere? This morning, I have had the alewife here earlier, complaining that her rebuilt alehouse has been destroyed already, demanding compensation for broken furniture *and* spilled barrels, *and* unpaid ale. There are men who look like they have fought ten battles in one day, whose injuries will render them useless for the time being, including you. It is hard enough keeping large numbers of soldiers under control, without you throwing your feud into the equation."

Wulfhere's hands shook as he took a mouthful of ale, wishing it was strong mead to calm his jitters. He stared blankly at his lord. His head pounded, and he felt sick. "I-I am sorry, Lord Harold," he managed to say. He almost heaved.

Harold sat back and continued, "We need cohesiveness in these times. I cannot have my men fighting amongst themselves when our security is threatened. Is it not bad enough that men like Alfgar have joined forces with our ancient enemy to destroy one of our major strongholds, maim, kill, and carry off its citizens without impunity? Is it not enough that our authority is undermined, our suzerainty threatened? Then men like you, and that fat braggart, Helghi, have to demoralize it further with your own petty squabbles."

Wulfhere's face reddened. He resented the way Harold referred to him as, 'men like you.' "My lord, this squabble, as you call it, is between Helghi and I. There has been a feud between our families for generations; it need not be of any concern to anyone else."

"The hell it isn't, Wulfhere!" Harold snapped, angrily. "At home, maybe, amongst your own. But here, men take sides. One faction joins forces with another, and the feud grows. I could have ended up with more than a handful of dead, or half dead warriors, if my men had not broken up the fight. Now Leofnoth of Stochingham and his son, have been dragged into it too… and so have *his* followers… and that of his son's. That enmity could grow, and new feuds take root. You can see how it snowballs, Wulfhere? I cannot have that."

Wulfhere bowed his head, and nodded shamefully. He knew that Harold was right, but it was all very well for *him*; it was not *his* daughter marrying into that family of ignoble degenerates. He suppressed the irritation he felt, and muttered a subservient, "Yes, my lord."

"We no longer live in the days of the bloodfeud. These are Christian times, Wulfhere," Harold said bluntly, "and, in plain terms, I cannot have this division amongst my lands."

"My lord, I have my reasons for breaking the betrothal contract," Wulfhere interjected. "I have not taken this decision lightly."

"I know that you were not keen to have this marriage for your daughter, Wulfhere, and you may well have come up with a reason for breaking the bargain, but as your lord, you should have discussed it with me."

For a moment, the two of them were silent. Wulfhere looked miserably at the ground.

The earl continued, "I like you, Wulfhere, we have long been friends, and your father was loyal to mine. I do not want bad feeling between us. But I cannot have my men, loyal or no, gainsay me."

"The man tried to rape my maidservant at his own son's betrothal... and in your presence too, my lord!" protested Wulfhere, unable to contain himself any longer. "I have two witnesses to vouch for that and one of them is your own man, the lad who got hit by the Wéalas' arrow."

Harold sighed heavily. He fingered his chin, thoughtfully, as if processing the information, and gave a whistle before saying, "That Helghi certainly knows how to act with honour, doesn't he?" He leant forward and cupped his jaw in his hand, as his knee supported his elbow. He looked downwards, as if there on the floor, was the answer to the puzzle.

"He is a drunk and an animal, my lord. You see now why I am so opposed to my daughter marrying his son?" Wulfhere said determinedly.

"And you think he is the only man who likes to drink? Judging by your behaviour last night, it would seem that perhaps you also like your mead a little too much." Harold stared at him condescendingly, as if to hammer home his point. Then his features softened. "Though I do see why you object. But it is not the fault of his son that his father is the man he is. By the Holy Rood, if I had thought that my Eadgyth would turn out like her mother, I would never have chosen her."

"Pigs breed more pigs, lord," Wulfhere replied stubbornly.

"When I met the lad, I did not find him so distasteful a person as you would have me believe. This has more to do with your dislike of his father than anything else," Harold reasoned. "It is this curse between you and Helghi that is the problem."

"The curse, as you call it, my lord, can never be lifted, so it seems."

"What of your daughter, Wulfhere? As I recall, she was determined to marry Edgar. Even so far as to burn down his homestead to prove it!"

"Freyda is content to marry Aemund now. She had a change of heart when she learned what manner of family she was to be married into."

"I see. So, Wulfhere, how do we solve this problem? How do I keep the peace? Now I have Leofnoth, and his son, to contend with. They will have their grievances, too, if I decide in Helghi's favour. Helghi wants your daughter for his son; you want Leofnoth's lad for her; and Leofnoth wants her for his son. But you have other daughters…" The humour returned to Harold's face and he smiled.

Wulfhere gave an involuntary moan, and put his head in his hands. He looked back at Harold, shaking his head. "Winflaed was but nine this springtime gone. She is just a little thing, and the others are barely out of the cradle."

"So, in three or four years or so, she will be of marriageable age. Anything can happen in three years. Edgar might drop dead of the pox by then, with a bit of luck, and his Godforsaken father with him. Helghi will have to be content with her, and Leofnoth's son can have your eldest after all."

"Can I think on it, my lord?" Wulfhere asked hesitantly. He felt sick to his stomach.

Harold gave him a stern look and shook his head. "No, Wulfhere. No thinking. It must be done. We must be rid of this thing between you and Helghi. There must be peace between your families. I cannot have this feud spill out into the rest of the community."

"What about the attempted rape charge?"

"I will speak with Helghi on that matter. He will know that if he ever tries such a thing again, I personally will remove that part of him he would not wish to lose!"

Wulfhere shook his head resignedly. How was he going to explain this to Ealdgytha? He knew that he was going to have to agree. Harold would not let this go, and Wulfhere did not wish to incur his wrath any further. There was nothing else for it. He breathed in deeply and said unenthusiastically, "I will agree… if I have to. But I am not happy, my lord."

"No, of course you are not happy, but it has to be done, Wulfhere."

Wulfhere nodded, solemnly accepting his daughter's fate on her behalf.

"Good. Problem solved. But next time you decide to go against my decisions, you will not get off so lightly, Wulfhere. You and Helghi will be fined for starting the fight, and Helghi also for gross misconduct against your servant girl. As for oath breaking, I will spare you this time because of the mitigating circumstances, but there will not be a second time. If Helghi has cause to complain again, then I will come down harder next time."

Wulfhere felt the resentment build inside him. He wanted to protest, but he knew it would be pointless. Instead, he remembered that he needed to speak to the earl about another matter. "That lad Tigfi," Wulfhere said as he got up to leave.

"What of him?"

"It seems Helghi wasn't the only one vying for my maidservant's charms that night."

"He does have a way with the women, but I do my best to keep my men under control."

"Not enough it would seem, my lord, for there is now a child, and the babe is undeniably his... the yellow hair is remarkably like his own."

"This is the maid who was almost raped by Helghi?" Harold laughed when Wulfhere nodded. "Well, I will give the lass her due; even an easily seduced woman has a right to be choosy."

Wulfhere did not see the funny side. "The lad should take some responsibility for the child."

"Countless times I have had to reprimand him about his wanton ways. I will deal with him, rest assured. He will accept his responsibilities. That Wéalas archer should have shot him where he could do no more harm!"

Wulfhere bowed, and left the earl's tent with a head that ached much worse than it had before. He was more disgusted with himself than ever. His efforts to disentangle one daughter from Helghi's web, had led to another being caught in it. He should have discussed his plans with Harold first; had Helghi been brought before the scīr court for attempted rape, there may have been a different outcome. But he was not entirely to blame. In fact, was he to blame at all? If Ealdgytha hadn't... *The whole thing was Ealdgytha's fault!* It was her constant nagging that had led to this situation.

Helghi had also been summoned to Harold's tent, and was smarting from the tongue lashing and fines he had received, but it was a small price to pay, he thought, for he would, after all, get his prize: Wulfhere's daughter, well at least one of them anyway. For most of his life he had been trying to think of a way to avenge his ancestors. Thanks to the actions of his love-struck son, Edgar, he had found a way, and Wulfhere had been playing nicely into his hands. The plan had gone awry somewhat, thanks to the, 'falsified', accusation levelled at him regarding Wulfhere's servant girl, and that idiot, Leofnoth and his son, but things were now back on track. Revenge would be all the sweeter for the patience he'd shown... a revenge that would be terrible. He, Helghi, would eventually be the one, who puts right the wrongs done by Wulfhere's family, to his family!

All he had to do now was bide his time, and get Edgar married off to the other daughter. And this time he would come for her to make sure. There would be a longer wait, for the child was not yet of a marriageable age. In the meantime, there were other things he could do to bring his plan to fruition, like getting rid of the other obstacles to his plan, such as Wulfhere's three sons. They would have to be dealt with... somehow... if he was to achieve his main goal. He would have to be careful in his deeds. Sureties should be put in place to guarantee, that there would be no reason to suspect him of any involvement in their tragic deaths. But he would be the victor in the end. *He would win this one final battle!*

Wulfhere returned to his camp, and found Leofnoth and the others, brooding under the shelter, huddled round the glowing campfire, with Cana cooking breakfast. All were in a sombre mood, nursing their wounds and headaches from the night before. Wulfhere sat down heavily next to Leofnoth by the fire. Cana offered him some pork and bread, but he pushed it away, still feeling nauseous. It was Goddamned cold, but he was sweating and had been sick prior to joining them.

"You look like a man who has just been given a death sentence," Leofnoth said, squinting at him through blackened eyes. He licked at a cut on his swollen lip, as if it hurt to speak. "What did the earl say?"

Wulfhere related what Harold had demanded.

"*Scite*, my friend, I do not have any more sons to save this daughter," Leofnoth said.

"If I break the oath this time, I think that would be the end of me." Wulfhere shook his head.

"The earl is right though, Wulfhere. Anything can happen in three years," Aelmer said.

Wulfhere made no response. He unsheathed his seax and began to sharpen the blade on his whetstone.

"I'll tell you what will happen."

Alarmed, Wulfhere looked up as he recognised the voice.

"Helghi!" Wulfhere spat after he said the name, as if it were poison in his mouth. Accompanying him were Helghi's kinsmen: ominous-looking, stocky men, with sinister eyes.

Leofnoth and Wulfhere, both rose to their feet, and the others also gathered around them, protectively.

"You dare to come here, *ceorl*, to better men's space. We are lords of men here, and this is no place for stinking swine," Leofnoth said. Wulfhere had not seen him so angry before.

"Then you had better leave, for as you said, this is no place for pigs," replied Helghi. "Smell them, lads?" He turned to the men behind him and they laughed, unpleasantly.

Leofnoth unsheathed his sword, but Wulfhere stood between them. "This is not your fight, my friend. Put away your sword." He knew that there would be hell to pay for all of them if there was another fight. "What is it you want, Helghi?"

"I come to shake hands on the new bargain Earl Harold has made for us. We are to get a daughter from you after all, it would seem." Helghi grinned in triumph.

Wulfhere snarled, and pushed his face into Helghi's. "You will get my daughter over my dead body!"

"Aye, I will if need be!" Helghi replied through gritted teeth.

Wulfhere recoiled as if Helghi's breath was toxic. Helghi, his hands on his hips, continued triumphantly, "We will come for her in three years, maybe sooner. When she is ripe for picking. You cannot stop it this time, Wulfhere."

Wulfhere growled, and slammed his palms into Helghi's chest. "*Horningsunu*! I'll kill you before that!" He grabbed his sword from where he had laid it and started to pull it out of its sheath; his warning from Harold forgotten. Helghi's cronies drew out their seaxes.

This time Leofnoth intervened for Wulfhere. "No, my friend," he said grabbing his sword arm, and holding it down. "You will not keep your daughter safe, as an outlaw, Wulfhere, which is what you will be if you break the earl's peace this time. Leave it to fate... and God. Besides –"

"Besides what!" Wulfhere said, angrily.

"That's your bad arm," replied Leofnoth.

Wulfhere relaxed his arm. He knew that Leofnoth was right; he would have to leave it to fate.

As they withdrew, Helghi called back to him, "I will win this war, Wulfhere! One way or another, you will not be able to stop me."

Wulfhere clenched his fists. He thought of Winflaed, his little bird, *Fléogenda*, tired and weary of play, sitting on his lap with her head on his broad chest. He would tell her stories and she would fall asleep; such a tiny thing. He could not allow her life to be blighted amongst the Helghisons. And he could not allow his blood to be mixed with that scum.

"What does he mean, 'he will win this war'?" Aemund asked.

Wulfhere felt a wave of nausea pass over him. His thoughts sickened him. "He wants my land. He wants everything I have," he whispered. He shuddered as if someone was walking over his grave. "It is what he has always wanted."

The fyrd was finally disbanded when Harold, despite the king's disapproval, decided that to sue for peace was the best option. Alfgar's actions had inflamed Edward into demanding war, but Harold's insistence on diplomacy prevailed. *Why should Englishmen fight each other, whilst there are wolves aplenty in the lands of the Wéalas, and to the northern isles, just waiting for the chance to invade?* He had refortified Hereford with a new ditch around the town's palisade. He built new gates at each entrance, with heavy locking bars to keep out the invaders. Ralph de Mantes had ploughed so much of his energy and reserve into his prized mounted force, that he had neglected the very basics of burghal defence: its walls. It had been a hard lesson for the people of Hereford.

Harold led the council which met with Alfgar in the hills above the River Wye, a little south of Hereford. Gruffudd was absent, but Alfgar was there to represent him. Harold negotiated peace terms with Alfgar, who, it was agreed, should be restored to all his previous possessions, including the earldom of East Anglia. Part of the peace terms incorporated a settlement for Gruffudd. Alfgar negotiated on behalf of Gruffudd, and the King of the Wéalas was given possession of territories, long disputed over.

Harold stomached this last with contempt. Alfgar's actions, although reprehensible, were at least halfway to being explicable. He had been goaded into behaving treasonably, and Harold was now certain, after his brother's confession, that intrigue had played a part in his downfall. However, Gruffudd was another story. Pardoning Alfgar was like forgiving a wayward son, but Gruffudd, and his countrymen, had long been the foe of the Englisc. The resentment ran much deeper with Gruffudd. He had been harrying the marcher lands for years, and had invaded Herefordscīr and fought a devastating battle against the Mercians which brought about the death of Alfgar's own uncle, some years before. He had not even had the courage to appear before them in person, instead sending his younger brothers, Rhiwallon and Bleddyn, in his place. But Harold knew that war with the Wéalas would come at a high price in more ways than one. Alfgar had proved that he was able to raise a considerable army, and needed to be brought back into the fold. Future conflict would have to be avoided at all costs, and so Harold, and the thegns of Hereford, would have to accept that the time for retribution was not yet come.

So, Lord Alfgar was reconciled with the king and his father. He and his son, Burghred, were also reunited, but their relationship would always be a precarious one. Burghred entered his grandfather's service rather than that of his father, for he was never again able to look his father in the eye. The betrayal was too much for either of them to bear.

Ralph de Mantes, the man whose hopes for the crown rested on this one battle, would never recover from his shame, and would forever be known as Ralph the Timid. As for William Malet and some of the other Norman knights, they thought it more expedient to return to Normandy. There they would enter the household of the Duke of Normandy to become the mounted warriors they had aspired to be under the King of Englalond and had failed. They knew that their fortunes no longer lay with the man whose high hopes of becoming the next king had been dashed so infamously.

*

Edgar waited for Freyda by their old meeting place. He hoped that today would be the day that she came. She always liked to visit the forest, even in winter, but it was a mild November day, and he was hoping that she would come. With the men out of the way, gone off with the fyrd to fight in the western lands, he would take his chance. He would ask her first; give her a chance to come willingly. He was convinced that, when she saw him again, and heard the words that he wanted to speak, she would melt into his arms as she had done before, and it would be as it has always been, before that *horningsunu*, Aemund, hardened her heart against him.

But what if she does not wish to come willingly? The thought had crossed his mind. What would he do? He obsessed about her day and night, thinking up ways to get her back. His stepmother, Mildrith, was the only one who would listen to his words of anguish, offering empathy and words of comfort. His father blamed him for the loss of Freyda, saying that he had no backbone. He was nothing but an idiot, a cripple, of no use to anyone, not even himself. Edgar detested his father for that, wanting to shout that it was *his* fault Wulfhere had reneged on the oath, for trying to rape that girl. Instead he kept silent, knowing it would not serve him well to disclose what he knew about that night, and he kept his hatred deep within him. One day he would show Helghi that he was not the fool everyone took him for.

His decision was made. If she refused to come willingly, he would take her, anyway. Perhaps she would just need time to come around to the idea that she was meant to be his, not Aemund's. If she still refused, he would take her, and get her with child. Despoil her. Aemund would no longer desire her if she carried his seed. Then she would have to marry *him*. There could be no other choice. Either this, or he would kill them both, for life without her would be too unbearable. They could die together, or live together; the choice was hers.

When she finally came, he gave her no choice after all. She came alone, riding into the forest on Aelfwyn. He set the trap, and she fell right into it. As she lay helpless and unconscious on the ground, he threw her limp body over the saddle of his horse and took her, secretly, back to Gorde. Aelfwyn returned home, some hours after she had left, the empty saddle, an ominous sign that something untoward had happened to her.

Chapter Twenty-six

The Rescue

It was that time in November when trees, having shed the last of their dying leaves, enshroud the ground in various shades of gold, leaving their naked boughs exposed to the approaching winds of winter. Released from their duties, Wulfhere and the others had ridden forth from Hereford to be home before the snows threatened to obstruct their paths. Ealdgytha was waiting for him in the courtyard, and even as he entered through the gates and before he had seen the terrible look of despair upon her face, he sensed that some calamity had befallen.

She was hardly able to speak. Her chin trembled, and tears rained down her cheeks.

"What is it?" he asked anxiously. But he already knew: Freyda.

Ealdgytha threw herself into his arms and sobbed. "Thank God you are home!" she cried.

The twins hurried out from the hall. "Freyda is gone, Father!" they cried in unison, their words, omens of bad fortune, echoing in his ears. She was gone!

"We think it is Edgar's doing," Ealdgytha said tearfully, pulling herself away from his embrace. "She went riding out on that horse of hers. I told her it might not be safe, but you know her... She would do as she pleased, as usual." Her tone was bitter.

"Could she not have fallen and lain injured somewhere?" Wulfhere asked, hopefully.

Ealdgytha shook her head. "The men have looked everywhere, scouring the forests and meadows. *He* must have taken her!"

Wulfhere turned to Leofnoth, who had just dismounted. "Freyda is missing. She may be at Helghi's."

Leofnoth jumped back into his saddle. "Don't dismount!" he called to Aemund behind him. "We have your bride to rescue."

Wulfhere turned to his sons. "You two boys stay here and look after the homestead with Aelfstan."

The brothers screwed up their faces in disappointment, and began to protest. "We want to come with you, Father," they said together. "Please, let us come with you."

Wulfhere studied the boys. They could be of use...but he had lost a brother because of Helghi. He did not wish to lose his sons. He put his hands on their shoulders. "Your mother needs you here, boys," he replied firmly, ignoring their pleas. He gestured to Aelfstan to take them inside. Sullenly they complied, and their father watched them walk inside with the assurance that the big blacksmith would look after them.

Then he turned to Ealdgytha and squeezed her shoulders. "We will be back with her. Do not fret."

She stood on her toes and whispered in his ear. "That is what I am afraid of." He withdrew from her, puzzled. He could not have known that Ealdgytha's fear lay in the knowledge of what Edgar might do to her.

Wulfhere and the rescue party poured into the village of Gorde, bringing with them the spears and shields that lined the walls in their lord's hall. Those who could ride, did so on Horstede's horses, others ran on foot. Some brought pitchforks, scythes or clubs, anything they could use as a weapon, willing to help their lord in any way they could in his time of need.

It was a freezing cold afternoon and dusk was not far off. The unsuspecting villagers of Gorde were getting ready for their supper. Pigs, goats, and geese, scattered as the invaders entered their village boundary, whilst little children ran crying to their mothers' arms. Men came running out of their homes to see the commotion and ran back inside, the braver ones to find a weapon, the less courageous, to hide.

"Helghi!" Wulfhere shouted, as he rode his horse over the hurdles surrounding the new longhouse which he and his men had helped to build. The others followed suit, crashing through the flimsy fencing of Helghi's badly maintained homestead.

Helghi came swaggering out of his house with Eadnoth and his kinsmen. They were all inebriated as Helghi was, obviously celebrating their return from fyrd duty. There was no sign of Edgar.

"You dare to set foot on my land?" Helghi roared at them.

"You have my daughter!" Wulfhere bellowed. Hwitegast pranced and snorted nervously beneath him. Beside him, Leofnoth, Esegar and Aemund, were anxiously anticipating Wulfhere's actions. Wulfhere sensed the tension from his companions, knowing that Leofnoth was fighting to keep Aemund in check. The lad was champing at the bit to kill someone and Wulfhere was concerned that his youthful bravado would get them all killed...but he knew how he felt.

Helghi looked baffled. "Have your daughter? Are you offering me another of your pretty girls, Lord Wulfhere? Why thank you, I do have another son, after all." He laughed animatedly, his eyes sparkling with mead, and his kinsmen laughed with him. It was not a pleasant, gay sound, but more like the cackling of demons.

"Just give her back to me, Helghi, or I will see to it that the whole might of Súþseaxa is brought down on you," Wulfhere replied, keeping his composure. He was aware of the gathering crowd. The age-old hostility between their lords had spread into the lives of the people. Helghi was not much liked by his own folk, but he was their *hlaford*, their lord and loaf-giver. Their fortunes were intertwined with that of his, and if his fortunes failed, so did theirs.

"Wulfhere, you have lost your wits, my friend. What in God's name are you jabbering about? You're talking like a man who has mislaid his mind as well as his daughter. There are no daughters of yours here. Not yet, anyway. But when she is, there will be plenty of entertainment for her, eh, lads?" Helghi made a lascivious gesture, grinning hideously.

Wulfhere noticed that Æmund had reached for his sword. "No, Aemund!" he shouted.

Leofnoth reached across the neck of his son's horse and put a restraining hand on Æmund's arm, whispering a firm "No."

Wulfhere quelled the disgust that was rising within him. He steadied himself and said, "I want Freyda back now, Helghi. Your son has taken her." He looked about him. "Where is Edgar?"

Helghi looked momentarily puzzled. "Wife!" he called, gruffly.

Mildrith appeared on the porch. She looked frail, frightened, and weary.

"Yes, husband?" she mumbled. Wulfhere saw the torment in her eyes as she glanced toward him, darkened by the shadows beneath them. How could Harold expect him to hand any of his daughters over to this beast, only to end up like the wretched young woman who stood before him? His daughter, full of life and gaiety, to become like this poor creature.

"Where is Edgar? Where is that fool son of mine?" Helghi bellowed at Mildrith.

"I will find him." She scurried away.

"If he has harmed her in anyway, I will hang him from his bollocks!" Wulfhere said, looking directly at Helghi through gritted teeth. "And then I will slice open his guts and feed his entrails to you."

Helghi's mouth said nothing, but his eyes said plenty. His hatred burned.

"Esegar, take some of the men and search the buildings. She must be here somewhere."

"Aye, lord." Esegar was about to dismount when an arrow hit his horse in the neck. The horse reared with a high-pitched scream, throwing his rider to the ground; then galloped off in terror. The other horses, spooked, pricked up their ears and sidled nervously, and another took off, his rider still in situ, bouncing precariously, after the first had bolted. Suddenly there was another arrow in the time it would take to reload a bow, and Wulfhere shouted to the men to dismount and form a wall. Released from their riders, the horses ran in different directions, snorting with fear and confusion.

"Esegar?" Wulfhere called. "Are you all right?"

"Aye, lord." Esegar scrambled to his feet.

"Get your bow!"

"Aye, lord. It's here somewhere!" Esegar scrabbled around on the ground until he found what he was looking for.

"Aemund? Take two men, get the horses, and keep watch over them. See that I do not lose any!" God knew he had seen enough horses die of late.

"Do as he says, boy!" snapped Leofnoth, when the lad hesitated.

"I came here to fight, not nurse the horses."

"Do as you're told, boy. There's time enough for you to die when you're older!" Wulfhere shouted, knowing that the courage of youth was often tainted with a foolhardiness which could get him killed; especially when loved ones were involved.

As Aemund reluctantly followed his orders, Wulfhere lined up his defensive wall with the men carrying shields in the front. The rest stood behind, brandishing their crude farming tools. Most of them were not real fighting men, they were simple farmers, but he had trained them for such times as this when needs must.

Still the arrows kept coming. Pauses between each arrow told him that there must be only one archer, but whoever he was, he was quick. The arrows either bounced or were caught in the shields, as the men covered themselves against the onslaught.

Even Helghi had been taken by surprise at the arrow attack. "Who the hell is firing at them?" he shouted, looking around at the mayhem with disbelieving eyes. Wulfhere and his men were arranging a shieldwall. He genuinely had no idea where the girl was. Like Wulfhere, he had just returned home from Gleawecestre, and had been imbibing with his kinsmen and the men from his village, when Wulfhere and his men suddenly appeared in his yard.

Grabbing Eadnoth, he shoved him toward his hall. "Get our weapons!" he screeched. "And anything that will hit a man hard!"

"Yes, Father!" Eadnoth replied, eagerly, as he ran to do his father's bidding.

"It's your son!" came the reply, from one of his cousins. "It is Edgar! Look! Up there, yonder, on the high ground, by the hoary old oak. He is there with his bow." Hengest was pointing to a tree-lined ridge, front right of Helghi's longhouse.

Helghi was soon surrounded by his kinsmen, readying their own line of defence. His gaze followed his cousin's pointing finger.

"Damned fool," he muttered, catching a glimpse of his son on the ridge, before he disappeared behind the great trunk of the oak again. He had picked a good spot to shoot from. Helghi was amazed at Edgar's show of nerve. *But what is going on?* he wondered.

"Did you see the girl with him?" Helghi asked.

"He has her," Hengest replied.

From his place crouching on the ground, his shield covering his position, Wulfhere rapidly formulated a plan in his head. He had forty men, and guessed that Helghi had less, but there would be more, hiding in their homes, and if they came out, the shieldwall would be exposed to their attack, should they decide to join the fight.

"Leofnoth," he called, "lead the rear, in case those cowardly bastards come out of their hiding holes to attack us."

His friend bellowed his response, "I'm there already!"

Wulfhere sniffed, thankful that he could rely on his old shoulder companion to pre-empt his orders. "Herewulf, lead the right flank and charge Helghi's men. Esegar, you help me deal with that bastard up there!"

"My lord!" Herewulf nodded, shuffling down the line to the centre of the right flank.

Wulfhere carefully lowered his shield and looked to where the arrows had been flying from. Someone was up there still; he was sure of it. Suddenly he felt the men on his right surge forward, as Herewulf, leading with a shout, attacked Helghi's shieldwall. Behind them, Helghi's villagers were running out of their homes and straight into Leofnoth's men at the rear of him. He heard them screaming and yelling as they clashed, shield upon shield, weapon upon weapon.

"Esegar, take out that fucking bowman!" he shouted at his fyrdsman and pushed Yrmenlaf toward him. "Cover him so he can reload his bow," he told him. Yrmenlaf's face looked confused. "Use your shield, lad!"

The arrows were flying in both directions as Esegar, having taken up a safe position, nocked and loosened his own missiles. Wulfhere's vision was hampered as he took cover under his shield. He guessed the line of fire was to the right of their position judging from where the oncoming missiles were landing. The fighting was growing wilder behind him and the screams of those who had been wounded rang in his ears. He had grouped his own unit in such a way that their shields would deflect the arrows, thus protecting the men fighting to his rear. Gradually though, his line was being drawn into the fight behind them, as Helghi's men seemed to be getting the better of Herewulf's.

The archer must have been tiring, for the arrows were coming more slowly. Wulfhere was amazed at the speed he'd shot with. Either the bowman was very fast, or there was more than one archer. Still, Wulfhere stayed locked with five or so of his men, holding off the arrows with their stricken shields. He turned his head to survey the scene behind him. His men were surrounded, fighting like maddened wolves. It was going to be a bloody fight, one that had been brewing for some time. Keeping his shield up, he whirled around and saw that the arrows had stopped, but still there was no sign of the archer.

"Wulfhere!" Esegar's voice rang out to his left. "It is Edgar! The archer! It is Edgar!"

Wulfhere's face tensed. It made sense. He was up there, on the ridge, hiding. Intuitively, he knew that she would be up there too. Perhaps he had run out of arrows, and was searching for Esegar's that no doubt lay scattered around him. Wulfhere moved away from the fighting, and crouching down with his shield protecting him, appraised the ground in front of him. He saw that the tree-lined ridge ran for about one hundred feet. To his left was shallow rift, crisp with the dead leaves of autumn. His eyes searched for a way up without being seen by Edgar. He spotted a crude track, trod regularly into the mud over the years. It was surrounded by brambles and high bushes. Along the ridge, nearer the other end of the slope, he saw the old oak with the wide trunk. Something in Wulfhere's gut told him that Edgar was hiding behind it.

His men were pushing and heaving behind him, enjoined with the men of Gorde in the dance of battle. He remained where he was, a hand shielding his eyes from the shafts of dying sunlight, filtering through the golden branches. He watched, squinting, looking for any signs of movement. He started, as Edgar emerged stealthily from behind the tree, carrying his bow, pointing downwards, in one hand. He was yards away, but Wulfhere got the sense of someone who was half crazed. Tied to Edgar's right wrist was a length of rope, attached to something else – or someone else, behind the trunk of the oak. Wulfhere knew it was Freyda.

"Esegar, cover me," Wulfhere shouted, as he ran a few feet up the slope. He hid himself halfway up, hunkering down under cover of a gorse bush. It was then that he caught a glimpse of her golden hair, and he knew that his instincts were right. *She was there.* He could hear the clash of men shouting and yelling in pain further down. He ignored it, for his aim was to get to Edgar, and then to Freyda. He saw Edgar raise his bow, and wondered again why Esegar was not firing his. But then an arrow whizzed a few feet past him, and pierced the trunk of the oak, inches from Edgar. Wulfhere's heart almost flew into his mouth. Freyda was dangerously close by.

He looked around, and saw Esegar standing by the edge of the rift with his bow, already loading another arrow. Wulfhere was about to lunge out from his hiding place and scream at Esegar that Freyda was there, when he saw Edgar yank her out from behind the tree and pull her close to him. The rope tied around his wrist was secured to her neck, and as he held her in front of him, he threw down the bow and put a knife to her throat.

When he saw her, Esegar lowered his weapon. Wulfhere was relieved. Certain that Edgar had no idea of his presence, he wondered if he could get up there without alerting him.

"Put down your bow, or I will slit her throat," Edgar yelled.

"Let her go, Edgar!" Aemund called out to him. "Don't be a coward and hide behind a girl's skirts. *Fight* me!"

Wulfhere was glad of the diversion. He began to creep slowly up through the tangled brushwood, keeping his eyes focussed on Edgar. He had seen her. Her hair hung loosely in disarray and she was blue with cold, wearing only a thin linen tunic, muddy and torn. He hoped that she had taken heart that they had come for her, but her pale face registered only fear. Wulfhere tried to push visions of Edgar tearing off her clothing and violating her, out of his mind. Somehow, however, the image was not of Edgar at all, but Helghi. It was Helghi… always Helghi.

"Stop this, Edgar, and let her go. It will serve you nought to do this!" A woman's voice shouted. It was Mildrith. She was approaching with her child in her arms, the little one that Wulfhere had once saved.

"Do as she says, Edgar," Aemund called to him. "Let her go! Fight me," he repeated. "Whoever wins can have her."

Edgar's eyes were wild. "She belongs with me!" he cried. "She was promised to me. She has given herself to me many times, in many places. Even now —"

"Edgar, please… no! Don't do this! If you love me, as you say you do, let me go!" Freyda spoke for the first time, her voice barely audible.

"Shut up!" he screeched insanely at her and held her closer. She winced as the knife cut her neck. It was a superficial wound, but it drew blood. Wulfhere could wait no longer. Removing his throwing axe from his belt, he aimed and threw it, careful not to hit her. Perhaps too careful, his aim went wide and landed in the trunk, missing Edgar's head by some inches. Alarmed, Edgar turned, and the knife slipped out of his hand. Wulfhere rushed him but stumbled on a root in the ground. He looked up quickly and saw Edgar fumble for his bow. He quickly nocked the arrow into the cord. Freyda tried to run toward Wulfhere, but Edgar shouldered her to the ground and pinned her with his foot.

Edgar steadied himself and drew back the arrow. Wulfhere stared down the line of fire. He was holding his hands before him defensively.

"Put the bow down, Edgar," he said slowly.

"If anyone comes near, I will shoot him. I will shoot the thegn of Horstede!" Edgar shouted, looking round at the others.

"I'll shoot you first, Edgar," Esegar called.

Edgar spun and released an arrow. "Then I will kill you first!" he cried, his voice shaking with emotion. It was a good shot. It hit Esegar in his chest, up into his sternum at the perfect angle, toward his heart.

Wulfhere saw that Aemund had lunged with his shield, but he had been too late to deflect the arrow. Esegar went down clutching at the arrow in his chest, his eyes wide with disbelief. Aemund grabbed the bow and quickly loaded it. Too late, though. Edgar had already reloaded and was aiming straight at him. He had been so quick that Wulfhere, paralysed with the shock, had not been able to stop him.

The madness that had gripped Edgar was fading. His mind was whirling; thoughts tumbling through a tunnel of insanity, back into dreadful reality. If only he could stay within the grasp of his madness! Then he would not know the dreadful thing he had done. His life would be worth nothing now. His father would still think him useless... and Freyda – she would not have him now. He had killed a man. A good man.

She had rejected his attempts to rut her. When she had refused to do it willingly, he had thought to rape her. He could not even do that right. She was repulsed by him. It was there, in her eyes, her face, the turning away of her head, as he tore at her clothes, forcing her legs to part. But he had not been able to go through with it. He had pulled away from her when she had sobbed, "If you loved me as you say you do, you would not do this to me."

But now he was a soul torn in two. His heart burst with the need for her, but he hated her, desperately. And that part of him which was filled with hate, had wanted to hurt her. The part that loved her could not.

"No, Aemund!" Wulfhere cried out, afraid that the boy's actions might cause Edgar to harm Freyda. He drew in his breath and then exhaled again, as Aemund reluctantly relaxed the bow. "Edgar, let her go. She is not yours. She is my daughter. I urge you to give her back safely and we will leave here, and you will not be taken or harmed in any way."

Edgar was looking over at the men still fighting around the longhouse.

"Do you want your father and brother to be killed?" Wulfhere followed his gaze.

Edgar raised his bow and aimed at Wulfhere. "I am going to kill you, Wulfhere, for all the things you have done to me — and my father. Years of oppression and injustice will be avenged at last!"

"Edgar, it is your father who is to blame for all this. He brought the horse that crippled you – set fire to my stables. He tried to rape one of my servants... the list is endless!"

"You lie! You have lied about everything to bring shame upon us and keep us down among men." Edgar pointed his bow at Wulfhere.

Mildrith, watching from the side-line, intervened. "Edgar, you won't get away with it. The scīr-reeve's men will come for you! You will be outlawed." She stepped closer to him, still carrying the crying child in her arms.

"Do you think that I care about that?" Edgar spat then closed one eye and took aim, readying himself to pull back the arrow.

"Edgar, no! Would you kill the man who once saved your little sister's life?" Mildrith shouted. "The fire, Edgar. Remember the fire. You were the cause of it. If it wasn't for Lord Wulfhere, Ealswith would have perished in the flames."

Edgar looked at her strangely. "W-what are you talking about?" he stammered.

"The night of the fire, I had left Ealswith in her cot, and the hut caught fire. Lord Wulfhere – he went into it, to get her out, even though it was dangerously enclosed in flames. He got her out – saved her life! He might have died, but he risked his own life to save hers, and brought her back to me. Your little sister would have died if not for him. And it would have been your fault!"

Edgar frowned.

"Edgar, let Freyda go," Wulfhere said, softly, taking a step toward him, grateful for the intervention from Mildrith. "I am begging you."

"You – beg me?" Edgar laughed, throwing back his head with a look of insane amusement.

"Let her go, you bastard!" Aemund shouted and aimed his arrow at him.

"Aemund!" cried Wulfhere. He threw him a threatening look, and gestured for him to lower the weapon.

"Let her go, Edgar. We can stop this now," Mildrith entreated him. "Edgar, he saved Ealswith. Now you must let him have *his* daughter now." She held her sobbing toddler out to him, as if to convince him.

Wulfhere's breathing was shallow; his heart pounded in his chest as Edgar stared at the floor, his face crumpled in anguish. He let the bow and arrow slip from his fingers, removed his foot from Freyda's back, and cut her loose. She ran from him into her father's arms, sobbing. He held her tightly, kissing her head and whispering endearments. When he looked up, Edgar was gone.

Wulfhere and his war band returned home, battered, bruised, and bloody. Seeing the state of his men as they left Gorde, he realised just what they had risked for him, while he bore not a mark upon him. Esegar lay lifeless across the saddle of his horse. The arrow that had entered his chest had pierced his heart, and there had been nothing anyone could do for him. Helghi had taken casualties too, it had seemed, his courtyard strewn with that of the injured and maimed. But he cared not for them. All he had wanted was his daughter back and to return home with his men unharmed. He was devastated at Esegar's loss, and grateful to those who had fought for him. It was not a good day.

As they rode through the village, the women came out to greet them. Wulfhere, grim-faced at their head, sat astride Hwitegast; Freyda perched in the saddle in front of him. He had wrapped his cloak around her to keep her warm, covering her hair that hung loose and wild. She looked tired, distressed, dirty and humiliated. Riding nearby, Yrmenlaf led the horse that carried Esegar, miraculously the only fatality for the people of Horstede that day. Wulfhere flinched when he passed Esegar's house, and heard his wife Godgyva scream upon learning of her husband's death.

A procession of lighted candles flickered in the dark air, as their bearers followed the convoy up to their lord's homestead. Wulfhere wanted to take Esegar's body home into his hall, where he had sat many a long night with him, drinking mead into the late hours by the warmth of the hearth. He had been his hearth-man and loyal shield-bearer. Esegar's loss would be felt dearly. As they entered the hall, they carried his corpse on a stretcher with his shield laid over him. The arrow remained broken in his chest. Someone had tried in vain to pull it out, but it was no use. It had pierced his heart. Wulfhere was one of the four men who carried him, and they laid him on a mead table in the centre of the hall. His attention was focused on paying his respects to his dead retainer, whilst Ealdgytha swept her daughter upstairs to her chamber where she could attend to her. The men whose injuries needed treatment were given over to the care of their womenfolk, as others lamented over the prone figure of the lifeless man. Just one death – but one death too many.

Wulfhere stood by the table as Godgyva weaved through the crowd of mourners, her hands clasping those of her children's. She let them go when she saw Esegar, and drew her husband's lifeless body to her breast, whispering his name more than once, kissing his pale lips, his cheeks, and his forehead.

"He is still warm!" she cried, letting out a howl of grief. She threw herself to her knees. Esegar's mother, Wulfgyva, and her grandmother, Eadwina, comforted her whilst her children, confused and afraid, sobbed beside her.

Wulfhere bent down to her, lifting her to her feet when her womenfolk could not rouse her. "Godgyva, I would give anything not to have lost Esegar today. He was a good man, and I owed him my life, twice over," he said humbly, doing his best to appease her grief. "I am bereft without him."

"*You* are bereft without him?" Godgyva retorted. She rounded on him with tears flowing endlessly down her cheeks. "How do you think the coming years will be for his children without their father? Think on that, Lord Wulfhere, when you sup with your children tonight and every night thereafter."

Wulfhere felt his face grow red with shame. He suffered her angry words in silence.

"Come, daughter, you cannot speak so to our lord," Esegar's mother whispered to her, and drew her away.

"He will be given a good Christian burial. And I shall see that you will have justice – and his *wergild* also." Wulfhere hoped that the receipt of the death price would be of some comfort to her.

Godgyva stood swaying with grief, a woman on either side of her to support her. Wulfhere's face glowed with her burgeoning contempt. "*Wergild?* You could not even get Helghi to pay the *wergild* for your brother when he died, because of your – your damned, stupid bloodfeud! When will it end, Lord Wulfhere? How many more of your men do you have to lose, before this curse that hovers over all of us ends?"

Wulfhere opened his mouth to defend himself, but his words stuck in his throat. She was right. His feud with Helghi was to blame for Esegar's death. Once again, he had dragged his people into it.

"Look at your men, lord," Godgyva continued, her pretty face contorted with grief. "More of them could have died today – and for what?"

"For my daughter's sake, woman!" Wulfhere exclaimed, the pain in his voice plain for all to hear.

Godgyva laughed ironically. "Your daughter? Is she worth any more than my Esegar? She too suffers, because of your feud, Wulfhere! All of us do! We all suffer because you are too proud to end it. My father once told me that this bad blood of yours and Helghi's stretches back through generations. Now it belongs to the village folk as well. It will only end when there is no one left standing! Your feud will be the death of us all."

"Godgyva!" snapped her mother-in-law, as Godgyva stood by the mead table that held her beloved husband. "Lord, she is mad with grief – knows not what she says." Wulfgyva then turned back to her daughter-in-law. "Come, Godgyva, we shall return to our house."

"I will not!" Godgyva cried. "I will stay here with my husband! It is my place... and my right!"

Wulfhere nodded to Wulfgyva that he gave his consent. How could he stop Godgyva from keeping vigil with her man? He went to the fire and stoked it. None of his tenants had ever dared to speak to him thus before. Yet he could not deny the verity of what she said. The feud was destroying them slowly, like a monster with its venomous tendrils, sapping the life out of them. Freyda's honour had been compromised, Winflaed was now in jeopardy, and his brother, Leofric, had now been joined by Esegar, in heaven. Esegar may not be the only fatality of the night either. Someone might yet die of the wounds they had sustained in the fight... and there he was, without so much as a scratch upon him.

He knew that things would have to change... but how was that to come about? Helghi was the main protagonist in this. He would not rest until he had destroyed everything Wulfhere held dear. No matter what anyone said or did to make things different, there would be no peace whilst Helghi still lived.

Epilogue

Freyda peered out of the porch and watched mournfully as Leofnoth and Aemund, bade their goodbyes to her parents. Yrmenlaf and Aelfstan brought the horses for them, so they could embark on their journey home, taking her brothers with them back to Stochingham. They had stayed for Esegar's burial, and now, the day after, they were leaving. Aemund had not even said goodbye to her. He had said very little to her since they rescued her. In fact, no one had asked her about her ordeal and how she was feeling. All anyone wanted to know was whether or not she had been raped. She told them that Edgar had not touched her, but she did not tell them that he had only stopped, when she had begged him not to. Better not to talk of that. Let them believe that he had not touched her at all, for they were men, and they saw things only in one of two ways. She was either raped or she was not.

Even so, she had seen the look of disbelief in Aemund's eyes whenever he looked at her. She had tried to understand his fears about what had happened to her, but she had not dreamed that he would ever distrust her. His indifference toward her, stabbed at her heart like a knife, so she kept her own counsel, though she longed to tell him how she felt when his gaze met hers. How she shuddered, when his disgust permeated the space in her soul, and filled her with shame; how she felt dirty, unclean and untouchable, and longed for him to sweep her into his arms, and tell her that she was safe. Only his touch would make her feel cleansed. Part of her was gone.

That was why they did not stay to discuss their wedding plans, she thought: because he could not bear to be with her. She heard Leofnoth tell her father that his son needed time to recover. It had been a great shock for him to return home, and find his bride-to-be had been stolen by her former betrothed. *What did they think she had been through?* All anyone could think of was how this had affected them. Not how terrible an ordeal it had been for her. She wanted to scream at them, *was it not me who had been kept in a vermin-infested hut, made to lie on a cold earthen floor for days in the dark?* And now, the one she had given up Edgar to be with, gazed at her with a face that showed only pity or disgust; and pity was not the same as compassion. Pity was something one felt for an animal that had broken its leg. Pity was the thing that one endowed upon a beggar with one leg. She was not a beggar, and she was not a dog with a broken leg. She was a human being who had been snatched against her will, held hostage, brutalised and suffered many hurts. And the hurt continued.

Although they had not said so in words, she knew in her heart of hearts that Aemund would not be coming back, and it broke her heart to know that all he cared about was his honour, and how everyone would know that another man had abducted his woman and had raped her, even though she had denied it. He had once told her that it hadn't mattered to him that she'd given herself to Edgar, so why did it matter so much now? Then she realised that he was just like all other males, whose honour was threatened.

Wulfhere and Ealdgytha, watched as Leofnoth and Aemund left. Then Ealdgytha turned to him and slid her arms around him. She was crying quietly. Wulfhere kissed her head softly.

"He will not want her now, will he," she whispered sorrowfully.

Wulfhere had not wanted to think about it. Yesterday had been focused on Esegar's interment. It had kept his mind from thinking about Freyda, but he wanted to reassure Ealdgytha that everything was going to be all right. "Of course they will. Freyda has assured us that she was not touched."

"Do you believe her?" Ealdgytha pulled away from him.

"I believe her."

"Wulfhere, I cannot understand! We have had a terrible year! What are we going to do?"

He held her in his arms and kissed her reassuringly. "It will get better, *deór heort,*" he said softly. He sighed as he held her close. It was as if chains had locked his soul within him, and he was a prisoner of his own making. He would never be free. He was weary and tired of fighting... fighting everyone: Ealdgytha, Helghi, Harold, the Wéalas.

They walked toward the hall, their hands entwined. It had begun to rain, and the air was freezing. Soon it would be deep winter, and Horstede would become a frozen wasteland. He still had wounds to mend. A new year was approaching. Would it be as bad as the last, he wondered? Surely it could not get any worse. But something told him, as they walked into the hall and the warmth of a burning hearth, the worst was yet to come.

HISTORICAL NOTE

This book was originally the first half of an epic saga that took me six years in total to write. It started with an idea... an idea that took hold in the form of a man, mentioned in a book that I had read called, *1066: The Year of the Conquest* by David Howarth. It was Mr Howarth's account of that remarkable year in history that gave me the inspiration to write about Wulfhere, mentioned by Howarth as the recorded landholder of Horstede. In Mr Howarths's book, Wulfhere's home in Horstede near the Sussex town of Uckfield was brought colourfully to life, filling my mind with delightfully intriguing images of daily life in Anglo Saxon England to the point where I had to get it out and onto paper. And thus, the beginnings of Wulfhere's story was born. Figuring that such a novel on a 'war and peace' type proportion would be too ambitious for a first novel, I decided to develop the saga into two books. The second is due to be published in the Spring of 2016, and hopefully will follow *Sons* in the shape of *The Wolf Banner*.

Nothing is known about Wulfhere other than what the *Domesday Book* tells us, that he owned 5 hides of land in a forest clearing. Upon this land lived his tenants, 5 cottars and 9 villeins. Between them all, they shared 7 or so ploughs with teams of 8 oxen and a water mill. Frustratingly, that was all the information on Wulfhere I had. My imagination has done the rest, creating a family and a life for him. My Wulfhere is not a perfect man and his neighbour, Helghi (also a man of Domesday) fared even worse in my version of their lives. So, the names of these two men and what land they owned is where the non-fiction ends and the fiction starts. The historical characters in this story are, I am sure, obvious to the reader and anyone of them can be looked up and confirmed. I have tried to be as accurate with what little is known of their personalities, as I can. I believe that very often, it is possible to gauge a character's personal qualities by their actions and the part they may have played in the events of the time in which they lived. I hope my creations have done them the justice they deserve, be it bad or good.

The Battle of Hereford is recorded as having been a major disaster for the English and their Norman leaders. There is no full account of the battle itself and I have drawn on my own knowledge and research of the warfare of the time. What followed is very sketchy and again, I have had to use my imagination and conjecture as to why Harold did not engage the Welsh and Alfgar in battle after following their trail into the Golden Valley, and personally, I believe it's pretty apparent that the armies of the alliance had broken up, the Welsh disappearing into the rocky fortresses of the Black Mountains and sources indicate that Alfgar went with his Irish-Norse to Chester to pay them off. The Welsh were very adept at hitting the border lands with lightening raids and getting back over the border into Wales and obscurity, very quickly! It was my aim to invent a plausible interpretation of the battle and I hope my readers have been satisfied. Alfgar's oldest son, Burghred, is not very well documented. I could find only one mention of him in my research and that was to do with his death. His defection from his father was entirely my invention. Some of the other characters in the Welsh camp are also historical including Rhys the Saes, who was not in my original edition of this book. Gruffudd's sister, Angharad, his sons and his half-brothers are also real characters of the time. I would have liked to have expanded Gruffudd's character further as I was quite intrigued by him. To the Welsh, he was a hero, the only Welsh leader of the time who had the gall and the stamina to take on the English with alacrity. Unfortunately, this book was not the place to do that.

William Malet is indeed a real character and plays a large part in the post conquest years. He was known to Harold Godwinson and believed to have been Godfather to Ralph's son as was Harold. His part in the battle of Hereford is another of my inventions.

If anyone would like to ask any questions about this book and the events of the time, I would be happy to answer questions if I can. My email is sonsofthewolf1066@googlemail.com

Read the follow up:

The Wolf Banner

Available on Ebook on

Amazon

Printed in Great Britain
by Amazon

83092524R00226